Also by Brian Aldiss

The Brightfount Diaries
Interpreter
The Male Response
The Primal Urge
Report on Probability A

The Monster Trilogy
Frankenstein Unbound
Moreau's Other Island
Dracula Unbound

The Eighty-Minute Hour
The Malacia Tapestry
Brothers of the Head
Enemies of the System

The Squire Quartet
Life in the West
Forgotten Life
Remembrance Day
Somewhere East of Life

Cretan Teat
Jocasta
Finches of Mars
Comfort Zone

The Complete Short Stories: The 1950s
The Complete Short Stories: The 1960s. Parts One to Four

Poetry
Songs from the Steppes: The Poems of Makhtumkuli

Non-fiction
Bury my Heart at W. H. Smith's
The Detached Retina
The Twinkling of an Eye
When the Feast is Finished

Essays
This World and Nearer Ones
The Pale Shadow of Science
The Collected Essays

And available exclusively as ebooks
The Horatio Stubbs Trilogy
50 × 50: The Mini-sagas
Supertoys Trilogy

BRIAN ALDISS

Walcot

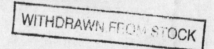

HARPER
Voyager

Harper*Voyager*
An imprint of HarperCollins*Publishers*
1 London Bridge Street
London SE1 9GF

www.harpervoyagerbooks.co.uk

This paperback edition 2015
1

First published in Great Britain by Goldmark 2009

A catalogue record for this book is
available from the British Library

ISBN: 978-0-00-748226-9

Set in Minion by Born Group using Atomik ePublisher from Easypress

Printed and bound in Great Britain

MIX
Paper from
responsible sources
FSC® C007454

To Ronnie
with remembrance of Ruth
with regards as always

God forbid that we should give out a dream of our own imagination for a pattern of the world.

– Francis Bacon
Novum Organum

Contents

Introduction

'You are free men, whatever that means.' So says Steve Fielding to some German soldiers, whose lives he spares during the closing events of a world war, in the freezing cold Ardennes. But Steve, as we learn in this complex unfolding of a life, is himself not a free man.

We find him first of all as a child, playing alone on a Norfolk beach – the beach that gives this complex tale its title.

Already, like a tide, doubt enters his life. Is he in danger? High on the dunes, a woman, almost a stranger, looks to see if Steve is safe.

So the question arises, to be solved if possible: do Steve's parents wish to get rid of him? In love, in war or peace – or in an uncertain interlude between the two – the uncertainty continues to tease.

As this delightful and complex story unfolds, the reader meets new astonishments and some strange old events.

Questions remain, but now there's beloved Verity – and a cheetah – and of course the sort of unexpected we all expect to meet.

A long and intriguing story unfolds before us.

Brian W. Aldiss
Oxford, 2015

PART ONE

1
Barefoot

At high tide, the sea lapped close to the dunes, leaving little sand to be seen. The remaining sand above the high tide mark was as fine as sifted salt. Spikes of marram grass grew from it like quills from a porcupine. No stones were visible. The small waves, white and grey, seethed against their limits. How lonely it was, this wild coastline.

When the tides began their retreat, they revealed first a line of pebbles, grey and black. The pebbles gleamed like jewels until the sun dried them, when they became as grey and inert as if they had grown rapidly old and died. Occasionally among the stones lay a small, dead crab, its up-turned belly the respectable white of death.

The pulse of the sea appeared to quicken; its faltering waves had left the slopes of the beach and were now retreating over level territory. Venturing down to follow this august daily event, you found your feet sinking into the wet sand, and so you kept moving. The sand squelched with every step you took, turned pale, went dark. Went *slurp*.

Stretches newly revealed were bare, immaculate, except perhaps for that baby crab, soft to the touch as you bent down to it. What caused it to die? Did crabs become ill?

Everything about you shone with a joyous newness.

The small ripples of waves as they rolled back towards their mother sea were transparent, and consequently looked as golden as the sand beneath them. They were so beautiful it was essential to pat them with bare feet, to jump up and down in them, splashing.

So you followed this grand *revanche*, as if you, too, were determined to get back into the real sea. You were hopping about in a world of ceaseless movement; these waves, or very similar waves, would never stop, would still be rolling back and forth in their interplay with the beach for eternity, or until you grew up, whichever time was the nearer. You felt very close to eternity because everything here was marvellous, and in this year before the nineteen-thirties had dawned, you had the entire beach all to yourself.

Look to left, look to right. Along the great expanses of beach, not a single person was to be seen.

All through that slumbrous summer you were there, playing on the sands. And in those bygone summers the sun shone always overhead, undeterred by cloud. The sun was there when you arrived on the dunes in the morning, pausing and taking in the whole wonderful spectacle, and when you departed in the late afternoon; at that time, the red ball of it was only just beginning to slope down towards those dunes.

The retreating waves swirled about a fishing boat. It was Mr North's boat, anchored on the sand. Mr North, rowing strongly, went out in it at night, when you were in bed asleep, with your arms about your golliwog. The sea eroded a bowl in the sand round the stern of the boat before retreating further, to leave the craft high and dry, a perch for the odd seagull.

At last the wavelets left the dunes as far away as possible. Their strength exhausted, they sank back into the embrace of the sea. The sea made little fuss as it swallowed them. This was the enchanted, the bronze, the salty and sublime, the interminable and august month of August, when everything is in compliance. The blue morning sky overhead was occasionally flecked with ribs of thin cloud, into which the sun was as yet still climbing.

Every day was calm and hot, in both reality and memory.

Very distant were the dunes, shallow as the breasts of an adolescent girl. They were perhaps half a mile from the lip of the sea. The sea was perceived as friendly, luxurious, playful, puppyish. You wore only a bathing costume and a round, grey, felt hat. You were completely solitary. You were able to exercise your imagination, free from interference. One year, you had a small wooden boat, which went exploring and survived many hazards.

On that stretch of fresh sand, firmer now, baked to the brown of the crust of one of your mother's pies, what adventures could be had! This was a newly discovered land, yours alone. It was the beginning of the world on which as yet no plant could grow, no animal would tread.

And there were rivers on this new-found land, miniature Amazons which wound towards the sea, sometimes deep, sometimes shallow, delta-like. They carved cliffs an inch high in the damp sand as they went. A spade, a wooden spade, could deflect some of their tributaries.

The sea, in its munificence, had also left behind, to punctuate this generous plain of sand, pools of various shapes and sizes. The sun glinted on them, spilling diamonds and daggers. You could lie in these pools; they were warm baths, more luxurious than any man-made bath. Little fishes were trapped here. Shrimps would come and tickle your toes. Sometimes you splashed, but never made much noise. You were in a secret, far-away land, where it was polite to be silent. You were encompassed, though, by a great shell of sound, sung by the sea in its conversation with itself; this was the resonant music of your happiness – though you were frequently unaware of it, or even of the fact that you were happy.

To either side of you the beaches stretched hazily into the distance, to Happisburgh in one direction, to Bacton in the other. No one was to be seen, even as far as all the way to where the view dissolved into vibrations of heat, nor was any ship to be spotted out to sea. Nothing lay between you and this unveiled nature, which would last for only a few hours, until the tide came rushing back to reclaim its territories, spilling over itself in rude haste.

You arrived barefoot on the beach. You had with you a rubber pail and a little paper Union Jack on a stick, a wooden spade and a bun wrapped in greaseproof paper in case you became hungry during the hours you are alone here.

Your mother baked the bun. You meant to repay her generosity by taking her back swarms of shrimps in your pail. She would throw the shrimps into boiling water and you would eat them together, on brown bread and butter, for tea. You were always distressed to see the shrimps go into the boiling water, although your mother told you that they died instantly. The idea of dying instantly held no appeal to a small boy only four years old. You did not know what it meant.

You spent days alone on the sands last summer, when you were only three. Your mother remained in the bungalow and read romantic novels by Norah Lofts, borrowed from the library. Norah Lofts and Ethel Mannin; of the two, she preferred Norah Lofts.

You stayed with her in a bungalow named 'Omega', which belonged to the family. You believed Omega to be the name of a flower, even when you were told it meant 'The End of Things'. The bungalow was built, in a way, at the end of things. The country seemed to you utterly remote. It was rare for anything but a farm cart to pass along the road at the foot of Omega's garden. The bungalow stood at one side of a pathway dignified by the name of Archibald Lane. When you walked up Archibald Lane towards the sea, you had a cornfield on your right. In those distant days, cornfields were gay, with red poppies and blue cornflowers, the seeds of which went into the bread to make it tastier.

At the top of the lane, just before the dunes, stood two old railway carriages, joined together to make one long carriage. Here lived the North family: a mother, a father and two quite big boys with sandy-coloured hair. They all had freckles. Your mother mistrusted people who lived in old railway carriages, but you were fascinated by them. You enjoyed being in the carriages, sometimes running from end to end in your excitement. Mrs North and her boys were kind to you. She sometimes sat you down and gave you a cold sausage to eat. Mrs North was freckled and pretty. Her eyes were blue. She wore an old blue apron. The North family were remarkably cheerful. You laughed a lot when you were together. Mr North was a fisherman; his was the boat high and dry on the sands. He slept in the day, when tides were low.

Sometimes when you were alone on the beaches for all the hours of the day, especially when the tide came racing in, you might turn and see Mrs North standing on the dunes, watching for you, shielding her blue eyes with a brown hand. You would wave. She would wave back.

You were busy. You were building a splendid castle on the edge of one of the warm pools. You were kneeling, determined to get the towers just right, when the water started to lap about your knees. You ignored it. You knew what it implied, but you are concentrating on getting the castle to look its best before the invading tide washed it all away.

The castle was completed. You stood up. Waves were racing across the acres of sand, covering them. You watched them, fascinated by the speed of the race. Soon the waters were dashing against the walls of your castle. It began to crumble. A tower fell into the flood. You removed the paper flag from the still surviving tower and put it in your pail with the shrimps. You collected up your spade. It was time to move to safety; but you wanted to watch the destruction of the splendid castle. It was a pity your mother was not there to see and admire it, but the beaches did not interest her.

The castle succumbed slowly. You knew you had better go; it was not so easy. You floundered through a pool now flooded by the new waters, then there was a deep gully to negotiate before you could reach the safe, dry slope of the higher beach. The gully looked deep and menacing now. You waded in. The current was fierce; it carried you sideways. You held pail and spade high. There was an unexpected pool underfoot. You staggered and went under. In your unwanted ducking, the shrimps were reprieved from the pot and the paper flag was washed away. You could see it go, but you were too frightened to do more than struggle for the safety of the shore. The rank water you swallowed in your ducking made you cough and splutter.

Once you were on the dry sand, you were cross with yourself for being frightened. Some way out to sea now, you could see a safe stretch of sand. But it was inaccessible, separated from the shore by a waste of water which heaved and tumbled in a hostile manner.

Would you say that this was the period of your life when you felt yourself to be closest to Nature?

Those sun-drenched, soul-drenched days alone? You believe I was in touch with all that was grand yet transitory. But who can speak for a lad only three years, four years old, when one's psyche is not yet developed?

What did you think about, there on the sands all day? Did you feel you were being encompassed by a great soul?

I doubt I was even aware of time – only of time as local, affecting the comings and goings of the sea at Walcot, and the possible arrival of teatime.

So you were sent to play on the beach?

I believe that was the case. Yes.

The sea and the time bound to destroy the finest castle you might build?

Of course. It was in the nature of things.

*

8

You sat and watched as the tide raced in. Well, you would be back again tomorrow, when that new world, ever fresh, would be revealed once more. Tomorrow, the little pools, the arcane rippling and ribbing of the sand, would be there anew; only you would be there to appreciate them. And there was still a whole week before the holiday had to end.

You looked up at the mackerel sky and it was then that there was a disturbance in the thin cloud, and a golden bird came speeding down. When it stood before you you could see that it was in fact vaguely human in form, seeming youthful, despite its long beard. You observed that it had no genitals.

It spoke. 'Have you been good today?'

You did not know what exactly to answer. It was obvious to you that opportunities for being 'bad' were strictly limited when you were alone on the beaches.

'Are you a Christian?' it asked.

You were forced to go to Church every Sunday. You had been given a little book into which you could stick a pretty stamp to mark each attendance. You recited the rhyme printed in the blank spaces.

Every stamp cries Duty done!
Every blank cries Shame!
Finish what you have begun
In the Saviour's Name.

The golden thing seems satisfied with this response. 'Do you say your prayers?'

You would have preferred it to have asked if you had enjoyed the day, but it had only tedious questions, such as those the local vicar might ask.

'Yes,' you said.

'Do you wish to get to Heaven?' it asked.

Again it was difficult to know what to answer. The day had been like heaven, with nobody to order you about, or be miserable at you.

9

'Not yet,' you said. 'Not while we're enjoying Walcot.'

The golden thing stood there. It finally said, 'Your time will come.' And then it zoomed back into the sky. You watched it until it vanished.

You decided to run home. You told your mother, 'Mummy, I just saw God.'

Your mummy said you must not tell lies.

'Perhaps it was just an angel. It was all gold.'

Your mummy frowned and asked if you had caught any shrimps.

'Does God have a weewee, mummy?' you asked.

Your mummy threw a Norah Lofts at you. 'Don't be so rude, you little so-and-so!'

The Norah Lofts missed you. You silently thanked God that Mummy never had a good aim.

2

An Adult Breath

Your mother liked being in Omega. She decorated it according to her own tastes. The living room was fairly dark; it had only one small window which looked towards the cornfields. It had hip-high wooden panelling painted a deep brown, thus adding to the darkness of the room. To offset this, your mother had scattered orange cushions about on the chairs and settee. She also had, stationed at strategic points, a number of gleaming copper jugs which she polished regularly. And there was a fine brass lamp with a frosted white shade and a clear glass chimney which she lit at dusk. The lamp shed its cosy light over part of the room. There was no electricity available within several miles of Omega.

The walls above the wooden panelling were painted white, and here your mother had hung a number of reproductions of paintings of flowers in bowls and vases. The paintings were glazed and bound in passe-partout. They most typically showed pink and white roses in a deep blue bowl, standing on a well-polished table. A petal had fallen and reflected its colour on table and bowl. Always a fallen petal, its hint of imperfection emphasizing the perfection of the picture.

Your mother was more than usually torpid and framed no flower pictures that night. She was a tall woman, heavy of body, heavy of face. She did her pale hair in a bun, bound tightly to the back of her head, like a supplementary brain. She was given to long skirts of woven material. She had within her the seed of a future child who was destined to take your place; but of this impending event you were not told. It was, as yet, your mother's secret.

She kept news of her early pregnancy, too, from her visitor. She was a secretive woman and did not entirely trust her visitor, whom she considered superficial. This visitor was younger and more vivacious than your mother. You knew her as your Auntie Violet. 'No shrinking violet, she!' your mother was apt to exclaim. 'Comes from Grantham, of all places,' she said, appalled.

Auntie Violet was sharp and pale of face, with beautiful arched eyebrows and a permanent wave in her hair which, despite its permanence, was frequently renewed. She had a neat upturned little nose, which you mentally labelled pert. She generally wore strings of beads which rattled across a generous bosom. Her flesh was pale and clear. She smelled delicious. Her clothes were bright, worn with belts which drooped over the upper reaches of her behind. Her shoes, at least at this moment, were bright red. You were fascinated by this flitting figure who drove to Omega in her own open-top tourer. Auntie Violet was married to your mother's younger brother, Bertie Wilberforce.

Auntie Violet smoked cigarettes in a long amber holder. Her lips were red. She had another endearing trait: she liked small boys and, in particular, she liked giving you treats. She had brought you a wooden glider. You ran outside to fly it; it flew well and meant many excursions between the crisp stalks of the cornfield to retrieve it.

While you were flying your glider, your mother and your aunt had a quarrel. Somehow you perceived this as you returned to

Omega. Auntie Violet stood smoking on the verandah, looking statuesque. She made a decision and said to you, 'I do not neglect my children. I love my children. And I love you, Stevie dear.' She bent and kissed you on the forehead. You were puzzled by this sudden display. You entered the bungalow to see your mother standing with her arms akimbo – always a bad sign.

While you were accustomed to your mother's moods, there was another worry on your mind. Auntie Violet was staying overnight. Omega contained only two bedrooms and the spare bed was in your room. You would have Auntie Violet sleeping in the bedroom with you. You were unsure how you should behave in this situation. You knelt and said your prayers by your bedside every night, as your mother had taught you; somehow, instinct told you now that Auntie Violet did not kneel by her bedside to say her prayers. It might be advisable to skip prayers this evening. And you hoped that God would be understanding, although he did not seem to have been particularly understanding in the past. He seemed, like your mother, to be a bit moody.

Several years later, when your auntie was thinking of committing suicide, she told you a remarkable story, which was to haunt much of your life. She said that for an hour or two she and your mother were not talking to each other. She looked hard at you and said that she was in your bedroom until the storm blew over, when the phone rang in the main room. Your mother had picked up the phone. Auntie Violet had listened to the conversation, and concluded that it was your father, your cold and distant father, who was on the other end of the line.

According to Violet, your mother said, 'Yes, high tide was at about a quarter-to four today … no, no, he came back as usual … we hope for better things tomorrow … it is likely to be windier, so the sea should be choppier … I can't do anything more, sorry … No, he doesn't mind being alone there … no, no one … if he was you know, it would of course be a regrettable accident … Don't worry. As you say, hope for the best. I don't want to discuss it … Good-bye.'

That is what your Auntie Violet told you she overheard your mother saying.

Your Auntie Violet was alarmed by the deductions she drew from this one-sided conversation. She believed it meant you were in grave danger. She did not know what to do and so she did nothing.

You were called for supper. Your mother instructed you to behave as Valerie would have behaved. You sat quietly at the table and ate your mackerel, mashed potato and *mange touts*. Your mother and Auntie Violet drank white wine from South Africa. They made polite conversation. The brass lamp with the frosted white shade shed a comfortable glow over the woven tablecloth.

You had been taught not to hum with pleasure as you ate.

The dessert was pineapple slices and cream. You luxuriated in the taste of pineapple, although it sometimes made your lips rough. You lingered over it. The meal being finished, your mother made Violet and herself some tea. She unfortunately brought up the case of the golden thing she said you pretended to have seen on the beach.

'I didn't pretend. I did see it,' you said.

'There's no such creature as this golden thing,' your mother responded.

'Perhaps he really did see something if he says so,' remarked Auntie Violet, casting a smile in your direction.

'You'll just have to go back tomorrow and perhaps you'll see it again,' your mother said, rather snappishly. After a short while she suggested you go to bed.

As you lay in bed, you could hear the murmur of their voices in the next room. At last, the bedroom door quietly opened. You closed your eyes and pretended to sleep. Your Auntie Violet entered, carrying a candle in a blue metal holder with a broad rim, with which you were familiar. The candle flame flickered in the draught of her entry.

Your auntie set the candle down on the bedside table you shared between you. She looked over at you. You feigned sleep.

14

She undressed. Her fragrance came to you. There was a moment when she removed her panties, letting them slide to the ground, and you saw the smooth arc of her back shining in the candlelight, and the innocence of her buttocks. Something within you was obscurely touched. Then her nightdress slipped over her head.

As she climbed into bed, the springs of the bed squeaked. Her head was on the pillow. You imagined she was staring towards you, and squeezed your eyes more tightly shut.

'Stephen,' she called in a whisper.

In a minute, she called your name again. 'Stevie.'

You sighed and turned over. It was very realistic. Then you sat up, to ask if she'd called you.

She said she knew you weren't asleep. She invited you to go over to her bed and have a cuddle.

Although you wished to go, you protested that you wanted to get to sleep.

She laughed softly and told you not to be shy. Again she invited you across that narrow space between your beds.

You felt yourself blushing as you obeyed. She opened up the bed and you climbed in. She put her arms around you and hugged you. She blew out the candle. You were in darkness together, the two of you, with her fragrance and her body heat.

She kissed your neck. You felt her tender warmth and found it more beautiful than you could possibly imagine. Without knowing how you could dare to do it, you wriggled about and put your arms round her neck.

'That's more like it,' she said. Her breath was adult, with flavours of nicotine and toothpaste.

You had no idea what to do next, although you felt something was required. She kissed you on your cheek, then lay there with her head on the pillow, her dark hair overflowing, and her lips against your cheek. You filled with happiness, only to find how like terror happiness is.

You blurted out that you loved her.

'Good, my little darling,' she said in a whisper. 'And I love you.'

Slowly and gently, she fell asleep. You struggled to sleep for her warmth and beauty. But eventually you did sleep.

The next day, your bright and loving young auntie drove away from Omega. You stood with your mother and waved her goodbye. Because you were so young and dominated by your mother, you were unable to put your feelings into words; they swam in you like fish that never reached the surface. For that reason perhaps, you could never name them.

In the same way, this grave and joyful event became confused with the idea of the gold thing which came down from the sky, both events being seen as in someway 'golden'. As time went by and you did not see anything more descending from heaven, you began questioning the truth of the experience, prompted perhaps by your mother's disbelief. But you never doubted the truth of climbing into your auntie's bed and being encompassed by her warmth and goodness. Indeed, in your adult life, whether consciously or not, you frequently sought to relive that transcendental experience in the beds of other women. It was only in those years of your childhood, when you were soon replaced by the baby girl to whom your mother shortly gave birth, that you sometimes wondered if your auntie had behaved out of a spirit of mischief, rather than a spirit of what you generally regarded as compassion.

Of course, as a four-year-old you were not clear about this matter. You never considered, as your aunt had done, that your parents had hoped to be rid of you by 'accidental' drowning. Only during Violet's disquisition did you discover – and great was your dismay upon hearing it – that those long summer days of contentment, playing in solitude on the beaches of Walcot, were intended to be your last: for what caring parent would permit a small child to remain all alone for so long, in circumstances which by their very nature held danger for the unwary?

*

16

In your innocence, such thoughts did not occur to you. However, on one occasion they came close. You were playing in one of the warm pools that dotted the great beaches. Shrimps and little fish were floating by you. You tried to trap one fish with an idle hand. It stung your finger with unexpected intensity. The pain shot up your arm. You could not bear it. You needed your mother's comfort.

Abandoning pail and spade, you ran back, nursing your hand, husbanding your tears, over the dunes, down Archibald Lane, to Omega. You ran inside, for the door was never locked.

Your mother had gone. No one was there. The bungalow was empty.

Mary's mother, Granny Wilberforce, had been staying for two days. They had gone. Father had driven them off for a jaunt somewhere. The familiar car was not in the driveway. They had abandoned you to the sands and the tides.

You lay stunned on the sofa, waiting for their return. After an hour you grew ashamed, ashamed of yourself, ashamed of your parents. You crept away, back onto the beaches, so that their neglect was hidden from them.

Here's an instance of your concealing your pain, isn't it?
Why do you draw my attention to it?
Because it becomes a lifelong habit. A habit that makes some people find you difficult to understand. Do you see that now?
I never felt my parents troubled to understand their son. That was certainly a pain I strove to hide.
Tell me why.
I suppose I didn't ... didn't want them to feel bad ... Because ... they already felt bad enough.

3

Almost Drowned

Quite late in your life there fell into your hands a leather-bound copy of the Holy Bible, which, you were told, had been owned by your paternal grandmother. This Bible had been a present from your grandfather to Elizabeth Harper when he was courting her. Later he would win Miss Harper's hand in marriage. A label inserted in the preliminary pages of the Bible read, 'From S.M.F. to Miss Elizabeth Harper as a token of his love'. And there was a date, May 1891.

The formality of this message enclosed within the pages of a Bible convinced you of the solemnity of a Victorian courtship. Possibly it also spoke of something slightly stiff in the character of your grandfather.

The evidence of your father's courtship of your mother was hardly more substantial, obscured as it was by the advent of war. Even before the Victorian Age was over, the nations of Europe were arming themselves against one other. In another August, an August graver than the one we have been discussing, war broke out after a shot was fired in Sarajevo. One by one, the nations were drawn towards the flame. Soon, all of Europe was at war. And your father was of an age to volunteer to fight. So the story went that young Martin Fielding became a pilot in the Royal Flying Corps, which at a later date became the Royal Air Force. He flew in Sopwith Camels, first of all on the Western Front and then in Mesopotamia. He shot down three German planes and became an air ace, with his picture in the *Daily Graphic*.

When Martin's plane crashed he was injured and spent some months in a hospital in Cairo – 'Cairo of all places', as your mother was frequently to say thereafter. In 1918, with the war ending, he was brought home on a troopship. The troopship moored a mile outside Southampton harbour, the troops fretting over the delay about getting ashore. It is here that Martin emerges from being 'Mentioned in Despatches' and becomes part of the folklore of your family. Martin dived off the troopship and swam ashore, in his impatience to meet again Miss Mary Wilberforce, to whom he was engaged. Another reason for his rebellious act was that he had become politicized by his wartime experiences. He had experienced the great division between men and officers and became a Socialist.

Mary Wilberforce lived in a sleepy cathedral town outside London. It was her younger brother, Bertie, who was later to marry your Aunt Violet; her older brother, Ernest, was killed in the Battle of the Somme. You can understand that all over Europe, people were scuttling everywhere, trying to pick up the threads of their lives, hoping to restore a normality that had vanished and would never return to the world.

Mary Wilberforce married Martin Fielding in May of 1919. Many marriages must have taken place in that year, as people strove to put the horrors of the war behind them and reconstruct their lives. You may ask why, if Martin was in such a hurry to get ashore and claim his ladylove, the marriage was delayed for almost a year. Certainly Martin, your father, had been injured in the war, but the wound had healed sufficiently to enable him to swim that mile from ship to shore. It seems not unlikely that he was suffering from some other type of malady, possibly picked up during his weeks of recuperation in the city of Cairo.

Although your father had to give up flying, he did not lose his love of aviation. In 1924, the year you were born, Imperial Airways undertook a commercial programme of flights across the world. Martin worked for Imperial before moving to Vickers Aviation, where Bertie Wilberforce was also employed. Bertie was a pilot. Bertie flew a Vickers 'Victoria', a troop-carrying plane, to Kabul in Afghanistan in 1929, rescuing six hundred people threatened by revolution there.

Martin was active in trade unionism, determined to obtain better pay and conditions for the workers. He made himself unpopular and moved to another company on the South Coast. The family went with him.

Omega was to be sold.

'We have to make sacrifices now and again,' said Martin, consolingly, to his weepy wife.

The last summer spent at Walcot was during the nineteen-thirties, when war clouds were gathering and the voice of the dictator of Germany was growing louder and shriller. You had a small, lively sister, Sonia, by that time. Your mother accompanied Sonia and you down to the beach. Your father was also there, during one of his increasingly rare visits. Politics taking up more of his time, he was a candidate to become Socialist Member of Parliament for the New Forest constituency on the south coast, following the death of Bernie Hale, the previous incumbent.

While Sonia and you played on the newly revealed stretch of beach, your parents sat nearby on deck chairs. Both were fully dressed; your father, you remember, wore highly polished brown shoes. They always kept anxious eyes on Sonia who, in conse-quence, was nervous, and did not like to splash in the deeper pools.

You were absorbed some distance away, chasing a small crab with your shrimping net. The intense murmuring silences of the sea were broken by Sonia's shrieks and your father's shouts at you. You caught the crab in your net before turning.

Sonia was lying on her back a few feet away, her hair in a shallow pool. She was crying in terror. Your father was ordering you to go to her aid. You popped the crab in your rubber pail and then ran over to her. While helping her to her feet, you could not understand why she had not got up of her own accord.

Your father was furious with you. 'Why didn't you hurry? Sonia could have drowned!'

'No, she couldn't. Her face was not in the water.'

He clenched his fist. 'She almost drowned.'

'No, she didn't, dad, really.'

'Don't you argue with me, boy!'

'I'm just saying her face –'

'She was helpless. You didn't care one bit, you little wretch.'

'I rescued her, didn't I?'

'Go back to the bungalow at once! Get off the beach! Go away!'

After tipping your crab back into the warm pool, you made your way up the beach.

'Come back, Stevie!' called Sonia. 'I'm all right! Really I am!'

You did not turn your head. You made your way down Archibald Lane without a tear. You went into Omega and settled down to read a book. You never in your childhood saw the beaches of Walcot again.

4

An Absolute Slave

Of course there were other Wilberforces, other Fieldings.

You recall various splurges with some of them, and with other friends of yours – indeed, splurges too with strangers. Splurges when you were half-boy, half-adult, ending up in Indian restaurants, swilling down glasses of Kingfisher lager, showing off, laughing 'fit to bust'.

You remember going off to pee one time, almost falling down the steep steps to Avernus, into the reeking, hot basement, realizing you were drunk, staggering, running your dirty hand over the dirty walls to steady yourself. Alien territory, sopping towels lying exhausted on the floor, doors marked successively STAFF, PRIVATE, LADIES, KEEP OUT. A fellow rushing by, throwing out a look of contempt as you were already unzipping, ready for the outpouring. GENTS, it said. And you smelt the urine/disinfectant smell like soup spilt on an oilcloth table cover. You tossed away in disgust from between your lips the half-puffed fag. It fell on the red-tiled floor. You directed a first splash at it to put it out, laughing weakly, then directing all your energy to the hard squirt into the china bowl, in which sodden things lay. You used your penis like a hose, amused to direct it to splash right up the wall. It writhed in your fingers, glad as a puppy for its master's touch.

You did not know then that a time would come when you would climb unsteadily down those same stairs, to that same urinal, this time going slowly, hobbling even, the frayed remnant of what you cherished proudly long ago already leaking into your trousers in anticipation and then, when you make it to the sordid bowl, unable to produce anything but an irregular drip. You would lean your arm against the wall and your head against your arm and you would spit into the yellow trail below. You would not be miserable exactly. You would just know that you had run out of spark and spunk and steam, and would be sort of semi-glad of it. But all this awaits you in the future.

You and all your pals.

Early in life you saw what old age and its captivities meant. You were fortunate, in that respect, to escape.

You mean I will not become a prisoner in my old age?
That is not my meaning exactly.
What do you mean?
Let us continue with your timelife story.
You worry me. What do you mean?
No, you do not worry. That's just a figure of speech. You will become old but never reach extreme old age.

You had a girlfriend at this period, as young as you but with plenty of female assurance. Her name was Gale Roberts, a rather cinematic name which bestowed glamour on her. Her mother was a big, hearty woman, who liked to praise things in general. She called you 'sensible'. When she despatched you and Gale to visit her

Uncle Norman and his wife, Tamsin, she described their tragedy in enthusiastic terms.

'She's totally incapacitated, poor darling thing! She bears her misfortune so nobly. And my brother – well, Norman's such a sweetie-pie! Of course, an absolute slave to Tammy, an absolute slave, he does everything, but *everything* for her. As you'll see, my dear.'

The visit proved a memorable one.

Tamsin Roberts had 'broken her back', as the phrase had it, when crossing a road in France and encountering a slow-moving vehicle. She suffered complex fractures of several vertebrae. Both Robertses were in their early fifties; to you they seemed vastly old. They lived in a small terraced house, the upper floor of which they let out.

When you rang the bell, Norman peeped out before nodding and letting you both in.

'Just doing a spot of cleaning,' he said with a laugh that affected at once to laugh at himself and to explain the floral apron he was wearing. Norman was a small, dry man with a sandy moustache and a large red nose. He clutched a yellow duster.

Tamsin was confined to an armchair in what had been their dining room, where she could gaze out at the small garden. Now she got her meals on a tray. Her husband, Gale's uncle, looked after her, doing everything for her; dressing her, undressing her, shopping and cooking for her.

Somehow they remained cheerful. The radio was always on. They kept two cats, Mike and Snippets, both tabbies. The cats hung about in picturesque positions on items of furniture, the one on the piano, the other on a side table. When they moved, they moved carefully about the little crowded room, full of its small tables, its china figures and its potted plants.

Gale presented the Roberts with a cake her mother had baked. They chatted of small things. Tamsin spoke in a flat voice, but appeared cheerful enough. Norman said he pushed her up the street and back in her wheelchair every day, when all the neighbours came out to speak to them.

'What a lot they are,' said Tamsin, looking slightly humorous as she referred to the neighbours.

As you and Gale were about to leave, Norman ushered you out, saying, 'Careful how you go. Mind the ironing board. I've just got to iron one of Tammy's nighties. I'll just shut the kitchen door. We love the cats so much; we don't want them to escape. We never let them go outside.'

So off the two of you went, carefree and skipping up the street, Gale swinging her mother's wicker shopping basket. You were getting to the stage when you might dare to kiss Gale.

'So what do you make of that pair of old crocks?' Gale asked.

'Your uncle's very good with Tamsin. Life can't be much fun for him.'

Gale sat down on a low wall, adjusting her dress so that first you saw a lot of thigh and then none. 'I reckon uncle enjoys being prison warden.' She spoke carelessly.

'Prison warden? How do you make that out?' You stood in front of her, your trousers all but touching her knees. 'I thought he was her slave. Isn't that the general idea?'

She tossed a lock of dark hair from her eyes. It immediately fell back into its original position, its lowest strands to rest on her rosy cheek. 'You heard what he said – about the cats, I mean. He loves the cats but is afraid they may escape. So they are stuck for ever in the house. Could be he feels the same about *her*.'

'You mean he feels Tamsin might escape?'

'Maybe he used to. You can see how insecure he is. He's glad she is stuck in that chair, unable to get away from him.'

Such a concept had not occurred to you. The novelty, the secrecy of it, thrilled you in some way. 'But what does *she* feel?'

Gale sighed and looked up at you with a contemplative air. 'Work it out for yourself. Could be she likes being a prisoner. She was always a bit valetudinarian, even when she was young – like her mum.'

'So you're saying they get on okay?'

26

'I'm saying it may not be the way it looks, with them both being miserable. Just could be it even suits them.'

'But you can't ask them —'

She reached out and touched your hand. 'Of course you can't ask *them*, silly!'

'What a bugger that you can't ask them straight out.'

But your mind was not really on that mystery of human relationships; it centred more on Gale's pretty, moist lips. You leant forward, clutched her shoulders and kissed her.

The world turned to gold dust about you.

You often wondered what sort of person Valerie had been in her short life. After the visit to the Roberts' house, you found reason to wonder about yourself. You had gone on this rather boring – as you initially saw it – visit to an invalid, simply to be near Gale. You were well aware of the life of the senses, even if, at that early age, you stood as yet high and dry on its shores. You were also aware of another life, one that might hinder or distract you from the sensual oceans represented by the tepid lake of Gale Roberts, and that was one to which she herself had directed your attention: the life of human motivation, so cunning, so unfathomable.

For which way had it been in the invalid's semi-detached home? Was old Norman the slave or the captor? Was she the dominatrix or the prisoner? Only slowly, as you sat upstairs in your bedroom, gazing blankly at the painting of birds quietly despoiling a wheat harvest, did it occur to you that both interpretations, such was the complexity of the human psyche, could be simultaneously viable.

Yet never did it occur to you that there were parallels here with your own unresolved dilemma; the Walcot problem.

5

'Bloody Cripples!'

When Martin joined Short's, another aviation company, the family followed him to Southampton, where Short Brothers was based. You saw little of your father. Politics kept him busy.

You remember an occasion when he had been addressing a small group of men on a street corner. He came home and told you that a policeman had appeared and said to him, gently but firmly, 'Move along there, there's a good lad.'

Your father had asked why he should move along. The bobby had replied, 'Because I say so, sir, if you don't mind.'

Your father was furious at this demonstration of power.

Looking back, you regret the disappearance of this kind of policing.

Your early existence was trapped between the two world wars, your later one by the Cold War. Your father provided constant reminders of the first war. The injury to his leg pained him continually; the broken bone had been badly set in the first place, and had to be re-broken and re-set. Throughout your boyhood, he was in and out of hospital. The aggravation increased his bitterness and his silence.

'Does your poor leg hurt very much, Daddy?' you asked him on one occasion, perhaps trying to curry favour.

'We all have to make sacrifices,' he said. It had become a favourite expression.

'Do you have to sacrifice us?' Sonia asked. As the spoilt one, she dared to criticize.

In fact, Martin had been lucky. He had survived the prolonged Battle of the Somme, a battle in which a million men had died – Germans, French and British – owing to a well-timed attack of pneumonia.

Your home was not generously provided with books. You remember one book in particular from those early days; it was bound in half-leather and consisted of twelve volumes: *The Daily Telegraph History of the Great War*. Through an absorbed study of those volumes, you gained an insight into the various hells through which your father had suffered and through which humankind put one another.

One painting reproduced in that book almost destroyed you with pity. The scene was in France; the ruins of a French town could be discerned mistily in the distance. In the foreground lay a wounded horse. It had to be left behind by the troops. The troops could be seen in the background, beckoning to a figure in the middle ground to hurry up and join them. But the figure in the middle ground lingered. His hand was raised in sad farewell to his horse. He it was who provided the caption to the picture: 'Farewell, old friend!'

You were inconsolable. You cried and cried until your mother became angry and left you to weep. The argument that this was 'only a painting' carried no weight with you, for you felt certain it was a representation of something that could have happened, where the innocent suffered along with the wicked.

Surely at that time, one of your admirable qualities was born and fortified: compassion.

For the first thirteen months of the family's removal to Southampton, you all stayed in a rented flat. Your father and mother could not find a house on which they could get a mortgage that they liked enough to buy. You were allotted a small room in the attic, where you were probably better situated than were the other members of the family. Sonia had a small room overlooking a banana importer's yard. The wallpaper was violently colourful and featured the endlessly reduplicated image of an animal with big ears driving a little red car. To this Sonia took strident objection.

'I hate it! I hate it! Take it away. It's horrid.'

'You'll soon get used to it, darling,' Mary had said, wearily. 'This was a child's room and, after all, you are a child, you know.'

Sonia screamed in response to this apparent injustice. 'I am not that kind of a child. I am a child hunchback! A famous child hunchback! I'm special. I can't sleep with this horrid thing hanging on the wall.'

'Valerie would love that wallpaper! Please don't be troublesome, dear.'

'It's not me. It's the wallpaper.'

But Sonia had to put up with it. And there in that flat you spent a confined Christmas. Before you had your presents, Mary insisted on crimping Sonia's hair. Protest as Sonia might, the tongs, the crimping paper, were brought to bear, and soon her chestnut locks were covered with waves like a sea of frozen gravy. The scorching smell still lingered round her head even when you sat down to dinner later that day.

Wished upon you was a girl of twelve, bigger than you and even more sulky, a girl of twelve with pigtails, by name Joan Pie. Martin had joined the local trade union. One of his docker friends had been struck by a falling girder. He was lying in hospital after a shoulder operation and his wife was ill, so Martin had generously volunteered to have Joan Pie come to stay with you all over Christmas and Boxing Day.

'I don't want to sit next to her,' Sonia said, after one second's inspection of the visitor. 'She's a pig.'

'Ooh, snooty!' said Joan Pie, and poked her tongue out at Sonia.

'Behave yourselves,' Mary ordered. But from then on, you two youngsters had conceived a hatred of this intruder into your uncomfortable quarters. You and Sonia were immediately united against her.

You asked your sister at the dinner table if she had ever heard of such a funny name as Pie. 'Fly is silly too,' Sonia said in a judicious manner. She asked the visitor, 'Do you know anyone called Fly, Pie?'

'Stop that, or I'll make you get down,' said Martin from his side of the table.

Now Mary was slicing and serving the Christmas pudding, doing it with slow care. You watched the operation like a hawk, alert for injustice.

Your plate with a slice of pudding was set down before you. Next, Joan Pie was served. Then Sonia. Suddenly, your mother exclaimed. Leaning forward, she rapidly switched your plate with Sonia's.

You were angry at once. 'Why did you do that?'

Mary waved her hands about. 'I gave you the wrong plates, that's all. Nothing else. Have some custard, Stevie.'

'How were they wrong?'

'Just be grateful for what you've got,' Martin said, sternly.

'Yes, be grateful for what you've got,' echoed Joan Pie, giving Martin a silly look, seeking his approval.

'You've got a bigger piece of pudding now, Stephen, so be quiet,' said Mary. 'Valerie would never complain as you do.'

You subsided. The Bird's custard circulated in its little boat. You all ate in silence. Christmas pudding, dark, reluctant to crumble, heavy as mud, comprising many unknown things, bizarrely pleasing and quelling to the taste buds, a thing of the Stone Age. Eaten once a year like a human sacrifice.

Sonia gave a shriek and plunged her fingers into the sodden mass on her plate.

'Look! I've got it!' She waved a little bright object, to which a squashed currant adhered. 'A sixpence! I've found a sixpence.'

You burst into tears. Well, you were only eight.

Only eight, but a bit of a baby.
You perceived that you had been swindled. It was a case of naked favouritism – And a reminder to me that I had been born into an unjust world.
No, the world has its invariable laws. It is human society which has established injustice.
Don't tell me any more. I don't want to remember –
It is necessary to remember, and to proceed.

After the meal, you had indoor fireworks. You and your sister loved indoor fireworks. There were paper mazes to which Martin applied his glowing cigarette end at the position marked 'Start', at which a spark went racing across the blank spaces to a destination it celebrated with quite a loud crack. There were sparklers you could hold and wave in dazzling patterns. There were folded papers that burnt into pretty ferns. There were flimsy paper cylinders to which you applied a lighted match and, as the paper burned down, magically rose and ascended to the ceiling. And there were snakes.

How you both loved the snakes.

By this time, you were in a better mood to enjoy the snakes. To comfort you, Sonia had whispered that she would share the sixpence, giving you half. Still grieving over the injustice, you had responded grumpily that it was your sixpence.

'It's not yours, it's mine, 'cos I've got it,' said Sonia, with some logic. 'So for that I'll only give you twopence.'

'That's not fair!'

'And if you don't shut up, you'll only get a penny, so there.'

The snakes came in two kinds. One form of snake emerged from a volcano. The volcano was very small and encased in green 'silver

33

paper'. It stood on a circular cardboard base. When the peak of the volcano was lit, little green flecks, closely resembling grass, poured from it, covering the base. Finally, the snake emerged, writhing realistically as it came. It was thin but, with what seemed like evil intent, it crossed the grass as if to attack. Then, mercifully, it froze.

Sonia and you were enraptured. But Joan Pie said, contemptuously, 'It didn't do much.'

'It would have bitten you if it could,' you told her.

'Stephen!' Martin said, reprovingly. 'You be nice to Joan or you'll go up to your room.'

The other kind of snake was bigger and more terrifying. That was why you liked it better than the grass snake.

This snake, possibly a python, was concealed in a small, black top hat. This Christmas, Martin had discovered a cardboard box full of the little top hats, left over from the previous year by the last tenant of the flat. You clapped your hands with excitement at the sight of so many hats.

'How Valerie would have loved them,' Mary exclaimed wistfully.

Your father set one of them on the table near the grass snake, struck a match and tried to light it. The hat would not burn. Martin burnt his finger instead, and swore.

'Try another match, daddy,' shouted Sonia, full of anticipation.

He struck another one, but it also failed to ignite the hat, and again he burnt his finger.

'Don't be daft, Martin,' Mary said. 'You can see they're old and damp. You'll only burn yourself.'

Perhaps he was annoyed to be called daft. He took the box of top hats and flung it onto the coal fire, which heated his end of the room. You and Sonia groaned your disappointment. Joan Pie stuck her tongue out at you both, enjoying your dismay. But the box caught fire. The next minute, a dozen huge black pythons came uncoiling out of the fire and across the hearth to the carpet. What a sight! Sonia gave a yelp of delight. Joan Pie ran from the room, howling with fear.

What a sight! What a triumph!

Your father seemed always to be standing, holding forth in those days, despite his bad leg. He was a big man, generally to be seen in a tight-fitting Aertex shirt. He had a broad face and steely eyes. His lips were generally compressed, as if with anger against the injustices of the world.

You remembered an occasion when your parents had been having what you thought of as 'a cold row'. Few words were spoken during their cold rows, but there was plenty of body language, of glaring of eyes and turning of backs. Your father had said, ill-advisedly, that his Socialist principles had been formed because he was shocked to find families like his wife's in penury.

'The Wilberforces' lot was much more humble than the Fieldings,' he said.

'I wouldn't say that,' Mary protested, stiff of face. She liked to think she came from 'respectable stock'. 'We weren't too badly off. When I was fifteen Dad had an indoor lavvy tacked on.'

A recital of your antecedents made you dizzy. It seemed to you that these dead people all became middle-aged shortly after their thirtieth birthdays, that they died in their fifties or sixties, and that they were poor in ways forgotten in the more prosperous present – your present.

'Take your mother's family,' Martin said, directing his words at you and glaring through you into the past. 'Zachariah Frost was grandfather to your grandfather. Where he came from, heaven knows, but his parents must have been extremely poor, since the story has come down that they had to remove Zachariah from school because they were unable to provide the halfpenny a week required to keep him there.

'A ha'penny! Think of that, Stephen!' He shot a corrective glance at you, huddled in an armchair with a comic.

You thought of it. You knew ha'pennies. They had the last king's head on one side of them and a sailing ship on the other. Those coins were often worn thin with usage, having passed through innumerable pockets.

'Zachariah became a cobbler,' Martin continued. 'He married one Jane Wilberforce. They lived in a small house in Brick Street, Newbury. Although she was a scraggy little thing, by all accounts, they produced two girls and two boys. The kids were brought up on jam butties. They were all Baptists – Buttie Baptists – and went to chapel every Sunday.'

'They were always religious,' Mary said, defensively. She was making a cloth cover in which to keep the week's *Radio Times*.

'One of those girls died aged three. A common fate in those days. Rickets, probably.'

'We used to have soap flakes called Ricketts,' your mother exclaimed, unable not to enjoy talk of the old days, despite the offence she had taken. Your father ignored her remark.

'Then the other girl, Hettie, her name was, she ran off with a foreigner and went to the Continent and was never heard of again.'

'I 'spec she wanted to escape the family,' said Sonia.

'Getting above herself, more like,' said Mary. 'The Continent! Of all places! Fancy!'

Father remarked in an aside that Paris must have been better than Portsmouth.

'One of Zachariah's boys was known as "Flash Harry". They say in the family that Flash Harry seduced the vicar's daughter. In any case, he went to fight the Boers and died in some horrible spot of Africa.

'The other Frost brother got a job in Utterson's, the hardware merchant. His name was Ernie, Ernie Frost. You picture him and his like in rough black suits, wearing caps when out on the street, where most of the lads like him spent much of their spare time.'

'Why was that?' you asked. You failed to see the attraction of streets.

He shrugged. 'Where else could they go in those days? Besides, the houses were so pokey –'

Ernie had the urge to improve himself. He rejected his surname, Frost, on the grounds that it was unappealing. He changed his name by deed poll to his mother's maiden name of Wilberforce. It was a rejection of all that cobbling and grubbing for the last farthing.

'Next, Ernie took up the banjo. He hired himself out to sing and play at parties. He had no wish to live forever in the back streets with a shared thunderbox. He had a daguerreotype taken of himself in a straw boater, strumming the banjo. Your mother can show it you. He must have been quite a lad, young Ernie. Leaving Utterson's at the age of nineteen, he became the delivery man for Ross, the big Newbury grocer. He worked hard and was reliable. Pretty soon, he was driving about in a pony and trap, delivering the groceries to the better houses of the district.

'That was how he met the young lady who played the organ at the Baptist chapel in Brink, just outside Newbury. Her name was Sarah Ream. She was a shy lass, though not without spirit, and she couldn't resist Ernie's charm and jollity. He coaxed Sarah to play piano accompaniment while he strummed the banjo and sang.'

'Oh, and they say that my mother never went near the chapel again,' Mary interposed, caught somewhere between shame and pride.

'Anyhow, Ernie and Sarah became a duo, quite stylish! The duo became quite fashionable. He wrote a song entitled *I Stand and Play My Banjo in the Strand*. It was printed as sheet music, and was very popular for a time.'

Your father sang, looking genial.

'The girls all fall for me
They ask me home for tea,
They think I'm grand.
They didn't ought to risk it
'Cos they know I take the biscuit
When I stand and play me banjo in the Strand,
Hey ho! I stand and play me banjo in the Strand.'

Sonia clapped the performance. Mary looked pleased and said she loved that old song.

'Ernie and Sarah got married and went to live in 33, Park Road. Although Ernie had no "background", as people used to say, his ease of manner served him well. With the help of local Baptists, he soon acquired four houses in Park Road. He became a man of substance and was appointed secretary of the local Baptist Church. He was never afraid of work, was Ernie. Sarah became director of the local Waifs and Strays House —'

So there you were, the fatal family four of you, in the cramped room. A light fitting hung centrally overhead, like the God in which you all more or less believed at that period. It was the only light in the room. On a side table stood the wireless, the only wireless in the house. A coal fire burned in the grate. On the mat in front of the grate lay a rug, and on that rug centrally stood your father, holding forth, as fathers did in those days, before they were deposed.

'Sarah and Ernie produced five children: first of all three boys, and then two girls, of which your dear Mother was the last to be born.'

Martin cast Mary an affectionate, if patronizing, glance as he mentioned her. The cold row was over.

'You can imagine that Ernie's increasing prosperity was shared by many of the lower classes at that time. Only four of your generations ago, Steve, listen to this, most people in England lived the sort of life Zachariah Frost lived; ill-educated, hand-to-mouth, having too many kids, dying young. Change since then has been incalculable, mainly thanks to the rise of Socialism.'

Socialism always backed science.

'These three Frost, or Wilberforce, sons formed an architectural partnership. Things were looking up. The town itself was expanding. The partnership built many of the rows of houses in which a new generation of engineers and artisans and other workers lived. It's all in the records. The sons all married young. They needed wives for social purposes. You'll remember your Uncle

Jeremy and Auntie Flo's little house, with its cheerful geranium window boxes?'

You did remember it. Uncle Jeremy's house was full of heavy furniture. The rooms smelt of mothballs. Sombre engravings of Napoleon's retreat from Moscow and similar improving subjects hung on the walls in heavy frames. Jeremy and Flo employed a little servant girl called Ann.

When you were taken visiting to the house, you used to run off to see Ann. She lived in the gloomy rear of the house until called. Ann was nice to you. Ann would even do a cute little dance for you. Ann was of obscure origin, probably illegitimate. She was quick and ardent, always smiling. What secret sorrows were hers you never knew. Nor did her employers enquire. Many feelings natural to earlier generations were necessarily repressed in the name of progress. When Ann finally climbed, late at night, to her tiny cabin in the attic, no one knew or thought to know what eternities of hope or disappointment she underwent there.

'Then the war came,' Martin went on, although this was on another occasion, just after your pet rabbit died. '1914. I'll never forget the date. August 1914. It was royalty brought the war about. The blinking Crowned Heads of Europe! The war gradually ground into action, swallowing up young men all over Europe and far beyond. Among those cast into the maw of this monster were the three brothers of the architectural partnership; your uncles, poor buggers.'

'Martin!' exclaimed Mary, reprovingly.

'I said beggars. Off they bravely went – Bertie, Jeremy and Ernest, Sarah shedding motherly tears as she waved them off on the train.'

'My poor mother! What she went through!'

'Two of the lads were captured by the Germans and spent most of the war in an Oflag. The third one, Ernie – a handsome youth of twenty-one – stopped a bullet at Passchendaele and died on the spot.'

'It was the Somme, of all places,' said Mary. 'I ought to know. He got shot in the Somme offensive. August 1916.'

'The Somme,' cried Sonia, bored with talk of war. 'That was where I got my hunchback.' She was sitting huddled in an armchair with Gyp, our Airedale, sprawling on her lap. Suddenly she threw Gyp off. 'I'm going to have an operation to get it removed.'

'Do stop that nonsense,' your mother scolded her. 'Valerie would never say anything like that.'

The dog sat and scratched himself, staring at Sonia with a look of amazement. Everyone was amazed by Sonia.

Martin pressed grimly on with his account.

'They say Ernie fell face down in the mud, was trampled over, got buried in it – never to play his banjo in the Strand again. Sarah, his widow, never remarried, poor lass.'

'She set up a teashop with a lady companion. It stood on what's now the Southampton Road,' said Mary. 'Valerie and I often used to go there in the old days.'

'The other two brothers, Bert and Jeremy, returned unharmed at the end of the war. Jeremy rejoined his Flo – her folks were no one much – and Bertie married Violet from Grantham, a member of the smart Parkins family. The Parkinses manufactured the latest thing in lawnmowers for the upwardly mobile generations. Violet is a bit of a goer – I'd say out of Bertie's class.'

'Don't say that,' Mary exclaimed. 'I wouldn't trust Violet further than I could throw her!'

Contemplating the idea of anyone throwing any aunties anywhere, Sonia burst into laughter. Her mother hushed her.

'Any road, at Violet's prompting, Bertie ceased to pursue his architectural career. He became instead a stunt pilot. Violet thought that was much more glamorous. He flew with Sir Alan Cobham's Air Display, touring the country and delighting audiences with his daring. Jeremy remained with the architectural business, sole owner. Bedazzled by his young wife, skittish Flo, he began to neglect his work. Gradually the business went downhill. Bertie finally gave up his flying and joined the sinking business. He and Jeremy built that little Baptist chapel down Greenacres Road.'

You imagined that old Zachariah Frost was a refugee from some starving stretch of the country, where life for the poor was even harder than life in the towns. Sonia drew a picture of him in crayon: a terrible old man with a big, hook nose and a hump on his back. Martin snatched up the paper and was furious at what he saw.

'You should show some respect, girl!'

Sonia jumped up, stamping her foot. She grabbed the paper back.

'It's me! It's not him! It's me, dressed up. Mind your own business.'

You would never have dared speak to your father like that. It would have provoked a beating.

'We've never had hunchbacks in our family,' Martin said. He enjoyed telling you and your sister about the family history. You listened more passively than Sonia. But you, like her, were obsessed with your appearance. Shutting yourself in your north-facing bedroom, you would stare at your face in the looking glass. Eyes of an indeterminate colour. But were you not rather *aristocratic*, by and large? Possibly lantern-jawed? What was a lantern jaw? Did it shine like a lantern? Lantern-jawed. You spent hours practising being lantern-jawed, walking round the room being lantern-jawed.

And still your father did his best to educate you in family history.

'We Fieldings became more prosperous earlier than did the Frosts,' Martin said. 'In the parish records, William Fielding comes into the picture with dates attached. Born in the eighteen-forties. His wife Isabelle – Isabelle Doughty, she was – was from the superior Norfolk family of Doughtys. Isabelle bore William seven children, no less. William himself was one of nine children, two of whom were daughters. Two of William's brothers died at sea.'

'We still have a record somewhere of the death of one of the brothers, James. James Fielding was Chief Petty Officer of the ship *Montgomery*. He died of a fever off the Grand Banks, aged twenty-five. A fine young man. His body was committed to the deep.'

Your father spoke these last words in a deep voice, as if to convey the depth of the ocean involved.

'What are the Grand Banks actually, Daddy?' you asked.

'Not the same as Barclay's Bank.' Perhaps he thought he had made a joke. 'No, the Grand Banks are off Newfoundland, and covered permanently in fog.'

'Did they push him over the side when he was dead?' Sonia asked. It was the first time she had shown any real interest in the account.

'His coffin was lowered over the side with all due reverence.' Martin gave his Aertex shirt a tug, as if to demonstrate.

'It may have been these deaths that persuaded William to settle in Swaffham and open a chemist's shop instead of going to sea. One of his sons, my dad, your grandfather, Sydney Fielding, established a similar business in Horncastle. He combined a dentistry with his pharmacy. In Horncastle were born all of Sydney and Elizabeth's children, one of them being none other than me, your father.'

Your mother was quite a bit younger than your father.

You feared him. He would beat you with a slipper even when you were small – say, two years old. After the beating, when your feelings were hurt as well as your behind, he would make you shake hands with him and declare that you were still friends. This you always did, fearing another beating if you didn't, but you never ever felt he was your friend.

'Never,' you swore under your breath, accentuating the word by becoming momentarily lantern-jawed.

When your father was not angry, he was morose. You remember watching him staring moodily out of your front window at the street. A little band of wounded ex-servicemen was playing there, with trumpet, tambourine and penny whistle. A cap lay on the pavement at their feet. The old soldiers could muster only five eyes and four legs between the three of them. You would often stand and look at them with a kind of puzzled sympathy, until they told you

Issues Summary   20/10/2016 16:53
Donabate and Portrane Library

Id :: 4000000326****
Name:: McClelland, Joanne

Item : Walcot / Brian Aldiss.
10-11-16
Item : Enigma of China / Qiu Xiaolong.
10-11-16

Total Number of Issued Items 2

Thank you for using Self-Service

to clear off. Your father regarded them icily through the window. He had no patience for those who did not, or could not, work.

'Bloody cripples,' he said, catching you staring at him. He had to fight against being a cripple himself, with his painful leg. Such disabled soldiers fell outside his socialist sympathies for the working man.

'Work's the saviour, young feller-m'-lad,' he told you. He often called you 'young feller-m'-lad', as if he could not quite remember your name. Perhaps he thought that a new breed of men would have to appear before wars ceased; men without the savagery that begot wars. You know he sometimes spoke to your mother of how the world could be redeemed. How God should send his Son down again, pretty promptly, and alter everything; yet his words were empty of any real sense of belief.

And Mary would sniff and say that these were awful times they were living in.

'It's the end of the British Empire,' Martin would respond. 'India has let us down. Remember when the present king held his durbar in Delhi? What a show that was. Those times are gone for ever.'

'Good old King George and Queen Mary,' your mother exclaimed.

'I've nothing against him, but what's he ever done for the poor? Look at the miners.'

And Mary would say, rather despairingly, 'Martin, couldn't we just talk about happy things?'

'Like what?' your father would ask.

She would gesture. 'Oh, can't we ever laugh? I long for humour the way you long for a pork chop.'

'You're too superficial, that's the trouble with you, dear.'

Your little sister, detecting something frosty in the air, perhaps another cold row brewing, would bang heartily on a tin tray with a spoon, while shrieking at the top of her voice her favourite swear word, 'Shuggerybees!'

You often wondered where Sonia got her high spirits from.

You were barely in your teens when you bought a book for twopence off a market stall. It was called The Old Red Sandstone. *You were attracted by the title –*

I don't remember it.

Yes, you do. Your father approved, because the book was written by a working man who became a geologist, a rare achievement in early Victorian times. What fascinated you were such dramatic passages as, 'At this period in our history some terrible catastrophe involved the sudden destruction of the fish of an area at least a hundred miles from boundary to boundary, perhaps far more. It exhibits unequivocally the marks of violent death ...'

Yes, I was thrilled by it, and by the idea of geology. Better than any fairy tale!

It was to play a part in your later life.

I don't think so.

We shall see, shan't we?

6

Earth Sciences

Before you were sent away to school – possibly the very reason why you were sent away to school – your remarkable sister Sonia had arrived in the world. Although she could never compare with Valerie, the perfect daughter, she immediately occupied your parents' attention. Your mother doted on her, absorbing all her, somewhat fickle, attention.

Your father, meanwhile, disliked displays of emotion. Perhaps his war injury reinforced his withdrawn character. Ignoring socialist principles, he sent you away to a nearby public school as soon as possible.

One consolation in this form of exile was the weekly arrival of your favourite magazine, *Modern Boy*. In the pages of *Modern Boy* you followed the adventures of 'Captain Castern of the South Seas'. Captain Mike Castern sailed a ketch about the Pacific Ocean. He had a crew of Kanakas, who would say of a dead man – and someone, generally wicked, died every week – things such as, 'Dat man he go big sky blong Jesus.'

At school, you developed an eccentric habit. There were certain senior boys whose looks were so peculiar in your eyes that you christened them with sentences from books you had been reading. That fellow with the swollen red face, suffering from some variant of acne rosacea, you dubbed, 'Morning dawned, red and angry'. Another fellow was 'The burly janitor replied'. Another was a thin fellow with a downcast air; he was christened, 'He watched it drain away without regret'. Another lumbering fellow was 'One excellence I crave'; but he left school early.

A curious protocol about these phrases dictated that you had to utter them obsessively to yourself whenever you caught sight of the boy to whom they referred. Often – for instance when the whole school was filing into the school chapel – the phrases had to be mumbled quickly, one after the other. The habit served to distance yourself from the other boys. You had contracted a splinter of isolation from your father.

You gave other boys of your own age, with whom you were more closely associated, exotic secret names, known only to yourself. You may recall Pyrodee Nangees, Trevor Birdshit, Fizure, Georgie Suckletrot and Gaspar de Peckubee. And a dull-looking day boy who became simply Fartadoo.

This inventive turn of mind caused you also to form with a friend a secret clique of two, called 'The Royal Society for the Overthrow of All Masters and the Government'. You and your friend were required to chant fifty times, 'We the Murderers will Overthrow all stinking rotten Masters – *pooh!* – and the stinking rotten Gov'ment, too.' The society flourished only for one term, to die of boredom since you were unable to dream up the means by which to execute your good intentions: although teams of well-trained cobras certainly entered into one of your proposals.

Following the example set by Hugh Miller's *The Old Red Sandstone*, you took to reading the strange books with strange titles you found in the library: *The Museum of Unconditional Surrender, Confessions of an English Opium Eater, On the Use of the Herb Slac, The Return of the Native* (the native what, you wondered), and *The End of the Imp*, translated from the Russian.

Among the strange books you were reading, cheek-by-jowl with Captain Castern, was one entitled *The Miscellaneous Writings of Sir Thomas Browne*. This volume contained many curiosities, including a paper on certain fossil remains discovered at Winterton. Winterton was the first place at which Robinson Crusoe was shipwrecked. It lies on the North Norfolk coast, not very far from Walcot.

Browne, a seventeenth-century doctor, said: 'Upon the same coaste, butt at some miles distance, divers great bones are sayd to have been found, & I have seen one side of a lower jaw containing very large teath petrified, farre exceeding the teeth of the biggest ox. It was found after a great flood neerc to the cliff, some thousand loades of earth being broaken down by the rage of the sea.'

Thomas Browne was mystified, as were you, by these great bones. Many years later, in the nineteen-eighties, the fossilized skeleton of a mammoth was found near Weybourne. Browne's animal was very likely a mammoth too, possibly from the same herd.

Your curiosity moved you to join a schools geological expedition in the summer holidays. A group of boys and masters were taken by ship to La Rochelle, from whence a coach conveyed you all inland to a small village called Beaussais. Outside Beaussais was an extensive dig, where the remains of a Roman villa that had been buried in an earthquake were being excavated. You all stayed in a small hotel just a kilometre away from the site.

The dig had been roped off. Topsoil, on which grass grew, lay in piles outside the ropes. All that had been revealed of the villa so far was a paved pathway with a broken pillar standing at one end of the path. To one side, a radial ditch had been dug, leading nowhere. Your companions were excited. You felt only disappointment; you do not know what you had been expecting. A revelation of some kind?

Your lack of enthusiasm was noticed by one of the masters super-intending you. He was not from your school. His face was roughly the shape and colour of a plum. His hair was well-oiled and curly. He wore khaki shorts and heavy boots, with thin, hairy legs showing in the exposed area between them. His name was Mr Loftus.

'Have you no interest in Roman villas?' he asked.

You thought, *what was another Roman villa?* but could not articulate the thought. You hung your head.

'A mile from here there's a more interesting site, where a mete-orite struck. Would you be interested in looking at that?'

His dark eyes regarded you rather contemptuously.

'Yes,' you said, although something in your head warned you to say no.

You went with Mr Loftus, following him up the slope. The ground was broken and stony. No trees grew, only clumps of bracken and furze; it was a landscape scraped bare.

Looking ahead at Mr Loftus's hairy legs working their way onwards, and Mr Loftus's boots, clumping along on your eye level, you conceived a hatred for all boots, reflecting that those who had power – the power represented by the boots – could do whatever they liked. You felt it to be your destiny always to be on an eye level with boots, plod, plod, plodding: boots with their studs, with their horseshoe-shaped metal shodding. There was a feeling in your stomach, totally unformed by intellect, that in only a few years – three at most – the world would be full of the clamour of metal-shod marching boots.

All your concerns about bursting into adulthood, a butterfly from a chrysalis – about how your career would go, about how you would earn money, about whether your friends liked you or secretly despised you – all those concerns would be kicked away by the legions of boots that even then were preparing to march in Germany, and out of Germany into neighbouring countries.

I am surprised you know what I thought then. I hardly knew my own thoughts.

They were deep within me.
You are not surprised. Nothing can surprise you here.
Yes, but those unspoken thoughts.
They were recorded. There are no privacies, no surprises here.

You climbed for about an hour before the ground levelled off. Mr Loftus continued to plod on, while you stopped to look at the view. From your vantage point, the country in the main looked flat. To the north, the serpentine bends of the river Niortaise gleamed in the sunshine. More distantly, the higher ground of the Sèvres region was obscured by a heat mist. Only faint noises arose from humanity below, challenged by nearer bird calls, plangent in the thin air. The sight of this beautiful sparse foreign land awoke vibrations within you.

You walked now on bare rock. Mr Loftus stopped at last. The boots were at rest, the knees of the hairy legs companionable together. Mr Loftus mopped his brow with a blue handkerchief. A whisper of breeze was keeping the temperature down in this high place.

'Here we are,' he said. He was breathing heavily.

'This is it,' he said. 'Few people know about this.'

He indicated a wide hole in the rock. Cracks meandered in several directions from the crater, like tributaries running into the sea. The interior of the crater was more or less smooth, except where a portion had been cut away. A rusty pick lay beside the cut.

'Get down in it, lad,' he said.

You did as you were bid, climbing into the rock. The lip of the crater came above your head, obscuring sight of anything beyond the crater but the blue sky. You recollected that experience much later in life. As you stared at the layered rock, Loftus explained what you were seeing. A thin broken dark band of what resembled rust separated two types of rock.

'The burn marks where the asteroid struck.' He squatted, so that his bare knees gleamed, to pick up a fragment and show it you. 'We call this stuff *breccia*. A small asteroid came in from space and left this burn signature in the rocks. It struck about forty million years ago, long before France or mankind itself was thought of. See how the stratum above the burn is quite dark. Then comes lighter rock. There, fossils begin. Just a few. I'd guess this darker rock signifies at least five hundred thousand years of ocean which followed the asteroid strike.'

He picked at it and laid a fragment in the palm of his left hand. 'What are the fossils?' you asked.

'Nothing important. Squirrels. A thing like a present-day fox –'

You listened to this matter-of-fact account, and all the while you were staring at the exposed rock face, the grits and stone of which Earth's crust was composed, which would have meant nothing to ordinary people. Yet, given knowledge – the sort of knowledge you longed to acquire – a terrestrial drama lay before you. It was an enigma which, given knowledge, could meet with understanding. This was an explanation for the terrible catastrophe, the sudden destruction, which had puzzled Hugh Miller. A key turned in your mind.

'It's amazing, Sir,' you said. 'Everyone ought to know about this place!'

'It's not important,' Mr Loftus said, indifferently. 'It's been examined and recorded. Hundreds of such impacts have been recorded all over the world. It goes to demonstrate what geologists already understand, that our planet, throughout the eons, has been constantly bombarded by comets, meteors, asteroids and assorted bits of rock.'

You had never before heard anyone use the phrase 'our planet' for the Earth. It seemed to weaken you, to make your legs tremble.

'All that time,' you murmured.

'From time immemorial up to the present day.'

'But it is important, Sir,' you insisted weakly.

'No. Not in itself. It's been recorded. Rock fragments have been analysed and their iridium content noted. It's now an item in a ledger in the Paris Institute of Geology.'

'Coo, I'd like to find something like this myself, Sir! What's iridium?'

Loftus went on to explain that the metal iridium was rare on the surface of the Earth, but abundant in the meteoritic dust arriving from space. You found it hard to tell from his attitude whether he believed you knew more of such matters than you did, or whether he thought you a complete ignoramus on whom further explanation was wasted.

You were entirely taken up by this connection between 'our planet' and the objects which arrived from distant places beyond your most fervid imagining. You were seized by a glimpse of the solar system as a whole. A new light, you felt, was lit in your intellect.

Yes, I think I did feel that.
I'm telling you, you did.
If only that light had not failed throughout many years of my life …
Isn't such knowledge, well, cleansing?
In some cases, yes.

Mr Loftus had pronounced the little crater to be without importance. But for you it was important; it set you on what was eventually to become your future career. You were not much interested in disinterring Roman villas; you wished to concentrate on the drama of battered 'our planet' itself, and of the creatures cast up on the beaches of existence upon it – for instance the creatures to be found in the old red sandstone.

As Mr Loftus extended a hand to help you out of the dig, you stammered your gratitude to him for bringing you to this remote spot, which chthonic activity had raised high above the ancient sea bed.

'You may care,' said he, in his dry voice, 'to remember the dictum of Goethe, who says, "Think in order to act, act in order to think."'

'Please, Sir, who is Goethe?'

'Why, he is the great German thinker, boy. Johann Wolfgang Goethe.'

Boy-like, as the two of you descended the hill, you again following the legs and the boots, you managed to assure yourself that you had discovered the importance of thought – of thinking about everything – long before this Goethe fellow came upon the scene.

Also at your school was a cousin of yours, by name Thomas Sidney Wilberforce. You never knew him well and rarely associated with him. Something about him you found disturbing; boy-like, you did not attempt to discover what it was.

Sidney was known to his class as 'Sad Sid'. He had suffered much as you had done; whereas you had soon grown out of it, Sid never managed to do so. His parents, Jeremy and the skittish Flo, rather like your mother, had not wanted a son. Flo had ill-advisedly set her heart on a girl, a little girl she could dress in frilly petticoats and fancy dresses, to be an image of her own, younger self.

Jeremy, gloomy by nature, became even gloomier at the sight of baby Sidney. He felt he had failed Flo. Indeed, his sense of failure had deepened during the war, when he had done nothing heroic, had never been in action. His war service had been spent on Salisbury Plain, organizing troop movements.

Sidney soon became aware he was unwanted; he drank in that impression with his mother's milk. He got up to mischief in order to draw attention to himself; the effect was merely to inspire further disapproval. In the market place one day, he happened to see a small girl in a pushchair, clutching a doll. Sidney snatched up the doll and ran off with it.

Now began a painful performance where Sad Sid endeavoured to act the part of a little girl, pretending to make a fuss over the doll, which he christened Dribble. Flo and Jeremy, entirely without understanding, were disgusted by this display. Sidney hated the doll. Dribble became a symbol of his degradation. For that reason, he took it with him everywhere. When laid horizontally, Dribble uttered a faint cry and closed its staring blue eyes with a click.

One day, you were invited over to play with Sidney. You did not wish to go, but Mary and Flo insisted you should be friends with Sid. You were baffled by Dribble. You would not hold it when Sid invited you to. Sidney dropped the doll on a hard floor. Dribble's china head broke open. The crude mechanism operating the eyes was revealed.

Sidney was appalled by what he had done. His face turned as pale as ashes. You stared down at the broken head in horror, thinking of your sister, Sonia. It was almost as if a murder had been committed: you asked to go home.

There followed a row in the Wilberforce household, about which you heard only remotely. Your parents spoke of it in a whisper. It was Sonia who found out about it and told you. Sonia was quite excited. 'Naughty!' she said, eyes gleaming. 'Shuggerybees!'

Sidney had done what he could to sort out his sexual confusions. He had persuaded a small girl called Rose Brackett to come into the garden shed with him. Sid had kissed Rose and she had pulled her panties down. Sidney had his shorts off, when the shed door opened. Jeremy stood there, forehead drawn in a frown.

'You dirty little tacker,' he exclaimed. Grabbing Sidney by the collar of his shirt, he dragged him from the shed – poor Rosie Brackett was quite ignored and ran home crying – dragged him up the garden path and into the house, calling angrily for Flo.

As Jeremy explained briefly what he imagined was taking place – shaking Sidney by the collar meanwhile – he gave the boy the odd cuff. With each cuff, he asked, 'Where did you get that filthy habit from?'

'It wasn't filthy,' cried Sid. 'I never even touched her.'

Another cuff.

Flo, in her apron, wrung her hands as she had so often done over her problem son, asking him, glaring down at him, 'What are we to do with you?'

What they did with him was send him to public school. That meant he would be away from home for most of the year.

One great interferer in family affairs was Claude Hillman. Claude had married your father's sister Ada, your neat little Aunt Ada. It had been another of those post-war marriages. You had heard Claude say once, when in his cups, 'Marry in haste, repent in leisure.' Both of your parents looked askance at Claude; their motto might have been, 'Judge in haste, disapprove in leisure.' But you liked lumpish old Uncle Claude, with his forced jollity, as with any jollity, however forced.

On this occasion, you thought he came out well, by saying, 'Sid only wanted a feel, didn't he? What's the harm in that?'

To which your mother had responded, 'The trouble with you, Claude, is you are mucky-minded.'

He laughed, unoffended. 'That's true, m'dear.'

You too could see the attractions of getting Rose Brackett into the garden shed and 'having a feel', as Claude put it.

But poor Sidney was in disgrace for some while. Jeremy drove Sidney through the college gates. To Sid's eyes, the great expanse of parade ground and forbidding buildings, all seemed to swarm with noisy boys, some running mindlessly about, some fighting, some standing still and moving their arms as if in semaphore.

Sidney, being brave, not crying, turned to give his father a farewell embrace. Jeremy became involved with the car's gears, staring ahead.

'Well, toodle-oo, old boy! Off you go!'

Sidney went.

Sidney had a troubled and delayed puberty. Puberty did not visit him until he was almost sixteen. He then became briefly known as 'Flasher Sid'. On his seventeenth birthday, when his parents gave him a pair of boxing gloves as a present, Sidney went to the bottom of their garden and hanged himself without fuss from a branch of an old apple tree.

The suicide caused shock waves all round the family.

'He was a nice, quiet boy, mind you,' said your mother.

'But he was a bit, you know, funny, mum,' Sonia exclaimed. 'He asked me once if I wanted to see his willy.'

'I hope you didn't say yes,' said your mother, keen that her daughter should remain unsullied.

'I did just have a quick look, but I didn't touch.'

You could see that Sonia was teasing your mother, but Mary was clearly shocked.

'Valerie wouldn't have looked, would she?' you said, teasing in your turn, with a sidelong glance at Sonia.

'Oh, you're so jealous of your poor sister,' Mary exclaimed. 'It's a horrible trait in you!'

Uncle Claude Hillman gave your father a wink. 'The kid was queer, wasn't he? 'Nuff to make anyone hang themselves.'

Your Auntie Violet had her own slant on the matter, saying to Bertie, 'Well, plants die from lack of sunlight. The poor kid died from lack of love and understanding, didn't he? They aren't exactly elements in which your flipping family specializes, are they, Bert?'

You can understand that at this time your mind was a confusion of ill-digested thoughts. You were of an age when your perceptions were extended, when it seemed to you that every day you climbed a new metaphorical hill. You had anxieties about what was truth, what false. You were keen to bring a possible life as a geologist into line with probity of character. Many connections had to be made, many decisions confronted you.

After leaving school, you went up to Birmingham University to study the new discipline of Earth Sciences. You knew of no other university offering such a course. You were proud to be an early student, and worked hard.

During your first term in Birmingham, your Aunt Violet came to visit you, to see how you were getting on. You were ashamed to take her to your digs, but Violet seemed not to mind. 'I like the poster,' she said, admiring the portrait of Che Guevara hanging on your wall. There she stood, perfectly at ease in the scruffy room. Your Aunt Violet was brightly clothed in something beaded and flowing. Gipsy earrings swung from her ears. She wore silk stockings and red, high-heeled shoes. You were overwhelmed by her appearance and hoped all your new friends saw you with this illustrious relation.

She removed, with meticulous care, your soiled shirts and pants from your rickety chair. She pushed aside some paperbacks and scribbled-on pieces of paper, to make a space on the table.

'I've brought you some plonk, Steve, dear,' she said, setting down on your table a brown paper carrier bag containing a bottle of red wine. 'I assume you drink?'

'Of course.' You did not wish to appear other than adult before this sophisticated aunt. The fact was that you had tasted beer and had not liked it, and the group of young men you mixed with proclaimed themselves Communists and were abstemious (and saw no contradiction in that).

Violet gingerly settled her behind down on your chair, tipped it back, put her feet up on the table edge, showing an extent of shapely leg as she did so, and eased off her high heels, so that they hung loose from her stockinged toes. She asked you what you were getting up to, now that you were free of parental control. You replied, 'I'm considering disowning my pater. I have already disowned God. My pater has been a bad and repressive influence. I reject his way of life. You know him, auntie, and I am sure you dislike him.'

'No, I don't really dislike Martin. I feel a bit sorry for the old blighter.'

'Feeling sorry for people does no one any good.' How grown up you were being.

'And your mother has a bit of a mental problem, as I suppose you know. Well, like poor old Bertie, in a way.'

Bertie was her husband, your mother's younger brother. But you were uninterested in Violet's troubles. You spoke instead of your own troubles.

You addressed her as if she were a meeting.

'You see, auntie, I have reached the conclusion that money should not be inherited. When a person dies, his estate, if there is one, should pass to the government. Within one or two generations, we would see a complete reformation of society. The public exchequers could then finance massive projects in housing and health and education. We might then expect a general moral reformation. Also, women have to be liberated from housework. Their intellects are limited at present.'

Violet gave a little laugh. 'That's certainly true of my intellect.'

She added, 'But who's going to put up with handing over their property to some government department? Not me, old sport.'

'Auntie, perhaps you don't realize,' you were being ponderously patient, 'that thirty-one per cent of the inhabitants of Britain live below the poverty line. Thirty-one per cent! That's disgraceful. That has to be rectified, in the name of justice. And humanity.'

Violet produced a cigarette and threw you one. You went over to get a light from her.

'Aren't things just as bad in Russia, where you get your ideas from?' she said, indifferently.

You then had to lecture her on basic economics. She sat there not listening, her pretty little chin in the air.

You embarrass me by recalling what I said on that occasion. What a prig I was! Do not feel embarrassed. You were attempting to digest recently learned facts and trying on what personality suited you best. We understand that adolescence is a difficult time.

'Don't believe what the capitalist press tells you about Russia, auntie. You're living under an illusion.' You were bending over your aunt to light a second cigarette. It did not occur to you to offer her a mug of instant coffee.

'I say, aunt, what beautiful legs you have.'

She looked up, giving you a flirtatious glance. Smiling she said, 'That's none of your business.'

'I wish it was, really.'

Violet removed her feet from the table and tucked them under her skirt. She announced there was something serious she wanted to talk to you about. Then she said, 'Oh, I can't. I'm made for the frivolous life. Besides, you're almost grown up now. You're safe.'

'What were you going to tell me, aunt, dear?'

She waved an elegant hand. 'Doesn't matter. There's going to be another war soon. You'll have to go, darling – serve King and country. Give your old aunt a kiss.'

You put an arm round her neck and kissed her lingeringly. An erection sprang up in your trousers. You knew she saw the effect she had on you.

She said, teasingly, 'You are a big boy! I'd better go, sweetie.'

She stubbed out her half-smoked cigarette. She put her shoes on. She gave you a straight look, serious but affectionate. 'Toodle-pip,' she said. You thought as she left how old-fashioned it was to say 'Toodle-pip'.

It was going to be a long while before you saw your aunt again. You would then be adult, war-hardened. But first you had to attend a funeral.

7

The New Widow

It was on the first day of April, 1939, that the Spanish Civil War ended. General Franco's forces had triumphed. 'Fascists!' your father had been shouting for some time. But not on that particular day. For on that particular day, he was standing with his mother, Elizabeth Fielding, by the bedside of his father, Sidney Vawes Fielding, in the Southampton hospital.

Old Sidney had been lying in a white-tiled cell, on a raised bed. He had been enjoying a last puff of a cigarette, clutching the cylinder in shaky purple hands. His countenance was the colour of the hospital pillow supporting his head. He suddenly raised that head from the pillow with a startled look, eyes bulging. 'I mean to say –', he began, only to fall back again, dead.

He had suffered from gastritis and lung cancer. He was sixty-nine years old.

Elizabeth clutched his cold, gnarled hand with both of her

delicate ones. 'Good-bye, my dear … my faithful husband,' she said, in her clear, but hesitant tones. This was after she had suffered her stroke.

Elizabeth Fielding had a more distinguished look about her than the majority of her clan. It could not be said that this was because of any particular facial feature, although her high forehead and delicate nostrils and lips were attractive. Her pile of white hair, secured by a small black velvet bow, gave her an impressive air. But her distinction lay more in the way she held herself stiffly erect. She had always been a silent sort of person, which had made you, when you were a small boy, fearful of her. The impediment in her speech, a result of the stroke, had hardly made her more garrulous. The family had not been accustomed to taking much notice of Elizabeth. If she resented this attitude, she wisely did not show it. She had, however, begun to show some partiality towards you, as if recognizing in your small person someone whose potentials were also overlooked.

In need of a degree of security, Elizabeth had married Sidney Fielding knowing him to be intellectually her inferior, as well as some years older than she. She tried to conceal this knowledge from Sidney, but such knowledge leaks out in many ways.

Sidney was never entirely satisfied with his wife, finding her often critical. He failed to relish her criticism as a way of advancing his own appreciation of the finer points of life. And so to their children, Martin and his brothers and sisters, that hidden dissatisfaction had a way of working through and shadowing their lives also. As to Martin and Mary's children, you often held beliefs that cast a shadow over what should have been your contentment, and their acceptance of you.

Various members of the family were summoned for Sidney Fielding's funeral. So the funeral took place a week after his death, on the day when Mussolini, having annexed Abyssinia, invaded Albania. This fresh sign of the rottenness of Europe was scarcely noticed by the Fielding and Wilberforce families. Or by you, for at fifteen you were enmeshed in the agonies and joys of your first love affair. You were pursuing Gale Roberts, who was proving by turns joky and elusive, affectionate and indifferent. This female behaviour was totally inscrutable to you. What Gale desired from day to day remained baffling; whereas all you desired was to get a hand up her skirt.

This problem had to be shelved on the seventh of April, when you and your sister stood by your parents' side at your grandfather's grave. Your heads were bowed. You wished to be sad, but Sonia kept nudging and winking at you, and exclaiming 'Shuggerybees!' After the ceremony, the two families, together with friends and spouses, gathered in your father's house for drinks and refreshments. They were greeted on the doorstep as they arrived by joyous barking from Gyp. Joy Frost, terrified of dogs, ran back to the car for refuge, and took some coaxing before she reappeared on the scene. 'Shut the confounded dog in the greenhouse,' demanded Mary. Although you loved Gyp greatly, you did as she ordered, smoothing his noble head before shutting him in.

Emma, the maid, served tea as soon as the guests came in. All were dressed in black, making family likenesses more apparent, the Wilberforces with their sallow complexions, the Fieldings with their aquiline noses, the Frosts with their tendency to be undershot, the Hillmans – or Claude at least – with their flushed faces and broken-veined cheeks.

Your parents' house gave off a slight greenish tinge. There were thick old green velvet curtains at the downstairs windows, destined to serve as blackout curtains during the war then looming. The furniture was heavy, and some of it shabby. It had been bought on the never-never at Heal's in London, shortly after Martin and Mary had married. The pictures on the walls of the living room showed Sopwith Camels and other ancient aeroplanes manoeuvring in clear blue skies. Mary had striven to brighten the room with bowls of flowers strategically placed, as advised in the pages of *Amateur Gardening*, to which she subscribed.

You were forced into the company of Joey and Terry, the two sons of Aunt Ada, your father's sister. Ada was there, still rather weepy from the graveside, with her husband, Claude Hillman, who was at this time of his life a stockbroker. Claude, your father always said, was 'a bit of a bounder'.

'Cheer up, old ducks,' Claude told Ada. 'Old Sid's time was up. He had a good run for his money, didn't he?'

'Oh, Claude, truly, "in the midst of life we are in death".'

He thrust his rubicund face at hers. 'Rubbish! In the midst of life we are in need of drink. Death'll have to wait until I've got a noggin in me.'

There had been a time a few months earlier when you had gone to play with Joey and Terry. They had stuck their hands in the pockets of their shorts and put their round, sand-coloured heads together. They contemplated you before asking, in no friendly terms, 'Do you know the system, sport?'

'What system is that?' you asked.

Terry had looked at Joey. Joey had looked at Terry. 'He asks what system,' they said to each other. Then, to you, 'Why, mathematics, of course. Do you know what numbers are for?'

'They're for counting,' you said, sulky under such interrogation.

And the two boys had laughed. They showed you a blackboard in their den. On the blackboard, cabbalistic signs mixed with numbers. Some signs were enclosed by chalk squares. Arrows indicated directions. You were impressed that they had various coloured chalks.

'What's all this "DOBD" in these red squares?' you asked.

Terry sniggered behind a grubby hand. 'Do or Be Done, of course.'

Summoning a protective indifference, you remarked that that was silly.

'It's our future. It's our system. We don't expect you to understand.'

But you had stayed for lunch in their house. Aunt Ada served cold stuffed veal with small new potatoes, cold, and a salad of crisp, sharp cos lettuce. Ada was a little woman with pale lips, very neat with her hair and clothes. Later on, not very surprisingly, Claude would leave Ada.

To see these two boys now in your own house, rapidly gobbling the snacks, aroused your hostility.

'Are you two still playing about with your stupid system?' you asked Joey.

'Our dad met Bertrand Russell,' Joey said, proudly.

It seemed unanswerable at the time.

Accompanying Claude and Ada were the Frosts. Joy Frost with pigtails, tied for the occasion with black ribbons, was Claude's younger sister. Her husband, Freddie Frost, adolescent in appearance, was regarded by the Fieldings as being rather loud. He was being rather loud now, saying cheerfully to Archie over his shoulder, as Emma poured more wine into his glass, 'Well, there's another one fallen off the old perch, eh, what?'

He nudged his brother Archie in the ribs in order to encourage him to share in the joke – Archie being always, in Freddie's judgement, too serious and quiet.

'Show some respect,' said Archie. 'Try the sausage rolls and shut up.'

You heard a good deal of shutting up in those days.

Of these Frosts, Joy at sixteen seemed to suffer the most grief. Her nose had been reddened by constant applications of a small handkerchief during the funeral. She confided now to her Aunt Ada, 'I've never been touched by death before – apart from the odd hamster.' Ada pressed her niece's hand. 'I know, my dear.' She repeated herself, saying, '"In the midst of life we are in death" – including hamsters.'

Meanwhile, Mary was welcoming in her stodgy older brother, Jeremy, who was looking about him for the fount and source of alcohol. 'Poor old pop, Mary,' he said heavily, laying a hand on her shoulder. 'Gone to his eternal rest, as they say. Still, not a bad life, I suppose. He certainly came up in society, didn't he?' He gave a short laugh.

'That's not a very nice way of putting it.' But it appeared your mother's thoughts were elsewhere, for she went on to say that she had heard on the radio that when certain kings could no longer satisfy their wives, they were put to death, or else the crops failed. She believed this was in some African tribe or other.

'Don't see what you are on about,' said Jeremy. 'We're no African tribe. Pop wasn't black, thank goodness.'

His younger brother Jack agreed, but said, sotto voce, 'No disrespect, please, Jeremy. Not in Mother's hearing.' He nodded towards Elizabeth.

'But I didn't respect him. He gave me a rotten childhood.' However, Jeremy had lowered his voice to make this pronouncement. 'Poor old bugger, all the same.'

Claude was interested in another kind of respect. He grabbed his two sons and addressed them confidentially. 'You two better behave respectfully to your grandmother. I happen to know that all of Granddad's money is left to her, so be nice to the old girl.'

'Will she be rich, dad?' Joey asked.

'Stinking rich, my boy. Stinking rich. So watch it!'

'Will we be rich, dad?' Terry asked.

Claude closed one eye. 'You go to work on it, old lad.'

All round the room and into the nearby breakfast room, muttered family conversations went on, the family being semi-glad to be called together.

'I don't know Hunstanton,' Jack Wilberforce proclaimed, as if bestowing a signal honour on the town he named.

Jeremy said, before holding out his glass for a refill as Emma came round with the bottle, 'I always felt a bit sorry for mum.'

'He gave Liz a hard time,' Flo agreed. 'She had more intelligence than Sidney, that was the problem.'

The lady referred to as Liz was the newly widowed Elizabeth, sitting alone in a corner of the room. Mary and Martin had escorted Elizabeth to a sofa, donkey brown and genuine leather, where she sat poised and elegant in her sweeping black dress. She wore a wide-brimmed black hat with a white rose attached to the brim. Elizabeth was in her late forties; her face, with its sharp features, was utterly pale, utterly composed, as she looked about the room.

Since her stroke, the old lady kept her ebony walking stick to hand; but the sofa suited her well enough because it had a high seat, from which it was easy to rise without assistance.

You went over to speak to her. 'I'm so sorry, Granny dear. Granddad will be greatly missed.' You added, 'By you, most of all.'

'It is character … istic of your mother,' she began, 'to wear a dress which fits – which does not fit, I should say – her. Properly.'

'Yes, Granny, but –'

She reached out and clutched your hand. 'Yes, it's about your granddad sad. But the over war … the Civil War Spanish is over. We must be small mercies. Grateful for –'

She paused, gazing upwards, searching for a word.

'Small mercies?' you suggested.

Later in life, you would come greatly to respect your grandmother. Moreover, it grew to be your opinion that Elizabeth was the one scholarly member of the family, apart from Jeremy's wife, Flo. Your grandmother, in your view and that of others, had not been well treated by her husband Sidney. Sidney had been too busy making money to care properly for his grand wife – or for her intellect.

Elizabeth had suffered her stroke three years earlier. Her intellect had carried her through. Sonia affected to be scared of the speech impediment. As Sonia happened to be passing, you grabbed her arm and made her say hello to her grandmother.

'Oh, I thought you didn't want to talk to me, Granny,' said Sonia, grinning and rocking her body back and forth in an idiotic way.

'Why should I … why not wish … to talk to you, child?' asked Elizabeth, scrutinizing Sonia with some interest.

'I thought perhaps you did not like hunchbacked children, Granny.' Sonia made an awful grimace as she said this.

'On the cont … on the contrary. I adore hunchbacks, child. Remind me of your name.'

'Oh,' Sonia gazed at the floor. 'I am sister to the adorable Valerie, who was perfect and not hunchbacked. Little Valerie-Wallerie was *the* world's most perfect child.'

You reassured your grandmother, pointing a finger to your temple, working it back and forth as if to drill into your brain. 'Sonia is a bit touched, Grandma. It runs in the family.'

Elizabeth made no direct reply to this remark, although she flashed at you something that could have been a smile of understanding. She fished in her handbag, took out a cigarette case and extracted a cigarette. When she had lit it and blown a plume of smoke from her nostrils, she said, not looking at you, but gazing rather into the room, where her relations were milling about, 'Why are your Uncle Bertie and Auntie Violet not here? Why did they not attend Sidney's funeral?'

'I'm afraid Mother doesn't approve of them. Well, at least she doesn't approve of Auntie Violet. She told Auntie she was not welcome.'

You did not add that you had asked your mother why she did not want Auntie Violet in the house. To which she had replied, loftily, that she was a good judge of character.

'Violet wears good clothes. Wears well. Them well,' said Elizabeth, now.

'Yes, but Mum says they are too expensive.'

The old lady inspected your face. 'Violet, I recall … Violet criticized your Uncle Jeremy. Jeremy's of his son, deplorable treatment. Poor Sid. Rightly so, to my mind. It's as well to speak. Brave to speak, um, out. A necessary adjunct. I say, adjunct of civiliz … our civilization.'

Lamely, you said, 'We were all upset about Sad Sid.'

'Suicide. Suicide is … sorry, suicide is always a family … A criticism, I mean to say, of the family.'

'We are a funny family, I must agree,' said Sonia. 'Look at their faces! But our sausage rolls are good. May I get you one, Granny?'

'No, thank you. Valerie.'

'No, sorry Granny.' Sonia vigorously shook her head. 'I'm Sonia, thanks very much. And I'm alive. Valerie is the one who is not alive.'

'I see.' Elizabeth spoke gravely, looking into Sonia's face. 'And was not Valerie also hunchbacked?'

'Oh, heavens no! Valerie was perfect, Granny. Everyone knows that. That was why she died, so they say. Died of perfection, like Jesus on the Cross. In fact, I believe I saw her at your husband's graveside.' She pressed her fingers to her lips. 'Sorry, shouldn't have mentioned gravesides.'

Elizabeth nodded thoughtfully, but she could not restrain a smile. 'Well then, Sonia, you should go far in life, and get into a lot of trouble on the way.'

She dismissed the subject. Again the inspection of your face. You liked your grandmother's intelligence, while finding it alarming at times. Her face still bore traces of a smile.

'I hope you learnt something, Stephen. From Sad Sid's death. Unlike your cheeky little sister.'

'Valerie?'

'Sonia.'

'I still feel bad about it, Gran.'

'Feeling bad is the same. Is not the same as something. Learning something.' She changed the subject abruptly. She tapped the end of her cigarette on the rim of a brass ashtray, which was secured in the middle of a weighted leather strap so that it hung comfortably over the arm of the sofa on which she was sitting. 'But that you know.'

She murmured the sentence to herself again, perhaps checking to see that she had got it right. 'But that you know.'

'Why should your mother have a say? Have a say over whether or not one attended? Attended.' She seemed momentarily to be stuck on the word. 'If her brothers and his wife attended … attended his father's funeral? Particularly when Sidney had a special. Special affection for Bertie. If you remember, dear, Bertie in his youth. In his youth, he flew … where?'

'Kabul,' you said.

'Oh dear, I must go,' said Sonia. 'I've just remembered something.' She slipped away, saying, 'I just want to see if Gyp has died in the greenhouse.'

'Yes. Kabul,' Elizabeth echoed. She watched Sonia's retreat with a slight smile. 'It's in Africa, I believe.'

'Afghanistan, Granny.'

'Of course. Quite right.'

You had no answer to her larger question. You knew only that, in the days preceding the funeral, terrible arguments had broken out between your parents. Some weeks earlier, Mary had ventured a few critical remarks regarding Violet to Violet's husband, Bertie. She told him that Violet was 'spendthrift', and had added the damning word 'gallivanting'. Bertie had become furious, vowing he would not speak to his sister again. Nothing had been said on that occasion about Violet's criticisms regarding the causes of Sad Sid's suicide; indeed, the word 'suicide' had proved too terrible to utter. In an endeavour to settle the quarrel, Martin had phoned Jack, Mary's other brother, asking him to intervene. Jack had accused Martin of going behind his sister's back. So a thunderous family row had developed, about which you knew nothing, walking into frosty silences as into a brick wall. Mary had said, 'I don't care who's died, I won't have that Violet here, flaunting her new clothes about the place! Neglecting her children! Making eyes at all the men!' And that ended the matter.

You felt for your grandmother, that calm and elegant lady. Anxious to detach yourself from your parents' quarrels, you said to her now, 'I really like Auntie Violet, Gran. She's ever so kind, you know.'

The remark appeared to make no impression on the new widow. In her halting way of speaking, she replied, 'People should not be small. Not small-minded. When there's a war. Particularly. A war. Now Mussolini. After all, on. Coming.'

You expressed agreement.

68

Elizabeth said, 'Oh dear, here is my dreadful Bella,' referring to her younger daughter. You thought she wished to change the subject, but she added, 'Violet brings a little family, I mean life. Into the family.'

There were pauses between her sentences. She would have said more, had not Joy Frost come to speak to her. You were squatting on your heels to bring your face on a level with your grandmother's. Putting a hand on your shoulder, Joy conveyed her condolences to Elizabeth. Joy had had her hair done for the occasion and had asked you earlier if you did not think she looked sizzling. You agreed she did look sizzling.

But Elizabeth was pursuing an earlier trail of thought. 'She has two children. At least two – Violet, I mean to say. A girl, Joyce. And a boy ... I've forgotten –'

'Douglas,' you reminded her. 'Dougie – the funny boy.'

'I had every wish, every wish. What? To be fond of them, you silly woman!'

Tears swam to Elizabeth's eyes. She turned her head away to conceal them, affecting to look out of the window.

'How they do pass, the years,' she said abstractedly to thin air. 'Yes,' you said – many years before you were able to respond to the statement with a genuine affirmative.

'Intellect ... unfortunately. Unfortunately intellect is no shield. Not against regret. I hope you two grand ... two grandchildren,' she gave you a swift glance, 'Will properly revere the ... What was it? Yes, what I just said. Intellect. My children, my children have proved lacking. Somewhat lacking in that ... that region. Department. Mm, yes, department.'

She essayed a smile. Being of an age when it was agreeable to hear adverse comments on your parents, you produced murmurs of reassurance.

Light filtering through your bay window made your grandmother's face, with its now prominent cheekbones, look as if it were made entirely of bone. In her clear, remote voice, she said, 'My grandfather had a small orchard. An orchard. An orchard of Laxton's Superb. Laxton's Superb. A delicious apple eating. Laxton's Superb. You don't see it now. Not now. No longer. Laxton's Superb, yes.'

She lingered over the name of the apple, apparently luxuriating in it. Reaching out her arm, stiffly, she stubbed out her half-smoked cigarette. 'I wonder who Mr Laxton was.'

While she had been speaking, her daughter, Belle, characterized by the old lady as the 'dreadful Bella', came across the room and sat down on the sofa beside her mother. She folded her hands in her lap and remained there with a vague smile on her face, as if expecting everyone to be content with her presence without her having to make further effort.

You wished to learn more of the family dislike of your favourite aunt. 'Granny, you were saying about Violet –'

Elizabeth had taken out a tiny lace handkerchief with which she dabbed her eyes. 'Bertie drinks too much. Far too much. From flying. A leg … a legacy from his flying days. It makes Violet – Oh!'

Her exclamation was long and cool, much like a sigh. You stood up. Mary shrieked in a refined way. On the other side of the room, Claude had told a lewd joke. Ada, stepping back in disapproval, had bumped into Emma. Emma had been bringing in a tray loaded with champagne glasses and a magnum of Moet & Chandon. She made a gallant effort to stave off disaster, but the tray was thrown into flight, crashing to the floor. The poor maid fell to her knees and covered her face with her hands. Joy Frost helped her to her feet, trying to console her, but Emma fled the room. Claude, Ada and Mary all rushed after her.

Elizabeth said, quietly addressing you and ignoring her daughter Belle, 'Many of the members of this family. Many members are half-mad. Mary, your mother, of course. Jeremy. Bertie. Possibly Violet. And of course … of course my husband … That was.'

She tried to hide her face in the small square of her handkerchief.

'I'm going to Venice,' she said, with a brighter tone. 'I've mind … made up my mind. My cats will. Someone will have to. Look

70

afterwards … have to look after my … You know, I just said it. Cats. I'm going to Venice to stay with my friend. My Dorothy friend. You and your hunchbacked sister are welcome to visit. Welcome if you can stand.' She gave a curt little laugh. 'Stand the company of old people.' She looked searchingly at you. Her eyes were red. 'I plan to be away. For some while. Four or five months away.'

But in five months' time, Hitler's Wehrmacht had invaded Poland, and Britain and France had declared war on Germany.

8

Kendal, of All Places

It was the morning of Sunday, 3rd of September, 1939, and your mother was having a weeping fit. She had a mixture of complaints, including the accusation that Elizabeth was cool towards her, that Sonia's hunchback was 'beyond a joke', that your room was always untidy, that Ribbentrop was a nice, handsome man, and that she missed Valerie.

Valerie. Your father groaned at the mention of Valerie's name.

Your mother had given birth to Sonia, as predicted when you were holidaying in Omega – though not predicted to you. You had been astonished when a little heavy nurse, wearing a starched uniform and a winged and starched head dress, arrived at your house.

'Is mum ill?' you asked, looking up past her massive starched battlements to her face.

'Not unless parturition is an illness,' she told you sternly, looking down.

You thought that parturition sounded like an illness.

Her name was Nurse Gill. She appeared to regard small boys much as she regarded other epidemics. Later she told you, as she stomped past, 'This time the child has survived. You have a living sister. Last time – dead, I'm sorry to say. Defunct – from something congenital.'

Here was revealed the reason for your mother having never acquired a great liking for you. There had been an earlier child of your parents' marriage, a girl, born in the year after their wedding. Had your father been carrying some unacknowledged disease, acquired when he was soldiering in the Great War, from the prostitutes of Cairo? In any event, for whatever malevolent cause, this baby was stillborn, cast up on the desolate shores of non-existence.

At a later date, when superstition had largely fallen away with the advance of medicine, to deliver a stillborn baby was no disgrace. But then – in that dreadful *Then* of the nineteen-twenties – Nurse Gill would have whisked the little body away immediately after delivery, hiding the corpse under a cloth – you visualized a tea cloth – possibly without letting the poor, suffering mother see it, or touch it; its fatal limbs, its unformed face with the eyes tightly squeezed closed, never to open.

No great wonder your mother developed a poisonous fantasy – as all fantasies are, at base, poisonous. Perhaps Mary could never convince herself her child was dead, since she never set eyes on it. In later years, mothers would have been permitted, encouraged, to hold this outcast from their fallible bodies, flesh of their flesh, their dead child, and so to offer it, if only for a minute, the recognition and love it could never return.

How greatly your mother desired another daughter as substitute for the dead one you could not imagine. Indeed, she poisoned her mind, and the minds of her children, by indulging in a fantasy, the fantasy that this first daughter had lived for six months and been the very image of perfection. The fantasy daughter even had a name. It was called Valerie. This consoling fantasy settled on

Mary's blood like a vampire. No living child could possibly rival, in Mary's eyes, the virtues of the dead Valerie.

When you emerged into the world, four years after this still-born girl, you entered a stifling imagined scenario of tragedy. Your mother could find no place for a boy amid the interstices of her dream. As for your father – unable to enter into this suffocating pretence – he was destroyed in a different way; estranged from your mother in a separation which further increased a propensity for loneliness in his nature.

'Valerie never did that,' she said when you broke a cup. 'Valerie would never make such a horrid noise,' she would say if you shouted. 'Valerie ate her food properly,' she said when you splashed your soup. At every turn, you were condemned by this unliving, but overwhelming, figment of your mother's imagination.

Later in life, you found that your mother had been visiting a psychotherapist in Norwich for some years during the period of your growing up.

Do you remember weeping?
I never wept.
Oh, indeed you did.

Your parents were at home on that momentous day early in September, and in a bad mood. Your mother was saying she felt cross with Neville Chamberlain. A gloomy silence ensued.

Martin said, meditatively, that September was the traditional season in which to go to war. In olden times, the peasants had got in the harvest and were free to be sent to fight for the lord of the manor.

'Never mind all that,' said Mary, irritably.

'It's a factor.'

'It's a bally nuisance,' Mary replied. 'Going to war with Germany like this. What does Ribbentrop think, I wonder? Valerie would have been terrified. Why can't we let Hitler get on with it? What he does on the Continent is nothing to do with us, is it?'

Your father replied, 'I've always said that if Churchill and Lord Vansittart didn't keep quiet, we would have to go to war again. Typical Tories … It's a fine muck-up and no mistake.'

'It is a mistake,' Mary said. Her knitting needles clicked together in anger. 'War again. We've only just got over the last one. People getting killed all over again.'

'But different people this time,' you said, attempting to console.

Your parents were talking in the sitting room. Martin Fielding had bought a small mansion, standing in parkland on the outskirts of Southampton, and a car to go with it. The plane manufacturers had promoted him from head of the 'heavy gang' to an office job on better pay. He remained head of the trades union chapel. You had seen him come home with several yards of cable under his coat, together with electrical equipment of various kinds. You had heard your mother protest, to which your father had answered, 'The bosses rob us men, so it's fair we should take something back.' And that settled the matter.

When you had asked Mary if dad was a criminal, she'd told you angrily to be quiet about it.

'Your father's a Socialist, and Socialists share everything.'

Your father's knowledge of the past, as revealed in his remark about the convenience of having wars begin in September, stayed with you for some while. He was knowledgeable, yet in other ways so stupid, so insensitive to others. It seemed a puzzle. How vexing were parents. But then, you considered it 'aristocratic' to be puzzled.

You had only one term at Birmingham University before you received a buff envelope. Inside was an Enlistment Notice saying you were required to present yourself at a nearby barracks for primary training. A postal order for four shillings was also enclosed 'in respect of advance of service pay'. You were Called Up.

Geology was forgotten, together with many other things. Your country needed you.

*

76

The men of the family went down to their local pub, The Black Hind, with their friends, and held a council of war. The date was 15th May, 1940, only four days after Winston Churchill had been confirmed as prime minister. You were with your regiment in Catterick, preparing for embarkation overseas. While pints were being ordered, to begin the meeting someone repeated the opening of the Robb Wilton monologue, 'The day war broke out, my wife said to me, *What are you going to do about it?*' But that, in fact, was the subject of their meeting.

Martin opened proceedings by announcing that he had already joined the Local Defence Volunteers. He advised all those over conscription age to join. Walter Pratchett, a young man working in a solicitor's office, said he had volunteered for service in the Royal Navy and would be away shortly. Many other men had plans to defend their country against invasion.

Claude Hillman, generally talkative enough, said nothing. He had been first in the pub and was drinking steadily. Martin asked him what the matter was.

'Quote from a book I read recently,' Claude growled. '"Sir, I have quarrelled with my wife and a man who has quarrelled with his wife is absolved from all duty to his country."'

'You and Ada again?' said Martin.

'She was the apple of my eye, really the apple of my eye. Now she's a crab apple.'

'She's borne you two children.'

Claude managed a smile. He tapped on the table with an index finger. 'Indeed she has, and mortal terrors they are. Her body – excuse me if I speak thus of your dear sister, Martin – her body was wild white winter, once upon a time. Now it has fruited and fallen back to autumn, season of yellow fruitlessness. War provides us with an excuse to get away from the womenfolk.'

Wally Pratchett was recently married and violently dissented.

Martin did not look particularly pleased, but other men seized on the topic of womanhood, saying that they hoped women

77

– whom they termed 'the good old girls' – would play their part in the conflict. Which is what happened. While the Third Reich ordered its womenfolk to *Kindermachen*, confining them to the home to make future soldiery, British women went into industry and agriculture and many other jobs, to fill vacancies left by men who had become soldiers, sailors or airmen.

When time was called in the pub, all had become intensely patriotic. They toasted Winston Churchill and staggered out into the spring daylight.

For a while, the Second World War had made little difference to your family.

After Emma the maid had fled, your parents employed a live-in maid, and a young boy who came in the mornings and did odd jobs. There was also a gardener, while a pony for daughter Sonia was installed in the paddock.

Sonia was afraid of this frisky animal; she insisted that the pony disliked her hump. Sonia went to a local school for girls, but this was holiday time. Her imagined hump was one of the devices by which she brought her mother to heel.

She taught Gyp to bark at the pony.

In any event, she never rode the pony. You established friendly relations with it. It was a three-year-old gelding, which had been christened Beauty. You led Beauty out into the field and let it canter about. After a while, when it was time to take it in again, Beauty would play hard to get, no doubt dreading a return to its prison of the stable. At other times it would come up to you shyly, gently, almost in a maidenly way, to gaze upon you with its large moist eyes. You would fondle it. Its muzzle was soft, although, when it opened its mouth, a set of large teeth were displayed.

Like every kind of animal with which man comes into contact, horses came into captivity. From Mary's goldfish swimming mindlessly round its bowl, the canary in its cage, to higher mammals like horses and elephants, all animals become prisoners of humans.

Only cats have never signed the contract; unlike their domestic rivals, the dogs, cats never submitted to leads or performed tricks, lounging about instead, in a very hands-in-pockets kind of way, and having naps in inconvenient places.

'Why don't you like Beauty?' you asked your sister.

'Oh, I don't know. P'raps, yes, p'raps because I'm *expected* to like her.'

'It's a he.'

Poor Beauty was later sold. 'Valerie would have liked a pony,' said Mary, with a sigh. 'Valerie was good to her mother.'

'Well, I think Valerie was a horrid creep!' Sonia retorted.

Your two parents were sitting together one night, by a coal fire, for the early September evenings were becoming chilly.

'I don't know what Sonia will do,' said Mary Fielding. 'These wars are so awful. We've been through one of them. Now another.'

She held a small handkerchief to her nose and attempted to shed a tear.

'Don't start that,' Martin warned. 'Wars are nothing to cry about. Got to be brave.'

'I was thinking of my poor brother, Ernie. Killed in France, in the early days of the war. I must get a cardigan.'

'Not France – the Somme. It's in Germany, woman!'

'Of all places.'

'Never mind that, think about what we're going to do now. This war is going to be worse than the last one, let me tell you that. For one thing, we are near the coast. We must consider what we should do in the case of an invasion.'

'Oh, Marty, how terrible it would be to have a house full of Nazis! Sonia will be so scared when she hears about it, poor mite.'

'We're all equally in the soup. I'd like to know what the heck Hitler thinks he's doing.'

Mary Fielding rose from her comfortable chair and went to gaze out of the window, as if to make sure that no one in boots was coming up the drive. She said, 'It's so horrible to think of war.

Once in our lifetimes was surely enough. Sonia will be so upset. You know how delicate her nerves are.'

'I suppose we could keep it from her.'

They began to discuss what they could do to deceive their daughter that peace still prevailed. The difficult question of the daily newspaper arose. The headlines would always be using the word 'WAR'. The paper would have to be cancelled for Sonia's peace of mind; but Martin enjoyed doing the crossword.

'Surely it's not much of a sacrifice to give up the crossword,' said Mary. 'Not when there's your child's sensibilities to consider.'

For a start, they called in Jane, the maid, and made her swear that she would say nothing to Sonia about the war. The maid, familiar with Sonia's outbursts, duly swore. Her mistress was watching her closely.

'Jane, you are looking tired. Why is that?'

Jane, whose real name was Henrietta – but all maids coming under the Fielding command were called Emma or Jane by turns – apologized and said there was a lot of work to be done.

'Nonsense,' said Mary, severely. 'After all, you work in a house where we have no mirrors – so, no mirrors to polish. You're very fortunate.'

'I do understand about the mirrors, ma'am,' said Jane, submissively. She knew the mirrors were banished by order of Sonia, so that she would never see her imaginary hump.

Your parents, assisted by the maid, began an elaborate deception. The delicate Sonia was accustomed to listening to the wireless. Martin removed a thermionic valve from their set, so that it no longer worked.

When Sonia begged her father to get the set repaired, he took it and hid it in the garage. As recompense, he bought his daughter a wind-up gramophone covered in red Rexine, and half-a-dozen records, with which he hoped to distract her. He secretly bought himself a new model Ecko wireless, which he concealed in his study, and on which he could listen to the news from the BBC. Sonia played the records. She quickly broke the one she did not like. The one she most enjoyed was called 'Impressions on a One-string Phone-fiddle'.

She liked to be taken out. Just along the coast was a teashop at which the family frequently stopped to eat cream teas. On one occasion when you had come home for a forty-eight-hour leave before proceeding to OCTU, your mother suggested a visit to the teashop for a special treat. Your mother was friendly, in a condescending way, with the two ladies who ran the teashop. 'Of course, they're just old maids,' she would say of them. 'Spinsters who could never attract any man to marry them.' Martin would try, with equal condescension, to explain to his wife that the men who would have liked to marry those ladies when they were young were very probably buried in the mud of the Somme.

So Mary Fielding rang the teashop before you set out. 'Oh, Miss Atkins. It's Mrs Fielding here,' she said in her most refined voice. 'I wonder if you would kindly assist us. Our dear daughter Sonia is so delicate we are forced to shield her from any knowledge of the hostilities with Nazi Germany. If my husband and I arrived at four o'clock, would you kindly ensure that no mention is made of those hostilities, either by your waitress or by the other customers?'

She listened to Miss Atkins' response. 'I quite see my request may raise difficulties, Miss Atkins, but not insuperable ones, I trust. Otherwise Mr Fielding and I may have to decide not to patronize your teashop henceforth. Oh, are you? I am surprised to hear that. Such a lucrative little business you and Miss Everdale have been running. Pack up if you will, but I would judge you will find the Lake District not to your liking at all.'

Mary put the handset down and turned to Martin. 'I never did! Of all the cheek! Those two spinsters are going to close down next week. They are going to live with a distant niece of Miss Atkins, in Kendal of all places.'

'It's cowardice,' he said. 'It wouldn't do if we all buggered off to the Lake District. How will they scratch a living in Kendal, I'd like to know?'

'Just because the Atkins woman has got an uncle up there.'

You drove to the teashop in the car with Sonia, not without misgivings. A bell on a spring tinkled as you opened the teashop door. A warm, encouraging smell of hot scones met you – the smell of peacetime, never to return. Miss Atkins greeted you all with her usual courtesy. She was rather an ungainly woman, her hair scraped back and tied into a bun with a length of straggling pink ribbon. Her usual attitude in what repose was granted her was to stand with her hands clasped before her; the hands were red from constant washing up. She was wearing the perennial apron over her dress. It showed a picturesque village street, with hills in the background and a notice which read 'Teas with Hovis', outside a half-timbered building. A customer wearing a tricorn hat was riding up to the building on a white horse.

'We are going to have to close down on Saturday week,' said Miss Atkins, with a sad smile. 'It is very inconvenient. You would like the usual cream tea, I expect, Mrs Fielding?'

Sonia's sharp eyes had noticed that bales of barbed wire were being unloaded on the harbour behind the teashop. 'Is all the barbed wire going to spoil your business, Miss Atkins?' she asked.

Miss Atkins looked flustered and adjusted the bun at the back of her greying hair. 'Barbed wire? Oh yes, they are going to do some repair work. They say it will take quite a long time. I'll get your order.'

'I heard they plan to extend the harbour,' said Mary, in an artificially loud voice, staring loftily ahead as if gazing into the future.

A man and his wife were sitting at the next table. Overhearing Mary's remark, the man turned, licking his thumb, and said, 'It's not that, my dear, it's the new defences –'

'Oh, quite right, quite right, I had forgotten,' Mary said. Extending her neck, lowering her head, she hissed across the table at Sonia, 'Just a typical vulgarian. He shouldn't be in here. Take no notice.'

'But what defences does he mean, Mummy?'

'Didn't I tell you? A gang of local men have been trying to steal the boats in the harbour … Oh, here comes our tray. Good. I'm terribly peckish, aren't you?'

'Can we go afterwards and see them putting up the barbed wire, Mummy?'

'We may not have time, Sonia, dear,' said Martin. 'Work is waiting for me. Pleasure must be sacrificed for duty, you know.'

Sonia looked across the table at you, her lips forming the word 'Shuggerybees'.

Miss Atkins arranged the spread on the table. Brown pottery teapot under its cosy in front of Mrs Fielding, hot water jug next, then milk jug. Sugar bowl with sugar tongs. Plates before each person. Pretty plates with floral decorations, now destined for Kendal. A dish with a pile of crisp light brown scones, still warm from the oven. A little pot of strawberry jam, with accompanying spoon. A large pot of whipped cream with a Devonshire motto on the outside of the pot, saying 'Goo Aisy on the Crame!' in rustic brown lettering.

'I'm sure we all will have to go easy on the cream in future,' Miss Atkins found herself murmuring, with another of her stock of sad smiles. 'Just one of the sacrifices we shall have to make.'

'Shuggerybees!' shrieked Sonia. 'Why does everyone keep on about sacrifices?'

'Be quiet,' Martin told her. 'Remember where you are.'

'Where am I?' Sonia asked, looking about in simulated terror. She waved her hands in front of her. 'Is it all a bad dream?'

'Yes', snapped Mary, ignoring her daughter, with a look to Miss Atkins which clearly implied, *No Tip Today!* 'We had heard of the terrible cream shortage in Kendal.'

'And not just in Kendal,' added Martin loyally.

'Where else?' Sonia asked, excitedly. 'Hunstanton? Are the cows dying?'

'We export most of our cream to France. And elsewhere,' said Mary. 'Perhaps to Sweden.'

'And Poland,' you added, helpfully. 'Because of the inv –' You stopped just in time, to add instead, 'the invalids there.'

Miss Atkins looked sad when she said goodbye to you all, standing at the door of the teashop, wringing her hands in her apron – much to Mary's annoyance.

On the drive home, progress was impeded by an army convoy of five-ton lorries travelling slowly along the road to the port. The troops in the rear vehicle shouted, whistled and gestured rudely at your family.

'They're laughing at my hump,' said Sonia. She waved happily to the men.

'Rubbish. They're just rude young men, like all soldiers.' Thus Martin, feeling uncomfortable about some of the ruder gestures.

'What are they doing, pa?'

'Doing? Doing? What do you mean? They're soldiers being taken somewhere to have a nice summer holiday.'

At last you arrived home. Gyp came out to greet you, wagging his tail. Sonia was still worrying about the soldiers' vulgar calls.

'I think I'm the prettiest hunchback in the world, ma. Why isn't there a beauty contest for hunchbacks?'

'Because you'd lose,' you told her, exasperated by her fantasies.

Mary told you both to be quiet and marched into the house, calling for Jane to get you all a pot of tea, despite the cream teas you had recently consumed.

Her daughter followed her, complaining. 'My hump is really pretty. The nurse told me so. She promised that when I die she will have me stuffed.'

'Shut up, Sonia. Valerie never had a hump and nor do you. You know mummy sacked that silly nurse.'

'She said that there were angel wings inside my hump and one day it would break open and then I could fly up to heaven.' She paused. 'I bet there's going to be oodles of blood when it does break open.' Pulling her little blue coat off and flinging it on the floor, she added, 'Hope I don't meet boring Valerie up there in heaven.'

Mary slumped onto her leather sofa and regarded her little daughter. 'That's all pure nonsense. Valerie would never have said anything like that. In any case, there's no place called heaven. Heaven is here in our nice home.'

Sonia sat on the curled arm of a second sofa, this one covered in viridian green satin, put her feet together and clutched her toes, so that her folded legs stuck out like wings to either side, and made a goblin face at her mother.

'If I haven't got a hump, then why don't we have any mirrors in this nice home of ours?'

'That's a silly argument. It's like saying that because we saw one convoy of troops on the road, England is at war.'

'Ha ha, what's that got to do with it?'

'Sonia, I love you dearly, but you are making me cross and you are ruining that sofa.' Mary pulled her regular, utterly-fed-up face. 'And pick your nice coat up off the floor.'

Jane entered with a tray of tea, set it down on a side table, opened a gateleg table and moved it to Mary's side. She set the tray down on the table.

Sonia, who had not moved from her position said, 'Jane, I'm a hunchback, aren't I?'

Jane hesitated. Sonia laughed contemptuously. 'Oh, you can tell me the truth. Ma won't sack you for it.'

Before the maid could answer, Mary said, 'Jane, you know very well Miss Sonia is telling fibs.'

Caught in the cross-fire, Jane said, mainly to the child, 'I'm sure I don't know what you mean, Miss Sonia.'

As she beat a hasty retreat, Sonia stuck out her tongue at the maid's back.

'Your sister Valerie would never behave like that,' Mary scolded.

'I hate that Valerie. I'm glad she's dead! I'd pull her hair if she was still alive.'

*

Next morning, Mary drove into town to buy groceries, and you and Sonia went with her. They passed the post office, which was newly barricaded behind a wall of sandbags. Sonia asked why this had happened. Her mother told her that the post office was being rebuilt; the sandbags were to stop hundreds of letters from drifting into the road.

Mary parked the car outside Randall's, the grocer, after dropping you off at the railway station. She ordered Sonia to stay in the car while she shopped. Sonia sat and fidgeted and read her comic. She became aware of a curious object rising in the sky above roof level. It was grey and crumpled. As it rose, it became plumper, gradually achieving a fat sausage shape with plump double tail. With a cable anchoring it to the ground, it turned gently in the breeze.

Sonia regarded it with wonder. Fitful sunshine made the object glow silver. It was frightening and yet beautiful. She climbed from the car and ran into the grocer to tell her mother.

'There's no such thing,' said Mary, indignantly. But the assistant serving her, who wore an apron and a pencil-thin moustache, said, 'I expect it's a barrage balloon. The papers said they were going up today.'

'So there!' said Sonia. 'The man is nice to me because he's sorry I'm a hunchback.'

'Will you stop it?' said Mary, angrily. 'Or I'll send you back to the hospital again.'

The groceries would be delivered that afternoon. When Sonia and her mother emerged from the grocer's and were back in the car, heading for home, more barrage balloons became visible. It was evident that the city was now ringed with them. They gleamed, serious and attractive in the sun.

'Goodness, aren't they pretty?' exclaimed Mary. 'How clever of the city council to rent those things from the army. It's the mayor's birthday, Sonia. What a pretty way to celebrate the mayor's birthday.'

'I bet Valerie would have been scared. She'd have peed herself.'

'That's so unkind, child. Valerie never wet herself. Not like you.'

Sonia never admitted she knew a war was in progress. She allowed her parents to continue their unconvincing deception for many a month, until the pretence ran thin and all concerned were exhausted. All, that is, except for Herr Hitler and Mr Churchill.

It makes me unbearably sad when you bring up that forgotten past again. What is the point of it, unless to make me miserable? Let the dead bury the dead.
Everything is recorded here, sorrowful or joyful.
But why? Why record?
Because it was enacted in the first place.
Then why was it all enacted, that everlasting artistry of circumstance?

'I expect you'll do reasonably well in your adult life, Smollett,' your headmaster said on your final day at school.

'It's Dickens, Sir,' you responded wittily, well aware of the head's flimsy grasp of names.

He peered at you through his rimless glasses, encompassing his ginger moustache with his lower lip, making that curious sucking noise which was the subject of so many imitations. 'So sorry, Dickens. I always confuse you with what's-his-name. He's also in the First Eleven. But you are bound to do quite well in the great world. Most of our boys do. I remember your father.' He added, 'I think.'

He shook your hand with a gentle resigned motion. You thought with some affection about this mild man when you were in the army and word came to you that your school had been evacuated to a place on the edge of Exmoor. You imagined the headmaster making his way across the quad in a heavy downpour. 'Oh, is it raining, Bronte? I hadn't noticed.'

You walked into town and caught a train home. Your trunk would arrive later by PLA. You were taking a break on your way to the Officers' Training Unit in Catterick, Yorkshire. You found your mother sitting in her conservatory, enjoying tea and cigarettes with a friend. She affected to be surprised by your appearance.

'How strange! And you're in uniform, Stephen. Good job Sonia isn't here. I was reliably informed that you were going to Catterick.'

'I am going to Catterick, Mother. I'm only here overnight. I'll get the nine-fifteen tomorrow morning, if that's okay by you.'

'It's rather inconvenient. The maid has yet to get your bed ready. And she's leaving next week, to work in a factory of some kind. We've been so busy.'

'Where's Sonia, Mother?'

'I think you know Mrs Thompson?' She indicated her friend, who was sitting tight, with a teacup poised halfway to her lips, her little finger pointing halfway to heaven. 'You might say hello to her.'

'Hello. Where did you say Sonia was, Mother?'

'Sonia is at RADA. I'll tell you about it later.'

'And Valerie?'

'Don't try to be funny.'

You retreated to your room and lay down on the unmade bed. You tried to think why Sonia had left school and why she was at RADA, where she might learn how to act but would not learn anything about – well, about all the other subjects of which the world was full.

You suffered the customary dismay at the indifference of your parents. Later, at the evening meal, you learnt that Sonia had been in some kind of trouble at school and had thrown an inkwell at her maths teacher. She had asked to leave school, to learn to act instead. This wish had been granted, although your father grumbled at the expense.

'I shall be leaving England soon, I expect,' you said. 'Soon as I get my pips.'

'Is that wise?' your father asked. He was still wearing an Aertex shirt.

'What do you mean, "Is it wise"? There's a war on, Pa. I'm going to fight for my sodding country. I have my OTC Certificate. What else am I supposed to do?'

'But you wanted to go to university and become a geologist, dear,' said your mother. 'It's silly to give all that up, isn't it?'

You became slightly peevish. 'It seems your pretence to Sonia that there's no war going on has affected your thinking. We've got to fight the Germans, see? The bloody Third Reich. It's a matter of priority.'

'I wish you wouldn't swear,' Mary complained. 'It's so lower class.'

Ignoring her, 'That's all very well,' said your father. 'But you have enjoyed an expensive education. You'll throw all that away in the army. The army's no place for education.'

'Not at all. I expect to become an officer.'

Your father pulled a lugubrious face. 'Officers get shot, you know, old boy. If you must serve, why not serve in the ranks? You'd be safer there.'

'I intend to become an officer, Father. I want to be able to shout at people.' By now you were six feet two inches tall and well-developed for your age. Entirely ready to shout at people.

Martin made a gesture of exhaustion, with which you were familiar.

9

A Good Old Row

So it was a fine March day in the year 1940. I was being told of my mother's psychoanalyst. Butter, sugar and bacon were already rationed, to Mary's disgust. 'We're cutting down on food. We're slimming. Your father's getting too fat,' she said angrily to Sonia, but already what was wearing thin was the pretence she had created for her daughter that there was no war.

Mary's psychoanalyst was leaving the district and moving to Exeter for safety. Mary went to her for one final session. By this time, she was on informal terms with Wilhelmina Fischer.

'I shall miss you, but I hardly think I need any more consultations,' she said, stretching out the final word.

Wilhelmina Fischer sat by an empty grate. She had changed her name and wore pale Lyle stockings under her heavy linen skirt.

'We all encounter obstacles in facing the realities of life,' said Wilhelmina Fischer, removing her pince-nez to gesture widely with them. 'But, *après tout*, realities are real and fantasies must not become real. The German peoples have fallen victim to an anti-Communist belief in their own powers, largely finding reinforcement in an Aryan myth of *Götterdämmerung*. It is a destructive myth which –'

'We're not like them, thank goodness,' said Mary hastily.

'But the British believe in the fantasy of white superiority, which may prove to be equally damaging.' Wilhelmina shook her heavy head so that her heavy cheeks wobbled.

'I can't see how that applies in my case. It's a generalization.' Mary realized, as she rose and thrust her right arm into her coat sleeve, that she had never liked Wilhelmina Fischer. Wilhelmina Fischer had contributed considerably to the miseries of the last few years. She made one feel one was mentally disturbed.

The women shook hands and bid one another farewell on the doorstep of the clinic.

'God speed,' said Mary, feeling, directly she had pronounced the words, that they were inappropriate.

While Wilhelmina Fischer was moving towards Exeter and extinction, you marched along Park Street, Southampton, towards Number 19, where Uncle Bertie Wilberforce and his family lived. You hoped that your uncle would be away.

Before you presented yourself on your Aunt Violet's doorstep, a young, chubby boy, of pink complexion, appeared from the back garden, round the side of the house, blowing a tiny silver trumpet of the kind to be found hanging off pre-war Christmas trees. The trumpet emitted a shrill note as the boy marched right up to you. 'Being carefree,' he said, addressing your Sam Browne, 'Being carefree is a thing like a motto, but I don't know what. I'm always being something. Not a motto, though. Ha ha ha.'

'Hello, Dougie,' you said. 'Is your mother in?'

'She's in charge of the Virol. Mistress of Virol! Know what Virol looks like? Like the mess what Lillie Reader made in her nick-nacks when our form were in the gym, swinging on the handlebars. We all laughed except Lillie.'

That silly forgotten scene … As he was speaking, another figure emerged from the back garden, pushing aside the buds of a hazelnut tree. It was your Uncle Claude. He looked somewhat disconcerted to see you standing there, but covered his embarrassment quickly.

'Morning, Steve! Just came to see how this young rogue was getting on at school. Must be off. Dougie, follow me, you little blighter.'

He grasped the boy's arm and began to drag him away, promising the child a stick of rock 'down at the port'.

You were slightly surprised by this encounter, but, after all, it seemed to be no business of yours. You were in any case more concerned with the impression your appearance would make on your dear aunt.

You were smartly dressed in your new khaki uniform, with the pips of a Second Lieutenant on your shoulders. You were fresh out of OCTU. Your hair was slicked down with Brylcreem and you wore a cap. Your shoes were shining. You had a moustache of a kind. When you rang the bell, Violet opened the door after some delay, looking flushed and dishevelled.

'Golly! Steve, I hardly recognized you in that get-up. Do you want to come in?'

Since she seemed reluctant, you said sharply that that was the general idea. She stood back. You entered the familiar hall. You recognized the heavily-carved hall-stand, with a mirror in its middle and a wooden bear's head snarling at the crown of it. A child's fairy cycle was propped against it. Of course, you remembered, Violet had two children, not only the garrulous Douglas, but his more silent sister, Joyce. It would be Douglas' bike. Thank God Joyce would probably be at school, you thought. There was something more intimate in your mind, which you attempted to keep from consciousness. You had expected that when your aunt saw you spick and span in your officer's uniform she would fall into your arms. Instead she was giving a little snigger and saying that you were, in her phrase, all done up like a dog's dinner.

'Better come into the kitchen,' she said unceremoniously, leading the way through to the rear of the house. Her face was flushed and unhappy. You felt annoyed because she had not kissed you; you had no concern for her.

You were not best pleased to see your Uncle Bertie there, in his old brown-striped suit, his tie badly knotted. He was leaning against the sink with his arms folded. The kitchen smelt stale and cheerless; you had remembered it as a cosy place. A plate with a half-eaten piece of toast lay on the table.

'We were having a good old row,' said Violet, with an imitation of her previous brightness. 'Do you want a sherry?' she asked you.

When you hesitated, she added, 'It's all we've got in this house of parsimony.'

'Because you've guzzled all the gin,' said her husband. He was regarding his wife with a look that seemed to contain hatred and fear. He then said, 'I don't want to come home and find Claude hanging round here again.'

'Sorry if I've come at an awkward moment, Uncle,' you said, with a tone intended to indicate that sorrow was only skin deep.

'There are plenty of those round here,' he responded, without removing his gaze from Violet. 'Plenty and to bloody spare.'

A large ginger cat, which had possibly fled the room when the row was in full swing, slunk back in, jumped up on a kitchen chair and curled itself into a ball. Violet filled two glasses with a dark sherry and handed one to you. Her hand was shaking. Taking the glass with a frown, you directed a look towards Bertie. 'You're not having one?'

'Can't afford to drink, my lad. I leave all that to your aunt.'

'Well, cheers!'

Neither of them made any response. Bertie continued to lean against the sink; he now gazed down at the floor. He seemed to have aged considerably since you last saw him. Violet, too, looked less bright and sassy than she had done. She was wearing no lipstick. She stood now on the far side of the kitchen table, her glass half-raised to her mouth. A clock was inset in one door of the kitchen dresser. It gave a loud tick.

'So you're an officer, Steve,' said Bertie with an attempt at geniality. 'Going to have a crack at the Boche, eh?'

'Sooner or later, yes. That's the general idea. I'll be in the tank corps.'

Bertie pulled a face, as if dismissing such an odd notion.

'We were all Socialists in my day. What made you wish to become an officer?'

'I wanted to be able to shout at people.' The phrase had become your standard joke. You expected people to laugh at it. You never saw below the surface – that it was no joke, that you felt your parents had mistreated you, that other people did not value you, and that you could get your own back by shouting and bullying.

Your uncle did not laugh. 'Your father tells me you were at OCTU. Who did you shout at there?' He shot glances at you before turning his gaze once more to his shoes.

You did not like the question.

'At an Officer Cadet Training Unit, you learn to control men. That's the essence of what being an officer means. You have squads of ordinary soldiers you have to drill. Discipline, you know, Uncle, discipline. Necessary in times of war.'

'Did the, what you call "ordinary soldiers", enjoy this drill?'

A vivid picture came into your head. You were standing erect at one end of the parade ground. The squad was three hundred yards distant from you at the other end of the parade ground, marching like robots, arms swinging, faultlessly in step, the noise of their progress echoing against the stern surrounding buildings. 'Straighten up there,' you bawled. 'March as if you mean it. Squad. Ri-i-ght. WHEEEEL!'

'They weren't there to enjoy it,' you told your uncle. 'They were in the army. They were just part of the system.'

'But you had a good time,' Bertie insinuated.

'Oh, leave the poor lad alone!' shouted Violet. 'I should hope he did have a good time. Why should he want to be in the bloody ranks? You're on embarkation leave now, aren't you, Steve?'

'How did you know?'

She looked puzzled. 'Your father told us. We're still speaking, more-or-less. Off to France, aren't you?'

'It's supposed to be a military secret.'

With feeble sarcasm, Bertie said, 'Don't want Adolf Hitler to know where our Second Lieutenant Steve Fielding is, do we? Might lose the war because of it.'

You sipped the sherry, before saying you were sorry to barge in in the middle of an argument, but had no wish to be drawn into it.

'Your aunt is spending too much money, that's all,' said Bertie, pettishly. 'That's it and all about it. She doesn't know there's a war on. She can't get it into her head. It's not an argument, it's a fact. I'm not made of money.'

'This stingy nonsense is just because I took Joyce up to London in the hols and bought her a new party dress.' Violet sighed and gazed up at the ceiling. 'Not a big deal. In any case, the dress was a bargain.'

'Bargains, bargains. That's all you ever think of.'

Turning away from her husband towards you, Violet said, 'What kind of father grudges his daughter a new party dress?'

'Yes, and what else? In the middle of a war –' Bertie was red in the face.

'We went to see a flick. So what?'

'Oh, have you seen *The Grapes of Wrath*?' you asked her.

'Oh, we wanted something light. We went to see Bob Hope and Bing Crosby in *Road to Singapore*. Ever so funny. They make a great comedy pair.'

'And sat in the best seats, of course,' sneered Bertie.

'I'd better be going,' you said. You were trying to suppress anger and disappointment.

Bertie thrust his hands into his trouser pockets, saying nothing. Violet accompanied you to the front door. She said she was sorry about the way things were. She gave you a fleeting kiss on the cheek and wished you well. Turning back as she was closing the door you saw tears in her eyes.

'Goodbye, my darling,' she called. You felt pretty irritated.

10

A Slight Change of Plan

The sea was slightly choppy. A chilly wind blew, driving cloud before it. The landing craft, with their freight of troops, tanks, guns, lorries and other support vehicles, lurched towards the French shore. It was the 20th May. German forces had already made huge incursions into France. In 1940, the war was going the Germans' way.

This detachment of the Tank Corps, known to some as 'Montagu's Marauders', were to act as reinforcements. After landing, their orders were to move immediately to supplement the defence of Paris. They were about to land on the beaches of Fecamp, a village between Dieppe and Le Havre.

As the ramp of the lead LCT came down, waves surged over it. You stood in the bows, wishing there was some way to stop looking pale. Major Hilary Montagu gripped your elbow, declaiming in a firm voice, 'A mighty wave Odysseus overbore: Quenching all thought, it swept him to the shore.'

You looked at him in puzzlement. Montagu already had his binoculars to his eyes, and was searching the shore for signs of activity.

'*The Odyssey*, old chap. Translated by someone or other. Have you never read *The Odyssey*? The world's greatest book. Tut-tut.'

You said nothing. Montagu was your superior officer, recently returned from India, where he had been in command of a company of Gurkhas on the North West Frontier. A lean and civilized man with a sudden temper which made him feared by both men and officers, Montagu had adopted a somewhat fatherly attitude towards you, for which you were grateful, telling yourself you could stand patronizing. You were so young.

At his signal, the vehicle engines started up. The bottom of the LCT grated against shingle.

'Come on!' shouted Montagu. 'Forward the Buffs!' He jumped into the spray. You followed, the troops behind you. The heaving water came up to your thighs, intent on impeding you. Shingle crunched underfoot. You were too intent on watching for possible opposition ashore to notice the cold of the water.

There was no opposition on the beach, only a French officer awaiting you by a pick-up truck. As you, Captain Travers and two Red Caps directed the traffic from the landing craft into line on the sand, shouting to the soldiers to muster on a road just above the low cliffs, Montagu marched briskly towards the French officer. They saluted each other, then shook hands. They hurried to the pick-up to send out wireless messages to base across the Channel, confirming that you had landed unopposed.

You marshalled the small invading force in order on the road, with scouts out and alert and all Churchills sending out blue exhaust. Two sandy roads divided, with a wood on one side of the main road and a field with cows grazing on the other. Some distance away was a house with a barn beside it, the whole making a disturbingly peaceful picture.

The major, returning from the French pick-up, said to you in an aside, 'Chap doesn't speak Urdu, or much English, but it seems we should get a move on. We proceed via Rouen. There's a straight road from Rouen to Paris, but we may encounter refugees en route.'

'Move immediately, Sir?'

'What else? Get on with it, Fielding.'

As you climbed into your tank, a faint siren blast sounded from across the water. Your supply ship was turning, leaving France to make the return journey back to England. At that point you felt isolated. You thought there were perhaps half a million British troops on French soil, many engaged in battles with the Wehrmacht, but none of them were anywhere near your detachment. You prickled with a sense of peril and excitement.

The vehicles rolled. You began the trek south-west on the more important road. Almost immediately, you encountered refugees. Many were on foot, travelling in families, fathers pushing prams loaded with provisions and cooking utensils; some were in cars of ancient vintage, with mattresses tied to the roof; some had carts, farm carts of various sizes, drawn by horses, with bedraggled sons and daughters of farmers who were trudging alongside the turning wheels. This was what the great French nation had been brought down to.

The road you were taking was raised above the level of the surrounding fields to prevent it from flooding. Many refugees had problems getting up on the road from the fields; carts had to be heaved with a united effort, babies and small children had to be carried, grandmothers had to be pushed, cars in some cases to be abandoned. It was a terrible scramble, involving shouting, cursing and screaming. The fear was always that Stukas would fly over and strafe the crowds. Fortunately none appeared; the skies remained clear.

But your progress was painfully slow. Some refugees, travelling on foot, seized the opportunity to climb on the sides of the tanks for a brief respite. You did not have the heart to order them off. Captain Travers had the passengers of his tank turned away.

*

Your company had landed at dawn. Cloud had blown away, leaving blue skies. Just before one o'clock you arrived at the town of Yvetot, to find much of it in flames following a German bombing raid. A mixed bunch of soldiers and *gendarmes* was barring entrance to the town.

Major Montagu handed over command to Captain Travers and went on foot to order the mayor to give us permission to pass through. He returned after ninety minutes, during which time the men had 'brewed up'. One of the men handed you up a mug of tea. Montagu looked grim. The mayor had been injured by a bomb blast and his harried second-in-command had no control over affairs. He claimed that bomb craters had closed the streets and there was no road open to Rouen: you would have to turn back.

The Major had persuaded or forced the man to sign a piece of paper, which he waved at the soldiery on guard. A large blond Frenchman wearing an old-fashioned helmet came forward and bellowed at the *gendarmes* to let the British tanks through.

Moving slowly along the shattered streets, you all had your first close glimpse of the destruction brought by the war Hitler had wished upon you. It was a still day. Smoke lay like layers of mist, generated by buildings reduced to smouldering wrecks. A car burned quietly, its driver hanging dead from its open door.

The hospital had suffered a direct hit. Injured persons were lying under blankets in the grounds, with unharmed people thronging about, nursing the dying, weeping, or trying to administer medicines or water to the wounded. A young boy was crawling on hands and knees towards the church, dragging a bloody leg.

The church and its grounds were crowded with frightened people; nuns went among them, smiling and gentle, to soothe or to pray. Two men in uniform were dragging a corpse towards the cemetery. When they saw your vehicles, they stopped and stood rigidly to attention, saluting your unit until every tank had passed.

All shops were closed. A once cheerful main street was completely dead. A queue had formed outside the shutters of a *boulangerie*. There were no signs of looting.

The number of bomb craters had been exaggerated. Your tanks experienced greater difficulty negotiating the rubble of collapsed houses strewn across the thoroughfare. It took two hours before you had picked your way through Yvetot, and were on the road to Rouen – or 'the road to ruin', as the troops put it.

What were you thinking at the time? Do you remember?
I hardly thought. Oh, I suppose I was relieved in a way to see the devastation, the suffering. I told myself that this was how it had always been, that this was simply part of the tragic human condition. Or maybe I thought all that later, when there was time to think, when I was in prison.
Were you aware that this was a peak moment in your life?
No – for once I was totally preoccupied by the present.

You were not more than a kilometre down the road, and were passing through a grove of poplars lining each side of the road, when three Stukas came roaring overhead. The bombs they dropped whistled as they fell, to add to the terror of the attack.

No order was needed for you to dive for cover under or beside your vehicles. Hapless refugees fled to either side of the road among the tall trees, to crouch in ditches. Fortunately, the bombs did little damage, exploding in nearby fields.

'Stay where you are,' Montagu shouted. 'The blighters are liable to come back.'

Indeed the planes did come back. They wheeled and returned from the north-west, flying low down the road, machine guns blazing. Many refugees were hit; several were killed. Some did not die outright; screams of pain and terror rang out long after the planes had gone.

You heard a dog yelping terribly with pain. Suddenly it was silenced.

You had First Aid kits with you, and administered what help you could to the injured. A peasant woman, herself with a badly damaged shoulder, sat nursing a dead child. Over and over, in a choking voice, she cried, '*Putain de bordel de merde! Putain de bordel de merde!*' You let her drink from your water bottle.

A ragged hound was lapping up blood on the road. You kicked it aside. The scene was one of chaos, of splinters, of ruined limbs. A horse lay struggling in its death agonies, entangled in reins. It had broken a wheel of the cart to which it was attached. One of your troop, a young soldier called Palfrey, put his rifle to the horse's head and shot it. He helped three men to cut the horse free and drag its body and the ruined cart to the side of the road. An adolescent girl, seemingly unharmed, was leaning against a tree, covering her face, weeping.

Your wireless operator called to the major. An RT message awaited him. Montagu beckoned you to follow him. You stood by the wireless truck while he spoke intermittently in an incomprehensible language, all the while watching the chaos nearby. He finally pronounced an English 'Out', and returned the handset to the operator. He locked his hands behind his back and spoke quietly to his two officers, Captain Travers and you.

'I thank God that a comrade of mine is in the Southampton HQ. We once took a holiday in Ootie together. We can *bolo* in clear Urdu to each other. Security is maintained – I doubt many Huns *bolo* Urdu.

'The news in whatever language is extremely poor, gentlemen. Advanced German Panzer columns have overwhelmed Amiens and Abbeville, on the River Somme. In case you don't know, those cities are not too far distant from here; about sixty miles.'

He nodded towards the north-east.

'Now the Panzers are heading this way. We aren't making the progress we had anticipated. The Germans are making the progress we did not anticipate. We are in some danger of being cut off. The Prime Minister of France, Paul Reynaud, is talking of giving up the struggle.'

'I always said the French were a bunch of cowards,' said Travers. He was a wiry man with a lean, hard face, handsome in its way.

You had always found him reserved and unfriendly. 'I'll wager they lose their nerve.'

Montagu frowned, but let the remark pass. 'If France packs it in, we shall have a few problems on our hands. Indeed, we have some already.' The nod of his head was directed towards your men, who were standing in front of their vehicles, rifles pointed at a group of ten or more men and a woman, who were attempting to take possession of the two supply lorries.

One of the soldiers fired his rifle in the air, low over the heads of the advancing group.

The major removed his hands from behind his back and marched briskly to where his men stood. He addressed the French mob in English. He told them that you were a detachment going to help defend their capital city, that their actions threatened to upset military plans, and that the Boche were closing in rapidly on their position.

'In other words, clear off, the lot of you!'

Whether the refugees understood what he said was doubtful. But his firm, reasonable and authoritative voice had its effect. The mob slunk away and returned to help their wounded comrades.

'*Danke schön*,' said Montagu calmly, turning back to you officers. 'Now then, I have received orders for a slight change of plan. Somewhere to the west of here lies the city of Rennes, in Brittany. About one hundred and seventy miles away as the crow flies. There's a firm in Rennes called Colomar, part British-owned. Their HQ is on the Place de Bretagne, a main square, *thik hai*?'

'What's all this to do with us, Major?' Travers asked.

Montagu continued as if he had not heard the question.

'Colomar currently hold three-million-pounds-worth, sterling, of industrial diamonds. We don't want this haul to fall into German hands. You, Fielding, what are industrial diamonds used for?'

You replied, 'They are essential for the manufacturing of machine tools, and tools necessary for making armaments.'

'Full marks. The way the war is going, we do not want these diamonds falling into German hands, for obvious reasons. Our orders are for one of us to press on immediately to Rennes, take charge of the diamond stock, and to transport it to Saint Nazaire, a port on the south coast of Brittany at the mouth of the River Loire. I gather there may be some difficulty in persuading the company to hand the diamonds over. However, we are armed and they are not. A persuasive point.'

He stood there sturdily in the middle of the road, looking at you.

'Rennes is a long way from home. Why is it up to us, for God's sake?' asked Travers.

'Because we are on the spot, Captain. We happen to be British troops farther to the south than other units.' He spoke briskly, before turning to you.

'Fielding, you are young and brave, I am delegating you the task of taking one of the vehicles and collecting the diamonds from Colomar.'

You asked why there was this sudden change of plans.

'Better ask the fornicating Germans that.' Montagu continued with his instructions.

'You will drive with the diamonds, going like the clappers, to St Nazaire in the south, where a Royal Naval ship will deliver you and the valuables back to Britain.'

You were horrified. 'Why me, Sir?'

As you asked the question, you remembered the OCTU report in a stray roster you had caught sight of. There lay a summary of your qualities: '6ft 2ins. Good-looking, good accent. Knows how to handle knife and fork. Officer material.' Nothing was said there about a capacity to collect diamonds from a distant French city.

'Why not Captain Travers, Sir?'

Montagu gave a low growl.

'Captain Travers has a poor opinion of our French allies and does not speak French. You do speak French, Lieutenant. You are young and foolhardy. You will do well.'

'But, Sir … well, I can't deal in diamonds, Sir. I'm a Socialist.'

In a quiet voice, Montagu said, 'Don't be a bloody fool, Fielding. There are larger issues at stake than your political conscience. The whole continent of Europe totters on the very brink of falling to Hitler's armies. Britain will then stand alone. We need those industrial diamonds and so do the Huns. We must secure them. Take one of the *gharies* and two volunteers and a Bren gun and off you go. *Jaldhi*!'

'Not my tank, Sir?'

'The *ghari* is much faster. Stop arguing and go, will you?'

'What's the name of the ship I have to rendezvous with, Sir?'

'You'll find out when you get there. Starting from now!'

You stood poised to move. But there was a further question, born of the danger you were all in.

'What about you, Sir?'

Montagu gave you a rictus that passed for a smile. 'The rest of us will continue on to "Gay Paris" as ordered. The way you are going, away from the immediate combat, should be less dangerous. If you get a move on.'

You found yourself reluctant to leave the presence of this forceful officer. 'Hope you make it, Sir.'

Montagu put his hands behind his back and stuck his chin in the air. 'I rely on the motto of the Montagus, forged on the Khyber Pass, *Numquam wappas* – Never backwards!'

11

Carnage on the Road

The vehicle Major Montagu referred to as a *ghari* was a five-ton lorry. Among the few supplies loaded into the back of it sat Private Furbank, manning the Bren gun. Private Pete Palfrey was driving the *ghari*. You swung yourself up into the front seat beside him.

You were entering the hilly country to the south of Bernay, where no refugees filled the roads – where indeed it seemed there were no inhabitants. Signs of human occupation were few – a barn here, an old tractor there, a dilapidated house with a picket fence. Apple trees lined the road, in full blossom, turning hedges white and pink. But not a man with a spade, not a woman hanging out washing, not a child leading a dog along. It was as if the tribes of mankind, having finally got things going, had themselves gone.

Here the spring had come, in contrast to the carnage you had witnessed in Yvetot, the season announced in the trumpets of daffodils by roadsides, and not only there. Cuckoos called from

107

nearby hills. Other birds sang, warbling from tree to tree. The spring enfolded them with its calming presence.

And it rained. It was but a shower. You kept on driving.

Dusk was falling by the time you reached a tiny village on a crossroads, by name Monnai.

'Stop here,' you told Palfrey. He drew up at the side of the little street, where the houses crouched against the pavement, looking as if they had closed for the duration of the war.

Furbank came round to the window and asked where you all were.

You responded with an order. 'You two go and find if there's somewhere we can eat. Keep your rifles ready for trouble.'

Palfrey said, 'We don't speak the local lingo, Sir.'

'Use gestures,' you replied. 'Go!'

You were feeling shocked beyond words. You could not rid your mind of the images of carnage on the road, of bodies stripped of clothing and skin, blood-red and glistening, like something in a butcher's window. The horror of it would not leave you. Yet you feared it would one day leave you. It was your new knowledge – knowledge that in fact you had known all along – that scared you; that there were madmen loose in the world, that people were meat. You were disgusted with … well, with everything, including yourself. You vowed you would be a vegetarian from now on. Nevertheless, you were feeling hungry.

Furbank and Palfrey came back with a big, red-faced man, his face fringed by a line of beard. He wore a striped sweater and a pair of old corduroy trousers.

You opened the *ghari* door to him. He put out a beefy hand in welcome. You shook it. He said he understood you were English. You agreed, in your graduate French. He declared that he knew only two words of English, 'coffee' and 'wine'. He laughed at his own shortcomings. You followed suit. He said that if you and your men would do him the honour, he and his wife would like to give you some supper.

108

You were grateful and accepted.

He asked you what your vehicle was called. You answered 'Ghari', for you had taken to Major Montagu's Urdu for 'lorry'. The Frenchman said he now knew three words of English. 'Ghari!' he said. You had to drive the ghari off the road to his orchard.

The man's wife was a kindly woman who, directly she saw your pallor, brought you and your companions glasses of calvados. You felt slightly better. She provided you with a good solid meal and a rich red local wine to go with it. You were given cushions on which to lay your heads in the ghari; you already had blankets. You were parked in the man's orchard, surrounded by blossom. After that generous meal, you all slept well. Your sleep was mercifully dreamless.

The French couple were up even earlier than you in the morning. They gave you croissants and cups of strong coffee for breakfast. You thanked them for their kindness. You would come and see them and repay their hospitality when the war was over.

They stood and waved in the road until you were a good quarter kilometre away. You feared for them when les Boches arrived.

You made good time. Sometimes the roads seemed almost deserted, apart from the odd farm cart; at other times they were busy and you had to pull over to the right-hand side of the road. At one point, on a road lined thickly with trees, you encountered a considerable body of French motorized troops, heading towards the north-east. The commander of the troop was suspicious. He halted the column and came to inspect you.

You climbed slowly from the ghari and saluted him. He was a tall man with a withered face and a black military moustache. He returned your salute and asked who the devil you were. You replied in French that you were a British detachment on a mission to Rennes. He told you you were going the wrong way to meet the Boche.

You explained your mission. He said that the Germans would never get as far as Rennes. But there was a whisper of doubt in his voice. You exchanged a few remarks about the enemy, and you stressed the fact that the British were fighting alongside their allies. He became more cordial. His name was Capitaine Philippe de la Tour, commander of a Breton battalion advancing to engage the enemy. He offered you a *Gaulois*. You stood together in the road, smoking. He remarked on how young you were. He was thirty-two.

The trees branching overhead were still. Everyone waited for you. Except the Boche.

The capitaine was friendly and curious. He inspected the interior of the five-tonner. Finally, he asked if there was anything he could do to assist you. You mentioned petrol. He had two men bring up two full jerry cans to stow in the rear of the *ghari*. He enquired if you had French money. You were forced to admit you had none. He tut-tutted and summoned his paymaster, who was made to pay out five hundred francs, which he did with a bad grace.

You were most grateful. You shook hands. The capitaine embraced you, for you were comrades-in-arms. You saluted smartly before he turned away and marched briskly back to his vehicle. It seemed as if your heart rose to your throat and almost choked you.

That night, you were somewhere near Fougères. You did not know where anywhere was, or how far it was, for all signposts had been removed – an indication that someone, if not the capitaine, must believe the Germans might get this far. The countryside was broken and wooded. You pulled into a firebreak between tall beeches. You ate Army iron rations and settled down to sleep on the boards of the *ghari*.

The sound of distant explosions roused you from sleep. You climbed out quietly, so as not to awaken Palfrey and Furbank, to see what was to be seen. The trees cut off all distant vision. They stirred uneasily in an increasingly strong breeze. Planes were flying overhead. A town further along the road was getting strafed, presumably Fougères. You were sleepy and climbed back to your blanket.

110

Suddenly Palfrey was shaking you.

'Wake up, Sir! There's a dogfight going on. Wake up!'

You were cold and heavy. Only gradually did you become properly alert. The roar of aero engines brought you to your senses. You climbed out after Palfrey. Furbank was standing with his back against the *ghari*, looking up at the dull dawn sky. His face was grey and drawn, as if he had aged twenty years overnight.

One flickering searchlight was probing the air. A number of planes were manoeuvring, spurting paths of tracer. Slow French fighters were taking on the speedier Messerschmitts. From the ground, it all looked harmless.

You watched in fascination as a plane was hit. It began to spiral earthwards, with a tail of flame.

'It's one of ours,' you said, almost to yourself.

The burning plane flattened out, as if the pilot were recovering control. Still it flew lower and lower.

'Look out!' yelled Furbank.

The plane crashed through the tops of nearby trees at great speed, flaming, flaming, as it rushed towards where you stood.

Did you run? Who could remember in that moment of extreme terror? – All you recall is that gigantic fiery thing, like vengeance itself, disintegrating as it sped through saplings, smashing into your lorry, spewing flame and metal all about.

You were hit by a fragment of metal. You went down. Terrible noise. Then the crackle and crash of everything burning.

Into the silence and blackness came strange dreams, incoherent, confused and confusing. Gradually you realized you were recovering consciousness. You could not move.

There was a roof overhead. You were lying in a hut of some kind. You thought you were at home. You could hear the sound of water. You believed you were a boy again, back at Walcot.

You passed out.

When consciousness closes down, all manner of other senses occupy the darkened stage of your mind. These are, in many cases, deeply rooted myth figures, inherited from a long phylogeny, the roots of which precede the human. If only you could examine them! But the net of consciousness is not there to effect a capture.

Slowly the dark tide receded. You sprawled on the very shores of awareness, taking in little or nothing.

You found that someone – and this was real – was lifting your head in order to give you a drink. It was not always water he presented you with. Sometimes it was milk.

You became more able to take in your surroundings. It was not unlike a baby being born. You were conscious of pain. You struggled to sit up. You were alone in something much like a cowshed, covered with an old army greatcoat. Beyond the open shed door lay woodland, where sunshine was visible in slices amid the dense foliage.

When you made an attempt to get to your feet, you groaned with the pain. In response, a figure appeared in the doorway, an unkempt figure in ragged khaki uniform.

'Christ, I thought you'd never come fucking round,' it said, in tones of relief.

You seemed to recognize the man but could not recall his name. He came and squatted by you.

'I wouldn't try to get up. You've got a nasty gash in your leg.'

You lay back, exhausted. You managed to gasp a question, asking how long you had been unconscious.

'It's been ten or more days, I reckon.' He gave a laugh. 'I started carving notches in a tree. If you'd have died, I'd have been stuck here alone. I've not a fucking clue where we are.'

When you apologized and said you had forgotten his name, he told you he was Pete Palfrey. 'You're Steve Fielding. We don't have no ranks, you savvy. Not here in this bloody forest.'

You had no wish to dispute the matter with him.

Memory was returning. 'A bomb hit our *ghari*! My God!'

'Only it weren't a bomb. It were a bloody French fighter plane, full of fuel. A Morane 445.'

You were astonished by his knowledge.

'We done aircraft recognition at school. Moranes were never a match for the Messerschmitts.'

'Moraine? A funny thing to call an aircraft. A moraine is a heap of debris left by a retreating glacier.'

He made nothing of that. 'Well, it's just a heap of debris now.'

Pete Palfrey was a little younger than you, with a lad's slenderness. His unshaven whiskery state made him look older. He had attended a grammar school in Leeds.

'How's the *ghari*?'

'The *ghari*, as you call it, were blown into little bits.'

'And Private Furbank?'

'Him likewise, poor sod! His name were Gary too.' He paused meditatively. 'I heard as he was a bit of a one for Navy Cake.'

He added that when you were able to walk, you two could go and inspect the remains of the crash. They were not far away.

You learnt to hobble about with an improvised crutch. Your surroundings narrowed your consciousness. You marvelled at the resourcefulness of Palfrey. He had reconnoitred the area and had discovered a nearby farmhouse. Careful observation confirmed that it had been deserted. The back door was unlocked, had, in fact, no lock on it. The occupants had left in a hurry, leaving utensils and clothes and various other belongings behind. Palfrey had carried a mattress out to the cattle shed for you to lie on.

Two cows had been left in a field. Palfrey had milked them.

Desperate for food, he had found some flour and had baked a kind of bun, flavoured with sultanas from a pottery jar. He had found an old wireless in a downstairs room, and listened in, but could not get an English-speaking station.

You stood in a small clearing. You asked him if there was a bicycle at the house; he could cycle into Fougères and get help. He had thought of that, he said dismissively. There was no bike. Nor did he intend to leave you.

As you were talking, a heavy bird fluttered overhead, battering its way through light twigs. You exclaimed in surprise.

'What the hell is that?'

'It's a feral hen,' Palfrey said. He dug into his pocket and produced some grains of corn which he scattered on the path. The hen landed and pecked at the grain. It was a gaunt bird, clucking to itself, darting swift, suspicious glances here and there as it ate.

When you raised your crutch to kill it, Palfrey stopped you.

'Don't be a daft bugger! These chickens lay eggs. We need eggs. I'm hoping to get them to settle here, to save me having to traipse up to the house where they roost all the time. Someone might spot us.'

It appeared that a number of hens had been left behind when the farm was evacuated. Left to run free, they had regrown their wings and rediscovered the art of flight. They were not your only source of food. Palfrey had made a catapult, which he used with deadly accuracy to stun and then kill squirrels and, on one occasion, a rabbit. These morsels you cooked on spits over small fires. Palfrey was expert at skinning the animals, and at building fires.

Your admiration for his resourcefulness grew. You thought of a play in which you had acted in the days of the Sixth Form, entitled *The Admirable Crichton*, written by a then popular playwright. The play concerned a wealthy family who had a butler named Crichton; the butler went with the family on a cruise, to serve them as usual. When the family were shipwrecked, the butler proved himself the superior man and saved the family from starvation. You had known the play well, for you had played the role of the admirable Crichton yourself. Sonia had come to see you acting. Now here was Private Palfrey, rejoicing in a similar role. While you had lain unconscious, this city lad had learnt the arts of survival in the wilds.

Slowly your leg healed, at least in part, for it continued to trouble you. You followed Palfrey along a faint woodland path and came to a place where the trees were blackened by fire. They surrounded the burnt-out remains of the crashed plane and your lorry. Both machines were skeletal. A dog was chewing something. It threw you a guilty glance over one shoulder and slunk away into the undergrowth.

114

The two of you stood there, silenced by the grim spectacle. Of Gary Furbank and the French pilot there was no sign. They had either been consumed in the fire or feral dogs had devoured their remains.

'Seen enough?' Palfrey asked, with a sneer.

But you rooted about to see what could be retrieved. Not everything had been consumed by the blaze. You found a box of ammunition, still sealed, miraculously intact, overturned in rough grass. You insisted that Palfrey and you dragged it back to your lair.

There was still, you considered, a war to be fought.

12

'War or No War …'

There was some mercy in the restriction of your awareness to your immediate circumstances. You never thought of your home. I will tell you briefly of something going on there. Are you prepared?
Yes.

Mary Fielding was having the room she called her lounge redecorated. Two decorators in overalls were hanging the new wallpaper. She stood watching them. She had moved her goldfish into the kitchen for safety.

'War or no war, we've got to have the place looking smart,' she said. 'People may call.' The men agreed. They had voted for Martin Fielding in the previous by-election.

Mary was restless. She looked out into the garden. Unable to think of anything else to say, she retreated and went into the kitchen. Martin had left the house early for a meeting at work.

Theirs was hardly a marriage, she told herself. Steve was gone. Of course, there was Sonia … but Sonia was away at acting school. The home was so dull without Sonia.

She retreated to Valerie, the ghost eternally at her side. Valerie would have stayed with her, would have found her interesting. Valerie. She would be quite a big girl by now. She wore little frilly dresses, with frilly petticoats beneath. She had ribbons in her hair. She was always smiling and happy – as good as gold.

Mary acknowledged to herself now that Valerie was dead, had never lived, was a fantasy; yet it was a fantasy that consoled her, as far as she could be consoled. Not just dead even, but had never had life, except in the shelter of her womb. Perhaps, after all, Valerie was better out of it, out of the world.

She went back to watch the men working. Valerie followed, meek, but faint.

Someone was ringing the front door bell.

As Mary left the room, the older decorator straightened up and eased his back. He worked with his son. This youth was a poor droopy thing with a bad case of acne. He was due to be called up; he had a verruca, which might save him from the infantry. When he was gone, the old man would be alone. But perhaps interior decorating would not be needed any more in wartime.

He lit up a Wild Woodbine and gave one to his son.

'Take a break,' he said. He sat himself down on a sofa covered by dust sheets. He drew the smoke into his lungs.

His father had been a general carrier, and had died at the age of fifty-one, of drink and misery. This son of his, now puffing away at his cigarette, one of five children, often daydreamed of a wise old man with long white hair and a white beard, dressed in a trailing hessian garb – a very kindly, wise man. Perhaps he had seen a picture of such a sage, perhaps in the pages of *Everybody's*. He knew he could never be, or even meet, such an ancient. Like his father, he sucked at the Woodbine.

Mary went slowly to see who it was at the door. She knew the decorators stopped work directly she was not present. A messenger boy stood on the doorstep; he apologetically offered her a telegram in a buff envelope.

'What is it?' she asked, drawing back from it.

'Dunno, ma'am. It's a telegram.'

Mary accepted it with a word of thanks. She was sure it was bad news.

She turned away, closing the door, and ripped the envelope open. The message had come from the War Office. It announced that Second Lieutenant Stephen Fielding was missing in action, presumed killed.

'Oh, dear.' Mary bit her lip. How could they hide the bad news from Sonia? The poor girl would be so upset.

She stood there, crying a little, telegram in hand. Valerie watched. Of course it was typical of Martin to be away when he was needed.

13

'We're Okay Here ...'

Palfrey was squatting, engaged in scooping out a hole in the ground. He was barefoot and half-naked. He worked with concentration, biting his lower lip. When the hole was about the size and depth of a washbasin, he placed a piece of tarpaulin in the bottom of it, smoothing it out carefully. From a cup standing beside him, he poured water into the improvised bowl.

You were curious and watched the operation with interest. You asked Palfrey what he was doing. The explanation, curtly delivered, was that insects would fall into the cavity and drown. They could then be fed to the hens, or possibly eaten by the two of them.

'I can hobble,' you said. 'If we take it easy, we can walk into Fougères and get help.'

'We're okay here,' said Palfrey, without looking up.

You were astonished by his reply, and repeated that you both needed to get into Fougères, to rejoin your unit.

'We're okay here,' Palfrey repeated in an indifferent tone of voice. He smoothed down the sides of his trap without bothering to look up.

You tried to speak lightly. 'This Robinson Crusoe thing is all very well, but we are soldiers, you know.'

'I'm not. Not no more. I've had it as far as soldiering is concerned.'

'You are still a soldier, Palfrey. Nominally, at least, under my command. I'm ordering you –'

He looked up, blank-faced. 'Fuck off,' he said.

Various noises disturbed the peace of the woods. Aircraft frequently roared overhead. From a distant road came more continuous sounds of convoys on the move. The war had not stopped just because you and Palfrey had stopped.

Your leg grew no better. The femur itself had probably been splintered. You tried to persuade Palfrey you would do better to move into the farmhouse. Palfrey would have none of it: the farmhouse would be a target for the enemy or for marauders, he said. In that he soon proved correct.

You had hobbled up to the house, hoping for fresh bandages. Already green things were springing up on the walls of the building. Bushes grew from the guttering, hanging down like unruly hair, nodding as you passed. A feral cat was about, running off when you came in sight. In the barren kitchen were rat droppings. Grasses were springing up through the floorboards.

You were desperate to have news of the outside world. You opened up the back of the wireless set, to find the shrivelled corpse of a little mouse there. You removed the thermionic valves to clean them one by one. The set was powered by an accumulator. You polished up the connections and switched the 'on' button.

The set slowly warmed up and began to speak in French. You tuned it carefully and soon found an English wavelength. A man was talking in a BBC accent. You switched off then, to wait for six o'clock and the news, afraid that the current might fail at any moment.

You waited in the dimness of the deserted room. Nothing stirred.

At six o'clock, you switched on again, and so you heard the announcer state, in measured tones, that France had capitulated and had signed an armistice with Nazi Germany. Arrangements were being made to evacuate the British Expeditionary Force.

You were frantic. You remained in the house that night, listening to sundry scratchings and scamperings, the sharp little destructive teeth of history. You waited for the early morning news, when a BBC announcer would announce the day's date. You had no idea how long you and Palfrey had remained in the woods. Palfrey had long ago given up marking the days with notches on a tree.

Morning dawned. You switched on. You learned that the date had crept to the 23rd of June. You had been in the woods for just over four weeks.

The speech Prime Minister Winston Churchill had made earlier in the month was then repeated over the airwaves. Churchill said, 'Even though large tracts of Europe and many old and famous states have fallen or may fall into the grip of the Gestapo and all the odious apparatus of Nazi rule, we shall not flag or fail ... We shall fight on the beaches, we shall fight on the landing grounds, we shall fight in the fields, and in the streets, we shall fight in the hills; we shall never surrender ...'

The great voice faded to a whisper and was gone as power died.

You rested your elbow on the old table and your forehead on your hand, and you wept. Your shoulders heaved and you cried your heart out.

You did not hear the creak of floorboards. Only when a strange voice spoke did you look round, startled. A man dressed in a shabby black suit stood nearby, pointing a rifle at you.

The new arrival had a long face with an angular jaw emphasized by side-whiskers, black and white in colour. The pupils of his eyes were extremely pale and shaded by bushy eyebrows. He was a narrow man, narrow about the shoulders, shallow in the chest. His age was about forty, as nearly as you could judge, and he said, grimly, 'We all have reason to weep. You most of all.'

He was speaking English with a French accent.

You raised your hands above your head. You turned round in the chair and asked if he intended to shoot you.

The man seemed to think this a reasonable enquiry. He said, 'I have been keeping a watch. You broke into this house, which is not yours.' He paused uncertainly. 'But foreigners have broken into this country, which is not theirs. There is plenty of shooting. One more shot would hardly need entry in God's accounts. But perhaps there is shooting enough.'

You were perplexed by these reasonable remarks, considering that the newcomer kept the rifle pointed towards you and his finger on the trigger.

'Why should you shoot me? If you wish me to leave here, I will. Is this your house? You left it unlocked.'

'It belongs to a distant kinsman. Are you open to reason? If you rush at me, I will certainly shoot.'

'Having a stranger aim a rifle at me makes me reasonable. I'll get out.'

'No, you won't. Not until I say so. Ah … remain seated!' This order because you had made to get up from the chair. He jerked the rifle, so that your hands rose again.

You recovered from your surprise and became angry.

'What do you bloody well want? You're French, aren't you? I'm English. So we are supposed to be on the same side in this war.'

'A supposition is a belief *sans* proof. In a war, everyone is an enemy. I hope you might prove an ally.' He bit his lower lip nervously.

'I'll never prove your ally while you point that bloody rifle at me.'

He gave you a mirthless smile. 'I am your friend. See, I don't shoot you, and I could do it, with ease. Though it is not my habit. A bad habit. Lower your hands.'

He gave a brief shrill whistle. A woman entered the room, holding the hand of a child who was dragged forward. She wore a dark green dress which hung to her ankles, and what looked like a man's shooting jacket over it. Her face was pale and pudding-like, as if made of part-cooked dough; her eyes were of a grey-blue colour, bright and intelligent.

She nodded to you, not in unfriendly fashion. The small boy she was clutching wriggled to get free, but she held him firmly. She told him quietly, in German, to keep still.

The man said, '*Schön.* This is time for introductions. My name is Gerard Geldstein, this is my wife, Helge, and our little boy, Pief. We are not ill-intentioned persons.' He gestured towards the others with a slight bow, as he might have done in a theatrical production. 'We have also a little girl, but she will not come in. She is afraid of you. And your name is, Sir?'

You introduced yourself, saying that you needed to get to Rennes as soon as possible. Geldstein said that Rennes was already being over-run by the Wehrmacht. 'It is a risk to anyone human to go there.'

You exchanged a few words. Pief, the small boy, was released and walked slowly backwards, step by step, until he could jump out of the open door.

Geldstein's proposal was that Palfrey and I should accompany the Geldstein family as armed escorts. They needed to travel. He knew of a safe place where it should be possible to wait out the war. Everyone, he claimed, needed an armed escort in these dreadful days.

Your ambition was to get back to your unit; however, you were still lame, and Geldstein convinced you that the wood in which you were hiding was of small extent, and would shortly be combed by elements of the Wehrmacht, at which point you and Palfrey would be caught and executed.

'Where is this refuge of yours?'

'South, by ninety kilometres. To travel such a distance, we need someone who can seriously shoot under pressure. Like a soldier. Like you, Monsieur Fielding.'

That made your decision for you. Going south meant being nearer the port of St Nazaire, and the possibility of getting a ship back to Britain.

So it was that that night, you and Palfrey set off in Geldstein's small van, accompanying Geldstein, his wife, the boy Pief and his sister, Brenda. Geldstein drove steadily and slowly, not using headlights. When another vehicle approached from ahead or behind, he would pull into the side of the road; there you would crouch anxiously until the other vehicle had passed. You had your rifle ready and were sitting on the box of ammunition you had salvaged from the destruction of your *ghari*.

You travelled south on by-roads. Never had you experienced France as a dangerous wasteland, inhabited by predators. As if Geldstein's paranoia was infectious, the dense belts of trees on either side of the road, black in the moonless night, became animate beings waiting to close their teeth on passers-by. Just as alarming were the villages through which you drove – seemingly untenanted, without light, squat, blind, waiting to be woken into hostility.

No sound came from this outside world, except for the bark of a dog when you passed a farm, or the cry of a night bird, giving solitude a voice.

Once, you passed two men, rifles slung over their shoulders, tramping wearily along in the centre of the road. At the sound of Geldstein's engine, they ran to one side, to hide among the unwelcoming foliage.

At every junction of the road, there might be a trap prepared; indeed, at one crossroads, ill-glimpsed, a tank waited. But it too seemed as dead as the villages stranded on the route. This was what invasion brought with it, social life in catatonia, sleep, or paralysis imitating sleep. You might have been feeling your way through a land of horror and the supernatural. The mist gathering after the midnight hour reinforced an illusion that you traversed a territory of the dead.

You kept watch out of the rear window of the van, anxious about pursuit but, as the kilometres slowly unpeeled, you too were lulled by the monotony of suspense. Despite the chill air, you fell asleep over your rifle.

When the van had covered ninety kilometres at not much more than twenty kilometres an hour, Geldstein turned the van off the road. The vehicle bumped and dawdled along a firebreak lane between forest trees. Intimations of dawn struggled in the eastern sky, rendering the crusty outline of a ruin in silhouette. The Geldsteins had reached their destination. With a final jerk, the van stopped and the engine died.

14

Over the Boundary

Do you wish to learn more of that other world to which you had belonged?
No. My mind is locked into that dreadful time I knew.
You must attend to what was happening. For completeness.

Both your mother and your father felt grief for the loss of their son. Martin took pride in the black band Mary sewed onto his jacket. Sonia was away in London; they agreed it was best not to upset her by informing her of your supposed death.

Martin had decided that wartime life must go on as usual. As a Socialist MP his duties included the captaincy of a constituency cricket team, known as the Scallywags. An annual match was played on the field behind the gasworks – the Scallywags versus the Morgan Memorial team. The Mike Morgan thus immortalized had instituted the matches back in the mists of time: 1912, to be precise.

In this year of 1940, getting two teams together had presented unusual difficulties, with so many men in the armed forces. Martin, now forty-six, had officially retired from the team the previous year. Now he was back at the crease, and was conducting a search for cricketers with the same dedication he showed in hunting for Labour voters.

The match was traditionally played on the weekend nearest the 14th July, birthday of the legendary Mike Morgan. The captain of the MM team was Pat Atterbury, known to the Scallywags as 'Pratterbury'. Pratterbury had experienced the same difficulties in raising a team as had Fielding. Nevertheless, on that precise Saturday, the two teams gathered to do battle.

Meanwhile another battle had begun, the fight for supremacy in the air which became known as the 'Battle of Britain'. The Luftwaffe pilots in their Messerschmitts were regarded as the precursors of an invasion. The RAF pilots in their Spitfires and Hurricanes rose to the skies above southern England and shot down as many German planes as possible.

But that afternoon the skies were quiet when Martin Fielding, bat tucked professionally under his right arm, went in to score against the forces of Pratterbury, taking his place at the crease and demanding Middle and Leg of the umpire.

Among the few spectators were Mary and her brother Bertie, down for the weekend. Bertie had left Violet at home to look after the children. The MM side boasted a spin bowler named Bernard Ames who had once played for Hampshire. Ames was near fifty now, but did not lack cunning.

Martin and his partner 'Wiggy' Wiggington settled in and began to score. Martin became more confident as over succeeded over. The determination grew in him that, if this were to be his last game of cricket, he would do what he had long wished to do, to hit a ball over the boundary. Then he could always remember his success – and perhaps other men in both teams would remember it too, saying to each other in the bar after the match was played,

'But do you remember that day when old Fielding knocked that pill right over the boundary?'

His chance came with the last ball but one of an over. Ames had let it go slightly wide of the off-stump. Martin stepped forward and struck the leather with all his might – indeed, with more might than he knew he had. Thwack!

He stood and watched the ball fly. It was the perfect shot. The MM fielders also stood and stared. The ball flew ever on, high over the shed both teams used as the pavilion, travelling as if it would never stop. It vanished over the fence into a scrap dealer's yard. A distant clang announced its landing.

Never had anyone there seen such a shot.

'Oh, well played, Sir!' exclaimed Wiggy. 'Right over the boundary, by gum!'

Even the opposing players burst into applause.

Next ball, Martin was out, bowled middle stump.

The Scallywags won that memorable match by twenty-one runs. Celebrations followed. Martin was the hero of the hour. The ball he had struck into the scrap yard was never found.

Wiggy was not only a cricketer. As the Reverend Archie Wiggington he was the vicar of the local church. He had an idea he put to Martin over a pint of Courage.

His suggestion was that Martin should write a pamphlet to be called 'Over the Boundary', which would describe his epic of sportsmanship, and lead on into a discussion of how Faith played a part in the great game of life. He intimated that Martin might go as far as to declare that worship of God would ensure that one was never bowled out.

Martin saw that by writing this pamphlet he could further disseminate his name; that as a Socialist it would do his reputation no harm to be linked with both religion and the manly game of cricket. He agreed to Wiggy's proposal. Wiggy would see that the pamphlet was printed and properly disseminated throughout the diocese.

Back home with Mary and Bertie, he discussed the matter.

Bertie had little to say. Martin asked if Violet was all right.

The answer Bertie gave was oblique. 'Not much demand for architects in wartime. You can't control women any more than you can control the weather. I'd join up if I weren't so old. Did you ever think that most of us pass our lives quite inarticulate? I mean, about the things that really matter to us?'

Martin gave a chuckle and said that he was not going to be inarticulate: he was going to write about his life for the vicar.

Later that evening, when Bertie had caught the train back north, Mary reproached her husband. 'He and Violet have fallen out a bit. He says she spends too much money on clothes.'

'How much?'

'Oh, don't be tiresome, Marty. There's a difference between men and women when it comes to clothes. Couldn't you sense he and Violet had fallen out?'

'I saw something was up.'

'Well, try not to be so thick-skinned.'

'What's he mean, "inarticulate"? He was always a bit of a chatterbox, wasn't he?'

Martin sat down to write the opening paragraphs of his Boundary book later that very evening.

Next morning, the BBC announced that the RAF had shot down twenty-five enemy planes over the counties of Southern England.

15

Le Forgel

The chateau in the Forest of the Bouche had been destroyed by fire some years previously. It had been abandoned and was now being consumed by a different agent of destruction, the ivy. The calloused walls were covered by the plant's green tendrils. Within the walls, however, a shelter had been built from fallen timbers and other materials. It was into this shelter that Gerard, Helge, Pief and Brenda Geldstein, together with you and Palfrey, moved, early that July morning.

In the manner of those who are stranded anywhere in any wilds, you all set to to expel from the new premises any wildlife that had entered there, from spiders and earwigs to rats and foxes.

Geldstein wanted his van to be concealed from the air. To this end, you and he went into the woods to cut down some young trees. As you worked, you studied Gerard. He had taken off his shirt. His white body glistened with sweat. Dressed, he had seemed rather puny. Naked, he appeared more solid; apart from a brief curl of hair on his chest, he could have been made entirely of bone. After each stroke of his axe, he would stand still, a hand cupped to his ear, to listen for any suspicious noises signalling an enemy approach. When the trees were felled, they were dragged to the walls of the chateau and the foliage propped there to conceal the van.

An amount of mistrust existed between you. Gerard had taken your and Palfrey's rifles and the ammunition. He did not confide and remained forever watchful, saying little. Nor did Palfrey's behaviour reassure him. Palfrey remained unfriendly and had increased his 'wild man of the woods' aspect. He would not sleep in the chateau shelter with the others, having constructed a secret lair somewhere in the forest.

So it came about that, missing company, you talked more and more to Helge Geldstein. As you grew accustomed to her, you saw that her face was not unattractive, while her serene personality gave her eyes and general expression a pleasant air. She was stern with her two children, but you saw good reason for that, surrounded with hostility as the Geldsteins understood themselves to be.

It was Helge who gave you gradually to accept the difficulties of their situation. German occupation threatened both her and her husband, Gerard, because he was a Jew, and because she had been a journalist in Hamburg, where she had spoken out against the increasingly powerful Nazi party. She had been forced to flee when her life was threatened.

The fear and strain she had undergone had made her ill. Gerard, then a widower, had given her sanctuary in his house. They had become mutually dependent on one another, both potential victims of the Nazi regime, and had undergone what Helge called 'a sort of marriage ceremony'. She laughed when she pronounced the words, only to sober immediately and say that she feared their two dear children were illegitimate, and so under threat on those grounds, quite apart from the fact that they were half-Jewish anti-Nazis.

Hearing these words – although he understood no English at this time – Pief raised his right arm in the Nazi salute and shouted 'Heil Hitler!'

'That may not save you, my darling,' said Helge with a sigh.

As you learnt their story, you inevitably became more involved with the Geldstein family. Pief was a hyperactive boy and seemed to be the more disturbed of the two children, but when you got to know them better, you saw that Brenda also had her problems. She spoke little, and was always to be found hanging about her mother's skirts.

Luftwaffe bombers frequently roared past overhead. On such occasions, Brenda would run to Helge to be cuddled, and snuggled on Helge's breast, thumb in mouth, eyes tightly closed in anxiety.

Your leg refused to heal. An area of heat and pain maintained itself along the outside of your tibia, where a swelling remained. You were forced to hobble about slowly.

Close to the rear of the chateau ran a stream, a tributary of the river a few kilometres away. It was Helge who first investigated the stream when drawing water from it. She announced that there were fish in it. You hobbled with her to look. Sedges bearded the water's edge, together with little stiff-necked yellow flowers. Helge gathered some of the reeds, carrying an armful back to the chateau. There she wove a basket in which she claimed you could catch fish. You duly sank the basket by one of the banks of the stream, and waited. Although her scheme was not entirely successful, you did catch some small fish after waiting patiently. But after all, what was there to do but wait?

The idea occurred to you that you could steal Geldstein's van and drive south to St Nazaire. You rejected the thought almost at once. The Jew had trouble enough; besides, you had become, in effect, his right-hand man, and had slowly grown to like him.

Gerard had a long conference with his wife, both of them speaking in low tones, after which Helge set off through the trees every morning, taking Brenda with her. She returned in the afternoon. Neither she nor Gerard offered any explanation for these missions.

'I followed her to the edge of the forest,' said Palfrey. 'She goes into a village down there. Suppose she shops us to the authorities?'

'Why should she do that?'

He shrugged, looking at you contemptuously. 'Why trust these foreigners? She's a German, isn't she? For all we know they're both just bloody crooks.'

'Gerard was Curator of the museum in Fougères. He told me so.'

'And you believed him, you prat!' He turned and swaggered away, back into the thickets.

On the following day, Helge returned bearing a sack of groceries. The small Brenda trudged wearily behind her.

Seating herself on a bench in the shelter, Helge called you and Gerard to her. She said that at last she had found a reliable woman in the village down the hill, a village called Le Forgel. This woman's husband had been captured by the Wehrmacht, captured, tortured and killed. She was very bitter, had quarrelled with her neighbours and had become rather a hermit. She gave her name as Marie Bourmard. Marie claimed to know which of the villagers were collaborators and could not be trusted, and which could.

Her promise was that as long as she was able, she would provide food – bread at the very least – twice a week for the fugitives in the forest. She would leave the food hidden in a certain hedge she had shown Helge. Helge would have to collect it from there.

Gerard was shaking his head and looking grim. A discussion began.

'Are there Germans in Le Forgel?', Gerard asked his wife.

Helge shook her head. 'Marie told me that lorries and convoys regularly drive past on the crossroads just outside the village, but there are no Germans in Le Forgel itself. It's just a cluster of small houses.'

'If any Germans come to the village – so little even as one of them – then this arrangement must stop. You understand?'

She gestured. 'Then we shall starve. We cannot live on small fish.'

'We'll find more food here in the forest.'

'Or we kill the German.'

'Don't be stupid, my dear! If you kill one of the Germans, the whole village is destroyed in retribution. Better to starve.'

'And our children?'

'You heard what I said. This damned war can't last for ever.'

You intervened at this point to ask if Marie from the village could be trusted.

Helge wiped a weary hand across her brow and face. 'We have to trust someone.'

You told her you would go with her, armed, to collect the food, just in case there was a trap.

'You must always go a different way, so you do not leave a trail to guide people to us.' So said Gerard.

'Of course. I'm not a fool.'

It seemed as if he trusted you more from that time onwards. He showed you his reason for choosing this particular ruin for a refuge. He had come here previously, when pursuing his work for the museum. He had found a door blocked by wreckage; by dragging away the wreckage, he had been able to pull the door open. A flight of stone steps led down into a dungeon. This dungeon would be their last refuge if enemies approached. Once inside, he had fixed a piece of wood panelling which could be dragged by a rope to cover up the existence of the door. He showed you the contraption with pride.

You viewed this bolthole with some scepticism, but said nothing.

Gerard stared at you. 'Maybe this cellar was once a place of injustice. What does that matter to us? It will be our refuge.'

'Good, Gerard. Good.' But you realized your tone was gloomy. A false door offered little protection.

'What's the matter? Such terrible injustice is done to us, then we seek out a place of injustice.'

You had heard him chopping logic before this, but could not decide whether or not he was trying to be funny in his way.

'I only wondered about people searching this place. Would they not easily find the door?'

He swept this remark aside, to ask if you had read the works of Aristotle. When you admitted you had not, Gerard said grimly that he would give you lessons.

16

A Lesson in Aristotle

'After all', Gerard said, 'you might expect me to take a personal interest in justice since, as a Jew, I have suffered injustice all my life.

'As a young man, I was keen to study antiquities,' he told you, staring at you with those pale eyes of his. 'When I left university, I won a prize which entitled me to go with an expedition of French antiquarians and experts to study antique works of art in Greece. That expedition helped shape my life. I found myself with two men, greatly my seniors, on the Greek island of Assos, where there is a remarkable collection of sarcophagi.

'I should explain,' he said, 'that the Greek word "sarcophagus" comes from two words meaning "flesh-eating". These coffins were made of a stone which was reputed to devour the flesh of any corpse placed within them.

'I had been on the island for two weeks when I became interested in a certain young lady. She was a lace-maker, and sat most days on her doorstep making items of lace to sell on the mainland. She it was who told me something of the history of the island, when I persuaded her to take a coffee with me. We went into the only taverna on the island. In the fourth century BC, she said, Assos was ruled by a tyrant or king who had an appreciation of learning. It so happened that Aristotle, who was a Macedonian, not a Greek, arrived to stay and work on Assos. He became friendly with the tyrant. They would hold long conversations by the light of a single oil lamp, until the night waned before the approach of another day. It was then that the tyrant's daughter brought food and wine to them.

'This daughter was young and beautiful and was attracted by Aristotle's powers of thought and argument. Speculation about worlds elsewhere – above all, about abstract worlds of ratiocination – were awakened in her breast.

'For his part, the youthful Aristotle was impressed by the daughter's virtuous good manners and patience in staying up until the middle of the night to fuel the conversations taking place.

'One day, so my lace-making lady told me, this daughter happened on Aristotle swimming naked in the Aegean. She impulsively disrobed and joined him in the water. Aristotle could not resist this bold approach. So –'

At this point in his narration, Gerard looked up from under his brows to make sure you were attending. You were attending.

'So,' he continued, 'Aristotle married the bold young lady because he very much longed to have sexual intercourse with her, this tyrant's lovely daughter.

'When I heard this story,' said Gerard, 'great was my astonishment. I had no idea there had been a Madame Aristotle. It humanized the man for me. Yet, why should I have been astonished? For Aristotle has much to say about happiness. I do believe that marriage is a way, if sometimes an uncertain one, to happiness, or at least to contentment.'

As he spoke, Gerard rested a benevolent hand on Helge's hand, since she was sitting close, listening to the story.

'All this I tell you, Stephen,' he continued, 'as a mere preamble to our discussion of Aristotle's works. Is it not the case that those of Aristotle's writings that survive have had a profound influence on Western philosophy, affecting the course of ancient, medieval and modern philosophy? Not necessarily because of the beauty of his prose, but because he, of all men, lauded contemplation and had something valuable to say on all manner of matters which remain of concern today, twenty-four centuries later.'

'I've had enough of this nonsense,' said Palfrey, who had been sitting on a log nearby, absent-mindedly whittling a stick. 'Who gives a fuck about this ancient stuff?' With that he was off, disappearing among the trees.

'There is a man impervious to contemplation,' Gerard commented. 'He who most needs it.'

He wished to talk about metaphysics to you because, he said, he saw in you a potential to become a good man 'when you grew up', as he put it. He spoke of the realization of perfection as entelechy, and feared that the war, even if you survived it, was a thing intrinsically liable to block entelechy. Gerard had read Aristotle as a consolation for the difficulties he had experienced in life. He regarded Palfrey as impervious to such teaching, but you not.

He talked long on this subject. You listened, trying to take in what he said, yet doubting a great deal, as you had doubted the Gospels when they were expounded. Nevertheless, what Gerard told you as you sat among the ruins remained for many years half-remembered, half-forgotten. What most impressed you was that here was someone, for the first time in your young life, who took the trouble to care about helping to shape your potential self. In that alone, it was of immense value – of more value than was shouting at people, which you had previously seen as a useful way of going about the business of life.

A little later on, Gerard spoke with you on the subject of happiness. He went on to state that Aristotle regarded some kinds of knowledge as a supreme good, although other kinds might be bad.

Gerard regarded knowledge of the Nazi fascist regime as bad, but only because the regime itself was evil. Evil might prove as infectious as influenza. Such knowledge was not conducive to happiness. But, Gerard argued, it might be claimed that a thorough knowledge of the workings of the Nazi regime could qualify as good, if that knowledge assisted one to avoid its clutches.

A worse person could be said to be he who exercises his wickedness against others. In Gerard's opinion, a homosexual man who seduces another into his practices is wicked, but the supreme wickedness is when any man exercises his wickedness so as to pervert an entire society. He mentioned Adolf Hitler as an example; Hitler had brought the entire German people, hitherto an upright and civilized people, into shame.

You spoke then, to say that, at the outbreak of war, the Parliament of Great Britain had debated whether the music of Beethoven, as a German composer, should be banned for the duration of the struggle. Parliament was enlightened enough to vote that it should not be banned. However, it was felt there was perhaps a different case to be made for the music of Richard Wagner, on the grounds that it was anti-Semitic and that Adolf Hitler enjoyed it. When an argument was advanced for not banning Wagner's music, it was on the grounds that Hitler, as far as we knew, enjoyed Beethoven's music also. Was this a false line of argument?

There the two of you sat, with Helge an almost silent witness, under the sheltering trees, while night fell with all its rustic whisperings, and a crescent moon rose in the sky.

You confided to Helge your gratitude to her husband for his interest in you, particularly while you were stranded in such unusual circumstances.

'You must look on this as your *Wanderjahre*,' she said, giving you a sad smile.

You went with Helge to collect the vital sack of food from the hedge. The method was that you remained a distance apart, Helge leading. Both of you kept a sharp watch for other people, especially as you emerged from the shelter of the trees. On each journey you varied the route.

You covered Helge as she reached the hedge where the sack was concealed. You never saw Marie, the deliverer of the sack. The sack was concealed in a little thicket. Helge collected it and then rapidly made her way back uphill to the concealment of the forest.

The day came when Helge was feeling ill, greatly to your and Gerard's concern. Pief jumped up and down, eager to go and collect the sack. Gerard was against it.

'My boy, you are the future. This present time will remain always in your memory, and I trust it will influence you towards a day when there are no vagabonds such as we in the world. You must remain here, under cover. The present is bad enough: we shall not put the future in jeopardy as well.'

You volunteered to go. You could hobble despite your injured leg, you said, smiling to show your confidence.

You went. You were slow and cautious. At the fringe of the forest, you paused, looking out from the partial concealment of a tree. Someone was standing by the hedge where the sack was usually hidden. You made out a slim figure with a hood over its head.

It seemed that this person had caught a movement in your direction. He shaded his eyes to peer up at the forest. You stayed immobile.

This other person pushed through a gap in the hedge and began the shallow climb towards where you stood. You eased your revolver from its holster as the figure came nearer. You saw then it was a woman approaching. Guessing that this must be Marie Bourmard, you stepped forth. The woman stopped. She asked in French if you were waiting for her. When you said you were, she came on and stood in front of you.

'You are that English officer?'

Again you said you were. She studied your face with a half-smile, as if she felt she was being impertinent. She nodded. She took you by the arm and led the way among the trees, saying you should not be seen.

'No food?' you asked.

Not bothering to answer the question, to which the answer was clear, she pushed the hood back from her head and said she had come to warn you that there were now Germans in the village of Le Forgel. An officer and a driver had arrived in a jeep in the early hours of the morning, with soldiers following in a truck. The newcomers had frightened everyone. They made them all get out of bed and go into the street in their night garments while their houses were searched. They were investigating villages in the area for anyone they called 'militants' or other suspicious persons who might be hiding there.

'So I cannot provide food until they go away again,' she warned you. 'I collect items of food for you from the villagers. It will be impossible to do it while these horrid men are present.'

'What rank are they?'

'The soldiers are gone. They found no one in their search. Just the officer and the driver remain. I don't know German ranks. The driver is just a young man. He seems pleasant enough and is good-looking. The officer … ugh!'

Marie had fair hair. Her face was pale but healthy, and entirely without make-up. It was clear she was frightened. She bit her finger while listening to your questions. The fear made her age hard to decipher.

'You are brave to come and warn us.'

'The hospital where I worked was bombed, so I am at home. Did I see you limp?'

'My right leg. It's getting better slowly.'

'Sorry for the injury.'

'You'd better be getting back. We'll keep a good look out.'

'I could examine your leg for you.'

'You'd better get back in case you are missed.'

*

You will recall your feelings – in the circumstances you had no alternative – as you limped back to the ruined chateau. You were melancholy, not for the lack of food, but for the involvement of the young woman in situations of danger and, to a lesser extent, of the wretched circumstances in which the Geldsteins and their children found themselves. It was a wretched thing that young Pief was encouraged to say 'Heil Hitler', even as a safety measure.

Such was the weight of your melancholy that a passing thought suggested it would be better to finish with everything and to go down to Le Forgel and surrender yourselves to the German officer.

This blight upon your thought extended even to your past: the Forêt de la Bouche became an analogy for the beach at Walcot, except that now you were aware of the danger you were in, whereas on the beach you had no such knowledge. Supposing in those infant days the incoming tide had swept you away and drowned you, then you would not have had to face this present dilemma. You would have escaped the war.

This despairing impulse soon faded. Gerard was as equable as ever, and Helge supported him. Palfrey, heavy of brow, suggested you go down to the village and shoot the Germans, but it seemed that even he did not take this proposal seriously.

Supper was merely a crust of bread, at which Pief complained loudly. Helge promised to catch more fish on the morrow. Pief cuddled against her. Afterwards, when the children were settled, you sat about talking as usual, by the light of a stub of candle.

Gerard said that, as you were English, he would quote the words of Bishop George Berkeley as saying that 'an idea can be like nothing but an idea'. You replied that Berkeley was an Irishman.

'Do not concentrate on inessentials,' said Gerard. 'An idea surely incorporates things.'

He went on to ask himself if in justice existed before the idea of justice. No doubt it did. For the idea to continue to exist, it must be transmitted to others than the originator, either in speech or in writing.

Here Helge spoke, to say that a German writer had written of the creation of ideas in conversation. The paper emphasized that frequently a speaker did not know what he was about to say – his words came spontaneously and might contain something that was new and had not occurred to him until released from its prison of silence, as it were, triggered by what the other person had said.

'So he would have no choice but to say it,' you remarked, in agreement. 'I can see that a writer might, when in full flow, stumble on something new in the same way.'

This comment Gerard ignored, returning to his favourite subject of injustice, from which he and his wife had greatly suffered. He said that according to his model philosopher, Aristotle, it was those who acted rightly who were truly happy because – here he thumped his knee for emphasis – pleasure was an experience of the soul. He had found pleasure in work, in being curator of his museum, of arranging things in sensible order so that they might have most meaning for those who came to look and learn. He considered himself a just man, but he had to live in a world of turmoil and injustice. He was deprived of pleasure because of his race; it was the deepest form of injustice.

Helge said that she suffered from another kind of injustice. She was persecuted because she reported the truth about the cruelty of the Nazi regime. She had been happy, the most pleasant of all feelings, because she dared to tell the truth. And for that she had been persecuted.

You then said that you noticed a dichotomy between pleasure and its opposites, pain and sorrow. That when you were sad you certainly knew it, yet when you were happy you were scarcely aware of it. Only in retrospect were you aware you had been happy. If sorrow were a stone, then happiness was a butterfly.

'So are you happy here or sad?' asked Helge. 'In this great sheltering forest?'

You could only answer, both at once. You asked what Aristotle had had to say about the gods. Did he believe in them? You said that although you did not believe in God, you sometimes felt His presence. It had become easy to believe in God in a great forest. Evidences of a woodcutter had been found. Neatly chopped logs had been discovered – those logs had fuelled your fire. Such men must have believed in God, so you claimed. As you gazed into the embers of your fire, you ventured to say that perhaps the forest itself was God, and woodcutters and forest and all were a part of God's disposition.

There you were so close to the truth ... And you forgot all about it later when you were back in what you call ... civilization.
Perhaps at that time, sitting there with them, I might even have claimed that civilization was a way of warding off God. My deeper feelings had been stirred by the encounter with the Geldsteins.

Such matters you three discussed for an hour or two, until finally you went away to sleep. You kept no watch during the night. It would have been too taxing for such a small number of people to stay awake during the small hours. It was because there was no watch that you slept so fitfully. Your dreams were full of fragments of attack, arrest and torture.

You were, as you claimed, both miserable and happy.

You were not out of the woods yet.

17

The Wehrmacht Pays a Visit

One of the countless trees in the Forêt de la Bouche began to shed its leaves. Slowly, over the previous weeks, its leaves had changed from green to a bright yellow – brighter still when the sun shone on them. A mild ground frost prompted other trees to follow suit, shedding their foliage. The great tide of the seasons was lapping its way down the hillside. The green went. The leaves went. Soon the forest was carpeted in yellow and gold and bronze to its very depths. And the nights became chillier, the hillside more frequently shrouded in a cloying mist.

As, in search of edible fungi, you wandered through the thickets of the forest, following almost invisible trails made by the cumulative progress of multitudinous small creatures, it occurred to you that through the labyrinths of your brain a similar transit of benevolent thoughts might in time wear a way through the

wilderness of your mind, creating something of the enlighten-
ment Gerard offered you. For you had some hope, not merely of
finding ceps, but of becoming a wiser being, like the author of
the Red Sandstone book, hardly realizing that, as the mushrooms
had their season, so too your aspirations were seasonal. A winter
was to follow which would freeze those hopes and ambitions for
mental well-being.

One night, when the moon was high and full, a shot echoed
through the trees. Immediately, you and the Geldsteins were alert;
you rose and stood awaiting a second shot. It never came. You
could not tell from which direction the single shot had originated;
there was no further shot to guide your hearing.

You stared into the perspective of vague trees, those sentinels of
autumn, seeing merely an entanglement of branches, fading into
the eternity of forest. It was then you felt a true visceral discomfort.
Each tree grew only for itself, struggled against its neighbours,
grew to overcome them, to overshadow them, grim, emotionless,
motionless: the very exemplar of Darwinian competition.

Another sound could be heard, faintly at first, the sound as of
a steam goods train labouring from a station.

'Shine a light,' whispered Helge.

'No, no!' said Gerard, laying a restraining hand on her arm.

Soon a figure could be seen approaching, detaching itself from
the ghostly landscape. Parts of its body were being revealed and
concealed by turns, as faded moonlight or tree-shadow caught it.
At least, whether friend or enemy, it was human. It seemed he was
carrying a sack. With his heavy tread, the man was kicking up the bed
of leaves in his path, the remembered noise of a steam goods train.

'It's only Palfrey,' you said, with relief, going forward to meet him.

Palfrey grunted by way of greeting and pushed forward to the
shelter. He bent and dumped his burden down. Pief ran squeaking
to see what it was. A dead boar lay at their feet. Its great head lay
resting on heavy cheek with dirt as pillow, its wide mouth gaping,
tongue and teeth visible, still steaming, little eyes open, blind.

Pief spanked the hulking body with both hands.

'Some food,' said Palfrey. He leaned back to ease his spine.

Helge wrapped an arm round his waist and kissed his stubbly cheek. 'Wonderful!' she exclaimed. 'How ever have you managed it?'

'I shot it,' he said flatly. 'I waited and I shot it.'

'Was it alone?'

'I've seen several.'

'Well done, Pete,' you said. 'We shall not starve, after all.' But you thought how inedible the corpse looked.

Gerard said nothing. Quite apart from his dislike of Palfrey, he feared that the sound of the shot could be heard in Le Forgel, awakening enemy curiosity.

The mist crept across the countryside, smothering details of fields, hedges and the distant roofs of Le Forgel. By dawn it lingered thick among the trees, so it was possible to light a fire and expect the smoke to remain undetected. Soon you were inhaling the smell of roasting boar, as Pief and Brenda insisted on taking turns to work an improvised spit.

You remarked to Gerard that here was pleasure, and pleasure unearned.

He smiled, saying lightly, 'This is not pleasure, Stephen. This is pure greed.'

You all ate chunks of that boar, burnt or almost raw, delicious in the mouth, blood seeping between the teeth and down the chin, to be swallowed improperly chewed, all in your eagerness. Pief and Brenda rolled about, gnawing on the bones they had been given and growling like small dogs in their enjoyment. The meat tasted extraordinarily good, a victory for nutrition. The mutilated body of the hog was then hung from a branch, where no wild creature could reach its remains.

On the following day, when you were all unusually somnolent, you received a visitor. You had not seen Marie Bourmard for three weeks; the season had declined since then. She arrived as before, a slight figure clad in a rough coat with the hood up over her head.

'It's a pleasure to see you again,' you said, clutching her hard, thin hand. 'Is all well in Le Forgel?'

Marie tossed back the hood, smiling. 'It is better. That German officer and his driver have left. It is almost like we are at peace again. So I can come once more to bring for you a little food.'

And she brought more than food. She brought bandages and ointment for your leg.

She said she would massage the leg first, and then apply ointment and bandage. You protested, saying your legs were filthy.

'It is a filthy time we live in,' she said. When she had done her work, she shyly kissed you on the cheek, to acknowledge that you were a man far from home.

Two days later, Marie returned after dark, when a light rain was falling. She brought no food, only bad news. The German officer had returned. He had again established himself in the best house of the village. It appeared he had gone to Rennes only to report, returning to duty to Le Forgel in an evil mood.

'Perhaps he is ticked off because he is not enough strict,' Marie said, with a chuckle.

The rain gathered strength, aided by a blustering wind.

You told her she could not return to the village in such weather. She must stay in your shelter until the rain ceased.

The rain did not cease. It fell with a stubborn determination, as if it had decided never to stop.

'Stay here for the night, Marie,' you urged. 'Sleep in my bed with me.' Your throat tightened with desire as you spoke the words.

You twain lay together fully dressed. When you tried to fondle her, she spoke of her religious beliefs. 'I am attracted to you, yes, but God watches our actions.'

You mocked her, saying it was absurd to hold religious beliefs in wartime, when France had been overrun by a ruthless enemy.

'It is then the Christian religion is most necessary,' she told you. 'I am fond of you, my English officer, but do not take advantage of me.'

You did not take advantage of her. There was some comfort, as well as torment, to be had in having a girl sleeping warmly by your side. You lay for a long while, listening to her quiet breathing. It brought no hope for the future but a consoling memory of the distant past.

Towards dawn, the rain abated. Everything dripped. Marie rose, kissed your cheek and left, to make her way cautiously down the slippery hillside.

A crisis struck the next day. Pief came running into the shelter, where his mother was washing some clothes.

'A man comes! A man comes!'

Helge corrected him. 'Is coming.' She looked grave as she called quietly to you.

Cautiously, you looked from the concealment of a tree. A grey-clad man was slowly climbing the hill, where the grass was still slippery from the recent rainstorm.

You watched him, judging his size. You felt no fear, where once you had been startled by a bird rising up from a nearby thicket with a clatter of wings. You had come into yourself.

'Hide yourselves,' you said. 'The Wehrmacht is paying us a visit.'

Calmly, Gerard ushered his little family through the door to their private hiding place in the cellar. You and Palfrey waited. Palfrey, before disappearing, signalled where he wanted you to position yourself.

So you stood tight where the trees were growing thinly, now seeing the approaching stranger more clearly. He wore a grey overcoat and had a peaked cap rammed on his head. There was no mistaking an officer of the Wehrmacht.

Your pulse quickened, but you reassured yourself that you were wearing a tattered battledress and were clearly a British officer. Supposing you were arrested, you should be treated according to the rules of the Geneva Convention.

The German halted when he saw you. He unholstered his service revolver. You slowly raised your hands, staying put where you were.

He uttered a challenge and moved forward, into the sparse outer limits of the trees, his eyebrows raised in astonishment. At that juncture, Palfrey launched himself from a high branch. Crashing down on the officer, he bore him flat to the ground. You ran to help, grabbing the German's revolver.

The officer gave no cry. He was badly winded, and hurt. Palfrey locked an arm about his neck and wrenched. A distinct crack sounded.

'Oh, no!' you exclaimed.

Palfrey looked up, savage of face. 'What you mean, "No"? He's our enemy. Had to finish him, didn't we? Ah, but that was neat! I always longed to do that!'

The German sprawled there, unmoving, ugly in death. Palfrey got to his feet and rubbed his ankle.

'We should have talked to him,' you said weakly.

He turned a rock hard face to confront me.

'Whose side are you on? How would we talk to the bastard? Do you speak German? 'Cos I don't. He pulled a gun on you. Don't be so fucking wet.'

'I suppose you're right. Sorry. Now we'll have to bury the sod. Before anyone comes looking for him.'

Gerard emerged from hiding, looked down at the dead man, gave him a kick in the ribs.

Looking to him for sympathy with your point of view, you began to protest at the killing. Gerard stopped you immediately. 'It's done, isn't it? What's done is done. Keep quiet.'

He stood gazing down at the body. 'Search all his pockets. See if there's anything we can use. He came to investigate that rifle shot a few nights ago, I shouldn't wonder.'

'Shut it,' said Palfrey. 'You ate the bloody boar, didn't you?'

'But once they find this rat is missing –'

'Bloody shut it,' Palfrey repeated. 'First things first.'

You were shaking. Without further comment, both you and Palfrey grabbed the dead man by the shoulders of his coat and dragged him into the undergrowth. A spade had been abandoned in the ruins. You went to fetch it. When you returned to the body, Palfrey was scraping back dead leaves with his boot.

'No brambles here,' he said. 'You want first dig?'

All the Geldstein family had gathered to look at the dead body. The children were silent, glancing up continually at their mother, who was hiding her eyes, weeping. No doubt they looked for clues as to how they should behave in the face of death.

'What are you crying about?' asked Palfrey, with a sneer. 'He was a Kraut, wasn't he? Don't worry.'

Helge turned a wet-cheeked face to him. 'I am also a Kraut, as you call it. What I am crying for is … is … oh, who can say?' She burst into fresh tears.

'It's the misery of the world, my cherub,' said Gerard, putting a comforting arm round his wife's shoulders.

Palfrey pulled a long face and shrugged. 'Better get digging. I'm going to keep a look out, okay?' He trotted off.

You began to dig. The earth was soft, but with plenty of root to slow progress. You worked. You sweated, and you worked. You now felt surprisingly content, saying to yourself, 'This is real life with a vengeance.'

After about an hour, you rested. Gerard took over the digging. Pief and Brenda still stood solemnly by and regarded the dead German officer. Brenda clutched her brother's hand.

'He really is dead,' said she, after deep thought. 'He really looks really dead. I bet he was really bad when he was alive.'

'I bet he tortured lots of people,' Pief said. 'I bet he'd have tortured us.'

Eventually, Palfrey returned to the site. He stood looking at the growing hole before saying, calmly, 'Another bloke is coming up the hill.'

You and Gerard stood and stared at him. Palfrey was thinking, solid in command of the situation.

'Okay, here's what we do. You lot hide behind trees. Kids, you follow your dad and don't make a sound, understand? Don't move.

Steve, give me the revolver.'

'What are you going to do?' you asked.

'I'll think of something.'

'Who is it? Military?'

He prodded the dead body. 'Could be this sod's driver. Get yourself hidden. Don't worry. I can sort it.'

You smarted under that patronizing tone, but nevertheless did as Palfrey instructed. You stood behind a tree. The others were already hidden. The children had long ago learnt to be mute when told.

Palfrey lay flat on the damp ground, facing the open country, covering himself with fallen leaves. You waited.

Minutes passed. Then a head appeared in the clearing. It bore blonde hair, close-cropped. Plain and beefy features, grey eyes, searching ahead. Then the torso became visible as he took another couple of steps forward. He waved his cap about. He was hot from the climb. He hesitated. The country was silent all round him.

Finding all was quiet ahead, he advanced cautiously to level ground. Standing by the first trees, he called out the name of his officer, a question in his voice. Only silence answered. When he received no other response, he took another couple of steps forward. He was now little more than twenty metres from where you were hiding. It was then that Palfrey shot him.

The noise was extraordinary. Birds flew up, startled, and smashed away through twigs and foliage to the free air. The driver – you later established it was the driver – was still standing. He turned to one side, his knees buckled, and he fell to the ground.

'Bloody good,' said Palfrey, climbing from his place of conceal-ment, shaking off leaves as he went to examine the body. You joined him. You stood looking down at the man. His mouth was open. His eyes were open, staring towards the sky.

'Another grave,' said Palfrey.

'We should hang on to their uniforms.'

'Okay, maybe we should – if you fancy stripping them.'

So you dragged the second body to where the first one lay.

Gerard shooed his children away. You pulled the greatcoats and the tunics off the dead men.

Gerard was wringing his hands. 'There can be dozens of them here tomorrow.'

You had been thinking. 'But Marie said there were just these two in the village. It will take a while for news of their disappearance to travel. How will they know where to search?'

He stared at you as if he thought you mad, his pale eyes on you, his long face haggard.

'Think, Stephen! Their vehicle must be parked at the bottom of the hill.'

'Yes, that's it! Bugger! We must move the car some distance away. A kilometre at least.'

Palfrey chimed in. 'Yeah, get the vehicle out the way. Then there'll be no evidence to point to this stretch of forest.'

'Yes, but –'

'Never mind the buts, Gerard.' You enjoyed contradicting him. 'We've got to move the bloody car. I'll go. I'll drive it somewhere. I'll walk back.'

'Your leg –'

'To hell with my leg. It's urgent. We must shift that car.'

'Good,' said Palfrey. He threw you the officer's cap and greatcoat. 'Wear these, Steve, and you should be safe enough.'

You grinned at him as you fitted on the cap. 'Just don't shoot me when I come back.'

He came closer and pressed the German revolver into your hand. 'Take this. It may help. For God's sake come back, won't you? I don't fancy being stuck here alone with the Geldsteins.'

'Don't worry.' You used his phrase.

He slapped you on the shoulder. A rough sign of friendliness.

The jeep was waiting in the lane at the bottom of the hill. After a couple of tries, you got the engine started. You set off at a careful pace, taking the first turning to the left in order to avoid the village.

You had driven no more than a quarter of a kilometre when

you reached an old stone bridge across a shallow river. You had a clear picture of what you should do next. You would put your foot down, bump across the coarse grass and plunge the vehicle into the water.

The vehicle might not be completely submerged, since the river was rather shallow. So you would climb out and wade ashore, leaving the car door open. A cow in a field on the other side of the stream would amble over to see what was happening.

You would limp back into the concealment of the Forêt de la Bouche.

Yes, the picture was clear enough. Yet not entirely clear. Gerard was your friend, your ally, but also your captor. Still you sat at the wheel, in a state of hesitation.

At last you came to a decision. You felt for the Geldstein family, and for Marie Bourmard – and indeed for Palfrey, who had become so formidable; but loyalty to King and country came first. And freedom. So you quelled your conscience: an easy task.

You drove over the bridge and headed south, towards the French coast and St Nazaire, without looking back.

PART TWO

1

What a Wild Man

The Southampton street was dimly respectable. A line of plane trees marched along it at regulation distances from each other. To one side, the even more select Prescot Close led off; on the other side, an alleyway sloped down to a waste area where boys occasionally kicked footballs about. It was as if urban geography offered a paradigm of how citizens might move up or down an ill-defined social scale.

The front gate of 'Grendon', 19 Park Street, was not quite off its hinges. All it needed was a good push and you were through, shoes crunching on the gravel of the drive. The front door of the house had been painted mauve. It was fashionably shabby.

The time was four-thirty of the late December afternoon and dusk had already set in when you rapped with the iron knocker on the door. After a pause, a light showed in the fanlight over the door, which was then opened a few inches. A pale pixie face peeped out at you and asked what you wanted.

'Does Mrs Wilberforce still live here?' you asked.

'Who is it?'

'I'm Steve, Mrs Wilberforce's nephew.'

'Who?' Asked with incredulity. You repeated your name.

'Hang on.'

The door closed. Belatedly it occurred to you that this pallid countenance belonged to your little cousin Joyce. You hardly remembered her.

The door reopened; there stood Aunt Violet. She was wearing spectacles; she had on a flimsy summer dress with a cardigan over it; she wore a pair of fluffy blue slippers on her feet.

'Steve, my darling, oh!' she exclaimed. She flung her arms round your neck; you clutched her round her slender waist and hugged and kissed her.

'Auntie, darling.'

'Come in, darling, come in. I didn't expect … Golly, what a treat! Come on in! I must put the blackouts up or they'll arrest me …'

In you went. You remembered the heavy hallstand, now draped with raincoats and hats. Violet led you through into the kitchen. A sewing machine stood on the table, together with some fabric and scissors and a large ginger cat. The cat sat watchful and monumental, surveying the visitor with narrowed eyes. A fire burned in the grate.

The room was dimly lit. Violet dragged heavy black curtains over the window.

'I'm trying to make myself a frock.' She laughed. 'Sorry for the mess. It's wonderful to see you again, my darling Stevie! You know we believed you were dead, don't you – according to the War Office? But you're not, are you? Have they kicked you out of the army?'

'Worse luck, no. I've got a bit of leave over Christmas.'

Violet switched on a sidelight.

The kitchen was smaller than you remembered. You thought of the limitless reaches of the Forêt de la Bouche.

The pale young girl was standing by the coal fire. She wore a dressing gown over a blouse and a short cream skirt. She was picking nervously at the hem of her dressing gown.

162

'You remember Joyce, don't you? She's away from school. Dougie has just broken up.'

'Into lots of pieces,' said Douglas. He gave a scream to show how painful it was. He had been standing quietly, summing up the visitor.

Violet nodded and smiled at him, otherwise ignoring the boy.

'Joyce had measles, didn't you, dear? Rather nasty for her ... So where have you been, exactly, Steve? Are you starving? I've got some drink here, believe it or not.'

In no time, the dress fabric was pushed aside, two glasses and a bottle of gin, accompanied by a small bottle of Angostura, were on the table. The cat leapt off the chair and sat alertly on a corner of the table, as if hoping for a drink. Violet said gaily, as she poured two healthy jiggers of gin into two glasses, 'Let's celebrate your safe return!'

You brought out a packet of Players Navy Cut. You both lit up. Your auntie no longer used a cigarette holder as she had done in more stylish days. 'It's wonderful to see you – you've grown a bit. Life's become so dreary.'

Douglas was fitting a penny into each eye socket. When the coins were securely lodged, he came blindly forward, hands extended in front of him. 'Think how horrid your face would look without any eyes,' he said.

'Your face looks horrid enough already,' his sister retorted.

'You'd really bang into things. It might do you good, stop you being cheeky.'

'P'raps you could grow buffers on your knees.' As he spoke, he pushed one hand into Violet's face.

'Go away, you little scamp!' she said, half-laughing. 'Go upstairs and read your book and leave us in peace.'

Douglas let the coins drop from his eyes, saying in surprise, 'Oh, it's you, is it? I didn't know you were here.' Nevertheless, he was retreating as ordered.

Violet exclaimed with some pride that anyone would think Dougie was half daft.

'Why only half?' asked Joyce. She took to stroking the cat rather hard.

You sipped your gin and asked Violet what she was planning to do for Christmas.

'Not much, I can tell you. Might take the kids to the panto.' She downed her gin. 'Golly, it goes to your head at once! Have another.'

'Where's Uncle Bertie, Auntie?'

She shrugged. 'He's been away for a few days, the old blighter. He's in a reserved occupation, like Claude – another scrounger in the family. Bertie says he's designing a new prison for German and Italian prisoners of war – if they catch any. Still, the Belgian government in exile have just declared war on Italy, so things are looking up.' She blew a plume of smoke into the air and raised her glass again. 'Well, chin chin! Lovely to see you safe back.'

'You're looking nice and slender, Auntie.' And indeed, now that she had become more frisky, and her eyes were gleaming, she looked more like her old youthful self.

She removed her glasses. 'Rationing helps. Joyce, dear, why don't you go up to your room and read your book? Sorry we're just in the kitchen but the rest of the house – it's a bit parky. I haven't laid the fire in the sitting room. Have to economize! Parsimony is patriotic. Or so they say.'

Joyce did not move. Like the cat, she continued to stare into the distance. Nor did Violet press the point regarding her going upstairs.

'How are your parents? Were they surprised to see you again? You're a hero, aren't you, Steve?'

'I came to see you first, Auntie. I haven't been home yet. I must ring them.'

She thought about this information, looking at you over the rim of her glass. In a more serious tone than hitherto, she said, 'Well, I'm flattered. Your parents are a bit rum, darling. I can put you up for the night, if you like …' Then, hastily, 'So what's been happening to you?'

'I got stuck in France after it gave up.' Joyce came to sit at the table with them, closely regarding you. 'How old are you, Joyce?'

'Six and five months,' she said. 'How old are you?'

'Coming up for twenty-one.'

Violet took over the conversation, such as it was. 'Well, come on, Steve, you got stuck in France. What happened? Tell us about it! Did someone pinch your tank, or what?'

'We had an accident.' You paused. 'I've been living in some woods for several months.'

'Golly, a Robin Hood life! What a wild man! What did you eat, and drink?'

As you began to tell her your story, you ran your finger absent-mindedly up and down a groove in the table. The wooden tabletop had been so well scrubbed its grain stood out so that it resembled the coat, you thought, of a wet polar bear. A red strand of the dress-making procedure had caught in the groove. You talked of your time in the Forêt de la Bouche, of the Geldsteins, of Palfrey and of Marie Bourmard, who had brought you food, and of the talks about Aristotle. You realized you had enjoyed that outlaw life. Or at least you enjoyed talking about it afterwards.

Violet listened intently. She clutched your hand, which lay on the table. A cigarette smouldered between her fingers.

'You must feel bad about leaving these people in the lurch.'

You did feel bad. But, as so often, you told yourself that the Geldsteins were safe enough, and that you had a duty as an officer to return to the armed struggle. Violet listened to your excuses, saying nothing, tipping more gin into her glass.

'So there was a woman with you.' Throwing a hasty glance at her daughter, she asked, 'Did you manage to seduce her?'

'No. 'Fraid not.'

'Why ever not? You must have been missing the girls.'

You gave a grin. 'Marie said she was Catholic.'

Violet made no immediate comment. Withdrawing her hand, she sucked on the cigarette.

'Can I have a fag, mum?', her daughter asked.

'No, you jolly well can't. Wait till you're sixteen.' Turning her attention back to me, 'Do you want a sip of my gin? Surely it was this woman's patriotic duty …' She caught something in your expression and dropped the subject. 'I'd better make us something for supper. There's not much in the house. Or I can send Joyce out for some fish and chips.'

'I'm not well yet, mum,' Joyce said promptly.

Violet made a funny face in your direction, raising her eyebrows, but otherwise abandoning the subject. 'So how many Jerries did you kill to escape from this wood?'

You told her how you had driven in the German army vehicle down to the south coast of Brittany, where a series of French fishermen had taken you round the peninsula in their smacks, from small harbour to small harbour. The last boat in the chain had crossed the Channel and landed you ashore near Brighton. From Brighton, you had been taken under escort to Aldershot. There, over the course of two weeks, you had undergone interrogation. Various intelligence officers had checked the details of your story. You were pleased to learn from them that Major Hilary Montagu had returned safely to England, following the fall of Paris.

At the end of the examinations, you had been given three weeks leave.

You also repeated that you felt guilty about leaving the Geldsteins.

'You mustn't worry about them, dear. It's their war.'

'Not exactly. It's our war, too. I'd hate them to get killed. They're splendid people.'

She asked you if you had been afraid of getting killed.

You said that no one wanted their life to end. To which she made no reply, beyond pulling a face.

'I'm so happy to see you again, Auntie.'

She turned and put a small shovel-full of coal on the fire.

Then she gazed at you thoughtfully, as if deciding what she would say next. She sat forward in her chair, glanced sideways at her daughter with something of concern in her look, before turning the great beam of her attention on you.

She said, 'You know I don't get on with your parents. I rather missed the bus with your mother. I will tell you why. There is a reason. It was a long time ago, when you were a small boy.'

'That is a long time ago. It doesn't matter now, Auntie, whatever it was. You think I don't know my parents are difficult to get on with?'

Her mouth set in a thin line. 'I couldn't tell you last time we met. You were at university, and a bit stuffy. You're not so bad now, I can see. This still matters – at least it does to me. You remember Walcot, of course?'

You tried to subdue a mounting sense of anxiety at what was to come. You lit another cigarette, slightly to delay matters.

Yes, you remembered the magical solitudes of that beach, the ripple of the waves – the very sound of summer – your contentment. And you remembered something else. Violet had come for a weekend in Omega and had brought you a glider. The weekend she coaxed you into her bed.

She was looking at you intensely across the table, her generous bosom resting on the table edge.

'You were such a sweet little boy – only three, or maybe four at the time. You were beautiful, with your frank open face. You had freckles then! I was worried because your mother left you to play alone, unsupervised, for hours on the beach, with the sea and its uncertain tides. But I have always had a dislike of the sea. A fear of its power, I suppose. There never seemed to be anyone else on all that stretch of beach. Not a soul to see if you were all right –'

'But I was fine, Auntie –'

'No, you weren't fine.' She shook her curly head. 'It wasn't fine at all. It was all wrong.'

She sniffed a little, running her open palm over her nose. You were both getting slightly tipsy.

Feeling uncomfortable now, you tipped more gin into your glass and drank, while the ginger cat looked calmly on.

You remembered Mrs North, who lived in the Walcot railway carriages. She would come occasionally to the edge of the dunes to see that you were safe. The memory of the gaunt woman silhouetted against the sky was accompanied by a sorrow you had never felt when you were a child.

'One evening in the bungalow – I remember it so clearly, it still sends chills through me – your mother was phoning your father. I happened to overhear her. And what Mary said …' Violet dropped her gaze, then looked you steadily in the eye. 'I was convinced by what she said that she hoped you would drown in the incoming tide. That the sea would carry you away.'

Violet began seriously to cry. She jumped up from her chair, hiding her face, running to a corner next to the oven, pulling a handkerchief from her cardigan pocket.

'Oh, Auntie, dearest!' You went to her, held her, kissed the nape of her neck, where fine hairs grew. As she subsided into sobbing, Joyce spoke contemptuously from her position at the table. 'She often goes on like this nowadays. It's the bloody war.'

Her mother said fiercely, 'Go up to bed, will you! I won't tell you again.'

Joyce slunk off without another word. The cat rose and followed, stretching as it went.

Violet used her scrap of handkerchief and, turning towards you in your arms, mopped her eyes. You felt her warmth and smelt her perfume.

'Steve, sweetie, do you believe me? It's been my guilty secret for so long. It was a plan between your parents to dispose of you. I'm convinced of it. Oh golly, I should have done something about it ages ago.'

'But why –'

'I didn't know what to do. Why? I've often asked myself; why? They did not want a boy, but –'

All of your troubled past seemed to return to you – the long years, the sorrowful years, all mixed with memories of Sad Sid, who had died from his parents' indifference.

'Mother's phantom child – Valerie ...'

'I should have done something about it. You know how trivial I am ...' – she was sobbing again – 'You couldn't go to the police and say someone was planning the murder of a small boy.' More tears.

'Oh, you are far from trivial. What could you have done?'

'I could have adopted you.' She pulled a face at her blank statement, at the bare idea.

You were still standing close. You kept your arms round her body while you digested this new possibility. You found it hard not to shed a tear yourself, so precious to you was her affection and doubt.

'But you didn't. How could you have done?'

'Bertie refused to believe me when I told him what I suspected. He told me never to think of such a monstrous – a monstrous thing. He stuck up for his sister, of course.'

You gave her cheek a light kiss, saying that she had married into the wrong family.

'Of course Bertie stuck up for his sister. We had quite a row when I told him. He hit me across the face. The Hero of Kabul hit me across the face. I hate him.'

Still you were amazed. All those happy days on the beach – not happy at all in reality. You longed to reject what your aunt had told you. 'But is it true? Their plan?'

At that, she managed a smile. 'You don't imagine I'm making all this up?'

'No, my darling Violet.' Now you had been told, you had to confront the full shame of the truth. Aristotle would have had something to say about ignorance as a source of happiness. You felt your own chill against the warmth and softness of Violet's body under her inappropriate summer dress. 'Thank you for caring, darling Aunt. Don't cry about it.'

'But how could they? How could they? It was criminal –'

Putting her head on your shoulder, she sobbed anew. 'You were such a sweetie.'

You let her recover. 'Sorry,' she said, and poured you both another tot of gin.

'You know what a weak and silly girl I am, Steve. I didn't mean what I said about the Jews and it being their war.'

'Don't worry about it, Auntie, dear.' You stroked her hair. You went back to the table and sat down, contemplating each other. You held her hand on the tabletop.

As if with sudden determination, she said, 'I must tell you another little family secret. I know it's not exactly what you came home for.'

You felt a slight alarm at what she might say next. The first shock had been entirely sufficient. 'Do you need to tell me?'

She attempted a smile before looking down at the table. 'It's like Walcot. Knowledge doesn't make you happier, but somehow you have to know. Maybe not knowing is worse than knowing, whatever it feels like.'

Violet then embarked on her story. 'It's about young Sid, your mother's nephew. Maybe it is connected with his suicide a few years ago.'

Jeremy Wilberforce sent his young son Sid to boarding school to 'toughen him up', as he said. This was back in the late thirties, when a great number of people were fleeing from Nazi Germany. It happened that at Sid's school there were two Jewish brothers – Bernie, the elder brother, and Peter, the younger. Whereas Bernie was a cheerful, outgoing boy, good at games, his brother, the younger by two years, was withdrawn and subject to casual bullying.

'This young boy, Peter, slept in a dormitory in a bed next to your cousin, Sad Sid – as the boys called him,' said Violet. 'At the beginning of the winter term, someone had thumped Peter and he was feeling wretched. He climbed into Sid's bed to be comforted.'

170

She gave you a sort of mirthless smile. 'He just wanted a cuddle. You didn't know about this, I suppose?'

You shook your head.

'So Sid cuddled the boy. As they warmed up, Peter got an erection, and Sid felt it. Although Peter was a small boy, he had a large, well-developed penis.' Again, Violet's rather mirthless smile. 'Sid had seen the big brother, Bernie, in the showers after rugger, and had noticed he was circumcised. Peter was not circumcised. His foreskin would not draw back when Sid started to play with it.' She stared at you, to make sure you were listening. You released her hand to take a gulp of the gin. 'It's a condition known as phimosis – I know because I've looked it up – quite common, apparently. I take a considerable interest in the male sexual organ, Steve.'

Your Aunt regarded you straight-faced. You laughed at her confession.

'Peter's prick interested Sid. He rubbed it until Peter, with a little gasp, came all over the sheets. He then crept away, ashamed, back to his own bed. But of course he returned another night for more of the same. It became a regular thing. His condition did not stop him needing a spot of pleasure.'

You were embarrassed by this second family secret and asked Violet how she knew all the details.

She replied that eventually Sid had gone, not to Flo, his mother, whom he feared, but to his grandmother, Elizabeth Fielding. He had admitted everything, blurted it out, admitting that as soon as Peter left his bed, Sid had masturbated himself to orgasm. It was his need to confess.

'You're telling me that Sid was, in fact, queer?'

'No, I'd say not. At the time of puberty, when boys' pricks grow and they can produce semen, the whole phenomenon is exciting – a source of pride and some anxiety. They like to compare notes. "Tossing off" is almost mandatory. I bet you did it, Steve! The point of all this is the time factor, really. Do you see the implications?'

You asked her what she meant by that.

'It's not about masturbation. It's the filthy Nazis, don't you see? The elder boy was circumcised in the usual Jewish way, when conditions in Germany were not too bad. Then the younger boy, then Peter came along. Jews were increasingly persecuted. And as a safety precaution, simply in order to protect their son's life – how different from your parents! – his parents did not have him circumcised. Why exactly? Because the lousy Germans, the Gestapo, checked up on such private matters. If you had had your foreskin chopped off, then you were a Jew, and off to the gas chambers with you.'

'But –'

'And it just so happened that because of the phimosis, circumcision was what poor Peter needed. And did not get.'

You put a hand to your forehead. You understood. Evil infected the flesh, as it did the mind. Poor, wretched kids. It was just as Pief Geldstein had been allowed, even encouraged, to say 'Heil Hitler' and give the Nazi salute.

'So Sid told Granny? He must have been pretty desperate to do that. Why Granny?'

'Perhaps, like you, he admired her intelligence.'

'But it seems so odd –'

'Everything in life is odd.'

You sat staring at each other until she spoke again.

'We do know he was desperate – and a bit unstable mentally. And of course Elizabeth is the most intelligent member of your dreary family.'

You tried to imagine your grandmother listening to such an intimate male confession. 'How did she take Sid's story?'

Violet sighed and gazed at the ceiling. 'You have to remember Elizabeth was born in Victorian times. She was shocked to hear the story. I'm sure she had never heard of such a thing as phimosis. In this case, prudery overcame intelligence. Her recommendation was that Peter should be expelled from the school. She told me the tale in a great flutter.'

'She told you?'

'She was so disgusted, so upset. I mean, penises! She had to tell someone. I had taken her shopping. She told me everything over a coffee. Golly, what a world we live in.'

You shook your head at this new misery.

'I was taken aback,' your aunt said, reflectively. 'In particular, I suppose, sorry poor Sid didn't have a more understanding reception. You little lads certainly get it rough.'

You both took swigs of gin. After a long silence, you looked at your aunt and asked what she had done about it, after she had heard the story from Elizabeth.

'I was pregnant at the time. I did absolutely sod all. As with you and Walcot. I was pregnant. And then Sid strung himself up, poor kid. It was too late to do anything. But what could I have done?'

'Yes, poor Sid. Poor Granny, brought up in another age –'

Violet covered her eyes with her hand, propping her elbow on the edge of the table. 'I'm a dead loss, darling,' she said at last, looking up with a kind of grin. 'Let's have another ruddy gin and a fag. Be cheerful.'

Were you comfortable in that claustrophobic room?
Cosy, not claustrophobic! Yes, I was comfortable.
Yet your aunt was confiding some uncomfortable things to you. What do you think you thought of her behaviour?
I loved – adored my dear aunt, and I believe she loved me. She was able to confide in me. I counted that as a blessing. I took what she said at face value. What else?

That night, you slept in Violet and Bertie's spare room, which overlooked their garden, where they now kept chickens to help with the rationing.

Dreams of the sea came to you in your sleep. Not the sea at Walcot, long ago, but more recent seas, where you lay on the decks of various French fishing boats, riding easily on the Atlantic. You heard the steady throb of a ship's engines, like a giant heart. High above you were the stars. You had visualized them once as cold and remote; now they seemed close and friendly, the same welcoming stars you might observe from England – the England to which brave men were risking their lives in returning you.

You wondered childishly if there were planets among those stars, planets containing civilizations older than Earth's transitory patchwork of cultures, perhaps millions of years older, where deeply wise – perhaps born wise – men and women travelled in great ships from star to star, conversing, sharing their knowledge and their speculations. With none of the muddle and strife afflicting Earth … perhaps having banished all cruelties from their natures. Dining decorously, and not eating animals they had killed. Or, if not men and women, then whatever those lofty beings did to reproduce their kind without all the torments that sexuality brought human beings. Such fancies dwindled into confused thickets of thought, then thoughts of Marie Bourmard, whose religion had stood between your lovemaking. You dreamed you were sliding your hand between her legs.

You woke.

Daylight was filtering through the curtains. Violet had entered the room in her nightdress, barefoot, bringing you a cup of tea.

'Steve! What on earth are you doing down there? What's wrong with the bed?' She looked down at you, half-astonished, half-amused, to find you lying on the floor.

You had grown unused to the softness of beds. The floor suited you better, and there you had slept the night through.

'It's comfortable here, Auntie. Come and try it.'

You lifted the blanket by way of invitation. You had slept naked. She gasped.

She set the cup and saucer down without hesitation and climbed in beside you.

'It's early yet,' she said in a whisper to herself.

As she got in, she hoisted up her nightdress. You saw her secret parts, almost like a secret smile. Next moment, her bare body was pressed against yours.

174

She kissed you passionately. She had applied lipstick to her lips. You returned her kisses. You rolled on your sides. Her tongue found its way between your lips, into your mouth. You wrapped your arms about her. She lifted her leg and guided your stiff flesh into her ready body.

'Oh ...' – a long shudder from her – 'my darling ...'

'Auntie, I've always loved you ... Always –' You could hardly speak.

You began to move in her. Slowly, sumptuously slowly at first.

2

Hoarded Biscuits

Another door. This door a grander one, and locked. No one at home. No parents when you wanted them. 'Par for the course', you told yourself. You sat on the step, resting an elbow on your suitcase. Your thoughts blew about like leaves in a windy driveway. The chills of winter had settled in.

Leave was a complex matter. Unexpectedly, life in the army was simpler: certainly with fewer emotional demands. Your beloved aunt had given you much. Once again you had been forced to think of Sad Sid's death and unhappy life. But overriding that was the riddle of your days on the sands of Walcot. As yet you could not bring yourself to believe completely in the truth of Violet's charge against Martin and Mary.

How could you approach your parents? Should you accuse them of – attempted murder? Should you say nothing? Should you be angry? But you felt too empty – empty and yet choked.

One implication you stumbled on was that if they did not love you, then you were not worthy of being loved.

All of a sudden, you got to your feet. You were too cold to await their return any longer. Besides, what could be said now that would affect what had happened some seventeen years or more in the past? And you would be glad to see Sonia again, even if you were not yet prepared to face your parents.

As soon as you started down the drive, it happened that your father's old Rover turned in at the gate. Your father braked. He climbed out of one door, your mother out of the other. The old dog, Gyp, followed, wagging his tail, advancing cautiously to sniff your khaki-clad knee.

'My boy!' Martin Fielding exclaimed. 'Good God, thought you were dead, killed in action – The War Office wrote –'

'Stephen darling!' exclaimed Mary Fielding. Rushing to you, she flung her arms round your neck and kissed you. 'Oh, if you knew how we've suffered. Our lives have been a misery. We thought you were dead. Why did you never write?'

You recognized the old note of reproach. Your mother seemed to have shrunk slightly. She was wearing a pink wool dress, the hem of which hung unevenly. You bent and patted the dog's head.

'Sonia's not with you?'

'Nottingham. Pursuing her acting career. Come on, Gyp, good boy. Home now.'

The three of you went into the house, followed by the dog.

'Valerie still here?' you asked sarcastically.

Father's cricket bats stood to attention in the hall. Mary took Gyp into the kitchen to drink at his water bowl. She hastened to make a big pot of tea. She continued to talk from the kitchen while waiting for the kettle to boil. 'You're lucky to have escaped some of the hardships here – pretty unnecessary –'

Martin talked in a low rapid voice, fixing you with an eager gaze. 'You'll want to know what's been happening. It's excellent that Churchill has taken our socialists into his coalition government.

It will give them experience for when we take over from the old brute.'

'When will that be?' you asked, startled.

'When the damned war is over, of course. When do you think? After what we're going through, things have to change.'

'Except cricket!' You gave a laugh. He looked angry, then recovered.

'There will be good opportunities for us all then. Aviation will be the thing — a better world, Steve, a better world. I want you to go into politics. Great advances will emerge from this terrible war. You can help sort the country out.'

'Dad, I can't sort myself out as yet. Sorry, I'm only on leave; I go back to my unit the day after Boxing Day. I, well, I feel I'm on automatic pilot. I don't really know who I bloody well am.'

Martin gave a snort. 'You don't have to swear about it. What do you mean, anyhow, "you don't know who you are"?'

Your mother re-entered the room, bearing a tray of tea. 'Luckily I have a packet of Macfarlane's biscuits.' She gave a giggle. 'I've been hoarding, naughty me!' She set the tray down and sank wearily into an armchair. 'We don't have a maid any more, you notice.'

'There's a war on, you know,' said Martin, clarifying the situation.

'So what have you been doing? We thought you were dead. Not that we're blaming you … Where on earth have you been?' Mary asked with emphasis on the 'been'.

'I've been in France.'

'France, of all places! Oooh, lucky you! I suppose the food was lovely as usual, despite the Jerries.'

'I was stuck in a forest, mother. A forest in Brittany. Food was a bit scarce. Sonia's in Nottingham, you say? Is she okay?'

You bit into the Macfarlane biscuit.

Mary's attention was easily deflected. She said proudly that Sonia was with a repertory company in Nottingham. This week, the company was performing *Henry V*. Men were so few and far between Sonia was taking the part of Henry. It was, Mary said, her big chance.

You laughed. 'Once more into the breech, dear ladies.'

Mary was indignant. 'That's unkind. How do you know what she's gone through? Ghastly digs. An unhappy love affair. The blackout –'

'She does modern plays too,' Martin explained. 'She was in a J. B. Priestley play last week. We're hoping she'll make a go of it. It's a hard slog for her and no mistake.'

'But she's enjoying herself?'

'Well, you know. I can't see much future in it for her, myself.' Father nodded his head sagely, as if the future were rationed along with butter.

While these and other conversations were continuing, you were suffering from an uncomfortable rumbling of the stomach. These two people were strange to you. Your mother had aged, your father had taken to brushing his hair in a peculiar way, in an endeavour to conceal its thinning. And had they disliked you so much that …?

Without doubt, they were pleased to see you now; they endeavoured to make themselves agreeable, pressing more of the precious biscuits on you. Yet they seemed disconnected from realities: they were dated figures, left over from another epoch. Without Sonia, the house seemed dead. The ever-unborn ghost of Valerie hovered still.

You took your suitcase up to your room, where you had insisted on having a phone extension installed. The room was in twilight. A lemon-coloured blind had been drawn down over the window. You dialled your aunt's number. When Bertie's voice answered, you set the phone back in its cradle.

Over a supper of cold mutton and warmed-up potatoes, you told your parents something of your adventures – of Major Montagu, of Palfrey, and above all of the Geldsteins.

'They don't sound very nice people to me,' said Mary. She lowered her fork and stared at you. 'I mean to say, they were outlaws in their own country, weren't they?'

'Their "own countries" had outlawed them, which is perhaps a different thing.'

180

'I don't see how that's at all different from what I said.'

'This Geldstein got you at gunpoint, didn't he?' said Martin. 'I don't understand how you became friends, as you claim.'

'At the very least we were allies in a hostile occupied country. You can understand that, I'm sure.'

'Really, I don't like to think of a son of ours having to associate with such people,' said Mary. 'Of course, I know there's a war on. I'm not criticizing – I don't want you to think that. And we are so glad you are still alive. When do you have to go back to the army?'

'Mother, the Geldsteins became my valued friends. We supported each other. He was an enlightened man. They taught me something about Aristotle, about happiness. My life had been so narrow –'

'Aristotle?' Martin chuckled. 'That dirty old blighter! I wouldn't think there was much you wanted to learn about him.'

'We talked about his ethics. Stuck there in a French forest, we talked about Aristotle's ideas, unlikely as it seems. It was intensely valuable. It opened my eyes to new aspects of life.'

'What new aspects exactly?'

You could not say. You could not explain to them.

'Still,' said Martin, 'You did desert these new friends, as you call them, didn't you?'

'Yes. I still feel bad about that. But I was no deserter from the British Army. I had to get back to England.'

Your parents made no further response beyond staring at you in perplexity.

'I'll make us a cup of tea,' said Mary, as she rose after carefully folding her napkin.

Gyp the Airedale had grown older and was less active. The house was smaller than you had remembered it. You saw evidences of poor finish everywhere, of wallpaper peeling, of damp in one corner of the sitting room. The photos of Sonia standing on the piano were fading within their silver frames.

In your old room that night, you felt bitterly that misery which Valerie had brought on you in your boyhood. You had been haunted by Valerie. Now that you were back, memories of her baleful existence were also back.

You considered that something vital had been missing, laying waste your childhood. A curtain of gloom descended upon you. You sat on the wicker-bottomed chair by the window and thought about your life. You could not define what it was that had been lost. Somehow, you were always perceived as having failed your parents. Now they appeared to you insensitive, stupid even. But it could be your arrogance.

Yet after all, they could have – should have – inculcated in you an ability to tolerate them at the very least, and to empathize with their point of view. To love them. Why had you not really loved them, even in those years when you had never reflected on the possible reasons why you had been left alone on Walcot's sands?

This new information – the reason why you had been left alone there, conveyed by your aunt – held a certain destructive power. It sank back in time to poison what you had regarded as a period of happiness. It might be that there was something destructive in Auntie Violet's nature; she could have kept her knowledge to herself. Certainly she had a dislike of your parents, and they of her; might she have a reason for wanting to turn you against them?

In discomfort you considered the matter. You chewed it over and over until you reached the uncomfortable judgement that your dear aunt should have held her peace. Supposing – supposing that her story was true – the fact was that you had survived. The danger on the sands could not have been so great.

Again your mind returned to those lovely expanses of beach: to the fresh, sweet smell of the sea; the murmur of the waves; the sun constant overhead; that joyous feeling of freedom.

It came to you that you had flown a paper kite at one time – a square kite, red and green, with a long tail. The kite rattled in the breeze high above your head, riding the blue air like happiness itself. You loved the sound of the kite: brisk, businesslike. A rare gull strutted by the wavering margins of the sea, sleek and alert.

You as a small boy again, lord of all you surveyed, sitting in a warm pool, watching the shrimps nibble at your toes ...

Never again would there be, could there be, a time like that. Realization of that finality came as a pervasive pain.

And then the war, gobbling up your youth.

If it was foolish of Violet to have spoken, perhaps it was also foolish of her to have climbed into bed with you; you conveniently forgot that you had invited her in. But at the thought of that conjunction, your senses caught fire, and you were, in a measure, comforted.

'Oh, Violet, dearest!' you whispered to the room.

Yet the questions held you unhappily enslaved, when you had thought yourself a free man. But, free? Free, when you were still in the army, and the struggle had still to be fought?

There was a passage in Aristotle's *Metaphysics* which Gerard had read out to you. He had written it in his notebook. You had committed it to memory: 'The arrangement of the universe is in fact like that of a household. In a household, it is the free members that have the least liberty to do whatever they please. Most, if not all, of their actions are prescribed.'

You could see how that applied to your parents, prescribed within their limitations.

'The slaves, on the other hand, and the livestock, have little to contribute and for the most part act as they please.'

There, surely, Aristotle was mistaken. That pony, Beauty, had enjoyed no freedom. The delightful maid, Ann, the slave of your uncle Jeremy's house, could never act as she pleased. Perhaps the war had freed Ann, as it had enslaved you.

It occurred to you that Aristotle had no clearer idea of the workings of the universe than you did.

Do you imply that you never acted as you pleased? Yet you enjoyed making love to Violet. It could be said that on the whole you enjoyed your exile in the Forêt de la Bouche. You seem a little confused.

183

Ha! Of course I was confused! And pretty despondent, being back home in England.

Your father made immediate overtures to you, and was thinking of your future.

You rejected him. Why was that?

How could I think of the future? I was only on leave – due to go back into the war in a few days time.

Of course! That war ... for many, suffering and death: for others, reprieves and excuses.

You rose and began to sort through your old chest of drawers. Some mementoes of childhood lay there, together with love notes from Gale Roberts, your first girlfriend. There was a whistle from a pre-war cracker, a Dinky Toy oil tanker labelled 'Redline Glico', an old yo-yo, a postcard from Uncle Jack in Jerusalem, and a box which still contained two Price's Night Lights.

You took out one of the little wax tubs. The night light reminded you of your fear of darkness as a child. You had been more frightened then than in the Forêt de la Bouche. The steady little flame of the candle had been soothing. Pleased with the memory, you lit the wick from your cigarette lighter and switched off the overhead light.

You stood in the dark, but the little light beamed steadily forth. As a small boy, standing in the same pose, you had come closer to Jesus, the light of the world. Now you put the thought away as too sentimental, reflecting instead on the darkness of the world, and how Britain saw itself as a solitary light against the night engulfing Europe.

The light symbolized your consciousness, lonely and isolated. You needed someone to truly love, and to love yourself. Useless to pursue your aunt when Bertie answered the phone. Such thoughts fluttered about you. You wondered if life would make more sense if someone, some being, were watching your mental struggles.

Now you know the answer to that.

Why did you not speak at the time?

Once the game was in motion, we could never change the rules.
Aristotle was evidently of no assistance at this juncture.
You mock me.

Nevertheless, the steady little tongue of flame from the nightlight was in itself cheering and beautiful. Such was your life.

You held the tub in your hands, relishing its mild illumination. Your mood lifted. Stripping off your clothes, you ran a hot bath and sank into it. You regarded your hard, muscular body with satisfaction, thinking how only twenty-four hours earlier it had been blessed by the embraces of Violet's body.

Next morning you would go to seek out Gale. But in the morning you would find that the Robertses had moved. Nobody could tell you where they had gone, for wartime England, grey wartime England, was full of secrets. 'There's a war on,' someone told you, as if you didn't know.

You slept this night on the floor, as you had done at your aunt's. In the morning there was no charming visitor to bring you a cup of tea.

3

Christmas at Gracefield

'For Christmas we'll be going to stay with your father's sister, Ada, and Claude, her husband, if you remember', your mother announced, after breakfast. 'You never sent them a card when you were in France, did you? Will you come with us? You don't want to stay here alone, do you?'

'And Sonia?'

'She's in Nottingham. I thought we told you. She has an acting career to pursue.'

She was putting a record of Ernest Lush on the radiogram. Ernest Lush in his high, thin voice sang of white doves flying. Mary was fond of the record. She held her chin prayerfully in her hands to show how fond she was.

Not for the first time, Mary was wrong. Even as Lush's voice ascended to the ceiling, a taxi was coming up the drive. You saw it through the window and went to the front door to find out who it was. The rear door opened and Sonia climbed out.

She waved on seeing you. 'Steve, have you got any cash? Could you pay the cabbie, please?'

The taxi-driver, to reinforce the request, stuck his hand out of the window. You put four pound notes into that hand. He gave you a wink and a nod. 'She don't feel too good. Look after her, Mr Soldier.' And with that he was off.

You carried Sonia's case into the house. She clung to you as she walked; she looked extremely drained. 'A kind man,' she murmured.

'He charged you just the same.'

'Yeah, he charged me just the same. Four quid – just from the station.'

Martin appeared in the doorway. 'Darling! This is a nice surprise! Come on in.'

From the background, competing with Ernest Lush, came Mary's voice, asking who it was. Martin told her. She came running, screeching welcome, and seized Sonia in an embrace.

'Go easy, Ma – I am a bit tender.'

'Oh, you're hurt? Poor little darling! What's the matter?'

'I fell off the stage.'

We all went into the living room. Sonia sank into the leather sofa. 'Shuggerybees,' she gasped.

'How thrilling to have you home for Christmas,' said her mother, nevertheless with a slight question in her voice. Father said Sonia looked tired and offered a dry sherry. She asked for a cup of tea instead. Mary bustled off to get it.

You sat down beside her and asked her what the matter was.

'Just tired from the trip – had to change trains. All the fucking trains are crowded. I'll be okay in a jiffy.' She gave you an odd look.

When she was drinking her tea, Mary sat beside her and busied herself smoothing her daughter's hair. Sonia made no protest.

'I'll go up and rest,' she said. 'Steve, could you carry my things?'

'Are you sure, dearest? Have you broken anything? You don't look well.'

'I'm fine, Mother. Please don't be tiresome.'

You went up to her room and dumped her luggage by the bed. Sonia shut the door and leaned against it.

'Christ, how they fuss. Steve, glad to see you. I never believed the War Office with their sodding telegrams. Something told me you were alive.'

You put your arms round her and you stood there, enjoying the embrace.

'Oh Christ, got to lie down.'

'You're ill, love.'

'I'm in fucking pain. I'll be okay, I've got some aspirins. I'll sleep.'

Sitting on the edge of the bed, she kicked off her shoes and lay down. You sat beside her and asked what the trouble was. She told you she had had an abortion, and the woman had hurt her. She emphasized the fact that it was a back-street abortion. 'A Nottingham back-street abortion at that. Can you imagine it? I couldn't believe I was pregnant. I'd made the guy wear a frenchie … How could I possibly have a baby? The mere thought! It would have ruined my career –'

'Who was the bloke?'

'What's it matter who it was? I had to do it. There was no love involved. Just as well.' After a pause, she went on, 'I had to get away. The thought of home suddenly seemed good – anything to escape for a day or two.'

You asked her when she had had the abortion. She said late on the night before last.

'Thank God you're here. I had to tell someone. But then … seeing them again … Mum would make such a bloody fuss. I can't bear to tell them. You won't tell them, will you? I'll say I fell off the stage.' She sighed. 'They'll believe anything. They're such bloody fantasists.'

She planned to deceive her parents as they had deceived her.

She added, 'Be like Dad – keep Mum', quoting a well-known Fougasse poster encouraging the British to be secretive in wartime in case Hitler was listening.

When your sister settled down to sleep, you spread the eider-down over her body.

'Where've you been all this while?' she asked.

'Stuck in France.'

'I thought you might have been. I rang your regiment. Didn't bring me back any perfume?' Then she said, with a pale smile, 'I know, don't tell me, there's a war on. I was only sodding-well joking.'

The Fieldings stayed at home on Christmas Day, out of concern for Sonia. Sonia's health improved, while she refused to accompany you all to the relations. She wished to remain on her own, quietly, since she had to return to Nottingham on the following day and was dreading the train journey.

Small gifts were exchanged for Christmas. You got a book on British Wildlife from your parents. Sonia gave you a little china figure of a milkmaid. She was treading the boards in *An Inspector Calls*, and had to be back in time for the evening performance.

You gave your parents a half-bottle of Johnny Walker and a bottle of Wincarnis. To Sonia you gave a torch with a battery. She told your parents she was having a wonderful time in Nottingham. In fact, she confided to you, she was having a wonderful love affair with the well-known stage set and costume designer, Adrian Hyasant. You noted his name.

'How's the hunchback?' you asked her jokingly. '"A Hunchback Calls".'

'Sod off!' she said, with a laugh.

That afternoon, you were treated to the melancholy prospect of your father standing in the kitchen, ironing the festive paper in which the morning's gifts had been wrapped.

He gave you his version of a jovial smile, saying, 'Better look after this paper, you know. And the string. There may not be any available next year. Paper is a weapon of war! Don't waste it. We all have to make sacrifices.'

It was easy, you thought, for parsimony to masquerade as patriotism.

The Hillmans lived not far distant, in the village of Cadnam. Their house stood in the middle of the High Street, behind iron railings. Martin, being employed on war work in the aviation industry, had a small petrol allowance for his Rover.

Ada and her husband Claude gave you a warm welcome, ushering you into the front room, where a roaring fire greeted you. The Hillman boys, Joey and Terry, were there, and were induced to come forward and shake hands. They had shot up since you last saw them, at grandfather Sidney's funeral, and were now in the unwholesome grip of early adolescence.

By the fire sat Sidney's widow, Elizabeth, her face the colour of old ivory, but serene and upright. She clutched the hand you proffered, saying, 'You've had some … some adventures, I hear. My plan is … as far as I have a plan … to sit … My plan is to sit the war … war out.'

Your father's sister, Belle, was also present. Her plan was apparently to sit out the war in silence. She smiled warmly at you but said nothing. You saw that she had become a good deal prettier than previously, and realized she could not be all that ancient – perhaps no more than thirty one – though that was bad enough.

Claude was in a roaring good humour, singing loudly, 'Ding dong merrily on high, Let's have a quick one on the sly …'

He advised everybody to make themselves at home, and began pouring liberal drinks. Claude ran a printing press and was currently engaged in well-paid war work which, as everyone knew, involved printing top secret pamphlets to drop on Germany.

Joey and Terry wanted to know how you had survived in the forest. You said, 'You told me you had a system. What's happened to it? Have you grown out of it?'

'Grown out of it!', echoed Joey incredulously. 'No, no, we've developed it, haven't we, Terry?'

'Out of all recognition. Except at basis it is recognisable.'

They sniggered together, changing the subject to enquire what it felt like to be a hero.

'Sounds like mumbo-jumbo to me,' you said.

'Get your hearing checked,' they said. 'How about a game of Monopoly?'

'We're bound to win,' said Joey.

In fact, you won, whereupon your cousins became sulky.

Ada had worked hard on Christmas dinner. 'A festive board indeed!' roared Claude, as the company entered the dining room, you supporting your grandmother with your arm. 'Better than a festive bawd, some might say.'

He began to recite, with a Yorkshire accent, ''Twas Christmas Day in the Workhouse, The paupers all sat there, Their faces full of goodness, Their bellies –' when Ada hushed him.

You all seated yourselves under festoons of pre-war paper decorations. Balloons, already wrinkling, nestled dangerously against the central electric light. Every plate played host to a Christmas cracker. Arms were gladly linked, the crackers pulled. Cries of delight, or laughter, greeted the puny gifts falling from the interiors of the crackers – little rings, minute combs, flimsy bracelets, a bakelite camel, dice, metal puzzles.

Riddles were read aloud: 'What sounds like a mouse, squeaks like a mouse, but is not a mouse? Answer: Two mice.' Groans and laughter.

'When is a door not a door? When it's a jar.' More groans and laughter.

Paper hats were applied to heads: red, green, blue, or mauve. A genial atmosphere prevailed while bowls of soup arrived, to be followed by a large goose besieged by sausages, enthroned on a large plate with gravy for a moat, followed by a convoy of dishes of bread sauce, redcurrant jelly, potatoes, mashed or baked, together with carrots and brussel sprouts grown in the frosty garden beyond the french windows.

Joey and Terry clapped their hands in applause. Everyone took it up and clapped loudly. Ada, flushed and triumphant, set the tray down before her and said, 'Happy Christmas Everyone, and Steve, we are so glad you are safe home and can be with us.'

You were gratified, and helped your uncle distribute glasses of redcurrant juice to everyone – or water from a glass jug if preferred.

Supported by your father, Elizabeth called for silence.

'We shall say grace … Grace for this Ada spread … This lovely spread provided by Ada … Ada and Claude. The pretend wine is a present from our friends … The Wades … our friends the Wades.

'The Wades family. The family lives quite close, outside Lyndhurst. It's quite close. And we are invited – all of us are invited – to Hall at the tea … tea at the Hall, is what I mean. To tea and dinner. Did I say that? A boar dinner, we are promised. With a performance of Shakespeare … Shakespeare. Of his play. *All's Well –*'

Elizabeth was interrupted by applause – again from Joey and Terry.

'Yes, boys. My daughter Belle will be taking part. A role in the play. We should … what? Yes, we should leave here at half-past three. In our cars at half-past four … after a rest. A sleep, after this lovely meal. And now –'

All bowed their paper-clad heads as Elizabeth said quietly, 'We thank Thee, Lord, for bringing us safely … safely so far through the war. Yet another war. And we pray that defeat … that defeat … that defeat will not be our lot. So we pray for Winston Churchill. The health and survival of Mr Churchill.' The old clear voice paused before continuing.

'And for what we are … what about to eat, we thank … thank God and the Fleet.'

'Amen', said the family, with feeling.

'This doesn't suit me,' grumbled Mary Fielding. 'I mean, I didn't bargain for this extra journey. Have we enough petrol? Who are the Wades anyway?'

Martin explained that Lord Lyndhurst, Benjamin Wade, was a member of the House of Lords, and was now engaged in important war work, in which it seemed Claude was playing a vital part.

'That shouldn't affect us,' said your mother.

'Oh, come on, Ma, it's Christmas. I don't hold with an old High Tory like Lyndhurst, but it may not be too bad. And we get a free meal.'

'His lordship is responsible for providing furniture for the NAAFI,' Joey interposed, knowledgeably. 'Important war work.'

The signs were that a visit to Gracefield House might indeed be not too bad. The fading light of day revealed a magnificent edifice sprawling at the end of a long drive, its four stories crowned by towers, pinnacles and crenellations; windows severe on the ground floor, windows jocular on the fourth. Not a light showed because the blackout was in force; seemingly completely deserted, the great house enjoyed an added majesty as it gathered gloom about itself.

Before the cars of the family had been neatly parked side by side, the doors in the front of the house were thrown open, emitting a strong fan of light, and an aged butler came slowly down the steps, flashing a torch, to greet and guide you all.

Your party were shown into a brightly lit hall from which several brightly lit rooms led. A large Christmas tree stood to one side, loaded with glittering points of light. A large dog of Irish wolfhound persuasion came slowly up and greeted the visitors without comment. To your eyes, it was an astonishing wartime exhibition of wealth and privilege.

Guests lined up to wish Lord and Lady Lyndhurst the compliments of the season. When it came to your mother and Martin's turn to shake his hand, she announced, 'Martin's working in Clement Attlee's office now, your Lordship.'

Lyndhurst showed his old tarnished teeth in a grin. 'I'd keep quiet about that, if I were you, my girl.'

Martin, red in the face, shook Mary's arm as they turned away. 'You ninny!' he said.

A huge volume of noise emanated from every corner of the house. The butler showed you into the room from which the greatest noise

194

came. With a whoop, Joey and Terry dived into the fray – the fray consisting of a surprising number of people, older men, younger women and many children; the children chasing each other about the legs of their elders.

A piano was being played. The pianist was an elderly man in tie and tails, striking the keys with vigour. He turned a shining face on the crowd, nodded and embarked at once on the carol, 'God Rest You Merry, Gentlemen'. The whole room joined in the singing with enthusiasm. You, Claude and Ada began immediately to sing, your parents coming in a bar-or-two later. You wished you had persuaded Sonia to join the party.

An aged servant circulated with a tray of glasses of mulled wine, while Elizabeth was shown to a seat in an alcove, from where she could survey the crowd.

'I never saw so much wine,' you said.

'When in Italy, we drink wine. Always wine,' said Elizabeth.

Shortly after the singing, a man of about sixty, with a ruddy, outdoor type of face, jumped on to the platform on which the piano stood and announced that tea and Christmas cake were being served in the next room. 'Don't eat too much cake, my dears,' he advised. 'Remember dinner is to follow anon.' Then the play would begin at nine sharp, after which there would be dancing.

Mary asked if the figure was Lord Lyndhurst. She was told not to be stupid: it was His Lordship's younger brother, Kim Wade, the famous artist, known, said Claude, as a bit of a blighter. He said this approvingly, and winked at Mary as he said it.

As people filtered from the room, its furnishings became more apparent. It was oak-panelled, the panels adorned with a number of oil paintings, most of them allegorical in character and framed in heavy gilt frames. The ceiling beams were elaborately carved.

'Where in the devil did all the money come from?' your father asked his brother-in-law, enviously.

Claude replied that the Wades had several generations of wealth behind them, but that, 'just when things were looking rather dim',

Felix Wade had secured a monopoly on the import of guano from South America. Besides being a natural fertilizer, the guano could be used to make explosives, as it had done in the First World War.

Belle slipped away wordlessly, with a smile, missing the generous tea to attend a last-minute rehearsal of the play.

Hospitality was certainly lavish. At the dinner, forty-four people sat at long tables while saddle of wild boar was served.

'They shot it on the estate,' said Claude. 'Enough to make any boar wild!'

The meat was served with quince sauce, and vegetables almost unheard of at the time were heaped on plates: lentils, celeriac and beetroot tumbling against each other in seasonal good humour. The pink slices of boar fell apart under busy knives. This feast! In wartime! Unimaginable!

'The chef is a French refugee,' a man by the name of Algie Cholmondeley told you. 'Certainly knows his onions – and his garlic.'

All agreed it was a delicious meal. You remembered the wild boar you had eaten with Palfrey and the Geldsteins. Even without the tracklements it had tasted wonderful, devoured in the depths of that unforgettable forest.

The curtain up on *All's Well That Ends Well* lifted at ten minutes past nine. The audience was considering being seated, and you were accompanying your grandmother. Lyndhurst had settled close to the stage, slumped in an armchair, with Augusta his wife beside him. There were cushions at his back. You took a look at him and decided that the founder of this unexpectedly generous feast was senile. However, chatting to the old man were an old lady with a high lace collar and a pretty young woman with bobbed hair. Attracted by the latter, you went over to speak to the little group.

The pretty young woman told Lyndhurst that you were one of the heroes keeping Britain free. 'I hear he has spent half the war so far camping out in a French forest, shooting all and sundry who came anywhere near.'

An ancient, gnarled face looked up at you. One eye was rather milky, but the scrutiny was sharp enough. 'I have a penchant for heroes, having been one myself, so to say, when the century was a great deal younger than it is now,' said the old man in a husky voice. 'What's your name, young feller?'

When you told him, he reached out a bony hand, the grip of which proved remarkably firm. 'Be nice to this young man, Augusta,' he advised his wife, who was standing stiffly just behind him. 'He may get himself killed before this confounded war is finished.'

'Do you ride?' Lady Augusta asked. She had a large, aquiline nose which dominated her face. 'You must come for a canter. We can lend you a mare if you lack one yourself.'

You thanked her, noting that the pretty young woman had seized the opportunity to disappear.

However, the pretty young woman pretty soon started screaming. It transpired that she was somewhat married, and had brought her Toddler along to the party. There was also a young husband, or someone playing that role, who had disappeared from the scene without greatly distressing her.

Now the Toddler was also missing. Some of the guests at once engaged in a sort of treasure hunt, crying 'Toddler, Toddler!' here and there. Other guests were offended by the fuss and preferred that the Toddler should remain hidden. 'Out of sight, out of way,' remarked one sporting type.

'Perhaps it has toddled outside,' said Lady Augusta, coldly. 'Where frostbite awaits it.'

'Not to mention the odd boar,' added Claude, with relish.

The thought of her Toddler outside and frost-bound caused the pretty young woman to shriek again. She looked, you thought, even prettier with her lovely mouth open and her lovely arms waving.

After a while, a sofa was pushed aside, to reveal the Toddler sprawled there. It was contentedly chewing a bone from His Lordship's terrier's bowl. The terrier lay close by the Toddler, watching the performance with every appearance of amiability;

his tail wagged in slow approval, at least until one of the sporty types kicked the animal out of the way.

The pretty young woman snatched up her child and gave it a good smacking to express her relief at its safe return.

'All's well that ends well, then,' Lyndhurst was heard to remark. He cackled at either his adroit reference to the play about to be performed, or at the pained cries of the Toddler.

You found yourself laughing sycophantically at this attempt at humour.

The audience settled down – even the pretty young woman and her Toddler settled down – as the play began. An elegant young Bertram strode forth behind the improvised footlights to recite the prologue:

'This is a Christmas frolic we cut short
For Shakespeare always has so much to say.
What's left are frolics of a naughty sort
But set in our New Forest, just outside,
Not in Will's France – now occupied.
We only hope that you'll enjoy our play!'

On trooped the courtiers, among them Helena, played by Belle Hillman, looking resplendent, red hair piled high with intertwined pearls, dressed in a stunning low-cut costume of white. Even more astonishing for this generally mute young lady, she spoke her lines musically, without hesitation. Unfortunately, her appearance was spoilt by the arrival on stage of the wolfhound, Chancellor, who proceeded to relieve himself against the curtain, to the delight of many in the audience.

In this abridged version of Shakespeare, Helena played her trick on Bertram, climbing at night, under cover of darkness, into Bertram's bed, as a substitute for his supposed beloved, Diana.

Bertram did not notice the difference in the women. He announced boldly, to the hilarity of most of the audience, 'I had my pleasure anyway – in the dark of night, all cats are grey.'

Because of his previous declarations, he was then persuaded he must marry Helena.

One of the minor courtiers assisting Helena in the deception was a character played by Terry Hillman. Other roles were filled by Lyndhurst's family or friends.

In conclusion, Helena spoke directly to the audience.

'My saucy tryst defies the pitchy night,
And now with tripping foot we'll make the dance
Disperse our darkness till the winter's worn.
For time will bring on verdant spring again
And briar shall bear green leaf as well as thorn.
All's well that ends well, and our play's well done.
Good night, fare well, and blessings, every one!'

Down came the curtain, to rapturous applause.

As the players took their bow, you heard your mother, in the row behind you, remark on the unpleasant nature of the play. 'Quite unsuitable,' she said. 'Insulting to women.'

'Great fun,' said your father, firmly. Your grandmother turned her stiff neck to say to Mary, 'How charming. A real Christmas. Real diversion. And Belle – so articulate.'

'That is so,' Mary agreed, looking severe.

A large gong was struck. The audience faded into the next room to mingle with the players. Much wine was tipped into many glasses.

A four-piece band wearing evening dress struck up with the latest lively tunes, As *Long as You're Not in Love With Anyone Else*, *Tuxedo Junction*, *The Hut Sut Song*, *Elmer's Tune* and *Night and Day*. It was the first time in your life you had heard live music, or seen it professionally played.

You stood on the edge of the dance floor, half pleased, half waiting, for what, you knew not. Terry passed, expertly guiding Belle, who still wore her Shakespearean costume.

A slender girl in an aquamarine two-piece, whom you had seen talking to Lord Lyndhurst's wife earlier, appeared at your side. With her short bobbed hair went plenty of make-up. She had a pretty Roman nose. She took you by the lapel in a proprietorial way.

'Hello, Hero. Why aren't you dancing? Surveying the battlefield? I guess you don't jitterbug?'

You had never heard of the jitterbug. You answered in a manner you considered appropriate for her amount of make-up. 'I'm a bit out of touch – almost a caveman. Until very recently, I was in France, being heroic.'

'You lucky thing. I bet the food was gorgeous. I used to love Paris.'

'Food was a bit short where I was.'

'Shame. When my pater was an attaché at the Quay d'Orsay, I practically lived off cassoulet, greedy little thing that I was …'

'I was rather far from the Quay d'Orsay. Hiding out in a wood in Brittany, in fact.'

At that she stared at you, summing you up, transfixing you with a pair of the bluest eyes you had ever seen. She raised her bright-nailed hands, giving a shudder which shook the major portions of her body. 'The provinces! So, no jitterbugging, eh? The Palais Glide it is, then.'

As you took to the floor in a foxtrot, she announced herself as Abby. She said she was a friend of Belle's. She was one of the Wade crowd – a niece of Ben's, she said, but down here just for the party. She lived in an apartment in Chelsea, with two other girls.

'Have you sort of given up on the army?'

'Oh no, I'm on leave. Are you rich?' you asked.

'Not rich enough,' she said.

'What do you do – apart from eating cassoulet?'

'Oh, this and that. I plan to have a shop, more or less. High class, not for the rabble. Worse luck, the premises were bombed out.'

'So you're not a Socialist, then.'

'For God's sake, no! Do stop quizzing me, darling.'

She asked you what you made of what she called the mob churning about the floor. Seeing you made very little of it, she supplied a description. There were plenty of women shuffling round the dance floor – 'mainly old bats', she said – but few men, and those mainly of under-conscription age. You, she said, were the exception that proved the rule.

'Quite a find,' she added. 'And I've got you. In a manner of speaking.'

As Joey drifted by with his arms about an older woman, Abby nodded towards him. She said that Joey and his brother were two youngsters taking advantage of the system.

'The system! I know they have what they call a system. What is it, actually?'

She came closer, looking up into your face, a gesture you were finding immensely appealing. 'It's simple. Look at Belle. Hasn't she opened up – literally?' She squeaked with laughter. 'Belle's one of theirs. Plus a lot of older women in this room. They're dashed grateful, don't you know? Husbands away or dead by now. Why do you think Belle has blossomed? She's the latest to benefit from their system.'

You were amazed, and sought to conceal the fact.

'You're telling me that my cousins well, they go to bed with Belle? She's their aunt!' Directly you had uttered the protestation, you had to think about what you were saying.

'Both of them together, I'm told. It's their system. Then they don't get too involved. Some of these old bags would cling like leeches to anyone young and randy.'

You experienced mild shock at hearing the word 'randy' issue from such encarmined female lips.

'But you're … How do you know this?'

She laughed. 'I'm sick of this music. They'll be doing the hokey-cokey next. Let's go somewhere and have a fag.'

As you left the room, you holding Abby's delectable smooth hand, she said, 'Oh, Belle brags about it.'

'And have you …?' You could not bring yourself to complete the question.

She dug a sharp elbow into your ribs. 'I hate the little bastards. They're so smug. You're much more my type: a bit apologetic.'

The two of you forged into the darkness of the back regions of Gracefield. Abby led the way. She guided you up the servants' stairs on to a rear landing, and from there down a long corridor, through a green baize door, to the front of the house. The dance music became fainter as you went. She opened a door at random. You entered a bedroom of a traditional kind, decked out with heavy powder blue swags of curtain, two armchairs of similar hue, an immense wardrobe and a grate in which a coal fire smouldered.

'A thousand miles from London!' Abby exclaimed, as if it were the stage direction in italics at the opening of a play.

The double bed was piled with the coats of guests. Abby switched on a bedside lamp and stood it on the floor beside the bed. She crossed to the door and turned the key in the lock.

'This'll do,' she said. 'Are you game, hero?'

You were enchanted by her. You took firm hold of her and kissed her lingeringly. Your hand went to her breast. Then you took it away and asked, 'Should we be doing this?'

'I've got a Dutch cap on, if that's what you mean.' She lowered a hand to your fly buttons. 'I hope you are not a prude. You're not going chicken, are you? We could be killed next week, don't you know?'

'Here and now, you mean?'

'Hitler's sending his doodlebugs to kill us all off, for God's sake.'

You peeled off your jacket while Abby pulled your trousers down.

'I'm not getting into the all-together. It's so dashed cold in here. Why doesn't Ben have better fires in his bedrooms?'

'Get your knickers down.'

She did so and you both collapsed on the bed. Your hand went down to the lively hairy quarters between her legs.

202

You groaned with delight. 'Oh, I need this, Abby!'

As the lady said, you might be killed next week. Meanwhile, there was this night, among all the coats, with this willing lady to delight you and to be delighted. She was certainly showing every sign of delight.

Later, as the car headed back to Cadnam, your mother, commenting on the surprises of the evening, said, 'Fancy Belle being so vocal! I didn't know she had it in her.'

'Many a time,' you said, with your head full of much more gorgeous surprises.

4

'Please Not to Shoot Us'

You were in Aldershot. It was Sunday. You were due to rejoin your regiment at one-pip-emma. It was ten-thirty of a chilly grey morning. Violet was with you. She had made her excuses and a neighbour was looking after the children. Even as you embraced, she had an apology to make. 'That awful Walcot business. I should not have worried you with it. I was a bit tiddly, Stevie. They're not trying to poison your tea, are they, I mean?'

'If so, I have survived so far.'

'Golly, isn't it cold? I must try and buy myself a new coat.'

You put an arm round her. You walked down the street. Every shop was closed. Men in uniform walked here and there, rather aimlessly.

Violet began to talk about her son. 'He's quite a problem, but so clever. Do you know, the other day I said something was larger than life. And Dougie asked me how large was life – could you measure it?'

You were thinking about Abby. She was related to the Wades. You knew from the moment you met her that you were in different classes, with different ways of life, whereas with Violet you were the same sort of people; troubled, slightly down-at-heel. There was, you reflected, much comfort in incest.

'He'll be a great man when he grows up, I'm sure. Perhaps he'll be a wireless announcer. Wear a bow tie and all that.'

When you came to a Methodist chapel, you both went in by mutual consent. You huddled together in one of the rear pews, clutching each other.

The service began. The Methodists had removed much of the Church of England's ceremonials. There was no psalm-singing, few responsories. The parsons in their grey flannel suits pressed briskly on with singing hymns and praying for salvation.

You joined in the hymn-singing, sometimes substituting your own words.

'Fatherlike he spends and tears us,
'Well our feeble frame he knows ...'

A Rev. Edith Morris ascended the pulpit to deliver a sermon. She was a short lady with short-cut hair, and she delivered a short sermon. The subject of the sermon was the contrast between gunfire and Hellfire. She said that Hellfire was by far the worse of the two: gunfire could miss you; Hellfire never missed.

'Not much hope for us, then,' said Violet, as you returned to the windy street. 'And you're going abroad, are you?'

'Yep. Europe. Should be in Berlin by Easter ...'

'Oh golly, Steve, sweetie, do take care of yourself.' Before she kissed you she added, 'This is such an awful time to be alive.'

You wore a greatcoat. You also wore a khaki wool scarf, wound round your head as well as your neck. It was freezing in the Ardennes, late in the remorseless January of 1945. With your hands in your pockets you asked the engineer crouching by your tank, 'So when are you going to get this tank started, Wood?'

The man's red raw face turned up to you in contempt. 'Like I said, Sir, the fucking anti-freeze is froze.'

'How can anti-freeze freeze?'

'And the petrol is froze in the fucking petrol tank. There's nowt we can do about it. I'm froze myself.'

'Get on with it, Wood.'

You looked across the bleak landscape. A platoon of American infantry was trudging doggedly across pristine snowfields, followed by two Jeeps. They were part of the rump of General Bradley's Twelfth Army Group. The whole country was in suspended animation, colour drained from it. The universal drab white was punctuated only by blackened trees.

'Those Jeeps are moving,' you told the engineer. 'Why aren't we?'

The man got up and straightened his back, hands on hips, leaning backwards. 'They was under shelter, most like. That's the Yankee army.' He gave you a look of hatred. 'Some of our blokes was froze to death in the night in our tents. Not like you officers.'

You had sheltered in a room in a ruined farmhouse and managed to sleep for three hours under a blanket. You had no answer for Wood. The Battle of the Bulge was almost won, with heavy Allied losses. Hitler had thrown thirty divisions into the attack, in a last gamble. The severe weather from mid-December onwards had halted the use of Allied air forces. It was discovered later that in the resultant ground battles Germany suffered one hundred thousand casualties, and the Allies almost as many.

'Get hold of some kindling, Wood,' you ordered. 'Light a fire under this bloody tank. We have to get weaving.'

By now the other Churchill tanks under your command were firing, belching acrid blue smoke across the site. Bodies of the men who had died during the night were being shuffled into the back of a fifteen-hundredweight, under the supervision of Sergeant Breeze. Snow began to fall again, carried on a stealthy East wind.

You turned to face the wind for a moment, to clear your head. The ground became speckled, as if with dandruff.

An English major drove up in a Jeep, goggles covering his eyes, otherwise almost entirely encased in frost. His driver was in similar state. He pulled up close to you. You saluted as he said, 'Get your tanks on the move, captain, chop chop. We rendezvous with the main column at 1600 hours, near Erve.' He gave a map reference.

'Beastly weather, Sir,' you said.

'Could be worse,' and he was off.

Three minutes later, you thought, 'Good God, was that Hilary Montagu? Sounded like him.'

At last the tank was started and you rolled on your way with the rest of the short convoy. It was almost impossible to see where the road was, except when the convoy was travelling through villages. All villages had been ruined in the last desperate advance of the Wehrmacht, or in their retreat, or in the Allied advance. The inhabitants had either fled or been killed, or died of cold and malnutrition. Houses were mere snow-locked shells. You felt you were driving through the end of the world.

'A fine fucking mess we made of this place,' your sergeant remarked at every village you passed through. You made no response. Inwardly you could only echo the sergeant's sentiments. A fine fucking mess indeed.

At one point, where two roads crossed, an American army ambulance had stopped. Two GIs with carbines slung over their shoulders were guarding it, while another man worked by the open doors. A doleful cluster of four inhabitants stood about, as close as they were allowed to get. You ordered the tanks to halt and climbed down to see if help was needed.

A burly corporal with a Red Cross armband greeted you. He pushed through the disconsolate villagers to speak, and tore you off a snappy salute.

'Good of you to stop, Cap. There's nothing anyone can do for these poor bastards. They'll likely starve to death.'

You were casting a glance at the disconsolate quartet of civilians. All wore trousers or slacks, were either hooded or had caps on their heads, and were bundled about by greatcoats or blankets. It became apparent that they were all women; the vagaries of conflict and climate had defeminized them. Snow clung to their garments.

'Can't you get them to hospital, Corporal?'

'No way: it's not our business. We're brewing up soup for them; I'm dividing K-rations between them. Best we can do. They don't speak English. Got to press on. Say, is Europe always like this? This goddamned weather?'

'Could be worse.'

He looked at you curiously, taking in your drawn features and the dark shadows under your eyes. 'You're the first Limey I ever spoke with, man to man. How's London town these days? Does London look like this motherfucking dump?'

'Thank God, no. A few doodlebugs coming over, otherwise we're okay. Where are you from?' Your breath formed in clouds about you. It was a pain to talk.

'Little old place called Blackfoot in Idaho. You know it?'

''Fraid not.' You grinned at one another. 'You ever heard of Walcot?'

The American gave a laugh, shrugging a beefy shoulder.

He said, 'You Limeys sure did a great job, holding off the Jerries all on your own for years. Mind if I shake your hand?'

You shook hands.

'What a goddamned fucking mess this war is. These Europeans will never recover.'

'It'll be spring some day. So we hope.'

He gave a shuddering laugh. 'I'll believe that when I see it.'

You clapped him on the shoulder; then you were on your way again. The villagers, swathed in what covering they could muster, remained where they stood; unmoving, conserving energy, turning into snowmen. The tanks rolled. The ambulance and its miserable cluster of humanity were left behind in the white distance.

There were five of you in Tank Chubby, as the men called it. You were in the lead Churchill with two more tanks making slow progress behind – just the three tanks of the squadron still moving. With your upper body exposed to the elements it was perishingly cold. Again, the snow renewed itself to blow in with an idle mercilessness. You had to keep wiping your goggles clear with a gloved hand.

The freezing wind rose to a howl. You were heading up a slight hill, crowned by a number of broken black poles which had once been trees, when your DR scout came roaring back to you. He slid to a halt by your tracks. A steady Yorkshireman with a boy's face, his name was Gould.

'Three Tigers over the hill, Sir. Don't seem to have any sentries posted.'

You gave the signal to kill engines. German Tiger tanks fired 88mm shells. Your guns fired 77mm shells.

'Guns pointing this way?', you asked.

'Two of them, yes, Sir. Third tank – well, could be burnt out.'

You signalled back to your sergeants in the rear tanks, saying to the despatch rider, 'We'll do a recce, Gould. You come with me.'

You trudged up the slope, the DR beside you. A young man with a bony, blistered face, capillary veins picked out in red by the chill; unseasoned, but obeying orders without question.

Around you lay the great ruinous landscape – all that was left of what had been Europe, as if cultivation had never come here, as if no man had ever inhabited the territory. To one side, patches of hedge showed black and grey, like tawdry body hair. Tanks had ploughed down most of the hedge, snow had blown in and covered the tank tracks. Distantly, the side of a barn showed; it too was without colour. It had been burning; now only strands of smoke – you smelt the taint of them – blew from its remains, thin as spiders' webs, wavering close across the spoilt land.

Yet one thing lived. From a broken branch, a thrush, its feathers torn by gale, uttered pure notes of song. To your mind came a fragment of a poem, to be instantly dismissed in face of the immediate peril:

... some blessed hope whereof he knew
And I was unaware ...

And what do you consider caused this desolation?
Well, the rise to power of Hitler. You mean the root causes?
The unfair peace terms forced on Germany at the end of World War I.
'Root causes' go much more deeply than that. Down to a fundamental
design flaw.
What do you mean by that?
With adventurousness, inventiveness, the will to succeed, goes a deep-
seated aggressiveness in humankind. Which is to be regretted.
Now you tell me.

You and the despatch rider flung yourselves down when you got to the dismantled trees. You crawled forward through two inches of snow. Your world was filled with noise, drowning out the song of the thrush. The wind screamed, loose and broken branches clattered above your heads, shaken as if by a gigantic animal.

You peered down at the enemy over the crest of the slope. It was clear the Germans had not heard the approach of your tanks, had not placed any look-outs. They were making a racket in their own right: a man in overalls was swinging a sledge-hammer, evidently trying to realign the shoe of a tank track. A group of men in grey Wehrmacht uniform were standing round, trying to light a fire.

While you were watching, one of the soldiers threw a mug full of what you judged to be petrol on their smouldering pile. Flames sprouted up from splintered wood, momentarily illuminating the faces of the men, then died as quickly as they had arisen, even before the men could warm their hands at the blaze. For a moment there had been colour in the scene.

As the DR had claimed, one of the Tigers was out of action. It had been hit and looked as if it was burnt out. The other two tanks were temporarily unmanned.

Cupping your hands round Gould's ear, you told him to stay where he was, on the look out, while you brought up the lead tank to the attack. He was to signal if the Germans showed signs of alarm.

Doubled up, you ran back to Tank Chubby. You had a four man crew and told them to prepare to open fire immediately the signal came. You gave the order to move forward. The Churchill crunched up the hill with agonizing sloth, doing under two miles an hour. Dusk was coming on, the snow fell more thickly, almost horizontally. Air was raw in the throat. You gained the crest of the hill and the DR jumped up, afraid of being run over.

The tank being repaired was in your sights: you bellowed the order to fire. The shell exploded on the casing just below the Tiger's turret. The soldier with the sledgehammer was hit by flying metal, and fell with his face smashed. The other Germans yelled and ran in all directions. You took aim and fired your service revolver repeatedly, almost without thought. Two men went down. Another shell exploded close by the other tank. The soldiers stopped running and raised their hands in surrender, faces turned anxiously towards you. Visibility was growing worse by the minute; as you switched on the searchlight, your two accompanying tanks rolled up.

'Well done, Sir,' said Sergeant Breeze. He ran up smartly and saluted. 'They must have been dreaming. Shall I get their guns and round 'em up?'

You told him to do that, and went slowly down to confront the surrendering Germans, your revolver at the ready. Your entire being was focused on the situation. You considered that this encounter had been so simple because some of the Wehrmacht and these Panzer teams had already decided that they were defeated, perhaps understanding that Hitler's orders for the Battle of the Bulge had proved his final mistake.

Yet many other armed groups fought on to the bitter end, with amazing courage, when all was lost.

You stepped over one of the bodies of the men you had shot, lying face down in the snow. Driving snow was already beginning to cover his body. Five men stood before you apprehensively, hands above their heads. They had bunched together. They seemed not to have any fight left in them. Their faces were thin and drawn. They had not shaved. All appeared to be in their sixties or seventies.

Your detachment stayed by their machines, on the rise, commanding the situation. The stand of mutilated trees, black from the western side, appeared white from this side. Only the DR and now Sgt Breeze stood beside you.

The sergeant said, 'We can't take no prisoners, Sir. Better shoot 'em on the spot, right?' He showed every sign of eagerness, facing the Germans aggressively.

'We can't shoot them in cold blood.' You thought, of course blood is cold in this bloody weather.

'That's what they'd sodding well do to us,' said Sergeant Breeze. 'No two ways about it, Sir.'

'Maybe, Sergeant, but we're not Germans.' Possibly it crossed your mind that you were fighting to preserve your way of life against the brutish Nazi way of life. It was certainly clear, as your sergeant had said, that it was impossible for you to take prisoners.

One of the Germans, a man with sharp grey eyes and cadaverous cheeks that were almost as grey, said, in English, in a faint voice, 'We surrender, good Sir. Please not to shoot us.'

You were in two minds about that. Killing in wartime was no murder. Indeed, your CO had commanded you, as a duty, to kill as many Germans as possible. Hatred and fear of the enemy would see to it that you carried out the order as thoroughly as possible. And yet, now that the war was almost won, these primitive drives, although fortified by official command, were losing something of their force.

'Why should I not shoot you?'

He put a trembling hand up to his jaw as if to steady it. 'I am family man, Sir. Please –'

Had you drowned as a small boy on the sands of Walcot, no murder could have been proved in the case. Nevertheless, your parents would have been guilty of murder. It seemed to you it would not be greatly different if you now despatched these old men standing helpless before you with their hands in the air: you would be guilty of murder, at least in your own eyes.

Trying to make up your mind, you stared at your prisoners. They had dropped their gaze to the trampled snow. Their faces were expressionless. One man had a trail of snot running from his nostril to his chin, about to freeze. A miserable group: conquerors turned victims.

Only a minute beforehand, you had shot dead two of this group without a moment's thought. It was absurd to argue that those soldiers had been in any way different from these remaining alive; they remained the hated enemy.

What was different – yes, something was different – was that you were no longer fighting to survive. You were now in control. You had the power of life and death over them, the power to decide. You would not be swayed by your sergeant. You must be swayed by your conscience. You came from a better way of life than did these old men.

'What have you fuckers got to say for yourselves?' Breeze asked the Germans.

They looked at each other. They did not know how to answer. 'How many innocent women have you fuckers raped and murdered?' Breeze poked his weapon at them.

Still they stood there, hands raised, as if mummified. One said, with his teeth chattering, 'Please to spare us. We are just soldiers like you. Made to fight. *Krieg ist schlecht.* War *ist* bad ...' The wind carried the words away.

'You started the fucking war,' Breeze shouted. Breeze was a big solid man with blue jowls, a leather sleeveless jacket over his uniform. He was pointing a Sten gun at the Germans.

Yet still as you stood there in the gale, revolver in gloved hand, a part of you, an atavistic part, lusted to kill your captives, to see them fall bloody to the snow – after all, they were part of the

214

nation that had buggered up your life. You could shoot. Why not? It would suit Breeze. You would be regarded as a hero, Mentioned in Despatches … Breeze would go home and tell them about you; with admiration. 'He shot the fuckers, just like that.'

Here in this howling wilderness, there was no law – only the law of strength and will. You understood that, without giving it a thought.

But. The idea came that if you shot these five men now, the scene might haunt you ever afterwards. You might replay it in your dreams over and over in succeeding years: the men falling, clutching their chests, soiling themselves in their pain, kicking out their death throes on the ground – perhaps another bullet needed there – the revolver having to be reloaded – stains of blood and urine in the tumbled snow – the men somehow in your dreams never dying – always continuing to die, their jaws agape, their faces ghastly.

Squeamishness rather than mercy, you complained to yourself afterwards, convinced you not to shoot your enemies.

'All right. Put your hands down. Stand still.'

You came to a decision. You told the DR to drop grenades into the turrets of each tank, 'just to make sure'. You were shouting to make yourself heard. When Gould did as ordered, the tanks flared up like small volcanoes. You ordered Breeze to search the captives and disarm them. He moved in upon them, rough as could be, throwing papers, cigarettes, pocket knives, from their pockets out into the snow as he searched them and took their weapons. When this was done, and the tanks still blazed in a lacklustre way, Breeze, looking grimly at you, asked, 'How about taking their greatcoats, Sir?'

'No. We'll simply leave them here and press on.'

'Orders say to kill the enemy, Sir. With respect.'

'Fuck the orders, Sergeant. This bloody war is almost won. These old bastards – Have some pity.'

'Right, Sir.' He stood looking at you, broad, raw face blank.

You contemplated the sorry group of prisoners. You said to them, 'You know that the Third Reich is defeated, don't you?

215

Defeated, *verstehen Sie? Dritte Reich kaput! Untergang!* The Russians are across the Oder and already on the outskirts of Berlin.'

The German who had first spoken English now said, 'Please, Captain, Sir, to make us prisoners! Else we must starve.' In his haggard face, his lips were livid.

You ignored the request. 'You are free men, whatever that means. You're bloody lucky we didn't kill you. Don't push your luck.'

As you made your way to the shelter of your tanks, Breeze called back angrily to the helpless men, 'Give my regards to Adolf!'

They stood there in the howling snowstorm, defeated, still not moving, not knowing where to move to.

'Poor bastards,' you said. You holstered your gun and made your way back to Tank Chubby.

Then you continued on the way to Erve.

5

Endless Carnage

The darkness was punctuated by lights. The ground was a churned mess of snow and mud: 'mashed potato and gravy' Wood called it. Vehicles were everywhere, some parked, others still arriving. From the REME sheds came noises of hammering and drilling. Ugly shapes of artillery were visible through the murk, light sliding down their barrels. Men were everywhere, briskly walking alone or marching in file. Shouting went on. Never an army without shouting.

The cold of winter still held you in its grip. You crunched your way over the smothered ground. You had but two thoughts in your chilled head: a meal now, and the drive for Cologne on the morrow. As you crossed to the officers' quarters, you passed an Other Ranks Mess, from which singing issued, 'While there's a Lucifer to light your fag, Smile, boys, that's the style …' You thought that many of the singers singing that sorrowful old song would not know what a Lucifer was. The lower ranks of the British Army preserved as fossils words and phrases elsewhere forgotten. These men remembered the old Great War songs, finding themselves in roughly the same situation as their fathers. *Pack up Your Troubles* was a folk-memory, precious in its doleful English optimism.

A marked feature of the rendezvous at Erve was that so many lights were showing, their beams criss-crossing in the snow. The Luftwaffe was at last defeated; it was claimed that more than three hundred German aircraft had been shot down on New Year's Day alone. The RAF and USAF now ruled the skies – when the weather permitted them to get up there. It could not be long before the long weary years of war would draw to a conclusion and Germany would capitulate.

'Thank fuck for that!' you said wearily to yourself. You longed for it to be over.

Having stashed your kit away, you entered the officers' club, a temporary accommodation in a hastily converted mansion. Groups of four or more men sat round tables, talking in subdued voices. At a table alone sat Major Hilary Montagu, a whisky by his elbow.

About him was still the aura that marked him out, at least in your eyes, as Hilary Montagu; but the few years that had passed since you last met had greatly changed him. His hair, cut in close military fashion, was almost entirely grey. His face had lost the healthy complexion which owed something to his years under the Indian sun. His nose was red and appeared to have swollen where its surrounding flesh had sunk, a change perhaps attributable to an increased intake of alcohol.

You stood before him, coming to attention. Since Montagu wore no cap, you did not salute. 'Good evening, Sir.'

He looked up at you, giving no sign of recognition. 'I'm off duty,' he said. 'Don't talk to me.' He then began a disquisition: he stared down at the battered tabletop as he spoke. 'Don't talk to me. I'm busy getting drunk, thanks. I once had a bungalow in Lahore. You knew where you were then. What I wouldn't give for a curry.

The Germans never took to curry, did they? That was where they went wrong. What I wouldn't give for a keema mattar right now. Go away, Captain. I'm busy drinking myself stupid.'

You said that you were Captain Steve Fielding. 'We were together in France, Sir, just before she fell.'

He stared at you rather drunkenly. 'Fielding! Christ, I didn't recognize you. You've grown a moustache. You look a hell of a lot older!'

'I am a hell of a lot older.'

'The damned war does that to us all … Sit down! Have a drink.' He reached out a hand: you shook it. He summoned a mess orderly to get you a whisky – and another for himself. You sat yourself down. 'I'm glad to see you again, Sir.'

'Didn't mean to be rude just then. Half-pissed. I look a whole lot older myself, I'm fully aware of that. The war grinds you down, endless carnage. These Krauts never give up, do they? I got a look at a Top Secret signal to SHAEF that reckoned the Yanks have lost upwards of twenty thousand men just this year alone, dead or captured. Carnage. It's insane.'

There was a wild look about him. His eyes darted here and there, never resting, as if seeking out a hidden enemy.

'Looks like it'll soon be over, Sir.' You lifted your glass to him.

'Can't be soon enough. I long for my bowler hat.' Something fixed and dead marked his gaze when he brought it forcefully to your eyes. 'Steve, we are trapped in a Breughel painting. A Breughel painting; artist who painted life as it was, not as it might be. There may be no end to this war, Fielding. It's all very well for Roosevelt to say British suspicions of Russia are unfounded. Once we've licked the Huns, we are going to have to fight the Soviet Union. You think it's cold here? Try Moscow!'

These things he appeared to be saying to himself.

He started up again. 'Steve, you know the Russians are far more ruthless than we are. The Germans are far more ruthless than we are. Or better coordinated. Or better indoctrinated, or something.

Why are we making such slow advances? Why aren't we mopping up the resistance and in Berlin by now?' Again the eyes flickering here and there.

As he took another gulp of his whisky, you said, 'Is it really that bad?'

He chose not to answer the question. 'How many tanks have 30th Division lost? Enemy fire, land mines … If the war stops for a moment, I'll be off. Go and live in the South Seas, like Paul Gauguin. I've had enough of the bloody whites, Huns or Frogs or English rozbifs. Or Yanks, of course. They all cause trouble wherever they go, the lot of them.'

'I'm sorry to find you so pessimistic, Sir.'

He gave a scornful 'Ha!' 'Pessimistic? No. Just appalled. I'm dead, Fielding. My soul has died within me. This eternal fighting, this endless carnage. What we're expected to endure.' He paused. 'Well, Steve, this isn't soldierly talk.'

It would have been trite to offer him consolation, even if consolation were to be had. You drank your whisky and called to the orderly for more.

'Trapped in a Breughel painting, yes. "Hunters in the Snow". Brilliant artist: Breughel knew what misery was all about.'

'I believe he must have lived somewhere near here, Sir. The Lowlands. We must be somewhere near Antwerp.'

'Near Armageddon, more like.'

You both slurped your whisky. You could hardly think.

'The painters, artists – good men, all. Had something better to think about than killing other men. The British had no artists in India. They were just interested in ruling the Wogs. That's what they implanted – no culture, read nothing. Sapper. Bulldog Drummond …'

Montagu evidently realized he was rambling. He fell silent, marshalling his thoughts. He rested his elbow on the table before him and his forehead in his hand, his gaze cast down at the stained surface of the table. Then he spoke in a level voice. 'But that's all past. All bally well past … We've got to push on tomorrow, before first light. We plan to push down the road to Cologne. I thought you were dead, old boy. Did you ever get to – Rennes, was it?'

So you started to tell each other your stories.

When France fell, Major Hilary Montagu and Captain Leonard Travers had attempted to walk to the Spanish border. They had reached Toulouse, only about sixty miles from the frontier, when they were arrested in a bar. A Frenchman shot one of the gendarmes arresting them, and was himself shot. Another man had joined in and Travers had been accidentally shot and wounded. Montagu managed to get away. He had crossed into Spain and had eventually been repatriated. Travers had not been heard of again.

'I sometimes wish I had stayed put in Spain. I met a young woman in Barcelona; a wonderful, lovely woman, Monika. A mulatto. Came from Buenos Aires originally. Always had a weakness for dark skins …'

He smiled and nodded to himself, his talk of going to live in the South Seas forgotten. 'I may go and look for her after this stinking war is over, if ever. No hope of getting back to Lahore: I'm too old for India service. Besides, we're giving India away. Monika's probably married by now, to some lucky bugger.'

In what you regarded as a drunkenly sentimental gesture, Montagu felt in an inner pocket and fished out a wallet. From the wallet he extracted a photograph of Monika. 'Have a dekko, Steve, old man.'

It was a black and white study that had been hand-coloured. You stared at an ordinary-looking girl with a string of beads in her hair.

'I've got a girl,' you said. 'A real peach. Her name's Abby.' You knew you were getting drunk. You did not care. The feeling of wildness, of losing control, was benevolent. You lit up a cigarette – one of Montagu's – and the two of you indulged in reminiscence: reminiscence of better times you had enjoyed, although the misery of the present cast a cloud over both past and present.

You were rather boastful about your affair with Abby, claiming a longer continuity of loving than had in fact been the case. You

221

did not mention the sexual episode with your aunt, alternating as you did between pride and shame at that affair: that salient point in your emotional life possibly marked the true dawn of your adult life.

And what had it meant to Violet? Was it something vital for her being or something merely incidental? Such questions were so difficult, you could not pretend they were in some way answers, and presented them to your senior friend simply as sexual conquests to be chuckled over.

But Violet was bound to burst through. 'Another woman I know. Got a kiddie who is going to be on the BBC – an announcer, she said …'

Thoughts of love and conquest, as the whisky went down, came increasingly to preoccupy your mind, while Montagu was telling you about what he termed 'the wily Afghan' who could steal a sheet from under you as you lay asleep, without waking you.

A red-haired man, another major, blundered up and sat himself down heavily at your table. He was clutching a whisky bottle, from which he took frequent sips. He and Montagu knew each other; he made no attempt at that drunken hour of evening to introduce himself to you.

'I've about had it up to here,' he said, in a Glaswegian accent. 'The bloody vehicles are falling apart faster than we can repair them. Men are falling apart as well. I'm i/c REME here,' he said, by way of explanation, addressing you. 'What I canne understand is why in hell the Germans don't pack it in. They must ken they're licked, yet still they go on bloody fighting.'

'You're right, Jock,' said Montagu. 'The Wehrmacht has been absolutely gutted, yet still they resist. The common soldier obeys his officer instead of throwing down his bondook. You have to marvel at them; they're fanatics. That's why I say the war will never end. Endless carnage, endless carnage –'

'Aye, it will continue on until doomsday,' said Jock, with gloomy relish. 'Disasters like Arnhem dinna help oor cause.' He said in an

222

aside to me, as he helped himself to a cigarette from a silver case, 'I was with First Airborne then. The fools dropped us at Nijmegen, ten miles or more from their bloody bridge.'

'I heard about it,' said Montagu, gesturing to the mess waiter for more whisky. 'Monty was to blame for all that.'

'Looks like the Russians will take Berlin before we do,' you said.

A lieutenant was entering the room, carried in on driving wind and snow. Shouts demanded he close the door.

Jock told you how he had spoken to a colonel who had been seconded to liaise with Zhukov's First Belorussian Front. He described the Russians as a ferocious rabble, advancing, killing and raping, while loaded down with loot – which included china lavatory bowls made by Royal Doulton, the likes of which no Russian had ever seen before. 'When we've knocked off Hitler,' Jock prophesied, 'we'll have to join up with the Germans and fight these bloody Russian barbarians.'

'It'll go on for ever, endless carnage,' said Montagu, lifting his glass to his lips. 'It's the death of the human spirit …'

The colonel commanding entered the mess, spruce and aloof, a man with a fine head and florid complexion, his backbone unbending. As he approached your table, Montagu, the Scottish major and you stood to attention.

He said in a friendly way, addressing Montagu and ignoring you, 'It might be a good idea to get some shut-eye, Hilary, don't you think? We are scheduled to push on for Cologne early tomorrow.'

'I'll see to it, Sir,' said Montagu. 'Will you have a goodnight drink with us, Sir? We were just talking about the Russian army.'

Without saying yes or no to the invitation, the colonel stood there rigid, not unfriendly, still unbending. 'We have to be grateful to Stalin and General Zhukov for killing off so many Germans on our behalf.'

The red-haired major showed no sign of appreciating this remark. 'Should we no be pressing on for Berlin, Sir, at a grander rate, don't you reckon?'

The colonel inclined his head in an odd way. 'We have our orders, Major.'

You were delighted when, as you parted from Jock and Montagu, Montagu seized your hand, shook it warmly, and clapped you on the back. Meeting up with him again was some compensation for the discontinuities of wartime. You staggered off to your separate rests.

Next morning at first light, the revving of engines began as you were finishing your plate of bacon and eggs.

'A spot of shooting in the night, Sir,' said your batman. 'About three hours thirty, it was.'

You nodded. 'Nothing to write home about.' You had heard nothing.

The batman was extraordinarily young. Britain was running out of seasoned warriors.

The parade ground was full of blue smoke when you appeared. Sergeant Breeze marched up and saluted smartly.

'All present and c'rect, Sir, ready to roll.'

Roll you did. The wind had dropped, the snow had ceased. It was a drab morning, drab but calm; heavy cloud enveloped the wartorn world. There were few impediments to your way. Vehicles found abandoned in the road were pushed over to one side. The desolate countryside was as empty as the moon.

The Germans seemed to have withdrawn in good order.

By late afternoon your convoy was crossing the bridge over the Rhine and entering the ruins of the city of Cologne. Major Montagu, standing in the lead tank, turned and raised a gloved thumb to you.

Not a house was left with its roof in place. Some buildings still smouldered, smoke drifting from gaping windows. Not a soul was to be seen in the suburbs of that great city. Once, a dog ran away in front of you, only three legs functioning. Distantly ahead, the spires of Cologne Cathedral rose. The cathedral alone was intact amid acres of rubble. You recalled that a man had joked that the cathedral owed its preservation to the fact that it was what the RAF had been aiming for.

Your trucks ground noisily over the broken road surface. You turned into a broader avenue; a ruinous office building, possibly six stories high, stood to your right. You caught a movement in a gaping shell hole, high on the fourth floor. You called a warning. Immediately, our bazookas were firing – off target to begin with.

Machine gun fire burst from the building. Out of the corner of your eye you saw that Montagu was hit. He flung up an arm and fell forward.

Almost at the same moment, the wall of the enemy building crumbled and fell across pavement and road, smothering you all in clouds of dirt and dust: a 77mm cannon had scored a direct hit. Your tanks were forced to halt. You climbed down and ran to the lead tank. Hilary Montagu was dying. His right shoulder and half his skull had been shot away. His blood flowed across the armour of his tank. It seemed his gaze met yours without seeing you. He gave a convulsive jerk and then he died.

You closed your eyes and buried your face in your hands.

Sgt Breeze came and respectfully escorted you back to your tank. So you drove on into the ruinous heart of Cologne.

6

Kiss Whom You Like

The war was over. After six years of struggle, the war was over. The struggle had been won. But at appalling cost.

What had been lost, although it was not immediately apparent, included many British investments overseas, especially in South America; chimeras of white supremacy in the East; the illusion of British supremacy almost everywhere; a kind of courtesy that transcended class barriers; the decline of some class barriers themselves; the release of tenure over what had been a *de facto* autocracy rather than a democracy, to which was related the disappearance of 'the respectable British working man'; the mistaken belief that Josef Stalin was any kind of benevolent 'Uncle Joe'; the beginnings of British disarmament, coupled with rearmament as the Cold War set in; the Home Guard, stood down without pay or ceremony; the hope that the end of war heralded a period of peace and calm; the crumbling of the Third Reich and the opening of the Nuremberg trials; the disestablishment of Shintoism in Japan and that country's surrender finally closing World War II; over five hundred thousand British nationals killed or wounded; the death of Franklin Delano Roosevelt; the seeping away of feelings of comradeship which had supported the British during their long struggle; the transformation of jazz into bebop; the waning of a decent English pessimism, together with the expectation that things would always stay as they were; the disappearance of family magazines; the failure of many British comedians to adapt to a new age, such as your old favourite, Billie Bennett, master of the once-prevalent style of concluding his act by spouting comic monologues: 'Her name was Wong, and in her sarong, She was blacker than blackest night. Her father had been a Royal Marine, But two Wongs don't make a white.'

These losses, many of which were to emerge only as the years wore on – as well as your personal grief over the death of your respected friend, Major Hilary Montagu – were as nothing compared with the joy of hard-won victory, after the long, slow grind of war. The crowds of people who surged down the Mall to congregate about the statue of Queen Victoria and cheer the Royal Family on the balcony at Buckingham Palace had no thought but to celebrate. The tribe was giving forth its last hurrah! Many Fieldings were among them.

You had received an airmail letter from Sonia:

'My dear brother,' she wrote, 'I was glad of your support when I rolled home some months ago, a bit the worse for wear. Just wanted to tell you that the big A went okay and I am not haunted by any Valerie replacements, thank G*d!

It has been a bit chilly in Hong Kong this last week. Even the whores have been wearing fur coats. So no early morning swims – if eleven o' clock is early. Now it is getting warmer again it's magic to be in HK. Away from f—ing Europe. I never dreamed …

We are the first group of actors to return here. A final bunch of the Japanese army were shipped out only four days ago. The city is very dilapidated and food is short, but we are okay. I have just eaten a gorgeous, massive egg fu yong, which is naughty of me just an hour before our matinee. It's wonderful to be here and I feel very privileged. I have a big part in *Worm's Eye View*. Not so big in *Hamlet*. One reason why I prefer modern plays to the classics. I realize I was awful in *Henry V*. Hope I'm improving.

I'm putting in for a part in *Sweeter and Lower* at the Ambassador's. Have you seen it yet? They say it's v. funny.

Hope you're getting lots of promotion!

Love,

Sonia'

Only two weeks after her letter arrived, Sonia was back in England and standing with you near the Queen Victoria Memorial in the heart of London. *Worm's Eye View* had enjoyed only a brief run in Hong Kong.

Both of you were among the crowds facing the palace on that great occasion, together with members of your family, your parents, Belle – no longer silent – and Ada, with her little girl Betty; Jeremy and Flo; Archie Hillman; and two members of the Frost family, Joy and Freddie. Freddie was now a large and attractive lad. As you shook hands with him, he said, 'I've missed the big show, Uncle', with some regret.

Several males among your relations were still in uniform, serving in other parts of the globe. You too were still in uniform.

People were milling about, aimlessly, happily, waiting for the Royal Family to reappear on the balcony. Freddie produced a mouth organ and began to play a lively tune, *The Kerry Dance*. Belle gave a cry and, seizing Martin, began to dance with him. The nearby crowd moved back like a tide, allowing them a small circle in which to dance. You seized Joy and danced with her, ignoring protestations from your injured leg. Then strangers too were dancing. Freddie switched to *I'm Going to Get Lit Up When the Lights Go on in London* and suddenly it seemed that everyone in the great crowd was singing and dancing.

There'll be love and there'll be laughter
And there'll be no morning after,
'Cos we'll all be drunk for months and months and months.

Laughter then, and great waves of happiness. You had survived. You had all survived. God bless you all. You and Sonia hugged each other. She was looking well after the short stay in Hong Kong.

The Royal Family appeared again on the balcony of the Palace. With them was the Prime Minister, Winston Churchill, waving his famous cigar to the crowd. The Queen waved and smiled. The poor old king did his best. His daughters, Elizabeth and Margaret Rose, waved in a dazed way.

How you cheered! How you loved them all, at least for that golden hour. They were The Family, the very symbol of British family life. How different, as someone remarked, from the grim old man in uniform who had so mesmerized the German nation.

'Oooh, isn't that young princess pretty?'

'Margaret Rose, you mean?'

'No, the other one, the taller one, Elizabeth.'

'Liz, we call her.'

Oh, the applause! The waves of joy! The war over at last! It was hard to believe. The war was actually over. Germany had been defeated.

Finally, the Royal Family departed indoors.

'Bet they're going to have a stiff gin.'

'Winnie will stick to whisky, I bet.'

'We ought to have a drink and a bite to eat.'

'Yes, if we can get through this scrimmage.'

A young sailor in a sailor's hat was pushing past. He suddenly seized Belle and gave her a resounding kiss on the lips. She returned it.

Mary was shocked. 'Really, Belle, don't be so common! That's not like you at all.'

'Oh, shut up, Mary! It's VE Day. I'll dratted well kiss who I like.'

'Whom you like, kiss whom you like,' said your mother, offended.

You all fought your way to a crowded little café just off Trafalgar Square – a cheap little café, your mother complained – with a large framed photograph of Winston Churchill hanging on the wall, but a haven nevertheless, air blue with cigarette smoke. A group of men in evening dress with women in elegant gowns had pushed some tables back and were dancing on a small floor space to the music, blasting from a radio, of Geraldo and his band.

Your mother asked the owner what there was to eat. He gave her a beaming smile. 'We run out of everything bar chicken sandwiches, love.'

'We'll have chicken sandwiches then.'

The way she said it struck everyone as comical. Your father ordered cups of tea. You protested – you wanted something stronger.

'Coming up,' said the owner, spreading his arms wide as if to emphasize his powers of hospitality. 'Agnes, dear' – to the waitress – 'tea for these ladies and gents.' He turned and rattled glasses and bottles temptingly together. Gins were served along with the cups of tea.

'Wish Auntie Violet was here,' you said, leaning rakishly against the counter and sipping the warm gin. 'Aunt Violet's such fun.'

'Oh, we don't want her.'

'Yes, Violet's fun,' said Freddie. 'Lovely woman.' He grinned and winked at you in a way that made you become deeply reflective.

Belle threw back her gin. 'Fun!' she echoed, with a scream. 'Blinking bloody fun!' She rushed to join what she called The Posh Party, shouting to Sonia to join her in the dance.

'Here I come, boys!'

'Oh, here she comes,' one of the Posh shouted, opening his arms to her. 'Magnificent! A redhead! We're in luck, chaps, Cleopatra in person.'

The radio was blaring. Soon, somehow, you all became engaged in the dancing. The light, the floor, the noise, the faces, the smiles, the shuffling feet – all shared, all contributed to the universal wave of joy as Geraldo blasted away – 'Don't sit under the apple tree, With anybody else but me …'

To your astonishment, Mary, after a second gin, had taken the photograph of Churchill off the wall and was kissing it. A lot of kissing was going on everywhere in the little confined space, amid cries of 'Whoopee!' One of the Posh ladies swung her necklace above her head.

Now Geraldo was playing *You are my Sunshine*. Everyone knew the words. Everyone was singing along. It was almost midnight.

'You are my sunshine, My only sunshine …'

The owner of the café hammered on his counter and shouted, 'Right-ho, folks, we've now run clean out of grub. We're CLOSED! I'm going to lock my door and then we'll all have a knees-up. One free drink each on the house; my treat! This is a ruddy historic day, blow me if it ain't!'

Everyone cheered him. Sonia, now promised a small role in *Sweeter and Lower*, as she had hoped, felt herself outshone by her Aunt Belle in the recklessness stakes. She rushed up and threw her arms round the owner, kissing him on both cheeks. 'Oh, you darling man, you darling you!'

The owner squealed in delight. 'Blimey, ducks! Me, I love you all! My dad got the DSC in the last set-to we had with the Jerries!'

'Bet they aren't celebrating much in Berlin tonight.'

'I should flipping well hope not!'

Then they danced. Your father danced. You danced. You all danced. You all sang. Tears filled many eyes. 'Please don't take my sunshine away …'

Ada lifted her daughter onto the counter. She kissed her smackingly on the lips.

'You just sit tight there, darling. You can watch your old mother going crackers for once!' She threw herself into the arms of a

232

stout gyratory person with a waxed moustache. Geraldo roared on. Dorothy Carless sang. 'The streets of town were paved with stars. It was such a romantic affair ...'

People outside banged on the door. No one let them in. No one paid any attention to them. You were all together in that wonderful little café, with that wonderfully generous host. You were British of whatever class and you had beaten the Jerries. You had won the war. You had won the bloody war!

It was a day to remember. The day life began again; no wonder you cried.

'Look, Steve, go and rescue your sister or I swear that man is going to do I-don't-know-what with her.'

'Look, mum, Sonia's a big girl now. If she wants a spot of I-don't-know-what, well, let her. After all, it is VE Day. There'll never be such a day again in the history of the world.'

You yourself grabbed a pretty painted woman to dance with. You too had a spot of I-don't-know-what in mind.

'What's your name?' you shouted in her ear.

'I'm Briony May,' she said. 'And my husband's in Singapore.'

You caught her scent; warm, elegant, carnal.

You were all so happy. It's difficult now to remember how happy.

7

Leaving Home

Another day. More whoopee.

You were dancing the quickstep with Abby in your arms, closely holding the delightful body which was Abby Cholmondeley. Everything was suddenly so modern. Abby was persuading you to take up a proffered partnership in the Acme Furnishing Company, which was currently being established.

'You'd be a full partner with Joey and Terry. The housing sector is booming. You know half-a-million new houses are going up right now? They'll all need furniture to stick in them.'

'Yes, but I don't really get on with Joey and Terry. You know that.'

The music sang away, compelling everyone to dance. The guy wearing evening dress who played the trumpet blew like an angel; *Holiday in Venice*, played in the style of Artie Shaw.

Abby's powder-white face and red lips were close to yours. You could taste the sweet health of her breath. She had joined the WRNS in the last month of the war and was wearing her blue overcoat. Provocative curls sprouted from underneath her nautical cap.

'You want to make money, don't you, Steve, darling?'

'Strike a light, Abby, I want to be a geologist! I don't want to sell furniture.' You were still crazed with passion for her and for that white body which had spread itself out so invitingly on Claude Hillman's bed.

'Please don't use that silly expression, strike a light! You're not in the army now. Acme's a bona fide company, if that's what you're worrying about.'

It was dark now, and those who had visited the Dome of Discovery were now intent on discovering each other.

'Yes, but Lord Lyndhurst is funding it, darling,' you told her. 'Don't forget, Dad's a Labour MP in Attlee's government. He wouldn't want me associating with a rotten old high Tory.'

'Honestly! When did you care what your father thinks? Besides, everyone's making whopping big profits these days. You know Uncle Ben has all that furniture under his control. It's a quick way to make a fortune.'

You were wearing your army greatcoat over a suit and tie. Light rain fell on you, as on the many other couples dancing beside the River Thames. The Festival of Britain had just opened and Sid Phillips and his Band were now playing *I've Found a New Baby*. Briskly, the pair of you gyrated to the music.

In the background stood the recently erected buildings of the South Bank, memorials to the New Brutalism and direct descendants of the spartan artillery casemates still dotting the East Coast, the grim naval fortress in Le Havre, the enigmatic flak towers and hideous observation posts, the personnel shelters, the Atlantic Wall, built by Hitler's Todt Organization, all of rough-board shuttered concrete; but now their wartime purposes were diverted here into peace and music and a single snack bar.

You stayed that night in a small hotel in the King's Cross area, where you slept with your arms round each other and your legs, where your juices had inundated one another, interlocked.

'I hate to say this,' she whispered, 'but you are so handsome. This gorgeous scar on your leg – and just heaven in bed …'

It was indeed something much resembling heaven to be in bed with her – your two naked bodies enmeshed in a physical rapture which seemed inexhaustible. You gave yourself up to her entirely, as she did to you. This was all you ever wished for, indeed more than you knew you wished for, as you clutched and groped the delicious declivities of her body.

Yielding to Abby's persuasion, you went to see Benjamin Wade, Lord Lyndhurst. The old man was reserved and shrunken, propped among brown satin cushions on a large leather armchair. The long, bony face was patched with liver marks. His brain was still working. His agents, he said, had located a munitions factory in the Midlands where were stacked what he called 'a few thousand miles' of steel tubing, no longer required now that, as he said, hostilities had ceased.

'Ideal stuff, tubes, to make chairs out of. Chairs and tables. Modern chairs, chairs that will stack; the up-and-coming thing. I own a factory in Southampton. Ex-army chaps to work there. Woven canvas needed for seat and back. War surplus stuff. Very low cost. Considerable profits to be garnered, and that quickly.

'My niece Abigail recommends you as a young man of probity. I need you to sign a contract here and now. You will help to keep those two young tearaways, Terry and Joey Hillman, in order.'

'I don't think I could manage that, Sir,' you told him.

'Nonsense. You've managed men. You were in the war and the boys weren't. You've been, so to say, tempered in the flame. They're afraid of you. Good businessmen, though. Ruthless, that's what matters. They've got a system.'

He gestured towards your leg. 'You're walking with a slight limp. War wound? Better get it fixed. The Labourites are setting up Beveridge's National Health Service, so you might get it done for nothing.'

You signed the contract. As you were pocketing your fountain pen, Lyndhurst leaned forward to say, 'Of course, you know Claude Hillman? Father of these two lads?'

'I do.'

'A bit of a fabricator, one might say. Told me he owns a race-horse at Newmarket. I checked: he doesn't.'

'I am sorry to hear it.'

His lordship inclined his head. 'I am reliably informed that you are related to Bertie Wilberforce, the architect – or an architect, should I say?'

Your reply was cautious. 'Bertie Wilberforce is married to my Aunt Violet, yes.'

'I know nothing about that. I do know the fellow did a poor job for me, building – or rather, one should say, rebuilding – the Methodist chapel in Southgate. Very shoddy workmanship; mortar fell apart after a year. Overcharged me, too.'

'I'm sorry about that, Sir.'

'Not half as sorry as I am.'

'I understand that mortar is not what it used to be.'

'Huh, nor are architects.'

You returned home to discover your father in his cricket togs, while your mother hovered excitedly around him.

'I'm captain of the Scallywags, Stephen,' he said proudly. 'We're about to play the Hamptonian Eleven. After this game I shall retire from the noble game. I'm forty-five and have more serious matters to attend to. This match happens to be a tradition, you see.'

'I thought you'd be in the Commons,' you said.

Martin narrowed his eyes, the better to observe his son. 'Not today of all days. This is an annual struggle, stretches back over a century. But I may as well tell you I am doing a good responsible job for my county.'

'It's really important work,' said Mary. 'Your father's dead against the CND.'

'Of course,' Martin said. 'Are you fool enough to believe that if we gave up our nuclear weapons the Soviets would meekly scrap theirs? Fat chance.'

Mary started telling you about Claude Hillman, whom she characterized as 'your mad Uncle Claude'.

'I hear he's saying he owns a racehorse.'

'Probably. He does tend to exaggerate.' She said that Claude was one of the CND marchers. He had been demonstrating peacefully outside the American Embassy in London, armed only with a couple of potatoes. The police were stuffing protesters into Black Marias.

'So one of the police says to Claude, "You aren't planning to throw that potato, I hope, Sir?" And Claude says no, he wasn't.'

Martin took over the tale. 'So as the Black Maria starts to move off, Claude shoves the potato into the exhaust pipe. Of course, the car stops; the Black Marias are immobilized.'

You gave a short laugh. 'That was pretty neat.'

'A crime against the state, nevertheless. They collared him and locked him up in the cells for the night.'

'Pleased to hear it,' you said, inadvertently making a move, undecided as to where you stood on that issue. But Martin knew.

'Yes, I've landed a post under the Minister for Health. We're going to transform this country, my boy!'

'Someone suggested I could get my leg sorted out, possibly by the National Health Institute. Is that so?'

'The National Health Service, you mean. Yes, now that Nye Bevan is the Minister, the plan's going ahead. It'll be up and running soon, never mind so many doctors are trying to stop us.'

'You mean to say that all injuries and illnesses are going to be treated for free?'

'That's the plan, yes. Free teeth, free spectacles. The country will become healthy in no time. My job's slightly different; I'm trying to relieve kiddie suffering. There are too many unfortunate children, most of them orphans after the war. Getting into trouble, causing mischief. Some of them probably demonstrating outside the American Embassy. My job is to arrange to ship them out to the colonies to new lives – lives full of promise and adventure.'

'Colonies? I thought we'd done with colonies.'

'You know what I mean. Australia, New Zealand, Canada.' He went into some detail, quoting numbers of orphans and future shipping dates.

'Do these children want to go to Canada?' you asked.

'They don't know what they do want; they're just kids. It's up to us to decide for them. But this afternoon, never mind that, I'm going to knock up a few sixes.'

He adjusted his red cap at a jaunty angle, nodding at you to make the point sink home.

'Good luck, Dad! Hope you score a century. I must pack, I'm going to live and work in London.'

Your father did not ask you what the work was. Instead, he said, 'You can surely spare time to watch your old pop hit a few boundaries, can't you?'

He was attempting pathos, this man who walked with a slight limp – just as you now did, from your wartime injury, he did from his injury in the earlier war.

'Oh, do support us, darling,' said your mother. 'It'll be a splendid afternoon. The WI are doing teas at four o'clock.'

'Sorry, folks, I want to catch the 3.40 train.'

'Why don't you buy yourself a motor car?' Mary asked.

'Can't afford it. Don't need one anyhow, in London.'

You walked slowly upstairs to your room, regretful that once more you had let your father down. You had watched him play cricket when you were a lad, and knew him to be a good bat and no mean bowler. He wanted you to see him exercise his skill. You denied him that pleasure.

You thought your father a mite pathetic. It was a time of disillusion. The nations gaining from the war had been the Soviet Union, now dominating Eastern Europe, and the USA, untouched by destruction, now enjoying a flourishing culture. Britain, aware of its moral virtue as the one country that had stood against Hitler, had emerged from the war impoverished, shabby, weary.

Once in your room, you began to root about aimlessly, uncertain what to take away with you. The sun shone into a corner of the room, where a butterfly net stood. From the box room, you pulled out a trunk with PLA labels on it. From the bottom of a cupboard you dragged out your old school tuckbox, with S. W. FIELDING printed on it in large white letters. As you lifted it on to the bed, your mother entered the room.

Mary Fielding's manner was unusually hesitant. She put a hand up delicately to pat her hair and adjust her bun.

'I – we are so sorry you are leaving home, Stephen. I do hope you know what you're doing.'

You took in her green dress, which reached well below her knees, realizing you had known it for a long while, as you had also known her slightly withdrawn expression, as if she were expecting a blow. The reference to your coming departure was a reminder that there had for long been a stiffness between you. It was a cause for sorrow, yet you could not be entirely clear which of you had first generated it; surely not the small child you had been, dependent upon your mother's good will. Valerie, that prevailing ghost, was to blame.

'Got to go, mother. The furniture business calls!' You attempted a note of facetiousness.

'I'm sad about it. I heard just this morning that a friend of mine, Wilhelmina, was killed when the Luftwaffe bombed Exeter. It was a while ago but I've only just heard. Her sister wrote to me. That horrid war! And now I find you are going to leave us –'

'It's a case of the fledgling leaving the nest, mother, I'm afraid.'

'We thought you intended to become a geologist.'

'Lots of houses going up, mother, all in dire need of furniture. Crying out for it, from Peterborough to Peterhead.'

The forced jocularity quelled her. But she moved forward. Absent-mindedly, she picked at the painted lid of the tuckbox, nerving herself to say, 'Stephen dear, there's always this distance between us. I wish I understood why.'

This was your chance to speak out, to ask her why you as a child had been left exposed to danger on Walcot beach, day after day. Perhaps there was a simple explanation: perhaps she had been unaware of the tidal threat; perhaps she had been too lazy, or too unwell to accompany you, letting you go alone because she understood there was something in your personality which required solitude even at that young age.

So you missed an opportunity. Why was that?
Cowardice? Compassion? How can you stand in front of your mother and accuse her of murder, or attempted murder?
How could you require solitude at the age of four? Surely not?
Oh, there were such distances … I don't know the answer. Do you?
I am gaining understanding. That's the object of the exercise.
You could not ask the question, for whatever reason. Possibly you sensed you would simply be faced by her denial, her stonewalling.

Instead, you asked her what had become of Valerie.

'Who is Valerie? I don't know the name.'

So there was a denial of knowledge.

You confronted her, not as a son but as a stern stranger, reminding her that your boyhood had been burdened by a phantom daughter by the name of Valerie, embodying a perfection neither you nor Sonia could rival.

'Oh, oh, that child! Was her name Valerie? I had forgotten.' She brushed back an imaginary hair from her face. Certainly her facial expression, her whole body language, was as uncomfortable as if she did remember. The sun had moved round, so that it now stained only a narrow strip of wallpaper by the window.

You said that you understood her motherly anguish in losing an earlier child. You pressed her to admit that it had been a daughter. She put a finger horizontally to her lips as if to hush herself. She said that the dead baby had been taken away from her quickly and she had never been informed if it was a boy or a girl.

'It was a girl, wasn't it, mother? A girl you had planned to call Valerie –'

Suddenly her right hand covered her face as she said indistinctly that, yes, it was a little girl, a little girl who had been delivered stillborn.

'My little little girl – Oh, my God –'

She was weeping. You did not tell her what Sonia had told you – that your mother had attended a psychotherapist, the sessions continuing for some years. You put an arm around her shoulders but made no other attempt by sign or word to comfort her as she had her brief cry out.

What would you say about this disproportionate mourning over a long-dead baby, at a time when Britain – and not Britain alone – was trying to come to terms with the horrors of Belsen and Auschwitz, and the deaths of millions?

Why do you bring that up? You were responsible for all that cruelty! Sometimes I am overcome by a terrible disgust of you and your existence.

No, you are not. Those are mere words from your locker. I shall continue.

'I must go to your father,' Mary said, quaveringly, mopping her eyes with a tiny square of handkerchief. 'I've made some sandwiches. You're always so resentful of me, Stephen. I don't know why. I don't deserve it. Don't deserve it at all. After all I've suffered.'

She left the room. You stood there by the bed, scowling with thought, unhappy, disturbed. It seemed that you stood apart from yourself, scrutinizing your own motives. Your reason for not feeling warmth for your mother was perhaps an excuse for your own cold nature, did you but know it. Perhaps she really was a kind woman and loving mother; perhaps it was simple trust in her son that had permitted her to let you play happily on the Walcot beach all day.

For you had been happy there. Perhaps it was Aunt Violet who had poisoned your mind against your mother, poisoned it with suspicion. Your dear Aunt whom you had loved and with whom you had eventually made love, had she nursed a jealous hatred of Mary?

The fact was that you did not understand either woman well enough to free yourself from suspicion, or from shunning both your parents.

You stood there in your room, looking out of the window, staring blankly at the semi-urban landscape: the garden, the hedge, the by-road running past and, beyond the road, tall elms in early leaf, with a line of semi-detached houses beyond.

You turned slowly and began to throw out the contents of your school tuckbox: an old pullover, an old pair of swimming trunks, a wooden monkey that could climb a stick, a paperback edition of *Darkness at Noon*, some once-loved magazines, including copies of *Modern Boy* containing the adventures of Castern of the South Seas. 'He go big sky blong Jesus.'

You were almost at the bottom of the box.

You pulled out some school exercise books, smiled at them, deciding they might as well go. Below them lay a spade. Sighing, you lifted it from its resting place. It was a child's wooden seaside spade, dark in colour, the grain standing out from use, making it look almost like fur. You ran your fingers down from the loop of handle to the blade. As you did so, that primitive sense of touch carried you back in time. Again you heard the ripple of tiny transparent waves on sand, the splash of your own footsteps in warm shallow pools. Again you felt – if only for a moment – the intensity of living free in the sun, totally alone on Walcot beach. Before you had learnt about loneliness.

But there were other things at the bottom of that tuckbox.
I have forgotten.
Nothing is forgotten here. There were fifty-two pencils lying there, unused.

244

Oh yes. I left them in there when I went to London.
What was remarkable about those pencils?
It was when I was in my adolescence – when I was what later was called a teenager. I went through a period of depression. I developed kleptomania. It lasted only for a few months but I could not stop myself. It was just pencils I nicked. As you can see, they're all unused.
You knew what you were doing.
I felt ghastly. I couldn't stop myself. I haunted stationers' shops. I was terrified of being arrested: my parents would have thrown me out of the house. And I felt guilty. But I just couldn't stop myself. I was humiliated to think I was a common thief.
What else do you notice about these pencils?
I never had any use for them. I kept them to remind me of that bad period. Oh, they all have little round rubbers at the top, all fifty-two of them; for rubbing out.
Exactly.

Then you were alone in your room again. The enveloping voice had faded. You were putting the spade aside, preparing to leave home, your usual self again, self-contained.

8
Old Children

The art class at Shirley Warren Grammar was in full swing. Heads were bent over paper, water and watercolours splashed everywhere, broken wax crayons lay on the floor, uncrushed or crushed, spilling little patches of colour on the dull boards.

The arts mistress walked among the desks, prompting or encouraging here and there. She paused by the bent shoulders of Joyce Wilberforce to watch as Joyce worked almost in a fury, now whirling a red crayon, now a black. She asked the child what she was drawing.

Joyce replied with one word, without looking up: 'God.'

She seized a yellow crayon and began making strong verticals.

Not without a hint of reproach, the mistress ventured that no one knew what God looked like.

'They will do now,' said Joyce. She still concentrated on her work of creation, without looking up. She was eight-and-a-half years old.

Why tell me all this?
It is a part of your lifetime.
There's a deeper reason?
Yes.

Both Joyce and her brother Douglas had been forced to leave their boarding schools and attend the local day school instead: expense had thus been saved. Douglas now walked home with his sister when classes were over. They were on reasonably good terms.

This afternoon, Douglas stopped to play football with some friends on a stretch of waste ground. A goal had been drawn in chalk on the wall of a ruined house. Recently, a much smaller goal had been drawn within the larger outline, to make goal-scoring more difficult. Six boys were running about, yelling, kicking the improvised ball. Joyce and a friend, another girl, looked on affecting carefully posed attitudes of nonchalance.

'Goal!' The yell went up. Dougie pranced briefly, shaking his fists above his head, enjoying his prowess. He ran off to join his sister. They made their way uphill through a side alley.

'We're a lost tribe,' said Joyce, assuming a croak. 'Far from home, in a jungle. We've run out of water.'

'Right. And the cannibals are after us.' They hastened their steps. 'We've had nothing to eat for days. We'll probably die. I think my leg's going to fall off.'

A mongrel dog trotted by. 'I just saw a wolf,' she said. 'The jungle's thick with them.'

Dougie tore a branch from a self-planted elder tree. Using it as a stick, bending his back, limping slightly, he said, 'We're old children. We got old during the Crime-Here War. There was rationing but they left us out.'

Now they went more slowly. Joyce extended her hands in front of her as if she were blind, or at least very short-sighted.

'Thousands of years old. I've got sixteen kids of my own; two of them are spastic, worse luck. My eldest is from Jamaica.'

'Night's falling.' Spoken in his wheezy voice. 'It will be a bad night. The native drums are pounding. Blood will be spilt. Like lemonade from a glass – sticky all over the table.'

'I see a light ahead! Saved! I believe it's our camp at last.'

In fact, what they saw was the mauve door of 'Grendon', 19 Park Road. Dougie's stick was thrown aside. Abandoning their roles, regaining their youth, the children scampered indoors, calling loudly for mother.

Violet Wilberforce was lying on the sofa, her feet up on its cushioned arm. She was scanning the pages of the *Daily Mail*. She wore spectacles to read with, removing them to greet her children.

'Back already, kids? How went the day?'

'Can I see Teddy Tail, mum?'

'I am dying for a slice of cake, Ma. I just scored a goal.' They flung down their satchels by her side.

Violet dropped the newspaper by the satchels and got off the sofa. She grabbed Joyce and hugged her. Douglas escaped laughing from her clutches.

Joyce unstrapped her satchel and produced her painting. Violet stared in some puzzlement at the furious black lines, out of which two blue and yellow eyes stared. A big red mouth was open in what was either a smile or coarse laughter.

'Wow, that's pretty strong, darling!'

'It's shit hot, I'd say.'

Violet tutted and wagged a finger. 'Don't use that naughty expression, darling. What's it meant to be?'

'It's the face of God. Can't you see?'

Violet smiled, shaking her head. 'I'm not very religious, sweetie. It's very good. Perhaps you are going to become a great artist.'

Douglas loomed near. 'It's rubbish. Where's the cake, Ma? Anyhow, Mum, why don't you be a great artist? You haven't got much else to do.'

'I wouldn't dream of such a thing.'

Although she laughed, Dougie looked thoughtful. 'Suppose I have a dream that my name is Henry Haircut, when I wake up would that make any difference? Or the world is made of toffee paper, say, there's not a kid that breathes –'

'Oh, do stop your nonsense. My nerves won't stand it,' she said laughing.

'I'm starving, that's why I'm delirious.'

'Delirious, you little scamps! Let's see if there's anything to eat. Dougie, you must have your Virol.'

'Urrrgh! I'll spew up!'

'Don't use that horrid word. And you won't spew, you like Virol. You know you like it. It's full of nourishment. You don't want to get TB, do you, now.'

'I shall spew up. I shall spew over the table and over the chairs and over the carpet. And over Joyce's picture.'

'You little monkey!' She made a rush at him and gave him a spank on his bottom. He fled round the table, laughing.

She went into the kitchen. She called out for the children to see what she had bought. They came to look; it was a new washing-up bowl, brilliant red in colour. Joyce grabbed it.

'Shit hot, Mum! What's it made of?'

'Guess … it's plastic. A new material. Isn't it lovely?'

'Shit hot!'

'What did I tell you about that expression?'

As she reached down the brown Virol jar from the kitchen dresser, she heard her husband, Bertie, coming in, slamming the front door.

As his hangdog face appeared round the kitchen door, the children fell silent, staring at him, waiting to see what came next. He moved forward and sat down at the table, pulling a funny face at Dougie as he did so.

Joyce slid her drawing of God across the table towards her father. He glanced at it before pushing it aside.

Violet gave him a smile and asked if he wanted a cup of tea. When he indicated that he did, she said she would put the kettle on. She showed him the beautiful new red washing-up bowl.

'More expense,' Bertie sighed.

He regarded his children. 'Well, little ones, and what did you learn today?' he asked, speaking heavily.

'I did that painting,' said Joyce. 'Didn't you understand it, Daddy?'

He glanced at it again, before repeating his question.

'We learnt about Henry the Eighth and his boring old wives,' Joyce said sulkily. 'I don't wonder he killed them off.'

'We learnt that the Red Sea isn't red,' said Douglas.

'Don't be rude.' He frowned at Douglas. 'I asked you seriously what you learnt. I want to know.'

'If you must know, we learnt about the Virgin Mary's womb and what it was. It's inside her. And Jesus was inside it.'

He showed no further interest then, watching as Violet cut them both a slice from a Swiss roll. With lowered voices, the children complained about the thinness of the slices.

'It's got to last till Saturday,' Violet said, with a sly side-glance at her husband.

Bertie flared up at once in his own defence. 'You know why we're hard up. You're such a spendthrift. You waste money: and the architectural business has collapsed. No one wants decent designs any more.' He looked pained.

'So that's why you have a menial job in that DIY place. Why don't you get a job in the car factory? You'd earn twice as much. Trouble with you is, you don't like manual work.'

'What about your father's firm? No one wants their lousy lawn-mowers any more. Everyone's buying Atcos.'

'It was the strike that broke him, you stupid fathead.' Violet's father had died recently, after a cerebral haemorrhage.

Bertie spoke more quietly, although still with rancour. He said that he had a brain, and that the owner of the DIY store was a friend – a friend who said that there were good chances of a raise after Christmas. Anyhow, he asked, why was Violet so mad keen to be married to a manual worker? He felt bad, he said, life had not worked out very well. Then he asked her for a cigarette.

Ignoring him, Violet produced a long spoon and dipped it into the jar of Virol. The spoon came out laden with the glistening, toffee-like substance.

'Come on, Dougie dear, you know you like it really. It'll help build you up. You've been looking rather pale lately.'

Obediently, Douglas opened his mouth. As she slid the spoon gently in, she cast an eye at Bertie.

'I'm out of fags. Buy your own.'

In a minute, she handed him a cup of tea. As he spooned sugar into the cup, he sighed heavily, 'It's a hard life and no ruddy mistake.'

'Don't swear in front of the kids,' she told him, 'and try not to make it hard for all of us. You're the breadwinner, aren't you? Drink your flipping tea.'

Joyce had found a drawing pin in the kitchen drawer. She pinned her drawing of God to the wallpaper. 'It's a warning not to quarrel,' she said, virtuously. 'He looks a bit furious with you, Daddy.'

9

Ex-Army Furniture

Your work took you to various parts of the country. This was the aspect of your work you most enjoyed as the years swiftly passed. On a clear frosty morning, you were driving to a corner of Northampton in your Rover, surveying the countryside in the distance.

Acme Furniture was a thriving business. Your factory in Shepherd's Bush employed twelve men, mostly ex-servicemen glad of a job. Money poured in. You collected cheap materials from various sources, bent them, stained them, machine-stitched or welded them together to produce workaday items of furniture which yielded healthy profits.

It was about maximizing this profit that you mainly thought. Whatever the discomforts of the Forêt de la Bouche, you had then been in contact with a living dynamism, as, to a lesser extent, you had been on Walcot's sands – you had lived according to tides and seasons. Even in the bitter chill of the Ardennes in the final months of the war you had experienced how aspects and accents of the natural world affected you. A primitive morality had been enforced thereby.

Remembering the past, you thought of the Geldsteins. Your desertion of them still preyed occasionally on your conscience. That little family should be safe, now that peace had prevailed. You had begun to feel sentimental about that period of your life, now safely over.

Now, moving rapidly, your head full of figures, through a countryside you considered uninvolving, you served merely an economic function.

It was not surprising that you were going astray. We need no talk of morality to understand that in returning to so-called civilization, you had lost something earthy which had been sustaining you.

It is easy to see this in retrospect. I was – let me put it this way, a novice in the ways of society. Doing simply what was expected of me.

Yes, you were weak.

You can say that. Yet I believed I was being strong – and aren't we about to meet a man with whom I was strong and firm? It was difficult to adjust to civilian life after the years of soldiering.

Certainly excuses are ready to hand.

You were about to investigate an ex-army furniture store. Acme was considering buying the contents of the store at a bargain price. You turned off the A5 to a side road, and thence to a track which petered out a mile from the village of Grimscote. You got out of the Rover and began to walk towards some buildings you could see ahead. The going was good at first: there had been a tarmacked road at one time; now grass grew over it.

You enjoyed the walk. Birds were chirping, green fields and unkempt hedges stretched in all directions, not exactly flat, although hardly undulating. Ordinary, extensive, traditional, temperate. This was the usual uninspiring English countryside, which must have left its imprint, you felt, on the English character. Nothing in particular existed on which one might fix the gaze, apart from a church tower standing on a distant and indistinct horizon. Nothing moved, apart from an odd flutter of bird wing.

Strands of barbed wire barred the old roadway farther along. A yellow notice warned that this was WD PROPERTY and that there was NO ADMITTANCE. Although the wire was sagging, it still held something of its old threat. You looked about and found that a path had been worn to one side of the metal post supporting the wire. You followed the path with care; it led slightly downward and the grass was slippery where frost, covering it earlier in the morning, had melted. Now those ordinary green blades gleamed freshly in the daylight.

The ground was uneven. You approached a cluster of buildings, mostly low brick hutments of the kind the military had been building two decades earlier, utilitarian hutments not intended to last or to be comfortable, or even warm. One building stood out from the others scattered near it, a larger structure whose curved metal roof gave it a resemblance to an aircraft hangar. You were undecided at first, but now directed your steps towards this larger building. The grass on the way grew tall and coarse. Something caught your leg. You found yourself falling.

Into a damp hollow you sprawled full length. Your right leg, the leg injured in France, sent out signals of pain. You pulled yourself into a sitting position, and saw your trouser leg had been ripped by concealed coils of barbed wire. When you tried to rub your leg, blood came away on your hand.

'Shit!' you exclaimed.

Once you got back on your feet, you found walking was painful but possible. You hobbled towards the barn.

'Hey, you, what do you do? Halt!'

The shout came. For a moment you could see no one. There were only the deserted buildings, standing solitary in the deserted landscape. To one side was a pile of felled tree trunks, bereft of branches, roots or tops; they were dark with damp. From behind them emerged a man, wielding a stick.

'I'm here on business,' you called. 'I'm hurt. I tripped over some damned barbed wire.'

The stick was lowered as the man approached; a small man, bundled into what had once been an army greatcoat.

'What do you want here?'

'I'm from Acme Furniture.'

'All right.'

He was a tough-looking man in his thirties, with a ruddy face and blue eyes. From somewhere behind him a woman's voice called anxiously, 'Who is it, Joe?'

He reassured her before coming up to you and proffering his hand, saying he had received your message.

'I see you are hurt, sir.'

'It's nothing, thanks.'

A beaming smile crossed Joe's face. 'A very English answer, sir, if I may say it. Do you wish I should take you straight to inspect the furniture storage?'

You were both slightly annoyed and slightly amused. 'A good idea, since that is what I came for.'

'I thought you should like perhaps to sit down and let my woman serve you some coffee.' He smiled inquiringly into your face.

'Thanks, but let's have a look at the furniture first.'

Joe led the way to the large building. Pulling a key from his pocket, he unlocked the padlock and, with a good deal of effort, pulled one of the two doors open to the extent of almost a yard. He led the way in.

Inside the structure it was freezing cold, as if the last of winter had been stored here for some future occasion. Joe pulled down a small lever situated near the door: a series of electric lights came on near the roof, each bulb hanging below a round white glass shade. They did little to illuminate an immense pile of furniture that was stacked high into every corner of the building.

You surveyed the heap with a certain wonder. Solid yellow tables were here, together with filing cabinets painted in camouflage green – though why indoor furniture should need to be camouflaged was a matter for debate – and an immense number of chairs; chairs of a variety of army uglinesses, with metal seats and wood seats and canvas seats, chairs of a now distant antiquity, creations of a now distant emergency. You understood how long ago the war was, even if the wound on your leg had opened afresh.

'There's nothing here we could use. Nothing we could adapt,' you told the waiting Joe. 'This lot's not for us.'

'But the filing cabinets, sir. With a repaint ... say in white, or cream ...'

You shook your head. 'They're far too clumsy for today's use, I'm afraid. Sorry about that. My visit is an utter waste of time.'

He said, 'The Ministry of Defence would be glad to have the place cleared, sir. You would not have to pay a great amount. Sold in the marketplace, sir ... on an open market, sir.'

'We don't work like that. That's not our business. You need a junk dealer for this lot.' You were annoyed that Joey and Terry had misled you in their description of the store's contents. 'New War Department Furnishings, various. Good Condition.' It had proved a fool's errand.

'I give my apologies, sir,' Joe was saying. 'Perhaps you will allow my woman and me to give you some coffee, sir, and also examine your leg.'

After he had switched off the lights and locked up, Joe led you to one of the low brick buildings, as meagre a building as could be designed by the combined brains of military men. You were introduced to Rhona, a woman with an attractive, worn face framed by straggling brown hair. Rhona wore no makeup. She had on a grey shirt with a brown pullover above it, and a pair of jeans. She welcomed you and guided you to a chair by a wood fire where you were able to warm yourself, noting that the chair on which you sat was an old metal army chair, painted a drab green, aspiring towards camouflage. Joe pulled off his greatcoat, revealing that he wore a rough grey wool suit beneath. He rubbed his hands by the wood fire.

The long narrow building contained only one room: a part of it had been curtained off. Rhona dived behind the curtain to prepare coffee. Joe sat himself down opposite you.

'Were you to remove your trousers, sir, I could repair them. My father was a tailor, and I learnt his trade as a young man.'

You had noted his accent and careful elocution, and asked where it was his father practised as a tailor.

After a moment's hesitation, he said, looking at you directly, 'This was in Nuremberg, sir, in Germany. Where the trials are held, sir.'

Rhona came to you with a steaming mug of instant coffee on a tin tray. She explained that Joe was born in Germany but now had British citizenship. 'You may consider we live in a strange wee place, sir, but it pleases us well enough. We had not a penny piece between us, so this job as caretakers suits us well. It's a quiet life, but I was born in a wee hut in the Highlands, so solitude doesne vex me.' She looked at you with her honest clear gaze, seeking your approval.

You smiled at her as you picked up the coffee mug.

'I have a respect for solitude,' you said. 'But since the war I have to struggle to make my way in the world.'

'Och, I fear I have no time for that kind of thing,' she said, with a slight gesture of either apology or dismissal.

'Is it the way or the world you mistrust?' you asked her.

She returned a sad smile. 'Seems I've cast my lot against the both of them.' She added, 'For better or worse, mayhap. My mentality isne fitted for the capitalist world, I'm ashamed to tell.' She hugged herself in the old brown pullover. 'This is a terrible time we're living in, and no mistake.'

'Has your life then been dramatic, sir, may I ask?' Joe enquired, urgent to cover his wife's confession.

258

You were unsure how to answer, but said that everyone's life had been dramatic in one form or another during the war. Joe nodded. Your remark led him to open up and tell something of his story. His father's tailoring business had not suited his adventurous nature. The family were poor. He had joined the German army. He admitted he admired Adolf Hitler at first. What worried him was the way in which crowds of people seemed to be hypnotized by his rabble-rousing oratory. (Joe used the German word, *Pöbel*, for rabble.) He asked, was it something in the people or the language that made them so easily roused?

All the while he was talking, he was stitching the tear in your trousers with neat, small stitches. You watched his rough hands working.

When the war broke out, Joe's unit was posted to Prague. Once the war started to go badly for the Third Reich, life became much harder. He was moved to the West. 'My good fortune was not to be despatched to the East,' he said.

In a pitched battle near Cologne he was captured by the British. Because he was slightly wounded he was taken to a British field hospital. After some days he was sent to England, to a prison camp near Liverpool.

Many of his fellow soldiers, also captured, dreaded bad treatment in British hands, as most had been indoctrinated to believe that this was the fate that awaited them. Joe, he now declared, had no such fears. His grandfather had served in the Great War, and had been one of those German soldiers who had played football with the British troops in No Man's Land at Christmas, 1914; this event had persuaded the family, despite all Nazi propaganda, that the British were decent people. So it had proved for Joe. In the Liverpool prison camp, they had been reasonably well treated. British women had come into the camp to teach the prisoners English.

Joe said, 'I was Josef Richter then. Later I became the Joe Rich I am now, sir, and one reason was because I liked the beauty of the English tongue as taught by those women, with the soft sounds and the hard sounds, different from the harsher German tongue. And I liked the many reasonable utterances I heard in that English tongue. And the uncertainties.'

Rhona said, 'He says the English language is like a good box of chocolates, with hard and soft centres. You can never ken the which you will taste next, but so much flavour is conveyed.'

Sipping your bitter coffee while Joe neatly patched your trousers, you felt submerged in their friendship. You forgot any embarrassment occasioned by sitting there in your underpants with Rhona present.

'But it is your national poetry that won me,' said Joe. 'Nothing to do with military superiority,' said Rhona teasingly.

'I fell in love with Rhona when she recited one particular poem.'

You sat there by the log fire, attending relaxedly while Joe recited.

'Listen! You hear the grating roar
Of pebbles which the waves draw back, and fling,
At their return, up the high strand,
Begin, and cease, and then again begin,
With tremulous cadence slow, and bring
The eternal note of sadness in.'

After the poem they sat in silence. Joe murmured to himself, 'With tremulous cadence slow ...' until Rhona said, addressing you, 'So do you have great expectations, sir?'

'I suppose I do.'

'Maybe it's a better idea to have low expectations,' she said, smiling sadly into the fire. 'That's the style me and Joe keep. We're content the noo, you might say, looking after this load of junk.'

'There's your trousers, sir,' said Joe, handing the garment over, neatly mended. 'Sorry for your accident, sir.'

You were driving away through that uninsistent English landscape, thinking about Joe and Rhona, thinking perhaps that they were all right as they were – surviving, as everyone had to survive somehow. You reflected on their meek submission to adversity, whereas you – A terrible choking sensation rose up in you and you had to pull in by the side of the road.

A welter of tears burst from what seemed like your whole body. There was no way you could stop it. A great misery tore you apart. The Second World War had ended fourteen years previously. You had never really spoken to anyone about what you and your friends had endured; no one who had been actively through the war could explain it to those who had not.

'Oh God, how can you live?' you said aloud. 'I live on sodding autopilot – How can you possibly, possibly – There's no meaning –'

How many had died worldwide in that ghastly upheaval of hatred and struggle? What was the estimate? Fifty-five million was it? Not just in Europe – everywhere: China, Japan … Fifty-five million – the population of the whole British Isles. Probably twice that. How could you know?

Fifty-five million. Falling into mud and shit and darkness … And those who survived; how could life ever be the same?

You sat there exhausted, almost without thought. The torrent had petered out, the storm died within you. You wiped the tears and snot from your face. It was useless to despair. Of course those of the new generation who had not gone through it would never know. Just as well.

'What a fuss you make,' you said in a whisper. 'For Christ's sake, it's a different world.'

You started up the car and headed back towards the A5 and London.

10

A Man About Town

The meeting with Joe Rich took place in the year of 1959, the year that Khrushchev visited the USA. Joseph Stalin had died in the spring of 1953, whereupon primroses had burst into flower all over Siberia. Khrushchev had denounced the terrible leader a few years later, but the confrontation between the West and the Communist world continued.

There was little you could do about the political situation, apart from worrying sporadically. Violet worried for her children; but Joyce was a child no more, and celebrated her twenty-first birthday. The grey and wearisome decade was all but at its end when the M1, Britain's first motorway, was opened between London and Birmingham. 'Good –' said Joey Hillman to Terry Hillman in your presence – you were taking riding lessons, the winter came and went–'Then we can open a branch in Birmingham. Plenty of money to be made in the Midlands.'

'It will be easier to get to Grimscote now, as if anyone would wish to,' you told them. 'But there was an interesting caretaker in the War Department store I visited. A German prisoner-of-war who took British citizenship, name of Joe Rich …'

The twins were not interested. Directed by Lord Lyndhurst, your company was rechristened. You were now CEO of the Britannia Furniture Co. Your friends in the company congratulated you. Slowly people had become more prosperous; many households now boasted a refrigerator and television set, while sales of furniture still held up.

One day in a news report on the TV, you thought you saw the Geldsteins, looking frightened, in a report on unrest in the East End. It was only a momentary glimpse, then they were gone. You wanted to get in touch with them, but were too busy.

You had a pleasant, if cramped, office with two secretaries in Hammersmith, whereas your cousins had larger premises in nearby Kensington, over a furniture showroom. You still found something sly about them, but both acted deferentially, and were punctilious about having your signature on all contracts and cheques.

You now lived the life of a man about town, and saw Abby whenever possible. You believed you were in love with her and that she was in love with you. When your mother became ill with pneumonia, Abby accompanied you to see her and to pay her respects. You were anxious to know what her response was to this different order of being, but Abby suppressed her sarcasm and was sweet and pleasant. However, two hours after arriving at your father's house, a phone call came which summoned her back to London.

'Crisis at the shop,' she said. 'Terrible nuisance. Many apologies, Mrs Fielding, but I must flee.' A kiss on your lips and off she drove in her little MG sports car.

You felt obliged to stay overnight to compensate for Abby's rapid disappearance. You slept badly. When the night paled, you threw on a dressing gown and went to walk in the garden. A light burned behind the curtains in your mother's bedroom window; the sight brought a twitch of guilt and compassion.

But the airs of an early autumn dawn were refreshing. You walked among the conventional arrangement of square flower beds which Mary had created, paying them no attention. In the windows of the distant line of modern houses, lights were beginning to show. A window on the outermost house still had a light burning. It had burned all night, as it had done previously; you remembered it. Presumably it indicated the room of an invalid, constantly in suffering.

As you began to mount a series of shallow steps to the lawn, you saw an animal ahead. The animal was in the act of crunching up the body of what had possibly been a rabbit, its sharp teeth snapping small bones. That was seen in an instant: in the next instant, the animal – a fox – was crouched and looking at you, brush low to the grass, sprung limbs ready to move.

You stood immobile, staring at the fox.

You looked into each other's eyes; the animal's blazed with life. There was no doubt that here was another conscious being, weighing you up. You opened your mouth to reassure it that you intended it no harm. Then, in a single moment, a single movement, it was gone, like a ghost into the bushes.

You walked up and stood where it had been, among the bloody remains in the spot where the kill had taken place. Now the day was lighter; lines of scarlet appeared among clouds on the eastern horizon. 'From a view to a death in the morning.' And you thought of Abby.

Yes, you 'loved' Abby. But there was little that was spiritual in that love, it was mainly lust, compounded by your wish to rise in the world. Like the fox, you had lived a wild life – a life in the wilds. Now you were captive to the capricious young woman. Should you not disappear like the fox, preserving your freedom, since with your admiration of her went a degree of disgust for yourself? It might be because there was no real deep affection between you that the affair – if that was what it was – had tailed on for so long.

The insight was only momentary, then it was gone, hidden in mortal bushes. Of course you loved Abby. Of course lust was involved, and the search for status and stability; it was but a human cocktail. If that was a captivity then so be it.

And you turned your back on the brightening sky, to re-enter the house, where Martin was laying the kitchen table for breakfast.

Certainly Abby Cholmondeley pursued other affairs. She ran a costumier's in Mayfair and often proved vexingly unavailable. You took up with other women, although your interest in Abby and all she stood for did not appreciably diminish. The weeks went by, winter came and eventually faded in a trail of snowdrops, and slowly England became less impoverished, while political uncertainties persisted.

Europe was slowly reforming itself as its nation states sought greater unity. Although the Treaty of Rome had been signed two years previously, Britain had not agreed to it. Under Prime Minister Harold Macmillan, EFTA was formed. Such groupings of initials continued. Although EFTA was no match for EEC, the population was more concerned with weightier concatenations of initials – the USSR and ICBMs.

Even Abby worried about the CND. 'I suppose your strange father is one of the marchers?' she said.

'No, he opposes it. CND has split the Labour Party in two.'

'Oh, good.'

'Of course you are bound to support Macmillan – he's so Edwardian.'

'Yes, Edwardian and civilized. One of the old kind, like Uncle Ben.'

You were always irritated by her political views.

'Where do you get to on your weekends?' you asked her. The two of you were drinking coffee from minute, white bone china cups, in the cluttered room behind her boutique, trapped between a rack of mini-skirts and a spider plant on a tall stand.

'Don't be so nosy, Steve. It's so fatiguing. If you must know I was down in the New Forest, riding. Everyone I know rides.'

'I don't.'

She stared at you, half-smiling, fluttering her eyelids. 'And you don't jitterbug. But you are quite nice in bed … on occasions.'

You almost proposed there and then, but two young women came in and demanded Abby's attention. She became enmeshed in new fabrics from abroad.

Later, you were in your Hammersmith office when a phone call summoned you to the Kensington office. When you arrived, you were surprised to find Lord Lyndhurst there, accompanied by Lady Augusta and a uniformed assistant. Lyndhurst walked with a stick and appeared more bent than he had when you had last seen him. The assistant helped him out of his coat. Augusta wore her usual air of having recently attended a justifiable execution, both grimness and self-satisfaction struggling for tenure on her arid countenance. Her husband was wearing a black velvet jacket with a sprig of rosemary in his lapel. His expression, as he looked about the office, was far less contented than his wife's. Joey hurried up with a chair upon which the lord seated himself, lowered down by his assistant. Joey hovered until Lyndhurst waved him away.

A great fuss was made while a clerk brewed coffee and brought a cafetière to the visitors on a tray. Lyndhurst ignored his cup.

'I am pleased to see you again, Fielding,' he said, without relaxing a vexed expression. He fixed you with his cloudy eye. 'I hear you are doing well. You evidently don't believe in the God of Failure.'

'I know no one of that name, Sir.'

'Bishop Clement's sermon on Sunday – Christian God of Failure. Made us what we are as Christians.' He gave a dry chuckle of compassion for the bishop. 'Lost his Son and all that, don't y'know. Unfortunately ended up on the Cross.'

'Mm, I see.'

'A rather forceful, should I say allegory, for a percentage of our population.' His face retained its contemptuous expression. 'The Bishop's a friend of Augusta's and mine. It's a matter of punctilio, actually, as much as anything, listening to his sermons.'

Augusta said, with some animation, 'Clement probably derives his lectures from eighteenth century books of sermons – of which there are many. The ideas may be stale, but at least it ensures the prose is sound.' It was difficult to determine whether or not she was being sarcastic.

'You probably don't attend Church, Fielding.' His Lordship spoke kindly enough. 'Godlessness having set in. I attribute godlessness to the boredom of Church sermons rather than television, a target for most commentators. The mob can surely be godless without the aid of television.'

'But "the mob" doesn't attend Church any more,' you ventured to point out.

His Lordship ignored the remark, instead raising his stick to indicate Terry on the opposite side of the room.

'I have come here regarding an important, shall I say, deal. Fortunately, Lady Augusta and I chanced to be staying at Claridge's. Less fortunately, your cousin Terry is overcome. Signs indicate that the God of Failure has got to him.'

He glanced up at you with a sort of evil merriment on his face, the milky eye adding to its mischief. You had already observed Terry, who sat at a desk with his head buried in his folded arms, his shoulders heaving as if he were weeping.

'Unmanly display of grief … Well, we'd better get this over with all speed,' said Lyndhurst. 'Joey, bring me the documents and Fielding here will sign them.'

'What's Terry's problem?' you asked.

Lady Augusta looked very severe, as if the question offended her. 'Their poor old dog, Vega, has just died. Faithful hound – sweet creature, friend to man and beast. And Terry is extraordinarily soft-hearted – absolutely adored Vega.'

'What was the trouble?'

'The trouble was that Terry was witness to its death throes' – spoken in a sepulchral voice.

You thought to yourself that you were seeing a new aspect of your cousin. Joey appeared unaffected by the death of their faithful hound, as he now briskly brought forward documents for your inspection.

'He's laying it on a bit thick,' Joey whispered. 'You know Terry likes to act. The sooner we get this over with, the better. You've only got to sign, then we'll take him to Claridge's for a drink.'

The documents showed that a company called Mayfair Holdings Ltd was prepared to buy Britannia Furniture from its shareholders for what you considered an amazingly generous sum. You remarked on this to His Lordship.

'EFTA rules, dear boy. Don't worry.'

According to the document, hastily scanned, the constitution of Britannia would not be altered. The money was to be paid directly into Parson's Banking Corporation, Isle of Man.

As you attempted to read the small print, Augusta went over to Terry, to comfort him. Terry began roaring with grief as soon as her hand was laid on his cashmere-clad shoulder.

'Dead! Friend of my childhood, dead! Who could replace my beloved Vega?'

'Hush, dear, hush. It's in the nature of all dogs frequently to die.'

Lyndhurst was tugging at your jacket. 'We must get the poor confounded fellow out of here. Can't have this noise going on. The balance of his mind is disturbed. Hurry up and sign and my man here will witness your signature. And by the way, Fielding, I understand you are romantically attached to my niece – well, niece-once-removed, Abigail Cholmondeley. Your engagement, if I may employ that term, has continued for sufficiently long. You have my assurance I approve of the match, dear boy.'

'Very kind of you to say so, Sir. I have indeed been romantically attached for many –'

'No need to go into details, thanks all the same.'

A good deal flummoxed by all this, you signed the papers, and His Lordship's man witnessed your signature. Only later did you start to wonder why Lyndhurst had not been the witness himself. Was it because he was the major shareholder of Britannia Furniture? Arthritis in his hand? You continued to feel uneasy, but there were other distractions.

Such distractions included the taking of riding lessons at a nearby stable, and enquiries regarding the whereabouts of the Geldsteins through Jewish refugee organisations and the Salvation Army. You also phoned your Aunt Violet, who sounded low in spirits – her children had left home and her family were all broke. There was your new apartment in Hammersmith to be attended to and redecorated, and a new kitchen to be installed. These and other occupations kept you busy, so that, together with a reluctance to think the sale of Britannia through, you set your anxieties aside.

Isn't that where all your species go wrong? You chase inessentials. Is there no meaning, no deeper meaning, to your life, which, if fully engaged with, would negate entirely all of these lesser worries?
I was caught up in the business of living.
But suppose living is not 'a business'?

11

A Break in Torremolinos

With the threat from the Soviet Union looming like bad weather from the East, the British people were the more inclined to tolerate dictatorships nearer at hand, and to flock to the beaches of Tito's Jugoslavia and Franco's Spain. The dictators of those impoverished states saw to it that charges were kept lower than prices on the more democratic shores in the south of France.

Your Uncle Claude realized that money was to be made out of package tours. Regarding you as a more reliable person than his own two sons, he persuaded you to accompany him to the town of Torremolinos in the south of Spain.

Torremolinos, with a convenient airport nearby, was undergoing rapid development as a seaside resort. Claude – good at drinking and making friends; the two habits often coincide – met a go-ahead young Spaniard, Francisco Lorca. Lorca was about to complete the construction of a large hotel called the Magnifico on the seafront.

Between them, the two men and their lawyers drew up a contract. Not that you were left out of the deal; Britannia was to provide the Magnifico with luxury furniture for its suites. 'Torrid Tours' was the name under which Claude operated. Lorca would receive a guaranteed number of bookings during the season.

The launch of Torrid Tours took place in a suite in the Savoy Hotel, a hotel favoured by the Fielding family. You were detained by traffic on the way there with Abby. The room was brightly lit, pop music played, the place thronged, so it seemed at first glance, with a number of young people, including attractive girls in miniskirts.

You did not recognize your uncle for a moment, although it was only a fortnight since you had been with him in Spain. In that time, he had shaved his moustache down to a thin line and had dyed his hair jet black. He now wore tight trousers and a black leather jacket.

As Claude shook your hand, he said, 'Steve, I am now Justin, okay? Claude is yesterday. Justin is now, comprenez?'

'Okay, uncle, but who are all these amazingly pretty girls you've got here?'

'Not "uncle". Justin. Okay? Just Justin. Justin of Torrid. Try to remember. The Press is here. I've got a gaggle of models – we're giving them a free trip to Torremolinos. Well, almost free. Publicity, you savvy?'

'But where did they come from?'

He took your arm in order to explain confidentially. Until yesterday there had only been women – mainly of the middle class – who dressed as their mothers dressed; dull, stuck in the mud. Now there were oodles of young girls, filling London, from the lower classes, who had their own way of dressing. Miniskirts up to their pert little bums.

'That's sociology, isn't it?' said Justin of Torrid.

Boutiques were opening up everywhere, he said. These girls, these boutiques, were changing London. London was swinging. Social

272

history was being made, and old Justin was riding the new wave. New opportunities, new opportunities … Justin told you all this excitedly.

'Yeah, and you see that chappie over there with a Pentax, snapping away? He's new on the scene, too. And Pentax spells a new view on life, believe me.'

You did not quite believe him, but you were amused.

Justin pointed to a young man dressed as he was, in tight trousers and a black leather jacket. 'Photographers. One or two are Italian. Yesterday these blokes were running pizza parlours, today, it's film. Believe me, Steve, suddenly the future's broken in.'

Abby regarded the scene coldly. 'I see. We're entering the Erogenous Zone. And where exactly does the money come from, to finance this new influx?'

Justin spread his arms wide. 'From the new magazines, of course. From costume designers, from banks, from movies, from commercials. From everywhere. I want you two to go on this first trip. A bit of class, eh? Stay at my expense in the Magnifico. Now, excuse me, I have to do an interview.'

As he hurried away, you saw that Sonia was standing relaxedly by one of the long windows, speaking at a young man holding a microphone within a few inches of her lips. A waiter pressed glasses of champagne into your and Abby's grasps as you crossed over to her. When the interview was over, she dismissed the interviewer and stood there waiting to be kissed. She said that she had been filmed earlier in the week, making a short commercial for Torrid Tours, which would be showing in the Torrid offices. She provided the comfortable presence, welcoming punters who had never left England before.

'And I hear you're going on the first trip to Torremolinos,' she said.

'We may do,' said Abby, cautiously. 'Are you?'

'Good heavens, no. I have a career to pursue.'

You were sorry to realize the two women did not like each other.

*

273

Abby consented to stay in the Magnifico only if you and she did not take the proffered charter flight to Torremolinos. You would travel on a regular flight, and in First Class.

'Don't be difficult, Abby, sweetie.'

'Not difficult, discerning.'

You arrived in Spain in mid-afternoon and took a taxi to the Magnifico. Heat shimmered and every dwelling was brilliantly white in the sunshine. In Torremolinos, a building site greeted you. The structure created to date was nested in bamboo scaffolding. Like the famous glass of water which is either half-full or half-empty depending on the temperament of the observer, the Magnifico was either half-finished or half-started.

'Don't go away,' Abby said to the taxi driver.

Concrete mixers were working, and men were uncertainly perched on the scaffolding, while derricks carried breeze blocks up to their level. Suites of Britannia furniture, delivered punctually as arranged, withered in the heat in what in due course would become the hotel car park.

A shabby blue coach arrived as you stood there rather helplessly, taking in the dismaying sight. From its doors poured the freeloading vacationers, models, photographers, maids and other servants. Francisco Lorca rushed from the grandiose entrance of the Magnifico to greet them, hair and arms flying.

'There is delay only!' he cried. 'Sorry for delay, peoples! Some workers don't work. But you are all welcome and I have many beautiful places for beds in our luxury lounges you will love!'

'But your fucking hotel ain't built yet!' cried one of the leading models, a young lady who went by the name of Barbie Salmon.

'All ground floor is finish!' Lorca cried. 'I invite you everybody to enter in and see it. Kitchen is all but finish. Tomorrow comes in the ovens. My lovely swimming pool is finish and needs only water. Come, please come.'

'Not fucking likely,' cried Barbie, to supportive shouts. 'We ain't staying in this awful dump. Might as well be back 'ome!'

'Let's go,' said Abby to you. No argument. You both climbéd back into the taxi.

What made you think that your uncle's hasty plans would succeed?
We did not realize that Britain was working to a faster clock than Spain, that was all. We were all go at the time.
You were simply swept along by the Zeitgeist.
What else is there, I ask you?
I regret there is nothing else.

A little way down the coast lay quiet Malaga. There you found a beautiful five star hotel, the Casa Bella. Your room was decorously furnished, its windows overlooking a small courtyard. Beyond the tiled roofs of the houses opposite lay the line of the blue Mediterranean, in which you would soon swim together. In the room was an ample double bed, on which you would soon lie together.

If the Magnifico was not entirely a success, Torrid Tours was not entirely a disaster. The craze to go abroad instead of to Butlin's Holiday Camps had hit the British. The Swinging Sixties *Zeitgeist* had arrived. But bigger charter holiday companies emerged like mushrooms sprouting from pasture, and so gradually Torrid was forced, first out to Montenegro, and then out of business.

Justin became your Uncle Claude again, and grew his moustache once more. 'The luck of the draw, old boy,' he told you vaguely, lifting his glass. 'Chin chin!'

12

The Disastrous Party

You and Abby were riding together, for you had progressed that far. You sat a fat well-fed mare, obedient and lazy, named Belinda. Abby announced that she was throwing a dinner party for Uncle Ben in two weeks' time. Uncle Ben would be eighty; the party was designed to celebrate the fact. She invited you. You said you would be happy to be there. By this time you were living – as Sonia eloquently put it – high on the hog, as indeed on Belinda.

'Then you can give a hefty donation towards the wine, Steve. Now that you're rich.'

You had no inclination to dispute that claim with her. 'How about my aunt, Violet? Can she come? She's rather down in the dumps at the mo.'

She looked at you, chin down, her beautiful eyes half-hidden by the peak of her hard hat. 'Your Aunt Violet? Awful name; is she common?'

'By your standards, most people are common.'

She laughed. 'At least she doesn't wear miniskirts, I assume. A bit dismal to drag your aunt along, isn't it? What weird vibes! Okay, though, if you wish to do so, I suppose it's kosher.'

She dug her stirrups into the flanks of her mare and was off at a canter.

You, perforce, followed.

So Violet Wilberforce attended Lord Lyndhurst's disastrous eightieth birthday party. She had bought herself a smart new gown for the occasion, and decked her neck with a double string of pearls. You hugged and kissed her and led her before Lord Lyndhurst to be introduced. It was the 12th of March, 1962, and Abby was staging the event in Gracefield House, his lordship's home, on the grounds that her own apartment was too tiny – she called it 'teeny' – for such an event.

'Do you happen to be any relation of one Bertie Wilberforce, m'dear?' Lyndhurst asked Violet when they met, showing his old tarnished teeth in a ferocious smile.

'I am married to Bertie Wilberforce.'

'Bad luck for you, then!' He gave a throaty chuckle. He was standing, propped up by an ebony stick over which he leant to say, 'He's a confounded poor architect, I'll tell you that! I hope for your sake he's a better husband than he is an architect.'

Violet gave a brittle smile. 'If he wasn't I wouldn't tell you.'

The retort amused the old man. He nodded considerably. He said, 'I see he can afford to deck you out in expensive dresses. No doubt you look, shall we say, better in that dress than out of it.'

'That's something you'll never discover, you cheeky old so-and-so!' She spoke without anger, half-laughing.

At that response, he gave a wheezy chuckle. 'Well, you're no chicken, you saucy monkey. Good luck, anyhow.' He turned to greet his next guest.

A lot of men stood about, faces lined, though not exactly old, as yet. They wore smart, unostentatious suits, made by discreet tailors. Some held glasses of kir or wine; others stood with hands behind their backs, alert but unspeaking.

You looked into a small side room, furnished with worn leather furniture. Claude – late Justin – Hillman was there. He acknowledged you with a curt nod and an inflection of his right eyebrow downwards, without removing his gaze from a television screen.

You asked him what he was doing at the Lyndhursts' party. Again you got the inflection of the right eyebrow.

'I'm on a roll, Steve,' he said, from the corner of his mouth. 'Confidential. Something new coming up …'

The Lyndhursts had a favourite Irish wolfhound, a great grey thing, thin and melancholy, with a pronounced backbone. This visitant was allowed to prowl among the guests, tolerating a pat here and there, to which it responded with a cautionary display of teeth, not unlike its master's. Abby made a fuss of the monster, who yielded his grin up at her, his tongue lolling.

'Chancellor, you dear old ghost! You're all a dog should be!' She introduced you to Chancellor; the hound was judicial at best.

The meal went cheerfully. The men who had waited for something revealed themselves to be good trenchermen, having little to say unless it was about the state of the stock market. With the venison was served a Château Miaudoux, Côtes de Bergerac. You had paid for it, as you had for the Laurent-Perrier Champagne. Lyndhurst ate little of each course but drank heavily.

He called to the wolfhound – 'Chance, here, old feller!' Chancellor appeared inclined to beg, but Lyndhurst told him it was demeaning to beg, and fed him a large portion of pheasant from his plate.

Making an exception for a lord, the men present moved round the table by one place for the dessert, in order to sit with fresh partners.

'How does Macmillan suit you as PM, Uncle Ben?' Abby asked.

His wife, Augusta, answered immediately, while Lyndhurst was drinking his wine, which trickled down the outside as well as the inside of his throat. Augusta showed her large false teeth as she spoke.

279

'Oh, Ben worked with Harold,' she clattered, 'when Harold was Parliamentary Secretary to the Ministry of Supply. They got on well, both being reformers, don't you know? You must remember that, Abigail.'

'Before my time,' Abby replied cheerfully, blinking her blue eyes at the thought.

'Nonsense, child,' Augusta added. 'There are some scandalous goings-on behind the scenes, but then, when weren't there?'

Lyndhurst set down his glass, continuing to clutch its stem. 'I hate the light-hearted way Harold behaves; not becoming in a Prime Minister; it sets a bad example to the country. I hate football,' – the table fell silent, as if familiar with the catechism to come – 'I hate the peasants who play football; I hate the idiots who attend the matches. I hate this new, so-called music, now being played. I hate English food; English seasides; the coarseness of English manners; the clothes English people wear; the way they agree with everything; the way they argue all the time; the cheekiness of the lower classes.'

The sting of this last remark was drawn by his wink at Violet as he spoke.

At this juncture, Chancellor, the Irish wolfhound, rose up and set its paws on the table, to stare up mournfully at its master's face.

'And most of all, I hate you, Vega!' Lyndhurst said, striking it on the head with a spoon.

As the dog sank down, Abby called out, 'Oh, Uncle, that's Chance! You know it's Chance! Vega has been dead for five years or more.'

You noted that.

'And the English – the way they talk, talk, talk.' He wiped his chin free of saliva, leaning forward to bang the table with his spoon for emphasis. 'We used to sail the seven seas … The way they talk – they're letting some of these bally oicks on the BBC now. I hate their jokes; their habit of swilling beer; "the pub"; their women; their ghastly little ill-mannered children; their aunties!'

Here, he again shot a not ill-natured glance at your Aunt Violet.

Violet put an elbow on the table and leaned across to the old man. 'The pale worn face of the English aunt is the backbone of English society!'

'Is it now?' He looked at her, smiling quite affectionately. 'Well then, get your elbow off my damned damask tablecloth!'

He continued with his disquisition.

'Above all, I hate ... well, I hate their elbows; their hotels, of course; their nasty, noisy motor cars – Morris, of course – that car manufacturer; George Orwell; Malcolm Campbell – why does he want to go so fast, I ask you? Their motion pictures; these, so-called "modern", plays – Ashburn's *The Entertainer* – *sheer* filth! The Americanization of everything! Give me the good old days before the war, when Britain was a stable place – let's admit it – fit to live in. I hate this National Health Service; I hate the French, with their superior ways; can't stand the Welsh; Lloyd George and all that ...'

As he ran out of breath, Abby said cheerfully, 'I expect you hate being old too, Uncle?'

He gave her a withering look, before saying in a low, growling voice, 'And I hate the young above all. It's an unnatural state of being, a pre-imago ...'

Everyone was looking anxious, when Lyndhurst burst out, 'Good Lord, I must be drunk, talking like this. Get me some more of that Armagnac, Reg!'

Reg, the butler presiding, poured half-an-inch of the golden liquid into His Lordship's brandy glass. The guests talked among themselves.

Among the diners sat the Bishop of Lymington. His plump face was full of smiles as he flapped a hand towards Lyndhurst, to say, in an unctuous way, 'I really don't think you believe a word of what you are saying, Ben. You're far too kind-hearted.'

Lyndhurst looked at the bishop from under his eyebrows. 'Do you believe a word of your sermons, Clement? All this business about our God being a God of Failure –'

'It was a metaphor,' the bishop responded, sounding rather disappointed. 'Failure is an honourable estate, like Marriage –'

'Utter balderdash!' exclaimed His Lordship. 'You might as well say indigestion was a – what did you call it? – an honourable estate …'

'So this is how the other half lives,' said Violet to you, *sotto voce*. When you assented, she added thoughtfully, 'Or perhaps it's just the state of being old, of decaying, when you hate everything that is alive and living … Poor old bugger.'

'You stood up to him well, Auntie.'

Eventually, the guests moved to the blue sitting room where, as Violet said, a pianist played Chopin and others played bezique.

Lyndhurst showed signs of flagging; Augusta was winning a hand at cards and asked Abby to escort her husband upstairs to his bedchamber. Abby linked her arm with the old man's and led him to the foot of the stairs, where he stubbornly insisted that he was perfectly capable of climbing them alone.

'Of course, Uncle. It's your birthday, do as you wish.'

'I saw Queen Victoria, don't you know? A fat little personage …'

He went slowly from stair to stair, gripping the banister rail, in part hauling himself up by it. Abby stood at the foot of the stairs to watch his progress.

'Got a photo of her somewhere,' he muttered, as he went. 'Somewhere …'

When he reached the topmost step, he let go of the banister. He tottered. Abby called out. He reached for the rail again, missed it, and fell backwards. He fell the whole length of the stairs, over and over, to land huddled at Abby's feet.

She screamed in horror. 'Uncle! Uncle!'

You came running. You knelt and lifted his lordship's torso; his old white head fell back, his mouth fell open. He gave a last sigh and was dead, neck broken in the fall.

Some of the dark-suited men gathered about his body, hands behind backs again, bowed slightly forward in the manner of vultures awaiting a feast. The bishop came and crossed himself.

'Sands of time have run out for old Lyndhurst, what?' said Claude Hillman, his tone of voice suggesting he hoped to lighten the gloom of the atmosphere.

Abby supported herself against the carved newel of the stair and wept. Augusta and other women came in a flurry of skirts as you wrapped your arms about the shaken girl.

'This marks the death of Old England, ma'am,' intoned Reg the Butler, who had been swept along with the tide of womanhood.

'Unfortunate,' intoned Augusta. 'Unfortunate in the extreme … It's not like Ben …' The bishop took her hand, but she pulled away from his clutch.

Chancellor the wolfhound threaded its way between the legs of the guests standing around, to sniff at its master's body. It lifted its old grey head to send a long howl echoing through the hall.

13

On the Grand Canal

You were dreaming that you were addressing a great audience on a serious subject. Inevitably, you began by including elements of your own life, but then seemed to go on to say of the universe that, even if someone gave humanity an explanation for its existence, humanity would in fact be unable to understand the explanation.

A huge figure rose in protest from the front row of seats.

She spoke: 'But Stephen, I'm your mother …' It was a withering condemnation. At this statement, a murmur rose from the audience. She continued, 'You never spoke like this when you were a boy.'

'Of course I didn't,' you managed to say, before the whole audience rose against you, roaring and laughing you off the stage.

You awoke.

What a terrible embarrassment! What a betrayal!

And it was the day, at long last, of your marriage to Abigail Cholmondeley.

The ceremony took place in St George's Church in Hampstead, shortly after the Cuban Missile Crisis. The crisis had prompted you to press her, just as, nine months later, there was a sharp rise in the birth rate, also prompted by that same crisis.

'I'm not getting married in the provinces, darling,' Abby had said.

Abby's parents were divorced. The reception was held in her father's home in Parson's Walk, where Nigel Humphrey Cholmondeley lived in some comfort. At this time, his ex-wife, Eleonora, was living with him.

The reception was lavish, with two hundred and eighty guests attending. Furniture had been removed from the room, although the walls remained hung with popular modern British painters such as Graham Sutherland, John Piper and Edward Burra. Among the guests, Wilberforces, Hillmans and Frosts made a good showing. Violet and Bertie were there, together with their adult offspring, Joyce and Douglas. Violet was wearing a new, floor-length amethyst-coloured dress. Belle Hillman had entirely abandoned her earlier mute period and was now being vivacious with a young blonde man called Roger Knee. Joy and Freddie Frost were not speaking to each other, but cheerfully barged into the conversations of others. Claude and Ada Hillman dressed up for the occasion, and strove to accompany their offspring, Joey and Terry, who were industriously touring the territory.

You asked Claude what he was doing now.

Ada answered for him, with a strong tone of disapproval. 'He is running a model agency.'

'How's it going, Uncle?' you asked.

'About as good as if I was the only model available,' he said, with a lopsided grin. 'These young females aren't easy to handle.'

'Then why are you always handling them?' snapped Ada, not expecting an answer.

Your mother was present, looking rather more human than in your nightmare; but Martin had refused to come to the reception on the grounds that the Parson's Walk house was a citadel of Toryism and it would never do for him to be seen there, occupying, as he did, his current position.

Eleonora, Nigel Cholmondeley's ex, was a smart, yellow-goldish kind of person, her coiffeur very smooth, merging almost undetectably with her skin, which was of the same tint. Her eyes, being heavy-lidded, sheltering dark golden eyes, gave her a languid air. She carried a remote resemblance to Abby. Eleonora was being charming to you, taking you about with a hand on your arm and introducing you to various noteworthy guests on Abby's side of the family. Among these guests was a ruddy-faced man in his sixties who resembled a prosperous farmer. His name was Oliver, an uncle of the bride.

He removed a cigar from his mouth to speak.

'Delighted to meet you, and congratulations, old chap,' he said, shaking your hand. 'You're taking on something, you know. Dear little Abby had an unsettled childhood; she's wayward, that's what.'

'Oh, she's not that bad,' said Eleonora, smiling, but sounding a cautionary note.

'Worse, dear, worse,' said Oliver. 'In the manner of all young women, of course'

At that moment, a young woman came up and proffered a dish of canapés.

'"And the silken girls bringing sherbet,"' Oliver, quoting, intoned.

'They're stuffed olives, Sir.'

Chuckling, he waved her away.

He said to you, 'I bumped into Tom Eliot once – tedious fellow, good poet though. I've come over to England especially to see my niece get hitched. My home's in Tuscany nowadays. Can't stand the English climate, y'know. I speak fluent Italian, of course; well-connected ...'

Eleonora said, 'Not as fluent as you think, *mio cognate*!' Turning to you, she said, 'Oliver's a bad boy. Oh, as what one calls a callow youth, he was pally with d'Annunzio, that terrible Fascist womanizer.'

With leisurely gestures, Oliver relit his cigar, using a pink-tipped match.

'Eleonora dear, you malign poor Gabriele! He was a literary man, a great protagonist of the arts. When he was ruler of Fiume, didn't he have the Sitwells to stay? I was there at the time, selling him a horse. He promoted the career of Tamara de Lempicka, remember.'

'He seduced her, you mean,' said Eleonora, waving cigar smoke away from her face. 'Tamara was young then and, oh, d'Annunzio was an ugly old man! But he seduced all the women. He was insatiable, a lecher of the first water. Second water, too, come to think of it.' Turning to you, Eleonora said, 'But his palace! Oh, it had been the home of the daughter – I have forgot her name – of Ricardo Wagner and Cosima Liszt. When I stayed there, I had in my quarters a dark blue bath and bidet. There is no such romantic place in this austere little island even today.'

'I suppose not,' you said. You had never heard of the people of whom they spoke.

You and Abby honeymooned in Venice, where you asked her who Tamara de Lempicka was.

'Oh, some bygone painter,' she said. 'Was she art deco style? Anyhow, a real degenerate – slept with everyone she painted, man or woman … including my mother.' She laughed. 'And that was just for a pencil sketch!'

'Did your mother get the sketch to keep?'

'Such scandalous lives in those times. It was what the English escaped to Italy for, from Byron and Shelley onward.'

'Yes, but was Lempicka a good artist?'

'That's like asking, was Byron a good poet!' Abby threw up her hands a little way. 'Oh, it's so tiresome not to know anything!'

You were in a vaporetto, chugging slowly along the Grand Canal towards its exit and the approach to the island of San Giorgio Maggiore. Both of you had about you a wild and windy look, although nothing but a slight breeze, product of your progress, ruffled Abby's hair.

You quoted Byron, to even the score. '"I stood in Venice on the Bridge of Sighs, A palace and a prison on each hand; I saw from out the wave her structures rise ..." What comes next?'

'Look!' Abby exclaimed, pointing to a building on the shore. 'There's the humble little Bauer Hotel! How lovely is the lacy stonework. Isn't it dainty, Steve? Who, long dead, can have had in mind such a design, and translated the thought into stone? Oh, there's the Rezzonico Palace – wonderful; in itself a world masterpiece. But why are you bothering about de Lempicka? She's old and unimportant. Her sitters are golden dummies!'

'I know Byron says of Venice, "The pleasant place of all festivity, The revel of the earth, the masque of Italy."'

'Why a mask? Look, feast your eyes, my darling Steve, that's the amazing Ca' Foscari, built in the fifteenth century. So fine, so delicate, so strong! It alone makes the fifteenth century worthwhile, I'd say. A truly magnificent façade, don't you agree?'

You agreed it was magnificent. The opium the hall porter had sold you both was taking hold now. 'Better than anything Uncle Bertie ever built.' You burst into laughter at the thought.

She was waving her bare arms about in a frenzy of expression. 'And when you think – all these buildings, artworks in themselves, contain so much artwork. Venice is a treasure house. There is more artistic merit on the banks of the Grand Canal than in all Britain ...'

'Artistic, yes okay, maybe, but religiosity too; overwhelmingly. I was impressed by the Tiepolo frescoes – that was different – on the ceiling of – which church was that? So many damned churches ...'

'The dei Gesuati.'

'There in those Tiepolos we saw pure form, pure colour, a sense no other artist conveys – a sense that there is a kind of divinity latent in the human race to which we can all aspire. Nothing religious ... maybe sacred. Aspiration; it means breathing out, doesn't it?' – you were talking wildly, not necessarily to your bride, trailing one hand in the grubby water rippling by – 'Certainly this great city of grime and stinks and magnificence encourages that belief. Thank God I am not bald. It would be a disaster not to have hair in this bejewelled city. A sin; a single sin.'

Abby lay back in her seat, sighing, her breast rising with the lift of her heart. 'Here is where what is mingles with what ought to be. All these remarkable canvases, depicting holiness in the richest Renaissance robes ... Richest Renaissance robes ... Why did we fall away from such standards? What can the modern world offer half so fine? Plumbing, of course; showers. Perhaps all these holy people stank. Europeans have such sharp noses. Why do you think that is? Negroes and Chinese have flat noses. Chinese don't smell, do they? Maybe it's sharp noses that have made Europeans so great. The Medici had big conks, didn't they? Big conks; big cocks ... sniffing, smelling out injustice.'

'How funny that rude words are all four-letter words.'

'Anglo-Saxons ... their words. They must have been rude all the time ...'

You pulled yourself up and nestled against Abby, tasting a square inch of her delectable neck.

'But Venice is a living memorial – well, not living, but you know what I mean – to injustice. Just to in justice.' You were not especially intelligible. 'For every patron of the arts there must have been a hundred labouring peasants and gonorrhoeas – um, gondoliers – men with hardly a pair of trousers to their name. The Italian tongue, the tongue, is so rich, full of words, of course, but most of those who speak it are so poor. I mean, you wouldn't really want to live here, would you, sweetheart? As Granny does?'

'There's another language; the physical language.' She slid a slender hand over the zip of your slacks. You took absent-mindedly to kissing her lips and the shining red lining of them. You said between kisses, 'Oh, the physical language – the physical tongue ...' You found you were stroking Abby's thigh, more from familiarity than philosophy. 'The dialogue of cock and cunt is the only true tongue; it must have come first.'

'You come first, darling.'

'I'm looking into it, as I'm looking into this fascinating part of you. Practice makes perfect. Ah, your grand little Grand Canal, here it is. I suppose we could have a screw here on the boat, right now, couldn't we?' You had your hand up her skirt and were gently rubbing the treasures you found concealed in her panties, as a miser polishes up his jewels.

'We're getting to the mouth of the Giudecca,' she murmured, vaguely. Her eyes were closed. 'Oh, oh, yes, that's it ...'

While you kept rubbing that teasing little spot, you were giggling and repeating, 'The mouth of the Giudecca, the mouth of the Giudecca ...' You paused for a moment in your hospitable ministrations to sniff with your nose and lick with your tongue your entrepreneurial finger. 'The old world had to give place to the new, and to you, lovely darling delicious you! I'll buy you an ice cream and you shall practise gelatio on me! You saw that canvas by Francesco Guardi, painted towards the end of the eighteenth century. It's called *The Ascent of the Montgolfier Balloon*, and there you see depicted our unjust friends, the Venetians, dressed up in rather ropey finery, gawping upwards like peasants' – with your other hand, you felt the delectable balloonlets of her bottom – 'as the hot air balloon ascends over the Giudecca. It's the new technology taking over, as it's taking over and over today.'

She wriggled, squeaked, sighed, impervious to your lecture. You rubbed the faster. You slipped down on your knees and kissed with merited fervour the seat and throne of her pleasure.

The boat forged on. It arrived at the much-quoted mouth of the actual Giudecca. It swerved to starboard. Before you, across the frothy waters, the island of San Giorgio loomed, the phallic tower of the church beckoning its saucy visitors.

'If only this journey, this voyage,' you said, laughing, 'this little sea trip, this excursion up the excursible, could go on forever ... or rever ...'

14
Elizabeth Sips
Her Wine

But of course it did not go on forever. Later that evening, you had a slight falling out, as newly-weds will, as surely as the tide turns. At *Frühstück* next morning (for there were many German tourists in the hotel) you were still feeling slightly aggrieved. You phoned Belle, your father's sister, and received from her your grandmother's address in the Calle Galina. You then made your excuses to an ominously silent Abby, and set off alone to see Elizabeth.

Since her husband had died, Elizabeth Fielding, now entering her eighties, was accustomed to spending some months every year in Venice. She stayed in the apartment of an old school friend, Dorothy Barnstable, who had made a prosperous marriage and who, at this time of year, went with her husband – whom she met only in the spring months – to stay with him and multitudinous friends by a lake in the Tyrol.

Elizabeth was attended by her friend's staff – two elderly matrons and an elderly man who, with his broad, bent back and wispy beard, reminded you of a Tiepolo caricature. The staff made it plain that they preferred Elizabeth to their employer, although whether this was because they simply enjoyed a change of dictatorship or were genuinely fond of the virtuous Elizabeth was never made clear, at least, not to Elizabeth, who preferred uncertainty to decision.

When you arrived, rather hot and tired, wearing a ludicrous straw boater which you quickly removed, your grandmother was sitting on a balcony in a capacious basketwork chair. A glass of white wine stood by her right elbow. The balcony overlooked the narrow-waisted Calle Galina, which fed distantly into the lagoon. As you came into her presence, Elizabeth set down a small, leather-bound volume she appeared to have been reading, entitled *The Variable Powers of the Human Mind*.

She was wearing a patterned satin jacket over a white cotton dress. Her white hair was beautifully dressed, with a dark velvet ribbon. She appeared, without much moving, somewhat pleased to see you. Music played softly in the background – if not a Boccherini string quartet, then something Boccherini-like. You settled yourself down on a second, inferior, basket-work chair. After a glass of white wine had been ordered for you, Elizabeth removed her spectacles and, indicating, with a languid hand a paperback book on the table beside the one she had been reading on the powers of the mind, began by saying, 'I would recommend …mend this book to you, Stephen … Stevie. You observe I have a … back … I have a paperblack. Oh, back is what I mean to say. Because … this is a paperback because … simply … because it is lift. More easy to lift.'

You noted that her speech impediment had grown worse. It may have been a good pair of Italian corsets that assisted her to sit so upright, yet Elizabeth seemed much the same person she had been a few years ago, when you and she had last met. A striped awning overhead shaded her delicate skin from the sun. Her face was bone pale, without make-up; her features were still sharp, unblunted, though blotched, by age.

'I have at home of course ... of course I have at home a hardcover. I possess a hardcover copy. The title is *The Museum of ...* Well, you can read. Read it yourself. *The Museum ... The Museum of Forgotten Memories ... of Unconditional Surrender*. By Ugreši. Dubravka Ugreši, yes. It is a memorable shattered ... a record of a shattered life. A memoir, I mean. In a way. A history of Eastern Europe. In a way. As all ... yes, really, as all our lives have been ... I mean, shattered. As yours, too. Yours has been.'

'In a way, yes, Granny. Shattered, I suppose, but we are accustomed ... I mean, that's how it is.'

She considered the remark. 'That's not artic ... not really very articulate.'

'I hadn't thought about it, Granny.'

She looked sternly at you; she had a flinty gaze. 'Here, you call me ... you call me Elizabeth. My name ... by my name, Elizabeth. I may be ... old. Though I am ... I yet possess a name.'

'I'm sorry, Elizabeth. I called you "Granny" only as a mark of respect.'

'No. You didn't. You are too old. I am too. Old.' She took a small sip from her glass; the wickerwork chair creaked as she moved. 'I shall become more old. The mornings ... it's in the mornings ...'

A silence fell. She sighed and smiled at her grandson.

'So what's this book all about, Elizabeth?'

'I told you. It is a ... it's a record of a shattered ... a somewhat shattered life. The English don't understand ... they don't understand the enormous ... What happened in Europe. At all.'

'I see ... No, perhaps we don't. I'm sure there's much in what ... in what you say.' You nodded then, vaguely upset that you could find nothing more exciting than agreement to offer her. You knew her for an intelligent woman. You found, in your need to meet with your grandmother, that you were almost imitating her way of speech.

'A book by my contemp ... my contemporary, G. F. Stridsberg – Franzi, she calls herself. *My Lives*. No, no, *My Five Lives*. You read it must. Perhaps you people don't any more. Don't read, I mean.'

'Yes, I do.'

'Then read *My Five Lives*. In order to stand Europe ... understand Europe. Wonderful, various – and the Balkans ... Most interesting. The English know nothing. Ignorant ... of such matters, nothing.' She took another sip of her wine.

'We are an island race, I must admit, and therefore insular.' Her lecture made you gloomy – her lecture and the truth of it.

'I don't care for the place. I like ... like Italy. Venice.' She closed her mouth and clamped her shallow jaw shut, to gaze out with a blurred, hazel gaze, at the canal and the waters beyond. 'Not to stay, of course. But to, what is it, visitair ... to visit. I miss my cats.'

'Cats really have no nationality.'

She asked after Abby's legacy, but you had no news on that to offer.

You sipped your wine. In the silence that followed, a snatch of song could be heard from the canal below. 'Sonia has the part of Isobel in an important production of *Measure for Measure*,' you told her. 'She's often in films.'

After a while, Elizabeth said, 'I met her. Ugreši Dubravka. She was passing ... just last year ... through. And Franzi Stridsberg once. Here. Very smart. Oh, very smart. Now I read John Ruskin. His Stones. You know, of Venice.'

You had nothing to say to that. You reached out and clasped her hand, which lay like a withered leaf on her lap. To your astonishment, Elizabeth immediately broke into song, to sing in a clear, small voice without the hesitations usual to her, 'And when I grow too old to dream, Your love will live in my heart ...'

You were moved. 'Are you happy here, Elizabeth?'

The wrinkles of her face elasticated themselves. She made a noise like a chuckle. 'Happiness? That question ... That's a young man's question.'

'Aristotle says that happiness must be earned by achievement.'

296

She was still grinning. 'Aristotle. I don't … I know nothing of his thoughts … thoughts on what my life has been, don't you see? Thwarted. Frustrated. That's what my life … Oh, well … And married. The Abby. Person you married. Too carnal!' She blurted these words out. You preferred to ignore them.

'Don't your grandchildren – well, doesn't the thought of them – make you happy?'

'Why should I? Stephen. Of course I'm glad. The war … you survived the war. But it has affected. The damned war … the wars … affected us all … My chiropodist … my chiropodist comes in an hour's … just an hour's time. Now this wretched Cold War. I must rest.'

She reached for a small silver bell on the table beside her chair; she rang it. A musical tinkle sounded. Immediately, the stout elderly attendant appeared by your grandmother's side.

'Stewart. Dash it, I forgot your name. It's Stephen. I'm so … I'm so fragile. Please excuse …'

She ordered her attendant to show you out. You kissed the ivory of your grandmother's cheek.

Raising her voice, Elizabeth said, 'Thank you for … Arrivederci, Stephen.'

You were going down her steep winding stair, a little sad.

You believe you loved your grandmother? Yet you said nothing affectionate to her.
I never thought of her as a cold woman, but she seemed so distant, perhaps because of her age.
So how do you feel about this meeting?
Mystified, perhaps. Gran was the bright one in our family. I'm sad about our inability to reach out to each other. I often feel like that – that I am remote; remote by nature.
Do you blame your mother for that?
No, not exactly. It was just that phantom daughter, Valerie, she set between us.

I believed in Valerie. It was near to madness ... Perhaps, on reflection, it was less the distancing that affected me than the sorrow; my mother's sorrow.
Not the war, then?
Sometimes one feels ashamed for surviving when so many were lost.

Perhaps prompted by a slight continued frostiness with Abby, you returned next day at a suitable hour to see your grandmother again. Again the stinks of the Calle Galina greeted you.

Elizabeth was adjusting dusky, dull red flowers in a bowl, possibly a species of camellia, in what she called her book room. She was wearing a long, silky house coat with wide lapels. Light in the room was dim. The jalousie was closed, filtering the sunlight.

She accepted a kiss before scrutinizing you with a slight smile. 'You prefer ... I cannot think ... my company to that of your bride.'

'I am taking the opportunity to visit you again.'

'Make love ... love to – while the relationship is good – her. Be wise. Enjoy it, the ... advantage. Beware. Spiritual. She's not. I must tell you, Sid ...'

At the time, you resented the advice, saying nothing in return.

Elizabeth stood quite still, with her back to the shuttered window, one hand on the table for support, the bowl of flowers before her. There was some resemblance to a portrait by Degas. She was silent, mustering her words, so that when she spoke, she spoke in a rush.

'In my youth and when I married ... married Sidney ... I was a prude. Upbringing, in part. Awful. Poor Sidney. Never to see me ... well, to be naked. Not completely. Now in age I am chaste. Perforce chaste. Venice, even in Venice – a lewd city as in thing ... in Byron's day. But I find in my mind ... in my mind I find ... discover that I am depraved. In my mind, the things I think of ... Not spiritual ...'

'Are there no young men, Elizabeth ...?' You did not need to complete the sentence.

'Only once. You are not a prude? Why do people ... speak ill of depravity? It gives ... when it gives so much pleasure?'

So she had shed her earlier prudishness, at least on the surface. You rubbed your chin, unsure how to answer.

'It doesn't lead to happiness? Is that a valid objection?'

She was stern. 'Tell ... tell me, what does lead to happiness? Inheritance?' She was thinking of Abby again.

You stood looking at each other across the table. It was not the occasion to trot out Aristotle. Elizabeth had gestured with her free hand, elegant, eloquent, against what was otherwise her stillness in the sweet dim room. It was hard to read her expression in the circumscribed light. Tension ran between you as you responded, trying to find a word of comfort for her, touched by her unexpected revelation.

'Perhaps something different is required for each individual. Not fame. Not even money. Yet not an absence of fame or money either. Sex. Love. But they, also, can bring their torments. I'd say, Elizabeth, keep depravity in the mind, where it belongs.'

She gave a curt laugh. 'You don't know ... happen to know a bisexual, a delicate man, suitable ... gentle ... gentle, genital ... willing ... Just once? I suppose not.'

'I don't, Elizabeth, I'm sorry to say.'

You contemplated each other. Then she dropped her gaze before dropping the subject.

'Do you care for fuchsias? They droop. Somewhat.'

Afterwards, you thought with sorrow about what she had been asking you for: a brief escape from her prison.

15

'I Must Love Abby'

You were walking in Hyde Park, enjoying a cool, late summer's day. You and Abby had moved into a smart apartment in Leinster Gardens, off the Bayswater Road. The early shine of marriage had worn off; you walked rather soberly, hands clasped behind your back.

This was the day of your thirty-ninth birthday. Abby had given you a light overcoat which you were wearing on your walk. It was undone, and flapped open – rather pleasingly, you thought. Joey and Terry had given you a print by William Hayter, which greatly pleased you. Your sister sent a bottle of brandy. Your parents had presented you with a copy of your father's newly published book about his life, and life in general, entitled *Over the Boundary*. You found you were scarcely mentioned in it ('born 1924'), while Sonia got a good deal of coverage.

You saw a copy of the book for sale in Hatchard's window in Piccadilly, together with a photograph of your father, his cricket cap at a rakish angle. He was 'The Sporting Politician', in journalistic jargon. Martin was now in the shadow Cabinet opposing Douglas-Home's government; the children of the nation were still benefiting from his attentions and being despatched to distant lands.

You were walking without a limp. You had been to an NHS hospital. Despite other people's worries, the operation on your leg had gone smoothly. The food had been deplorable but the nursing good: you had soon recovered.

Which was as well, for Abby was four months pregnant. She had had a miscarriage previously: in your depression, you had both turned to Purple Hearts. You sat about a lot, sometimes holding hands. You watched the BBC show, *That Was the Week That Was* on television, and derived some enjoyment from the Profumo affair. Yet somehow rather less enjoyment of life.

There had been a time before you were married when you and Abby had seen little of each other for almost two years. You had met a young academic called Briony Coates with whom you had an affair. You saw her first of all through an art shop window, buying a set of Cumberland pencils, and were attracted for one of those inscrutable reasons. Perhaps it was something in the way she held her head, or the way her face lit when she smiled.

Briony Coates was small and dark and had a surreal sense of humour. Her brown eyes were often downcast, or half-hidden by a lock of hair, as if to guard her inner self. She taught mythology at the nearby college. She was mild and sensitive and swam almost every day, sun or shower, in a small swimming pool in her widowed mother's garden in Canongate. Margaret Coates looked like a mouse: she was far from being a mouse. Her married life had been spent in Kenya with her husband, a big game hunter turned game park warden. She liked to talk about spiritual matters. She taught a weekend course in watercolour painting and was no mean painter herself; her oils sold in Bond Street galleries. She and Briony also made ends meet by letting out their first floor to lodgers. Much of Briony's time was spent reading, astronomy, psychology and mythology being her favourite subjects. While you were with Briony, those subjects attracted you, too.

Briony was calm, affectionate, amusing, and she and Mrs Coates welcomed you into their placid nest. You were free for a short while to move within those circumspect rooms, one of which housed a large Paul Nash watercolour, which hung over the fireplace. The lives of the Coateses were secretive and quiet, yet intense, in a way you found highly attractive. Its spiritual quality was something you thirsted for. Briony told you unexpectedly one day that her father had been injured in the war and had lost an arm, together with other injuries. Her mother, Margaret, had nursed him devotedly. He had died the previous year.

The Coateses, mother and daughter, played music on their ancient gramophone, mainly Wagner. 'So original,' said Briony once, after you had been attracted by the Vorspiel of Act 1 of *Lohengrin*, where the music seemed to emerge from a higher sphere, or from the earth itself. They often spoke of Wagner as a great musician.

'Wagner is superior to Beethoven, in my opinion,' said Margaret.

'Such amazing energy and accomplishment,' said Briony.

'I'd never have enough stamina to sit through *The Ring*,' said you.

'It does require endurance,' said Briony, with a laugh. 'And why not? After all, I read that Wagner based *The Ring Cycle* on Aeschylus's *Oresteia*.'

'Mmm,' you said.

You went away and read *Oresteia*, wondering at the powerful and majestic figures of a family which bestrode such death and horror.

'But families are a bit like that ...' said the mild Briony, when the subject came up again, 'or would like to be. I always admired Clytemnestra. It's true she is, well, a bit of a monster, but still, well, she has much to put up with.'

'Not quite the type for Canongate.' You kissed her.

'I teach mythology classes. They make you see murder at every turn in the road.'

When Briony acquired a more important post at Durham University, she moved north – and something in you was lost. Her pretentiousness, her gentleness.

Margaret Coates sent you an affectionate letter, inviting you to one of her suppers. You set it aside, forgot it, failed to answer.

You went to see Sonia performing in a John Arden play. Sonia was winning good notices. Her performance in the Arden play won her the lead role in the film *Loves of Mrs Meredith*. It was a great hit with audiences everywhere; this she made clear when she came to see you. Abby, back in your life, grew to like your sister, as she was inclined to like anyone whose prospects were good. 'Prospects' was a word Briony had giggled at. Sonia had met Christine Keeler somewhere at a smart party, which added to her interest in Abby's eyes. 'The little slut!' Sonia had exclaimed, enviously.

Into all these pursuits, and into the pursuit of making money, you entered with some determination. Yet there was a trace of feeling that this eagerness was forced, was 'put on', as a garment is put on to cover one's nudity. Briony, with her serene, nunlike countenance, was hard to forget. You corresponded, but the letters tailed off with time.

The war and its hardships were long past; there had been, not purity, but an integrity about the period, as if the human race, or at least the male portion of it, found its true being only when food was short, when necessity ruled, when lives were in danger, when one lived almost tribally – as if the demands of phylogeny for challenges dominated the trivial needs of ontogeny for a quiet, individual transit through the years.

What did one do about the flaccid routines of peace, when one's adulthood had been honed in the arts of survival? Regarding that time, of course, one could agree with Aristotle's definition: doing something one regarded as worthwhile, such as fighting for one's country, was the source of a ghastly happiness with which peace could not compete.

Moneymaking and marriage were not enough.

Just before your marriage to Abby, Briony had sent you a greetings card. She had written in it, 'Hope it works. Don't let it work against you.' You pretended it was just Briony's envy speaking; in fact, she knew you better than you would allow yourself to admit.

Possibly even Hilary Montagu in his disillusion had enjoyed the drama of despair. No, you dismissed that speculation as ridiculous; but at least Montagu had reached a fitting, if grim, conclusion. To live on into peacetime inevitably proved an anticlimax.

The intricacies of personal relationships – how insignificant they were. But how much perseverance they required!

There was Abby, so boisterous! And the self-effacing Briony, slipped for ever away into the past, to live her own balanced and inscrutable existence. You came to believe that perhaps human-kind's larger brains had developed, not because of struggles against severe weather, or carnivores, but against other men and tribes of men. The hunt had become a measure of man's intelligence.

Your attempt to discuss such matters with your male friends met with laughter. 'Who cares what they did in the Stone Age?' But I cared, and regretted my straying from the path of learning.

What was a married man to hunt in peacetime? Undeniably, many of the dealings of Britannia Furnishing were on the shady side, which provided some excitement, but it occurred to you that the Cold War gave politicians on both sides of the Iron Curtain something more interestingly akin to the hunting instinct.

Then there was science, the pursuit of knowledge. It certainly yielded positive rewards. You were interested in the reports of Crick and Watson, who had discovered the double helix, the structure of DNA. The genetic material of humanity and most animals had been revealed. You received an excited letter from Briony about the discovery – a bulletin, nothing more.

You believed that when Francis Crick announced in the pub that he and James Watson had found the secret of life, their joy, their victory, must have been almost unbearable. You looked at a diagram of this remarkable double helix. It was explained that 'the two sugar-phosphate backbones twist about on the outside with the flat hydrogen-bonded base pairs forming the core'. It took you many years of intermittent study before you could understand even half of it. The discovery represented for you a refinement and triumph of the old hunting instinct.

Abby was unmoved by this remarkable advance in science. Her own prospects were concerned with Lord Lyndhurst's will. Lyndhurst had left Abby a generous sum of money, but there were anomalies in the will over which lawyers debated, to their own enrichment. Various clauses were contested by Lyndhurst's widow, Lady Augusta. The resultant legal dispute promised to be a long one.

Slowly, your depression evaporated, or was set aside. Abby received you into her bed again, and once more became pregnant. This time, the pregnancy seemed to be going well. Indeed, even the international situation had improved. Although more and more American troops were being poured into Vietnam it proved to be the one occasion in which the British were not involved. At least President Kennedy had signed the Atmospheric Nuclear Test Ban Treaty. And everyone had been excited when he had recently delivered a peppy speech beside the Berlin Wall. Perhaps there wasn't going to be a nuclear war after all; perhaps people could die from natural causes.

Abby herself was cheerful. She sang little snatches of Mozart arias as well as a song called *Moon River* as she went about the flat. She listened to a lot of music, but had banned the Beatles. She consorted regularly with a group of female friends who met, among other occasions, in an upper room of a local hotel every Friday, to lunch, drink margaritas and smoke pot.

You asked her if it was wise to smoke pot while she was pregnant.

'I'm not changing my way of life for any foetus!' she said. You both laughed.

It was Friday.

As you walked in the park, a line of sturdy beeches cut into the sun's rays one by one. You thought about the foetus that had miscarried, which had grown for a while in your wife's body, and then had failed and died before it had truly lived. Abby was remarkably cool about the loss. Supposing the child had survived, it might be toddling by now. It would possess dolls or teddy bears precious to its heart. It would laugh and cry and sleep in its parents' arms, smelling of fresh excreta or Johnson's Baby Powder.

For the first time in this context, you recalled your childhood scourge, the phantom Valerie. You perceived it might be easy for such a fantasy to take command of one's mind, as it had your mother's. A whole world faded and disappeared when a child died prematurely.

Three elegantly dressed teenagers on horses clip-clopped by, their mounts gravely looking ahead down the long walk, the youths, two girls and a young fellow, not talking, simply enjoying the exercise and their command over the animals.

The thought occurred to you that perhaps galaxies were born in a manner similar to infants. Perhaps other universes had died unformed before this present universe had been born. The thought developed no further; it was too immense to contain. But supposing, you thought to yourself, there was an explanation for the existence of the universe and all the material in it, from galaxies down to thesmallest virus. Maybe the human mind would not be capable of comprehending that explanation.

Any more than you were able to visualize Abby's foetus growing up, becoming adult and – whatever it did then …

Human biology was not the best, although DNA did what it could. A pretty girl on a man's arm passed you on the path, walking smartly. You had only a glance at her face and at once your imagination sprang up. You thought what it would be like to speak to her, to hear her voice, her opinions, to dance with her, to kiss her lips, to see her naked, to lie with her, to experience the deep little well of her sexual pleasure. She had gone by, rapt in animated conversation with the wretch who undeservedly escorted her. You turned to see her from behind, her beautiful legs below her light blue skirt ...

She was an example of biology at its best. How had it been in the early days of the human race? Had women looked awful then? Had they had miscarriages? Had there been love as well as lust between the primitive human pair? You wondered idly about such questions without being able to provide yourself with answers. You had admittedly become rather shallow. Presumably the human species had not greatly changed.

But one's feelings changed, unfortunately. Abby still attracted you physically, but you hid from yourself the fact that you really did not greatly like her. You blamed your own inability to communicate; Abby was remote too, which did not help matters.

No, but I must be content. After all, I'm doing quite well. To be a geologist was just an idle dream, now I'm just – just a trader. Here's nature and beauty all around me. And I must love Abby as once I did. No man can expect to be happy all the time – not unless he has really achieved something. One must retain that perspective. So you reasoned.

Dusk was seeping into the English world as you approached your apartment. A light was glowing in your living room, spreading a fan of illumination across the gravel outside. You looked inside.

Abby had returned from her lunchtime binge. She was lying on the carpet, her body stretched parallel to the window. She slowly lifted one leg, massaging it as it rose. She then lowered it gently and raised the other leg, massaging it too. You knew she was afraid of getting varicose veins. She still owned her profitable boutique in Mayfair, and had put a manager in to run it while she was pregnant.

You watched with awe. Perhaps if you had been closer to your mother, you would not be so astonished by women. Your seed was in this lovely woman, busy turning into a baby. It was amazing what women did, what women were! You thought at that moment that women were quite, quite different from men. And if she had only lain a little more towards the window, you could have seen her panties; they were still of interest.

You had a vivid mental picture of that place between her thighs, and of her plump mons Veneris, with its thatch of curly brown hair. The memory of it and its scents rose before you, almost overpowering you with desire.

You shrank away, guiltily, in case she saw you there, a peeping Tom with an erection. All women ... all women ... you said to yourself. You thought of your Aunt Violet and of her welcoming secret places. Of Briony, swimming naked in her pool, her delicate breasts and toes. Then you mastered yourself, took your latchkey from your pocket and went to your door.

Unexpected shocks came along to jolt you both. Abby began to haemorrhage, at first slightly, one night violently. As if in a nightmare, you saw the blood seeping from her, spreading its stain across the matrimonial bed. The blue eyes flashed you a look of fear. You were both so alarmed, you got Abby into the car and drove her at two in the morning to hospital.

She was in the twenty-eighth week of her pregnancy. The bleeding was explained as *ante-partum* haemorrhage. She was sedated and went to the maternity hospital for further examination, while you paced up and down in the waiting room. A young doctor, with well-oiled hair, thick eyebrows and deep-set, grey eyes, came to speak to you. The eyes regarded you with compassion.

'I'm afraid we have a problem here, Mr Fielding. Your wife is not at all well. The placenta has become separated from the uterine wall. Not only is there considerable loss of blood –'

'How did this happen? What's gone wrong?'

'Such things do occasionally go wrong. Shall we sit down, Mr Fielding? It may be to do with lifestyle – a too active lifestyle, possibly. Too much drinking and smoking, for instance.'

'Smoking pot?'

'I'm afraid I can't say.'

'How's the baby, doctor?' There was a terrible pallor in the room from the overhead neon lighting. The pallor bathed your faces.

He looked very grave, and had to nerve himself up to announce that the child was dead.

'Oh, no …' You first thought was that you were cursed: this was what had happened to your mother before you were born; the accident that had brought on the storm of misery which had given birth to the phantom, Valerie.

'Can I go to Abby?'

The doctor said, 'She is asleep at present. We shall have to operate to remove the dead child. Can I get you a glass of water, sir?' He was very young. Perhaps he had not met with this situation before.

'No, thanks. Does that mean she won't be able to bear children in future?'

'Not necessarily. She will need time to recover, of course.'

You hid your face in your hands. 'Oh, my God …'

The doctor put a hand gently on your sleeve. 'It is a cause for grief, I know. However, if it's any consolation, I must tell you that one in every four pregnancies ends in miscarriage. We see so many of them here.'

From that day onward, there was a difference between you and your wife, as if both of you blamed each other for the other partners you had been with. Abby became a more reserved person. After a while, you realized her earlier beauty had faded away, together with something of her early verve.

One cannot be happy all the time. *It is almost impossible to be content. Perhaps when one is old it may be different … One must keep a perspective, even if dear Abby can't.* You thought she seemed to enjoy Joey and Terry's company more than yours. You're so stodgy, you told yourself.

You turned out to be short-sighted, rather than stodgy. You flew with her to Switzerland, where she could rest in a five star hotel in the charming old town of Neuchatel, in a suite overlooking the lake. You killed time while she rested: killed time considering whether you were a man without qualities. Had you had character only in those terrible war years?

Back in England, the brothers frequently took Abby shopping, an expensive diversion you despised. They were more 'fun' than you were. Terry had recently been over to France, where he had negotiated a deal with a huge furniture store outside Bordeaux and had contracted to sell them five hundred dining room suites. It was on that excursion that he had picked up the William Hayter print. He had also been paid for the furniture in cash and had not declared it. There were other dealings, too, which made you uneasy. You too were pocketing cash and hardly thought about it.

You were intermittently miserable. You did not like what you were doing, you did not know what was going to happen next, and while Hyde Park was fine, England was still rather drab. True, London was more lively than it had been for many a year; the London journalists labelled it 'Swinging'.

Young women, emboldened by the Pill, wore their hair and their skirts shorter, just as they shed the taboos under which their mothers and grandmothers had laboured. On stage and screen, in various dives and at pop concerts, in cars and by the side of the road, youth was voting for Free Love and the joys of sex without responsibility. You would be forty before long, but everyone else was outrageously young. When the Beatles sang *All You Need is Love*, they really meant 'All You Need is Youth'.

But for you and Abby, youth was disappearing, seeping away through the floorboards of a marriage.

The youths who worked for you in your factory were careless. The success of the West had depended, at least in part, on willingness to work. The willingness had disappeared with the new freedoms. You had been tempered by war; you were different from the new generation. Although the youngsters in fact had little in common with one another, what they did share was the fact that the priorities and pressures of warfare had missed them. They had no care for intellectual responsibility. Your well-concealed bad conscience was no match for their lack of any conscience at all.

Even the economics of the country were uncertain.

You felt your own situation to be uncertain. Perhaps all thirty-ninth birthdays were secretly like that. Some comfort was offered by the reflection.

Later that year President Kennedy was shot in Dallas, Texas.

16

A Modernizing Government

'Oh, Martin, you really should buy yourself a new suit, dear,' said Mary. 'Now you're going to be really important.' She and your father were standing in their bedroom as the latter prepared to go to Downing Street. He was standing in trousers and braces, trying to brush a little shine out of the cloth at his knees.

'I'm not going to kneel in front of Harold,' he said, with a brief laugh at the very thought.

'But you should look your best. You're not as young as you were. It's so important, dear.'

'We're Labour, my duck, not a gang of lordly Tories. Suits are hardly a priority.'

'Well, let me at least give your hair a trim. It's long at the back. It hangs over your collar.'

He struggled into his jacket and checked to see that his wallet was in place in the inner pocket. 'Don't fuss, my dear, or I'll miss the bloody train.'

She stood back to survey him. 'Just don't swear in front of the PM, that's all I ask.'

'Wilson's okay. He probably says "bugger" all the time, like a man of the people.'

'Are you going to take him a copy of *Over the Boundary*?'

He frowned at her. 'Are you mad?'

She smiled. 'I was only teasing, Martin, dear. Let me drive you to the station.'

On her way back from the station, Mary Fielding called in at the local fishmonger's to buy some whiting. She thought to celebrate her husband's elevation with a dish of whiting for supper, since she believed she did whiting well. They looked so pretty, done in breadcrumbs with their tails stuck through their eye sockets. She found the fishmonger in a gloomy mood.

Mrs Walker, who ran the grocer's along the street, also looked gloomy. 'Come forward please, Frances,' she told her assistant, not coming forward herself to greet her regular customer as she usually did. The little shop held pleasant smells of leaf tea and demerara sugar and other enticing things.

Frances was young and bright, and smiled as she asked Mary what she could get her.

'My word, everyone is gloomy today,' Mary remarked rather pointedly, casting a glance at Mrs Walker. A chair was provided for customers to sit on. Mary sat on it.

'I'm not a bit gloomy, Mrs Fielding,' said Frances, putting her head prettily on one side. 'I'm ever so happy. The Beatles are booked to give a concert in America. Fancy! Fantastic, I'd say. It was on the news this morning. I heard it when I was getting dressed.'

'Who may the Beetles be? I have never heard of the Beetles.'

'Oh, Mrs Fielding, bless! You must have heard of the Beatles! They're real great. The Fab Four, like. And John Lennon, he's –'

'Please serve your customers, Frances, without lecturing them,' said Mrs Walker, with asperity. She came forward as she spoke, smiling at her customer.

'*Please Please Me* is the recent Beatles hit, Mrs Fielding, and that is exactly and precisely what we aim to do here – please our customers.' She rubbed her hands together at the mere prospect.

'I have never heard of it,' said Mary, while returning the smile. In fact, she had often heard the song, which had become difficult to avoid; but she considered it somehow superior to have not heard of it, nor its singers.

Dropping the subject, Mrs Walker explained why there was indeed a certain amount of gloom about. It had been announced that what she called a big self-service shop was to be opened on the market square. It would undoubtedly take trade away from nearby shops, such as hers.

'Surely not!' exclaimed Mary. 'People will always want someone to serve them. They won't wish to have to serve themselves, certainly.'

'They'll get used to it soon enough,' said Frances. Then, possibly realizing that she had gone too far, remarked admiringly on the fur about Mary's neck, which the chilly morning had provoked her to wear.

Mary was pleased. 'Do you like it? It's rather old-fashioned for today. My mother always wore a fur; she had a lovely silver fox stole.'

'Goodness!' exclaimed the assistant. 'Did she ever get the poor creature back?' A few months on and Frances was working at the new Tesco's, earning good money and going out with a young man from Saffron Walden.

It was 10.53 when Martin Fielding was admitted through the door of Number 10, Downing Street. He was shown into a waiting room, where a Beatles record was playing, presumably to indicate that the dull days of the previous prime minister, Alexander Douglas-Home, were over, and a new, livelier epoch had dawned.

Martin had hardly sat down on a hard, Regency chair, before a brisk and smiling young secretary entered and announced that the prime minister would speak with him now. He followed her upstairs, past the portraits of the illustrious dead who had once occupied the premises.

He was shown into a long room, the walls of which were covered with a green flock wallpaper. A portrait of the Queen hung on the far wall, behind the prime minister's head. An open window let in gusts of rather fresh air. The room appeared full of young men and women, some of them engaged in stacking files on shelves. An older woman sat at a typewriter of an old-fashioned kind. At the other end of the table at which she sat was the prime minister himself. He was talking to another man who was standing beside him. In front of the prime minister were a pile of papers and a cup of tea. He was in his shirtsleeves. He nodded in a friendly way to Martin and waved a hand to indicate he should sit down, while he went on talking to the standing man. After a few minutes, he gave the man a folder and the man then departed. Martin recognized him as Jim Callaghan. He too gave Martin a friendly nod as he left.

Harold Wilson then turned his attention to Martin.

'Thank you for coming to see me, Martin,' he said. A slight trace of a Huddersfield accent remained in his voice. 'How's the wife?'

'She's fine, thank you, Prime Minister.'

'And your cricketing book is doing well, I hear?'

Martin was delighted.

'Yes, Prime Minister. It's reprinting.'

'Reprinting, is it? Good. It's an excellent read. A fine game, cricket.' He leant forward, elbows on table, and assumed a different tone of voice.

'Now, Martin, you've been looking after the nation's kids while we've been in Opposition. As you know, the nation's housing is in a deplorable state. To be frank, a worse state than the kids. My predecessor did nothing about it' – he smiled – 'just as well he has now retired to his rolling acres.

'It is of paramount importance that we pursue an anti-inflationary policy; show ourselves friendly to business. Nevertheless, we must build and be seen to build. Never forget that we're a modernizing government. We need to knock down a few slums here and there for a start; high rises look good. People see high rises, take note of them.

'It was one of the weaknesses of the Attlee government that Clem's house-building policy, ambitious although it was, was not implemented speedily enough. That must not be allowed to happen with us. We must build new towns in the North as well as down here in the South. Not forgetting Scotland – Cumbernauld's an example.

'Good shopping centres; to please the ladies, God bless them. We must aim for an additional ten thousand houses, mainly, but not exclusively, in the lower income bracket, up and going concerns by 1966 at the latest.' As if by afterthought, he added, 'And all with indoor lavs.'

Wilson paused and took a sip of the cold tea by his right hand, gazing at Martin meanwhile.

'At the next Cabinet meeting, I hope to propose you as Undersecretary of State for Housing. You'll find yourself under Tony Crosland, unless I give him Education. He can provide the putting up and you can supervise the pulling down. Or something like that.' He grinned. 'Do you feel up to the challenge?'

Hesitating, Martin asked about the nuclear arms race.

The prime minister inclined his head. 'We must proceed as if we are not about to annihilate each other. I ask you a second time, do you feel up to the challenge?'

'Well … er, well, I'd … I will certainly do my best, Prime Minister.'

'Good man. Confident but not over-confident, that's the way. We'll see how it goes. I know you'll do your best. Official announcement in two days. Keep mum about it meanwhile.'

It was over. Wilson rose and offered his hand. Martin rose and shook it.

'Miss Stebbings will show you out, Martin.' He turned and called to a man nearby to start instructing him about the ordering of the files. Martin turned and went unsteadily down the stairs, past Churchill, past Campbell-Bannerman, past Disraeli …

He told you later that his heart swelled at the natural kindness of the man, Harold.

Abby clapped her hands when she heard the news of your father's promotion. She gave you a kiss, exclaiming, 'What a clever family I married into!'

You laughed. You both lit cigarettes and had a drink. You again leafed through your father's book, now reprinting. One passage in particular teased you. You read aloud to your wife.

'I look at life this way. When you are the batsman, you stand virtually alone. Apart from your fellow batsman at the other wicket, you are surrounded by players who want to get you out. They are all sportsmen, they enjoy the game, but they are there to get you out.

'Does not this situation apply to the rest of life? You may well be part of a team, but the time comes when you have to stand alone and defend your wicket against all comers.

'Your rewards come when you have knocked the ball over the boundary a few times. You then return to the pavilion, or to your marriage, and there you are safe, sheltered, away from the public gaze. How you behave then is a private matter. But I would suggest that the rest of your behaviour is influenced pretty strongly by your performance on the field. You have a "self" which only you know. It differs from your flesh-and-blood self; it is inaccessible to others, and often even to yourself. Others can only sense it, for good or ill.

'It may be necessary to change that inner "self", perhaps by religious prompting, but certainly to change, as we change at the end of an over. This urge should not be resisted. The bowler's duty is to bowl, straight to the wicket and no wides!'

'Religion, cricket – spare me! I know nothing about either of them.' So said Abby.

'That's nothing to be proud of,' you told her.

Then followed your father's prescription for how to go about changing one's inner self, complete with cricketing analogies. You

318

found most of this laughable, yet you were uneasy. It was as if your father were addressing you personally. Perhaps he had you in mind when he wrote that passage.

And ... and you ridiculed yourself for finding Martin's image of himself as standing alone, defending his wicket with opposing players all round him, touching. It might indeed, in his father's none too subtle mind, be how he felt – isolated, with a son always indifferent, if not actually hostile, to him. But that was absurd, just as *Over the Boundary* was absurd. Yes, absurd, you affirmed. What Abby thought was neither here nor there. Your father was achieving something: which, you felt, was far from being your own case.

Your sister Sonia was also achieving something. Even while *Loves of Mrs Meredith* was still showing in cinemas, she had accepted the role of Medea in the new play by Adam Nightingale, *Morning for Medea*, at the Haymarket. The papers, the glossies, were full of Sonia, her life story and her face and body in various poses. She was toying with an invitation to Hollywood. She gave her age as twenty-nine.

'Only a few years out,' said Mary, protectively.

Sonia threw a party at the Savoy after her triumphant first night. You attended with the pregnant Abby – pregnant again, after many hesitations and prohibitions. Also there were Martin and Mary; Bertie and Violet, with Joyce and Dougie in tow; Terry and his latest conquest, Laura; Joey with his conquest, an underdressed Lily; and various other friends, as well as the director and entire cast of Sonia's play.

'Sonia's just terribly, terribly good,' the director told you. He grabbed hold of Sonia and pulled her to his side. 'She really becomes Medea.'

'Luckily, it's all pretence,' said Sonia brightly. To you she said, 'You're doing well, Pop's doing well, Abby is expecting and looks well, the family is doing fine. How did that miracle happen?'

'Britain is entering a new epoch under Wilson. Thank God he refused to let us be drawn into the Vietnam war. We're modernizing. The times are better.'

She flashed you a contradictory look. 'What you mean is how lousy the times were.'

'Pop's knocking down slums like billy-o!' you said. But you were uneasy. You believed that Sonia, despite her success, was unhappy. Taking her to one side, you asked her if all was well. She said she would write to you, so you knew something was wrong.

You caught a breath of her perfume – Blue Grass – Abby used it too.

Then other people swept her along on a tide of bonhomie. And there was scandal to talk about among the members of the family. Claude Hillman, once married to Martin's sister Ada, had gone off with a woman who ran a beauty salon in Carnaby Street. Joey and Terry made jokes about their father's disappearance from the family home, waggling their hands in mock desperation.

'He was always a bit of a blighter,' said Terry.

'He's having a last fling,' said Joey.

'We don't know it's his last,' said Terry, and everyone laughed.

The champagne corks continued to pop.

'How does Ada feel about it?' asked Lily, with a dash of acid in her tone. It was not a popular question.

Sonia addressed her captive audience briefly. 'My mother used to pretend she had a phantom daughter, by name Valerie. Valerie made my early life misery. Now I can be miserable in my own right – not that I am exactly miserable at the moment, with all you dear friends and all these expensive drinks around! Funny thing is, I have become a Valerie. I am now a phantom daughter – not a daughter at all, to be honest, but an actress instead. That strangest thing, an actress, where one week you are sitting on a sofa, pretending to knit socks, stage left, and the next you are busy murdering the rest of the family, stage centre …'

Everyone listened to her, nodding in agreement or laughing nervously.

'So I ask you to toast my mother, who taught me the fine art of dissembling!'

You drank your champagne with the rest, not daring to look at Mary.

There was dancing that evening; Abby said she felt too pregnant to dance. You danced with your sister and with the actress who played Clytemnestra, and with your Aunt Violet. She had shed her blue-rimmed glasses for the evening.

'I suppose you remember?' she said, gently.

'Of course, my darling aunt!'

She smiled and looked charming as you floated round the dance floor. 'There's a lot to be said for incest,' she murmured.

'Yes, it keeps it in the family.' You added, 'Don't cling so close or they'll begin to be suspicious.'

17

In the Alley

Dear Steve,   10th October

I never seem to get the chance to talk to you alone, but now I must write to you in my anguish. I don't really regard love as a defining centre of life; our parents maimed me by overdevotion. But at the moment love, desire, is destroying me. Shuggerybees, as we used to say, long ago in our foolish youth.

Did I ever mention the name of Adrian Hyasent to you? He's a very famous stage-designer. Also costumes, more and more. We met and fell instantly in love. Adrian was married. They have a child. I know it was wrong but I begged him to leave his wife and live with me. After all, it is the 1960's.

Eventually, Adrian did come to me. He spent the whole of that weekend crying. Crying, crying. About his bloody wife, about his bloody kid. In the end I got furious. He said it was his sensibility. And when Monday came, he went crawling back to them.

Can you imagine how I felt!!!

That should have been the end of it. It wasn't. I am obsessed by that beautiful man. He is superior to every other man I have met – and I have met a few. And slept with many. I am a bit of a whore, it must be admitted. It's easier for blokes.

We had then started work on *Medea*, beyond the read-through stage. For a week, we never touched each other, hardly even spoke. I hated Adrian, but I needed him. And my pride was hurt; I would go home late at night and dust and scrub and wash like an old mad woman. I was an old mad woman! Me, a star!

Then he rang me. He needed me in his life, he said. So we went out for a drink and – oh, Steve, I can't tell you. We just talked and talked – talked our souls out. It was my turn to cry. But we were sort of together again. Nothing else mattered.

Yet I can't bear living like this. I shall never stop. I never pass a day without anguish, never lie in my bed at night without longing for him. Will I ever be able to take him to Spain, a country I adore? To swim naked with him in the Med?

Life has cheated me. Just when I feel so low, along comes the offer of my life – another flick! This time a serious story. Nothing less than the title role in a class British movie called *Jocasta*, from the classical novel. Screenplay, Robert Bolt. It's the Oedipus story and they say it's going to be big. I must accept – my agent's fighting for more money up front. At least if it's shot in England I'll be able to see Adrian occasionally. I turned down a Hollywood offer because of him, the bastard!

Still we manage weekends together, now and again. What rapport, what tenderness then! The sense that everything is shared, that we accept everything about each other. Steve, I love Adrian so much I cannot tell you. His love for me must cause him pain too.

I feel I can never be free. Always I must live this half-life.
Sometimes the bitterness of it makes me feel old and ugly.
When I was a child, we used to pretend I was a hunchback. Now
I really have that hunched back. Only when I am in the glamour
of the stage or before the movie cameras – when I am being
someone else – does that hump disappear.

Of course I know you can't help. No one could. But any
comment on your foolish and perverse sister's predicament
would be welcome.

I know you have your problems too.

With my love,

Sonia

You read your sister's letter with deep sympathy. The anger came
later, anger against this fellow Hyasent, who was making two women's
lives miserable and, as far as you could see, taking advantage of them
both. You saw him as weak, as a parasite. You felt that when he had
actually left his wife, only to spend the weekend crying, Sonia should
have kicked him out of her life and had no more to do with the man.

After thinking hard in this vein, you wrote to Sonia expressing
your fears for her, your worry about her situation. Underlying the
sympathy flowed a deeper tide – the knowledge that your sister was
now in her mid-thirties, and that the biological clock was ticking
against her. Growing older was easier for a man than a woman,
although how anyone coped with the attrition of the years was
always a personal and secret process.

You sealed your letter in an envelope and went out to post it
in the pillar box along the street. It was that mild October day in
1965, when there was a demonstration against the war in Vietnam
– a war into which Harold Wilson had sensibly declined to send
British troops. People were running down the street as you left
the apartment block. You felt it was nothing to do with you. You
and Abby were arranging to go on holiday to France; Abby had
pressed you to buy a house there, where prices were so cheap.

It was a Hindu in the sixth century after the birth of Christ, whose name has not come down to the West, who discovered something missing from the abacus, that calculating machine used for centuries all over the world. After the figure *nine* came *nothing*, or 'zero', an Indian invention. Ever since that time, people in the civilized West have been slightly superstitious about *zero*, or anything with a *zero* in it. Such as fortieth birthdays.

It was on your fortieth birthday that your wife gave birth to a baby girl, whom you or she would later decide to christen Geraldine Augusta Fielding.

Abby was in the maternity hospital. There was no thought of your throwing a party, although you had taken a bottle of champagne to the hospital to share a glass with Abby – in the main to celebrate the birth of the baby, rather than your own.

Your parents came to Leinster Gardens one afternoon, once Abby had returned there, to visit you and the babe. They were going to *Medea* that evening to see Sonia on stage for a third time. Once more, you concealed your feelings. On sorting out some of Abby's clothes to take to the hospital, you had found two love notes in the pocket of her dove grey coat. Both were handwritten and from Joey, plainly indicating that he and Abby had been lovers and were talking about a secret love nest in Bordeaux.

Hatred against Joey boiled within you, that particularly toxic variant of the emotion which includes hatred of oneself and of one's folly – not to mention one's lusting after other women. Joey had always been a curse. It was part of his and Terry's so-called system, to take advantage of anything that was offered.

As to how you felt about Abby, all those feelings of anger and betrayal had to be sublimated. She lay in bed nursing your baby; it was your duty to love her.

So you tried to continue life as usual. You fostered your image of the man about town, and consorted with your friends. To those friends you said no word of what Joey had done; you feared it would make you a laughing-stock in their eyes.

For six days you kept a lid on your feelings. You struggled in a whirlpool of emotions, among which was a contempt for yourself for doing nothing. And the disease of blind hatred for Joey; a hatred that killed off all other questions, all reasoning. Only an insane cunning remained.

You bought a small hunting knife. You drove to Muswell Hill, where Joey had an apartment. You knew the place; you had been there many times, sharing a false friendship with the fellow. You parked the car some distance away. You stuck a false moustache on your upper lip. You walked, one hand in your pocket, clutching the knife.

The apartment block was bland and anonymous, built since the war. Its windows looked out onto a small square, Eden Square, surrounded by railings. Only residents in the square could enter the uninspiring little garden.

To one side of the block was a narrow alleyway leading to a back street. You went to the alley and stood watch, your mind black with murder. It was 10.07. You would wait. When Joey emerged, you would go up to him – walk? rush? – and stab him in the chest. Hold the little cur. Get an arm round his neck. Drag him towards the blade. He would struggle, you could choke him, jab the blade into his guts. Once. Again. Again. In his chest, a second time. See the blood pour out. Tell the bastard, 'You are going to die, you little scumbag!' 'Die!' 'Die!'

You would then throw him down. On the pavement. Maybe he would writhe – yes, yes, writhe in agony – before dying. Kick him. Kick him hard. Break his backbone. His skull …

What if there were passers-by? They would run off in terror. No one would interfere. You would have your revenge, then fling the knife into the railed garden. Run back to – No, *walk* back to the car.

What if Terry had also been fucking your wife?

You lusted for the attack. You were swollen with a terrible fury.

Someone was coming along the pavement, walking slowly. You hid the knife. He approached. You struggled to take control of yourself. It was Claude Hillman, in a shabby old check suit.

'Hello, Steve, what are you up to?' He showed no particular surprise.

'Oh, I was caught short, Uncle. Had to have a quick pee.'

'You don't look well. Are you okay? I suppose you are here to see Joey, but he's up in Middlesbrough today. I said I'd look in and feed his ruddy cockatoo.'

'Yes, Middlesbrough. Of course. I'll be off then.'

'Grown a moustache I see. Look, Steve, old boy, seeing as you're here … I've got a new project on –'

'Sorry, Uncle, I must go. Not feeling too well.'

'It's a false moustache, isn't it?' He was peering at you more closely. 'What have you been up to?' He suddenly changed tack. 'I just want a bit of help to get on my feet again.'

'Oh? So what happened to Torrid Tours?' You were shaking your head and blinking in a kind of fever.

He shrugged his shoulders and gave a false laugh. 'That one didn't really take off. You know what Spaniards are like. But if you could let me have two thousand quid – just for a month or two – I'd –'

'Uncle, I really couldn't. Sorry. I'm a father now, you know.'

'What, you're taking up burglary or something? It's nothing to you, two grand! Don't worry, you'd get it back. Trust your old uncle.'

You were looking about you, shaking your head, as if seeking a way of escape.

'Uncle, sorry, I must run.'

'Two hundred quid, then.'

You did run. Claude called angrily after you, 'Wait till you're up shit creek! See if I'll help you then!'

You were fortunate that circumstances prevented you from committing murder. Once I calmed down, I was ashamed of myself. I had taken no thought of the consequences.

No need for shame. It was a design fault. We never properly adjusted the endocrine system.

18

Blood on the Ice

For a while you scarcely felt human. You could not sleep for your murderous preoccupation. Just to talk to people was a burden; between you and the other person was a vision of the body falling, spraying blood. Even the face of your innocent child was partly obscured from your cognizance by that ever falling phantom.

Your parents came to visit you and Abby and the baby. It was another ordeal.

Mary commented that you looked rather downcast. You could not admit to Sonia's sorrows, or to Abby's unfaithfulness. Silence smothered you. You poured the parents drinks after they had inspected the cradle newly installed by your twin beds, and its contents, and had cooed sufficiently over the baby.

The baby bore their admiration with considerable equanimity.

'You don't seem at all overjoyed to have a baby daughter,' said Martin.

'Are you sickening for something, Steve, dear?' Mary, all solicitude, patted your hand.

You answered randomly. 'There's a spot of trouble at work, Mother,' you told her. 'Joey and Terry are scrapping. They – we – have a financial problem and the books don't add up. I try to stay clear of it.'

'In quarrel mode, are they, what?' said your father. He wore smart suits these days, with no shine at the knees. 'They always were a couple of little blighters, were Terry and Joey. They take after their father, thick as thieves. Bound to fall out eventually.'

'Yes, Claude's in hot water,' Mary reported. 'So poor Ada says. What that woman puts up with …'

'Anyhow, more importantly, have you noticed how clean the streets are?' said Martin. ''Specially to greet your offspring! Figures to be published by the Home Office next week will show that the litter in London's streets has decreased by 34 per cent since Labour came to power. It's a fine record.'

He looked so pleased, rubbing his hands together, that you became vexed. 'How on earth can refuse go down by a percentage, by any percentage? How is it measured? Does it include the findings from every street in London? In Greater London? Who is paid to go round measuring these things? It sounds like absolute nonsense to me.'

Martin shook his head sadly. 'You're talking rubbish, my boy. What do you know about it? Cleansing vans have multiplied under Labour. Figures are based on the number of vans cleansing the streets.'

'Oh, so there are now thirty-four per cent more vans, are there?'

Mary stamped her little foot. 'Stop it! Martin knows more about government business than you do, Stephen. Talk of pleasanter things. Pass the gin, please, Abby.'

Your mother sipped at her glass with an air of righteousness, the Peacemaker in person. She had taken to a fondness for gin, possibly under the impression that it gave her character. 'Just a drop for me auld age,' she said, smiling, in an approximate imitation of an Irish accent.

'There's trouble everywhere. I hope you're keeping your nose clean in that dodgy business of yours.' Martin followed up this hope with something more immediately on his mind. 'The US have been bombing the hell out of the Vietnamese. I know it's all part of the Cold War, but still …'

You remarked that President Nixon was beginning to withdraw American troops from Vietnam.

'Nixon's a good man, whatever he looks like,' Martin said. He sipped his martini with a judicious air. 'Still they're continuing to drop napalm on the poor bloody Viets.'

'Yes, and they are defoliating the place with this ghastly Agent Orange,' said Mary, adding, 'I never realized oranges could be so dangerous. What about your plans to buy a place in France? Are you really that rich, Steve?'

'Save something for a rainy day, old boy,' advised Martin.

'Property in France is amazingly cheap,' you told them.

Another visitor to Leinster Gardens to see baby Geraldine was Bella. She arrived on crutches, having recently been involved in a road accident in Belgium.

'She looks just like you, Abby,' said Bella, admiringly. Abby, being nice, attempted not to appear offended by the cliché.

Bella was looking very masculine, her hair trimmed short, wearing a grey, pinstriped suit. She was now the representative of the British Retail Consortium in an exclusive government department in Brussels. Her name was always mentioned, when it was mentioned at all, with respect.

She had heard from Martin of your plans to buy a property in France. 'Why France?' she asked. 'Why not Belgium? The Belgian cuisine is second to none. I know a little place in the Ardennes you would love …'

'No, I think not the Ardennes, thanks, Bella.'

Nevertheless, it was some years before you bought the property in Brittany. You had calmed down by then. Abby was unwell after the birth of Geraldine Augusta. You did not confront her regarding her affair with Joey, you simply kept Joey away from the house and watched Abby like the proverbial hawk. You partly blamed yourself for not loving her enough. Had she detected a hollow-ness in your affection?

Yet you did love her in a way. Intensely, in a way. How much time, you sometimes thought, you had squandered, pursuing her and the world she represented.

How little on Briony.

A factor very different from compassion persuaded you to keep silent on the matter of her affair with Joey: you could imagine Abby's lack of penitence. 'Why not?' she would say. 'Everyone's doing it!' There would be no apology or pretence to one. And, even more poisonously, with blue eyes flashing, the fashionable, 'You don't own me.' Indeed it was true, you did not.

So you kept your own counsel, as you had done in other serious matters. It was what to yourself you called 'keeping your trap shut' – no matter how much it hurt.

After many months of negotiation, and tiresome dealings with French lawyers, you bought a fine old chateau near the little town of Tremblay-en-France, some kilometres south of Mont St Michel. It amused you to think that you might have passed through Tremblay in 1940, in the days of the Second World War. Now the Cold War prevailed, but you were not going to let that spoil such pleasure as you could squeeze from life.

Chateau Aulnoy was named after the minor literary figure who had built it in the eighteenth century, in a vernacular style of stone with brick quoins and a fine, slate-capped tower. The chateau needed restoration and repair, and double-glazing of the fine large windows. You employed some excellent French craftsmen; carpenters, plasterers, decorators, wrought iron masters and others and put in an English overseer to supervise. You flew over once or twice to check on progress – and sometimes just to stand gazing at the building, thinking how lucky you were to own it, and how unlikely it had been that you would one day be able to afford it.

'It's entirely different from the chateau in the Forêt de la Bouche,' you explained to friends. Indeed, this was your triumph, you were back in France, out of uniform!

Standing in an empty and still dilapidated room, with its crumbling plasters and sombre Second Empire greys, you gazed out at the lake which had been one of the reasons for buying the property. Where the water came closest to the house a jetty stood, with a rowing boat moored there. It was a peaceful scene which, to your receptive mind, held a quality of the eternal about it, as if boat and jetty were designed to convey a pilgrim, not simply across a prosaic lake, but to more transcendental scenes.

And an image of North's boat, high and dry on the sands of Walcot, came to mind. At the Aulnoy lake, there were no treacherous tides.

Your thoughts drifted. You fell into that melancholy which was familiar to you, a melancholy of which you were as unaware generally as you were of your own breathing. Memories of Briony Coates returned. It occurred to you now that she might also suffer from the same prevailing gloom as you. Aulnoy was just the sort of place Briony would have loved, with its isolation and the waiting quality of the lake.

She could be seen in your imagination, dressed in her habitual brown; she would have walked this garden, would have been calm, clear eyed, affectionate. That was the worst of growing older: the torments of memory multiplied.

You felt that you loved the house as it was – despite the sounds of hammering – and were comfortable with its ruinous state. You could almost be happy there, just as you were almost happy with Abby and the infant Geraldine.

Why did you want this chateau?
Many of my prosperous friends were buying property in France. I suppose it was the fashion. It was a beautiful place; well worth having.
But why did you want it?

Oh, I don't know; to escape? You would probably say it was the Zeitgeist again. I could afford it. I suppose I wished to impress friends – and my family. 'Keeping up with the Fieldings …' And the lake; it was so placid, so peaceful …

It brought you peace of mind?

As you know, it just brought horror.

Abby became impatient with the slow progress of the restoration as months dawdled by. She put her foot down. The blue eyes flashed – you would take, she said, the child and some friends, and spend Christmas in the unfinished building. At least some downstairs rooms would be habitable by then, and a brand new kitchen would have been installed. You could hire a cook locally.

So the three of you flew in in mid-December, together with some smart Cholmondeley friends whom you hardly knew.

The Chateau Aulnoy looked glorious in the frosty hours of daylight, seeming to stand aloof from merely temporary affairs. There were thickets on the far side of the lake, trees and bushes coming down to the water's edge, their foliage at present powdered with frost, so that you suffered no shortage of wood. Soon fires were blazing in all the major rooms. The friends brought in bunches of holly with which to deck the place. At night when Geraldine Augusta was in her cot asleep, the guests played Murder and hid in mysterious places about the rambling corridors.

You drank local wines as you sat on rugs on the bare floorboards: furs of reindeer, the hairs of which adhered to your clothes. You ate oysters, suckling pig with gnocchi, and imported Christmas puddings with brandy butter and thick cream.

The weather was cold, but fine and still. You all voted it 'Excellent Christmas weather!' You drank a lot and laughed a lot.

You were borrowing money heavily. You had a bank account in the Cayman Islands and were siphoning money from your company. Did you not feel you were doing wrong?

334

I was simply behaving as many successful men behaved.
You thought your way of life was successful? Not reprehensible?
I certainly didn't think so at the time. Our lives were totally harmless
in comparison with the politicians who had got us into the dreadful
stand-off with the Soviet bloc. You know, sorry to go on about it, but
I had survived a horrendous war. I felt I deserved a more luxurious
life. And then there was the Cold War – certainly not of my making
– when we could all have been wiped out by a nuclear strike after a
four minute warning! We had to live while we could, enjoy ourselves
while we had the chance.
We should have granted you greater reasoning powers.

Abby gave you a striking Christmas present: a mating pair of
black-necked swans imported from the Falkland Islands, together
with a little wooden shelter for them. Was the gift guilt money,
you asked yourself? Nevertheless, the pair of you, well wrapped
up, sallied out, with Geraldine carried papoose-like, to establish
the birds by the side of the lake. You tossed them some grain, not
venturing too close. The proud creatures hissed their disapproval,
but appeared subdued. They ate the grain and did not venture
on the water.

As you returned to the house, your father phoned to wish you
both a Merry Christmas. You responded warmly. Martin said that
Mary was feeling unwell and announced that the Soviet army had
invaded Afghanistan.

'Why on earth?' you asked in amazement.

'Because they can,' came your father's reply, over a crackly line.
'The blighters.'

'But no one does any good going into Afghanistan. The British
fought two Afghan wars and got soundly trounced. Doesn't anyone
learn from history?'

'It seems they don't. How's the weather with you, Steve?'

'It's freezing cold. We've just been out there. I wonder there's
no ice on the pond.'

335

'Keep warm, old boy!'

You thought increasingly well of Martin as you and he grew older.

'Oh, these bloody Soviets!'

'What a terrible period of history we're living through.'

Such were the Cholmondeley verdicts when you told them the news of the Soviet invasion. But in came Abby bearing a bowl of a punch she had made. You all took a brimming glass full of it and toasted one another.

Later, you wrapped up well and walked into the village; there you bought French newspapers. The Afghans were portrayed as heroic. A particularly brave group of them called the Taliban was attacking the Soviet invaders. They were seeking economic support from the West.

'What can the Soviets hope to gain?' your guests asked each other. 'It's absolute madness.'

'The Afghans are Muslim. It's a religious war.'

They gazed out of the broad windows of your chateau, agreeing that Tremblay was a most beautiful refuge from worldly terrors. You were complimented on discovering it. Everything outside was frosty and still – 'Like a Dutch painting,' they said, without specifying to which painting they referred.

The black-necked swans stood together on the bank of the lake, hesitant before its still waters.

'They can't mind cold water,' said Abby, with a giggle. 'They come from the Falkland Islands, where it must be freezing most of the year. I'm sorry I chose such a cowardly pair!'

But no, the birds were now on the move. They spread their wings, flapped them, gained some height, and took to the air, flying just a few feet to splash down on the lake.

With a great resounding crunch, much like the sound of steel closing on steel, ice shot across the surface of the water. It was instantaneous. Suddenly the surface closed like icing on a cake. The swans had disturbed still water, remaining unfrozen four or five degrees below freezing. Disturbed, the water immediately changed its state. Becoming solid, it locked the two unfortunate birds in its grip.

You onlookers gasped with horror.

The swans struggled, but could not free themselves. Their legs were held in the ice. They screamed in their frustration; their wings beat vainly until they were exhausted. There they remained, captive.

'Can't we go and rescue them?' one of the Cholmondeley guests asked.

Picking up the general agitation, Geraldine began to cry.

'Wait! Look!' It was your exclamation.

From under the bushes on the far side of the lake, two rust-coloured animals came creeping. After them came a smaller animal, most probably the pair's cub.

The foxes gingerly approached the ice margin, bellies near the ground, noses to the air. The larger of the two tried the ice with a tentative paw. He, if it was a he, then cautiously ventured onto it. The ice held. The watchers saw him glance back over his shoulder as if beckoning. The vixen in her turn slunk on to the ice with many a hesitation.

Seeing the foxes some distance away, the swans fell silent, arching their necks, while fighting more vigorously to escape the grip of the ice.

The vixen found the ice safe. She turned back and nuzzled the cub until it too stood on the ice. Seeing this stage of the threat, the black-necked swans began to beat their wings in a frenzy to free themselves: they were unable to loosen their legs from their prison.

Now the three foxes were sure of their footing, they hesitated no more. They raced across the ice on their nimble black feet, and fell upon the swans.

Struggle as they might, crying terribly, the swans were torn to pieces.

Abby fell screaming to her knees, clutching her head. Geraldine also screamed.

Blood spread across the surface of the ice. The foxes went relentlessly about their meal.

You closed up Aulnoy and returned to Leinster Gardens. Such was your haste, you left fires burning in the chateau grates. Abby seemed on the edge of a breakdown, swearing she would never return to Tremblay. You had to sell the place: it was accursed.

'That's not rational,' you told her. 'We've only just bought the bloody place.'

'What the hell does rational mean? Were those horrid animals rational?' She was all but shrieking.

'According to their lights, yes, completely rational. Don't be so silly! They have to eat. They had to feed the cub. It's the law of the jungle.'

Gloom settled over you all. 'You should have shot those foxes,' Abby said at last, in a sulk. 'You would have done if you'd been a man!'

In sudden fury, you shouted, 'Don't lecture me, you bitch! I know you've been screwing Joey! I should have shot him, the little bastard!'

She drew back, pale of face. 'You don't own me!' she said.

On the last day of the year, a black car drew up outside the apartment in Leinster Gardens. Two men got out of the vehicle, to knock at your door.

When you opened it, they charged you with responsibility for financial fraud involving the purchase of Britannia Furniture by the fictitious company of Mayfair Holdings. You were complicit as Managing Director. Your signatures were on all the documents. They required you to help them with their enquiries.

Other matters of serious fraud were involved.

'Steve!' Abby cried, holding out her hands to you.

But you were resigned. You gave her a look of hate.

'It's your fault. It's the law of the jungle,' you told her, as they marched you off.

PART THREE

1

A New Line of Thought

You were confined in D Wing. The discomfiting racket of the prison; the shouts, the clanging of doors, the banging of trays, the jangle of keys, the stink of the place, got through to you. All harsh male sounds afflicted your ear. The hardest aspect of confinement was the deprivation of female company. You were forced to resign yourself to it.

It happened that Britain and other countries in the West were entering a period when the lives of women were much discussed, and new interest and knowledge were applied; when womanhood was scrutinized afresh and freshly valued. Not only woman's beauty and grace, but also her capabilities, her powers. Her vital function in the state. Too bad that womanhood was not also confined in your prison, you thought.

The contraceptive pill was changing society, leading perhaps to a period when the uses and employments of men were underestimated.

Your wandering thoughts strayed to the lives of men, as you reflected on the peculiarities of your own life. You longed to read a learned book on the various struggles and existences of contemporary men. You would have preferred it to have had an informal title, and to have been informal, perhaps 'The Lives of Blokes' – indicative of the gender which still scratched its armpits. What did men do to establish themselves before their own eyes? How did they do it? The difficulties besetting those who knew no father as model, or had rejected the father as model: 'Fatherlike he spends and tears us. Well our feeble frame he knows ...'

You thought how once, men – almost every man jack of them – had been serfs, peasants, or had fought. In those dark centuries of the past ... But now! If you were skilled at kicking a football, or if you were moderately capable of singing, then your path was reasonably clear, at least for the years when you were in fashion, while you collected Rolls Royces, or mansions, or younger women.

But alternatively, there was the hard route of learning. Or the way you had chosen, the primrose path of making money; although, to be frank, it had hardly been a matter of choice, rather just a matter of things happening. You had no firm hand on the tiller of your own destiny; you were afloat on a tide of lust and greed, those pleasant vices you concealed even from yourself.

And so the idea of change, the longing for a change, seeped like a rising tide into your mind. You resisted the prospect, being slow to realize it was already fermenting within you. By reading, you diluted your hours of solitary introspection between those grey walls. In one of the books from the prison library, donated by the League for Penal Reform, you came across some old Jacobean plays. In one play, an illustrious duchess asks: 'What would it pleasure me to have my throat cut / With diamonds? Or to be smothered / With cassia? Or to be shot to death with pearls?' An unlikely and philosophical enquiry for a woman about to be strangled, perhaps: yet it seemed a relevant question to ask of your past life, where to be a rich bloke with a wealthy and haughty wife appeared a satisfactory way of being, indeed, a bloke of stature.

Doors slammed, keys jangled, raised voices sounded. Somewhere, a prisoner yelled continually.

You thought over again what you had already thought.

The Duchess of Malfi's question, *What would it pleasure me to have my throat cut / With diamonds?* seemed immensely apt, immensely moving. You had cut the throat of any body of spiritual life you had once enjoyed. Yes, it was more difficult 'to be a bloke' when the war was over, and with it all the fear and courage and deprivation of that time of hostilities, yet who in their right mind would wish for wartime back? There had to be a new way; perhaps the budding European Community was a new way, or part of it. But what of the individual, the bloke on the Clapham omnibus? You recalled the saying that fine feathers made fine birds; but not, presumably, if the feathers were stolen. Somehow, you had fallen into a habit of stealing, although you were aware that to steal was wrong; prison drew your attention to the fact. You were, ultimately, glad to be imprisoned. Glad, even with the two tasteless, half-cold meals per day. The authorities did not let you starve exactly, though your meditations rolled like a sea without a shore.

Many of those imprisoned with you, being reckless, had performed heroic deeds during the war. They had failed to adjust to the demands of peace; lawlessness had entered their blood. When they had done their bird, they would break the law again.

One night, you dreamed you were walking in a garden with Abby. High clipped hedges arose on either side. You asked her if she was well and happy.

'Yes,' she said, but her face indicated a negative. Her expression was ghastly; the look was that of a dead woman, so that she turned her head away to hide it.

Startled, you awoke. You believed that the dream signified the realization that your marriage was dead. You stood with your face against the cell wall and wept.

Your marriage was finished and your whole life had reached a dead end.

A psychotherapist visited you. You enjoyed looking at her, with her clear skin and clear eyes. You were willing enough to talk to her; you told her your spirit had withered and died, the rigours of war had killed it. She suggested you were feeling guilt because you had survived. You said that if your spirit died, then you did not survive.

She said, 'Since you dare to breathe those words, then your spirit is not dead, and you should encourage yourself to see that it lives more fully.'

'I'm thinking,' you said, by way of a joke, 'of writing a "Life of Blokes".'

She suggested that flippancy would not help; it was, generally speaking, a defence mechanism. Deep retrospection might prove more helpful to you, while you should remember that Buddhists regarded guilt as self-indulgent.

Probation officers visited your cell in order to help you think over your situation. One of them, a Jamaican woman named Beryl, suggested various Open University courses you might take. You chose to study Earth Sciences, and so your thoughts were slowly drawn away from yourself to greater things, to a study of the processes of the planet itself, and the vastly complex interlocking mechanisms of the biomass, working upon the Earth.

You studied. Something in you quickened. You read various books.

The prison library was full of trash. Among its children's books and crime novels you dug out a large novel entitled *The Man without Qualities*. The very title attracted you. It proved to be a translation from the German, and was recommended by an illustrious person. You could see it was full of fine writing, but could not grasp its overall meaning. In that respect it resembled life.

If you could not understand this book, why keep on reading?
I felt I too was a man without qualities. No, a better answer is that

344

such is – was – my nature, that I preferred something I could not
fully comprehend to something I could easily comprehend.
Good. That's a sensible answer.

You began to take more interest in other prisoners. For the first
time, you attended 'Association', or free time. You tended to divide
your fellow prisoners into the intelligent and the near-imbecile,
although the borderline between the two groups was indistinct.
One man in the intelligent group attracted your attention; you
were convinced you had met him before, in the great outer world
of illusory freedoms, but could not remember where, or who he
was. You had not known each other well ... Or for long.

One day in the gym, you spoke to him.

'No, I don't know you. We never have met, I am certain,' he
said, bowing his head to one side in a rather sad way.

It was that slightly unidiomatic turn of phrase, 'we never have
met', instead of the customary 'we have never met', which unlocked
your memory.

'You're Joe! Joe Rich!' you exclaimed. 'You are – or were – the
caretaker of that War Department store, wherever it was – off the
A5 ... Aren't you?'

He held out his hand. Now he was not sad, but smiling sadly.
A warden watched you shake hands.

You both asked simultaneously what the other was doing in prison.

You said that you had led a useless kind of life; self-indulgent.
That you were frankly not sorry to have a time in your life when
you could think things over and review your mistakes. Even as you
made the admission you were proud to do so, believing such an
admission to be unusual – perhaps something that other blokes
would not have thought of saying.

Joe Rich said that he now remembered your visit. 'You would save
my stay in this place if you had buyed all the furniture Rhona and I
guarded. Winters in Grimscote are cold. I burn a wooden table or a
wooden desk in the grate to keep us warmed. I thought no harm in it.'

'Why not? No one else wanted the damned things.'

Joe nodded. 'As you say. As I also said. No one wanted that obsolete furniture. But yet, they were not my things to burn. Once came officials for inspection from the Department of War. They carried what do you call it – yes, an inventory! An inventory of all that should be in the store. Much of the wood things were missing; chairs, tables … I confessed I had used them on my fire, to keep my woman and me warmed in the winter. So I was arrested. And here I am, my friend.'

'You mended my trousers – did a splendid job!'

He gave a laugh. The warden eyed him.

You swung on the parallel bars and asked, 'What happened to the furniture – the stuff that was left in the store?'

'Military lorries came and took away everything. It was all to be destroyed.'

'Yet still they sentenced you to prison!'

'Three months only.'

'But how grossly unfair!'

'No, my friend. Not unfair. Just! I took things and used them that were not mine. Therefore I was a thief. It is only justice that I am in this horrid place.'

'Joe, I'd call that unjust. There is such a thing as necessity … I think I believe in necessity more than I do justice. Justice is man-made.'

'So was the wartime furniture …'

You hoped to see Joe again the next day. He was not there, nor on the day following. He had served his three months, was discharged and had returned to Rhona.

All the same, that conversation with him had started a new line of thought. You had claimed to yourself that you had made a confession other men would not have done – that you were glad of the respite in prison to think over your sins. That claim was untrue. Doubtless, many others had admitted, while being locked up, the error of their ways.

You thought for a while about furniture. The furniture business had made you and others a lot of money – bought you that chateau in France, for instance. Whereas, furniture had merely kept Joe and his wife warm on winter nights. There was an enormous difference when you considered the matter; Joe's was the more unusual case.

> *Let me ask you how you see yourself at that period.*
> *Confused. All the parts of the body change in seven years. The psyche probably undergoes a similar change. It's only things like passports and dental records that identify myself as I was before I was sent to prison.*
> *That imagined, or perceived, lack of continuity is a weakness with which we shall have to deal.*

You followed up the perception that you were not unique – that you were just a bloke. Your silly notion about blokes had been subconscious preparation for admitting to yourself that you were nothing out of the ordinary; indeed you were just a cheat, an agent of fraud. Why had you become that cheat? Because you had considered yourself as somehow different from others.

Which had permitted you to be 'above the law'.

You stood facing the cell wall, legs slightly apart for balance, resting your forehead against the clammy tiles, breathing deep, lost in a maze of thought.

You thought back to a poem about a beach, part of which Joe had once quoted to you:

... the world, which seems
To lie before us like a land of dreams,
So various, so beautiful, so new,
Hath really neither joy, nor love, nor light,
Nor certitude, nor peace, nor help for pain;
And we are here as on a darkling plain ...

A deep bitterness flooded over you as once again you thought of all those vulnerable childhood days spent on the beaches of Walcot. All the while unknowingly under a prevailing indifference, cruelty; as in that poem. And as in that poem of Matthew Arnold's, you had soldiered too long on that darkling plain.

The argument in your mind was then carried a step further. You considered yourself unique, different from others because of what you had been told happened – or rather, had failed to happen – long ago on the Walcot beaches. You were a child whom some higher power, unspecified, had spared.

Whom the gods love they first make arrogant.

This uncomfortable trail of reasoning, through a forest of hesitations and denials, finally reached a conclusion: you had lived under an illusion – much as your mother had, to take a parallel case – and now you were free of it.

Free! That wonderful word, tasting good in the mind even in captivity!

Yes, we admired the struggle in your limited mind to uncover the truth about yourself. You did find it and that made you jubilant –
Oh yes, you dear accursed alien thing! Happy indeed! Happy even in that Aristotelian sense of deserving to be happy! Maybe for the first time, truly happy, happy –
Now you exaggerate. Remember you – or the French – have a saying that nothing is ever as good or as bad as we imagine.
But the funny thing is, I was happy just to see myself as an ordinary fellow – the very thing I would once have hated.
That is certainly no ordinary matter.

And for the first time you felt a closeness to that monstrous thing telling you your story. Oh, that prison cell, that solitude, that revelatory disquisition with yourself … all in shades of grey.

*

Martin and Mary came visiting. Mary was complaining that the prison was over a hundred miles from home; you explained to her, as to a child, that you had no choice regarding into which prison you were cast. Martin was at his most jovial, Mary at her most shrinking. Martin had brought a film crew along. He had special dispensation to film your meeting.

'Some of the fellers in the department rib me,' Martin told you. 'They say I've got a wrong 'un for a son, but I take no notice of them.'

'I'm a bit "beyond the boundary", am I, Father?'

'You shouldn't talk to the boy like that,' Mary told her husband. 'He's still my precious son, whatever he's done. Aren't you, dear?'

'There are seventy-five thousand inmates of British prisons,' Martin told you. 'We are building more prisons. The system is under strain; you are fortunate to have a cell to yourself. Are you lonely?'

'A bit.'

'"A bit," he says!' Mary exclaimed. 'Of course he's lonely. Misses his wife, I'm sure.'

'What's the news of Abby? She never visits me.'

Your mother put on a mean face. 'She's gone to live on her family's estate in Gloucestershire. She's seeking a divorce from you. How can you blame her, after all?'

Martin was annoyed, although he controlled his face for the cameras. He told Mary she should not have told you about the divorce; they had agreed beforehand not to tell you about it.

'He's brought disgrace on the lot of us,' she said. She began to sniff, mustering up a tear. 'I hope you pray to God for forgiveness, Stephen, dear.'

Your frustration showed. 'Mother, don't you remember how you used to pretend you had a daughter called Valerie, who did not exist?'

'No, I never did!'

'Yes, you did. You had a firm belief in Valerie, it caused me endless misery. Do you now have a firm belief in God, who equally does not exist?'

349

Mary turned away, muttering about your blasphemy.

Martin's visit was shown on the Midlands TV News that evening. 'A minister takes an interest in the prisoners behind bars in one of our new prisons,' said the commentator. You had become 'the prisoners'. Your name was not mentioned, nor your relationship with 'the minister'.

Sonia visited you on another day. 'I can't stay long, love,' she told you. 'Adrian's outside in the car, waiting for me. I hate this dreadful prison smell; I suppose you're used to it.'

'I suppose I am.'

'What are the loos like? No, don't tell me, let me guess. Are you surviving okay? I've brought you a cake. No file in it.'

'Thanks, Sonia. Yes. I'm doing an Open University course in Earth Sciences.'

'I guess it passes the time.'

'Yes, and more than that. You're still with this chap Adrian, then.'

Sonia spread her hands. 'You could say ...'

'How's the career going?'

'Smile when you say that! Day after tomorrow I'm off to the States. Hollywood calls! That's why I came to see you today.'

'I'm glad you came, darling. Enjoy Hollywood!'

'Whatever, I shall enjoy it as much as I enjoy anything. All pretence, of course ...'

'How's Aunt Violet?'

'She hasn't been well this winter. She sends you love – I nearly forgot. She's getting on a bit. God, I'm going to hate old age ...'

Alone again, you meditated on what people endured. Sonia seemed never to be happy. Curious how Joe Rich was perfectly content to serve his sentence, believing it to be just. Aristotle had had a great deal to say about justice, 'When he wasn't swimming with a woman off the shores of the Isle of Assos,' you said to yourself. Some of the basic principles of Western democracy had been formulated by Greeks in their mild Thracian climate, where the living was fairly easy. Those principles had taken root in Northern Europe, where life was harsher than in Greece. You speculated on the hardships survived in the winters of past centuries in the North. The artist Brueghel had painted the onslaught of the first great European winter descending on Christendom in his superb canvas, *The Hunters in the Snow*. Winters had always been dreaded.

It was a time for cogitation. You thought of that ferocious wartime winter in the Ardennes, when Hilary Montagu had been killed, along with thousands of other men. Winters were times of cold, hunger and darkness, illness and death. For almost two thousand years, methods of lighting and heating had not improved. It was believed that devils walked in the night; certainly something carried the old and the very young away in the small hours of February months. Central heating had banished such devils. Life had become remarkably easier since the Second World War. Had people become softer since then? If they had become softer, what then of their moral values? Improved? Deteriorated? Much the same?

The fact was that many or most people nowadays lived an indoor life, although the thought patterns of Ancient Greece had been generated through a more outdoor and sunlit existence. Did that matter? Or did not the effect of an indoor existence, lived among small rooms accessible through narrow doorways, bring its own mental shortcomings?

A priest visited you in your cell. He could not answer such questions when they were put to him. But he told you that he deplored the prison system. You were inclined to disagree; you had begun to feel you were making moral progress.

For all that, the days became longer, the weeks dragged, the grey months spun themselves out, the year passed with all the sloth of a glacier, inching its way to the sea ...

351

2

Guernica

PAMPHLET: 'At this time, in a situation so remote from the metropolis, everything is as silent as it would be in a region wholly uninhabited. The moon shone bright; and the objects around being marked with strong variations of light and shade, gave a kind of sacred solemnity to the scene ... They had not ridden far, before a hollow wind seemed to rise at a distance, and they could hear the hoarse roarings of the sea. Presently the sky on one side assumed the appearance of a reddish brown, and a sudden angle in the road placed the phenomenon directly before them. As they proceeded, it became more distinct, and it was at length sufficiently visible that it was occasioned by a fire. Mr Falkland put spurs to his horse; and, as they approached, the object presented every instant a more alarming appearance. The flames ascended with fierceness; they embraced a large portion of the horizon; and as they carried up with them numerous little fragments of the materials that fed them, impregnated with fire, and of an extremely bright and luminous colour, they presented some feeble image of the tremendous eruption of a volcano.

The flames proceeded from a village directly in their road. There were eight of ten houses already on fire, and the whole seemed to be threatened with immediate destruction.'

It is all darkness, all fire, all pursuit and persecution. Injustice prevails, oppression is a system, terror ubiquitous. I read this book over and over. I write about it. No one will accept what I write. Can I be alone in perceiving the truth of what William Godwin wrote then, and what exists now? This indeed is things as they are.

This little island; think of it. Think of it sunk in an eternal war. Once a new tribe swarmed here, over our marshes and ditches and thickets. They grew into armies; those armies stormed down on the tiny towns of the period; on York, on Lincoln, on Peterborough, on Wells. Everywhere they went they killed or converted. They were called Christians. The country burned under their banners. They had no mercy. Prayer was their battle cry.

But spare no pity for those they conquered – those people were savages. They lived in filth and drank from puddles. They did anything vile. The men sold and slaughtered women as they did cattle.

Some of those who survived pleaded for mercy from the Christians. There was furtive intermarriage; the marriage of hyenas to jackals. And, as has been done ever since, the Christians built monuments to their war. They constructed stone cathedrals. Some of these memorials still stand. They were built on the edge of unconquered lands, as warnings to the enemy. Ely Cathedral confronts the wild Fens. Similarly, the religious in those states which once went under the name of Byzantium built their churches to face, and outface, the Ottoman lands.

This is the custom. Picasso painted his great canvas, *Guernica*, to commemorate similar atrocities: when the Nazi Condor squadrons utterly obliterated that quiet Basque town of Guernica. So every village in England erected a memorial to the slaughter of the Great War, preserving the names of humble villagers who died in it. Now the Americans are making a movie, *Apocalypse Now*, to celebrate the horrors of the Vietnam War. Every age has its own style.

All these monuments are to remind people of the savage past and of their own savage present. How did we win the war against Nazi Germany? Because most of the men pressed to fight for this country – men like my father – were inured to hardship, lived miserable and constricted lives, had such low expectations. Not the officer class, of course, but the officer class had been incarcerated in public schools, institutions expressly designed to harden them, to mould their inmates into bullies, captains and moustached majors.

Now we have won that struggle, we invite some of those who fought on our side to come and work for us at menial jobs. I refer to the Jamaicans, a jolly unruly sort of people, instant anathema to the majority of British citizens on the grounds that their skins are black, their songs of sexual liberality. Here's a new people to persecute!

So this nation, which contains more drunkards, more syphilitics, more pregnant unmarried mothers than the rest of Europe combined, claims to be a pure race. What can be greater or grander than to be an Englishman?

Daniel Defoe put that matter into perspective:

In eager rapes and furious lust begot,
Betwixt a painted Briton and a Scot.
Whose gend'ring off-spring quickly learn'd to bow,
And yoke their heifers to the Roman plough:
From whence a mongrel half-breed race there came,
With neither name nor nation, speech nor fame.
In whose hot veins new mixtures quickly run
Infus'd betwixt a Saxon and a Dane.
While their rank daughters, to their parents just,

Receiv'd all nations with promiscuous lust.
This nauseous brood directly did contain
The well-extracted blood of Englishmen.
And those who do not fuck are never chaste
But claim frigidity of higher taste:
The wish to be superior runs
Like semen over England's sons.

Defoe with my help, yes!

With things as they are, there is no escape. Those imprisoned under our systems of 'justice' are more victims than villains – the innocent who get gulled, the weak who get led astray, the orphaned who have never known security. Those who escape imprisonment are forced by circumstance to take advantage of others.

It is not that there is Good or Evil in the world: there is only Necessity; necessity the millstone, necessity driving us over the barren heath.

CALEB

3

One of the Poor

You found yourself, in the middle of this, your mortal life, wandering in that area of London where Finsbury merges with Bethnal Green, and Shoreditch lies to the north. It was a poor part of London, the refuge of many failed or oppressed lives. Broken pavements, impoverished terraces and pokey shops marked the area.

At the end of the 1960s, when many claimed that London was still swinging, this area had become the target for town planners, anxious, in the name of respectability, to improve appearances.

The sands of time had passed slowly through their narrow-waisted glass. The American astronaut Neil Armstrong had landed on the moon during the final days of your incarceration. You had hardly noticed. Now you worked in Scrutton Street, where you had taken a job as a packer in a warehouse after twenty-six months in prison. Your employment was rendered the more uncomfortable by the way in which your fellow employees had discovered that you were a 'jailbird', whose wings had been clipped, and resolved to treat you accordingly, sometimes in scorn, sometimes in fear, always with an attitude.

Currently, you were delivering an invoice to an office a few streets away. Drab though the streets were, your eye, accustomed to the greys of prison, was caught by splashes of colour; a shop sign, a red pillar box, a striped awning, a florist with bright bouquets of flowers placed on the pavement. You walked slowly, digesting these sights of freedom, when a notice, executed in pokerwork on a small board, claimed your attention. The notice read 'G. & H. Geldstein, Flats for Rent, Second floor.'

Your condition had greatly changed. You had felt yourself victimized. As the due processes of the law untangled themselves in various lawyers' offices and in court, you saw that the attractions of making money had lured you into a system whereby others made money at your expense. The really significant amounts of currency had gone into Lord Lyndhurst's purse, filtering, with rather less reward, by a trickle-down effect, into the systems and pockets of Joey and Terry Hillman.

As the evidence piled up against you – for who else had signed numerous documents ceding money to various fictitious companies? – you had felt indignantly that you were simply an innocent bystander caught in a system you did not bother to comprehend.

However, in the cool of your cell, you had had time to think the matter through; you came to different conclusions. Those conclusions, although not flattering, were arrived at by intellect. They condemned you for foolish greed. You had not regarded it as grasping at the time, but grasping it was, even if you had been surrounded by systems of greater greed generated by others. You thought often of the foxes at Chateau Aulnoy, devouring the swans on the ice. The greedy certainly included your cousins, Joey and Terry, who had escaped the law entirely; they also included your wife, Abby.

You had dreamed a prodromic dream in prison in which your marriage to Abby was dead. Abby had left you as soon as the verdict had gone against you. She had sold her couturier's shop for a healthy profit and had taken Geraldine away to live on her parents' estate near Birdlip Hill in Gloucestershire. In your chastened state of mind, you were not unhappy to be free of Abby; Abby had been a character in your illusion. The little girl was remote from you.

You were free to consider how greatly you had been misled by various illusions; by the stillborn sister, Valerie; by the mirage of a prosperous life with a classy, blue-eyed woman; above all, by the false security of your holidays on Walcot sands.

You were now preparing to begin life, if not anew, in a more frugally-oriented state of mind; the prospect excited you. And first of all you needed a roof over your head, away from your unfriendly associates at the warehouse; a place in which to study.

Eventually, you were to forgive Abby. And, having forgiven her, realize there was nothing to forgive. Lust and circumstance had thrown you together, something not greatly different had caused you to part. As to which was the stronger, the accident of character or the accident of circumstance, that was hard to say. You had read somewhere that in infancy it is fate that moulds character, and in adulthood character that moulds fate.

Unsatisfactory, no doubt, but close to the truth. As close as one ever got to that abstraction ...

But what was fate doing with little Geraldine?

It was hardly to be expected that you were jubilant as you climbed the creaking stair, which turned a narrow corner to the door of the office of G. & H. Geldstein, on the first floor above the cycle shop in Scrutton Street. You felt you had overcome a baser part of your character, and were now ready to face the next adventure in your life.

You tapped at the door on the landing and were invited to enter. You found yourself in a smallish room overlooking the street. It was poorly lit; an overhead light was burning. The room contained a table and desk, and a bookcase untidily full of books and papers. A map of the area hung on the distempered wall. At the table near the door sat H. Geldstein and at the desk sat G. Geldstein.

G. Geldstein was on the phone, talking and gesticulating. He glanced up at you but gave no sign of recognition. H. Geldstein asked you if she could help.

You stared at her. She stared at you. She had grey eyes in a pale face. Her hair was dyed blonde. She wore a navy blue jumper and had bright red fingernails.

'Helge!' you exclaimed.

At that, she stood up. 'Steve?' she asked in a hushed voice.

You could only nod. She rushed round the table and you embraced each other, calling each other's name.

The man at the desk put down the phone. He wore glasses over his pale eyes. He was almost bald. He stared across the desk, standing with his hands on it for support.

'Steve? It is Steve Fielding, no? I don't believe it! I can't believe it!'

'It is, it's our Steve!' Helge cried. 'From the French forest!' Tears ran down her cheeks. She stroked your face. Then Gerard came out from his desk and also embraced you.

'My dear boy, we thought you were dead! Thought you had been shot!'

He was sobbing. By contagion, Helge began to cry noisily. You too cried, making up the trio.

'People have thought that before. Luckily, you're all mistaken. I'm alive and kicking. And you? And the children?'

All three of you were crying and smiling and laughing. Gerard was looking much older, yet he executed a little caper. He removed his spectacles to mop his cheeks and stare at you with those strange eyes of his. 'Too much, too much ...' he kept saying. 'We were so upset when you disappeared. We felt the conviction that the Krauts had got you.'

Your escape from the forest had not been forgotten. 'My dear friends, I feel so bad that I deserted you. But once I was in that confounded German car … I remembered then that I was an officer in the King's army. I felt I had to get back to England. England in the toils … But, please forgive me for leaving you behind.'

Gerard clasped your hand. 'Do not feel like that. You had to do your duty. That we understand.'

'And England – now we understand that,' said Helge, between tears and laughter. 'Its sort of kindness – at least it lets you alone! Those were such desperate times,' said she. 'If the Germans gave you a car …'

But you thought you saw that, despite their protestations, they did resent your abandoning them. You inadvertently shook your head.

A moment's silence settled on them. Then Gerard spoke.

'I will lock up the premises, my friend, and we shall go and sit in the Queens Café down the street, and sit and drink some wine and talk all about ourselves and –'

'And how it is by some miracle that we all three happen yet to be alive,' said Helge, finishing her husband's sentence.

Gerard tucked his spectacles into his breast pocket, switched off the overhead light, and ushered you and his wife out before him. Once outside the door, he turned and locked it with a brass key. How you were smiling, could not help smiling.

'Oh, to think I've found you again!'

All three of you went down the turn in the creaking stair and on to the pavement and along until you reached the Queens Café; there you entered. Gerard shook hands with his friend the manager and you made your way to a little cubicle at the rear of the room, where the seats had high backs like church pews. You sat down, still unable to stop smiling at each other. The manager brought a lighted stub of candle and, without being asked, a bottle of red wine and three glasses. You drank each other's health, clinked your glasses, drank again, and then clutched one another's hands across the table.

'It's wonderful!' you said. 'Wonderful! I've always wondered what happened to you – and here you are, alive and kicking …'

'And also owing me money too,' said the manager, interrupting. He was a plump man, wearing a stained white waistcoat over his stomach. He was standing in the aisle, leaning against the high back of your seat, smiling genially to see his happy customers. 'They must remain alive until they have paid me all back!' He roared with laughter.

'Take no notice of him,' said Geldstein, with a flourish. 'He is Harry Heflin, only the father-in-law of my daughter, Brenda.'

'What? Brenda's married?' you exclaimed.

'And expecting,' said Helge. 'She's twenty-eight, you know. Twenty-eight years and a-half-a-year. How the years fly by!'

Yes, how the years had gone, you thought, as you plunged into reminiscence. The longer you looked into their faces, the more familiar they became. They were now more lined, yet these were the faces of those on whom you had depended for company and affection during the long, shipwrecked months in the French forest. To be again in their company was to feel that affection renewing itself, flowing in like a tide.

Speaking in chorus and alternately, Helge and Gerard told their story. Once you had left the hideout to dispose of the German vehicle and had not returned, they had become anxious. The fear was that the Nazis had captured and tortured you, and would soon be coming in force to scour the forest near Le Forgel. With the cooperation of Palfrey, they had moved with the kids further into the forest, only to be captured by a bunch of French Resistance fighters.

'Pretty grim men,' said Helge, with a giggle and a shiver.

The fighters had not known what to do with the family. At first, the Geldsteins feared they were to be shot; Helge's German accent told against them. It was the children, Pief and Brenda, who saved the day. Resistance fighters did not shoot children. Eventually, they had conducted the family to a small hamlet in what was regarded as a safe zone.

'We travelled hidden under straw in a cart drawn by an ox,' said Helge. 'Pief hated it because he said the straw tickled. Poor boy, he sneezed all the way.' She began to cry again.

After two nights of travel, they arrived at the hamlet of Saint-Aubin, near the River Semnon. There they lived in a cottage, protected by some of the Resistance fighters. Among these fighters was a schoolmaster from St Malo who gave the children some tuition. Once the Soviets entered the war against Germany, local Wehrmacht patrols became rarer, and life passed uneventfully until the war ended. They had managed to get to England with the financial assistance of Harry Heflin, who was a relation by marriage to a cousin of Gerard's.

'They are forced to eat in my café to pay me back,' interposed Harry Heflin, who had gone to the front of his premises but kept coming back to listen to the story.

'Had we but known ...' said Helge, with a heavy sigh, winking at you. 'So much of indigestion ...'

No, they had no idea what had happened to Palfrey. Maybe he had become like Tarzan of the Apes, and remained in the forest.

'And what like was your imprisonment in prison?' asked Helge of you. 'Was it very hard?'

'Not quite as bad as public school,' you said. She sniggered, unsure whether you were joking or not, hiding her mouth behind her hand. 'Now I'm looking for a room somewhere.'

Gerard struck his fist on the table so that the wine slopped over the rim of his glass.

'There, my dear valued friend, G. and H. Geldstein can certainly be of assistance!'

The room in Blackall Square had a shallow bay window which looked out on the street, and across it to the playground of a primary school. At some time in the past, the room had been painted light blue. It contained a bed, a cupboard, a gas fire and a small, solid table which fitted neatly into the bay. The chair that accompanied it was painted the same blue as the table.

This was the room Gerard Geldstein was letting you have for twelve shillings per week. It was in Number 12 Blackall Square.

'For Number 12, you pay me twelve shillings,' Gerard had told you. 'Aren't you lucky I don't put you in Number 35?'

Number 12 was a three-storey house with a cellar, which had been converted into a laundry for the soiled linen of Gerard's Indian restaurant in the street adjoining the square. Most of the other rooms stood empty.

Gerard installed a small television set in your room. You watched its flickering images rarely; you had to study. You were entering a new phase of life.

Now you were alone, your thoughts returned to Briony Coates, that quiet academic lady. Now, you reflected, you would be a better companion for her. You wrote to her.

Eventually a reply came. She had married a very quiet (under-lined) American, who was going to take her to live in Boston. She said her mother was well and wished to be remembered to you. Briony sent you love.

You found later that the Geldsteins had leased Number 12 from the local council in order to accommodate the Hindus who worked in two of Gerard's restaurants: the Cobra and the Madarchod. The Indians had assured him that 'madarchod' meant 'ray of sunshine'. The staff had left Number 12 in protest at the squalid conditions.

You began to understand their point of view. Every Saturday, Pief, the Geldsteins' son, brought the soiled linen from the restaurants to launder it in the basement, whereupon brownish steam percolated through the floorboards into your room. Pief said that the Madarchod was doing good business because Indians in the neighbourhood seemed to be amused by its name.

'I tell my father he should name the Cobra also Madarchod, so that it can prosper as well,' Pief told me on an early visit.

There was no bathroom in Number 12. However, a bath had been installed in the lower rear hall. It was too awful to bath in, but you could wash under its running tap.

You had washed yourself by this rudimentary means one morning, when a voice spoke nearby. You were surprised. You had been told there was another occupant of the house, who lived upstairs, but in your first week you had seen no one.

The voice asked a question. 'What was Schopenhauer doing at this time on the morning of March 2nd, in the year 1811?'

Wrapping your towel around your neck, you went and took a look up the stairs. Half-way down, all but hidden in the gloom, stood a lanky figure. It was barefoot and wore a torn pair of jeans and a soiled T-shirt. You formed no very favourable impression of it.

'What are you talking about?' you asked.

'I asked you, what was Schopenhauer, the German philosopher as possibly you know, or don't know, doing at this time on the morning of March 2nd, 1811?'

Annoyed, you said, 'How the fuck should I know?'

'Well, considering,' said the voice, spinning out its sentence as its owner took a step lower on the stair, 'considering that it's getting on for eight in the morning, I should reckon that Schopenhauer was getting out of bed!' He gave a laugh resembling a dog's bark.

'Very funny.'

The bare feet reached the bottom step but one. 'I was making a philosophical point. Poor bastard, you have no sense of humour, I see.'

So began your acquaintance with Arturo Blake, the not particularly distinguished author of 'Guernica' and other pamphlets.

He went under the name 'Caleb'. He was a scruffy character in his forties, who worked in Hounslow Park as a groundsman. His skull was shaven, he had two large protruding ears like bat's wings, and a sharp nose in his blue-jowled face. He claimed that his mother was Spanish, and that he intended to return to Barcelona as soon as he had the money for the fare.

You became friends, or at least drinking companions. Most nights the two of you began to visit the Gardeners Arms behind the square, drinking beer with an occasional whisky chaser. But before you scarcely knew him, before you scarcely liked him, you heard him hectoring an old working man. The old man, whose name was Bert

Sparrow, had been talking to a friend about coinage withdrawn from circulation. He claimed he had a farthing somewhere in his pockets.

'They was useful, was farthings, in my young day,' he declared.

Bert Sparrow proceeded to turn out various objects from his right hand jacket pocket. Out came a tangle of string, a folder of matches, a safety pin, a small penknife and other miscellaneous articles.

Observing this, Caleb pitched in with a sneer.

'You see, you're choked with objects! Useless objects. You're a hoarder, Sparrow! It's like your damned English drawers. Open any drawer in this country, I don't care whatever, try any piece of furniture, and what do you find? What's hidden in those stinking drawers? Endless things! Clutter! Scissors, thimbles, stamps, sealing wax, a missing playing card, tickets, old theatre programmes, boxes of tin tacks, postcards, pencils, tin whistles, yo-yos – all sorts of junk!

'Do you see it's like your minds? Your minds are full of clutter; empty of real thought. So, old currency? Throw it away! It's no damned good! If it's not current, it's not currency, *entiende*?'

The old labourer was visibly taken aback, as much by the eloquence as by the reproof. He managed to ask, 'What about the drawers in where you comes from? Are them any different?'

Proudly, Caleb declared, 'In Spain, drawers are empty. We have clear minds.'

At this you intervened. 'But that's because you had a civil war. So much was destroyed; houses were looted. Here we've been more fortunate; no civil wars for centuries. The country has remained intact.'

'Who asked you?' Caleb enquired, swivelling round on his chair to confront you. 'Intact, you say? *Stagnant*, I'd say.'

Old Sparrow's friend said, mildly enough, 'If you don't like it here, why don't you go back to where you comes from?'

It happened that next morning, a beautiful sunny morning. You were walking to work when you met Caleb, strolling, hands in pockets, in the opposite direction.

Not wishing to appear unfriendly, you bid him good morning.

'It's splendid!' he said in return, jerking his face with its sharp nose sharply upwards, perhaps to indicate the blue sky.

'Not too bad,' you agreed.

He stopped abruptly, in dramatic pose, hands out of pockets and extended with fingers wide before him.

'Not too bad? Not too damned bad? Oh, you English people! How I despair of you! You are so negative! It's a wonderful morning for once and all you can say is, it's "Not too bad".'

You forced a laugh. 'It's just a figure of speech.' But you were annoyed, not only with Caleb, but with yourself. The man had a point.

The garden of Number 12, long neglected, had turned into primal swamp. Still you liked to walk there. Two gardens away, over three garden fences, you could see tall cages. The cages were where old Bert Sparrow kept his flight of pigeons. Every morning he went in his soiled cap down the garden to let the pigeons out.

As soon as the doors were open, up the birds flew with a great clatter, to wheel above Blackall Square. Their wings seemed to beat in unison. Up they went! It was a sight to lift the spirit. You watched and wondered how the birds managed all to wheel to left or right in unison. How did they arrive at that perfect synchronicity? If only you could solve that one problem …

Round and round went the pigeons in the bright air, over the square, to return at last to Bert Sparrow, who had their food waiting for them.

Nearby were less splendid sights; pavements were cracked and broken, the roadway had potholes, the houses themselves were uniformly shabby. Weeds or bushes grew in what had been tiny front gardens, where old bicycles rusted. You observed that as inhabitants died or moved away, their houses, all owned by the council, were shuttered up with corrugated iron panels over their windows, and the house left to decay.

'The place is a shitheap,' Caleb said, with his usual brand of malicious glee.

'My belief is that those who are practically down-and-out,' you told him, 'find this ruination more congenial than they would an array of modern, glass-faced offices with everything spick and span.'

'Is that how you feel about it?'

'Well, how do you feel, Caleb?'

He gave his bark. 'Believe me, I wouldn't change a thing.'

The poor old square had been built in Victorian times for a respectable lower-middle class of clerk. With the disappearance, or at least the winnowing, of that class after World War Two, the square was neglected, the council allowing it to go downhill. The old lived here; the old and the shabby.

Various assets had been installed to assist the luckless who arrived to live out their tumble-down days in the square. You went rather hesitantly, pursuing your own downward path, to a bathhouse which had been established in a flat-roofed prefab building at the top of the square. The bathhouse was run by an ex-army sergeant you heard people call Colin. Colin ran the bathhouse with military precision.

You paid sixpence and were given a clean towel and a new sliver of soap. You were shown into a cubicle where you climbed into a spotlessly clean bath. There was plenty of hot water. You liked it and went there often.

'Yes, it's worth twopence,' Caleb said.

'Sixpence. Colin charges sixpence.'

'Colin, as you call him, charges me twopence.'

'Sorry, sixpence.'

Caleb jeered. 'He charges you sixpence because he thinks you're posh. He can see I'm the scum of the earth.'

Other amenities included a small Co-op in Willow Street. Willow Street led into the square. It had begun, and continued to be, poorer than the square – its terraced houses lower, their front doors and window fittings cheaper. The Co-op was a bare little shop, with wooden floorboards and dim lighting. Two women served there. They understood poverty; they would cut you half of a small white loaf of bread, or a half of the traditional quarter-pound pack of butter. You shopped there frequently, guiltily enjoying the novelty of being broke.

If you went there when rain was coming on, or there was a strike on the buses, the two women would trot out a number of familiar phrases.

'That's how it goes.'

'It never rains but it pours.'

'No use complaining, is it?'

'What do you expect?'

'Typical!'

You were, in a sense, only visiting. You had a hidden knowledge that your life would lead elsewhere; you were educated, you had been somewhere. The permanent denizens of Blackall Square were genuinely 'broke'. Old ladies, seeing you going frequently to the pillar box in Willow Street, deduced that you owned a bottle of ink; they would come knocking at your door and beg for a fill of ink for their fountain pens.

'Why don't you tell them to clear off?' asked Caleb. 'Oh, I see it now – you like to do good in your small way.'

'Any harm in that?'

He grunted. 'You shouldn't encourage them. Damned spongers.'

Another asset was the small TV set Gerard had given you. On it you fell to watching a strange, continuing, series of dramas entitled *The Prisoner*. A man with a political background was imprisoned on a fantastic island from which he tried to escape. Every week, his attempt was foiled. Within this negative structure, an extraordinary story was unfolded.

On the nights when *The Prisoner* was showing, you would not drink at the Gardeners Arms with Caleb, for fear of missing an instalment.

Caleb came to watch one instalment with you. He was baffled.

'It doesn't make the sense,' he said.

'It's surrealism. It doesn't have to make sense, not in a literal way.'

He smote his forehead with the heel of his right hand. 'Now I see the meaning you tell me! It doesn't make sense because it is an imitation of life, yes?'

'Something like that.' You laughed. Then he also laughed. Most fictions were designed to make sense, those that did not were most true to the way people lived through their existences, so *The Prisoner* was a masterpiece. You particularly identified with the hero, imprisoned on his island just as you had been imprisoned. He raised his fist to the heavens to cry, 'I am not a number. I am a free man!' While you were watching one episode, a knock came at your front door. Irritated, you went to see who it was. A lad of possibly fifteen stood there, holding two books.

He spoke politely. 'Sorry to disturb you, sir. My dad bought two books off of a stall in the market. He don't want them, says like they're above his head. He thought as you would like 'em, seeing you're, well, you're educated, like.'

'What are they?' you asked, snappishly.

'See, they're about time, and dad's a watch-repairer, like, so he thought they'd be up his street.'

'All right. Thanks. Thanks very much.' You took the books, hardly giving them a glance, eager to return to *Prisoner*. 'I'm busy, engaged in something.'

The lad, blank-faced, said without emphasis, 'Dad reckoned they would be worth a quid to you.'

It happened you had a pound note in your pocket. You paid him with it and then shut the door in his face.

The books were both by a Dr Fraser. You remembered your earlier love of strange titles. One of the books was called *Of Time, Passion, and Knowledge* – a large book, necessarily so to contain three such challenging qualities. The other was more slender, *Time As a Series of Irreconcilable Conflicts*. You began to read the latter volume as soon as the episode of *The Prisoner* was over.

You read, 'Personal identity has been recognized as a trouble-some and elusive idea, even a mysterious one. This elusiveness is hardly surprising if we recall that the Self, like all identities, is said to function in the external world; although, unlike any other kind of identity, it registers only partly on the external landscape ...'

You were astonished. Personal identity was exactly your problem. You began to read the taxing, but illuminating, Dr Fraser.

You often ate in the Madarchod, where food was cheap. If it happened that Gerard came into his restaurant when you were there, he would greet you warmly and sign your bill so that you did not have to pay. Sometimes, when he came round with his rent book to collect the rent, he would unfailingly extract the money from Caleb, but would often enough say to you, with a sad smile, 'Let us pretend we are yet in the French forest, where no money is needed.'

Sometimes, when you and Caleb went into the Gardeners Arms, you would meet old women coming out of the public bar with jugs of porter in their fists; you were a long way from Swinging London now. In that pub, Caleb liked to drink heavily, and talk.

'Among philosophers, I like best Schopenhauer. He's such a miserable bastard! He sees how our will distorts our lives. We will our own disasters. Like, why did I come to Britain?'

'You had to escape from Franco's Spain, didn't you? You found Spain an even worse place than England. Why come here if you were going to hate it? Why run it down all the time? Why not try France?'

He showed his teeth at you – already the drink was beginning to tell. 'I hate the French. They ruin a nice country. I don't hate the people of this country. I love the awfulness, its dilapidation, its attitudes far from modern here. I wouldn't change a thing.'

'You hate everything, Caleb. You're a destroyer at heart.'

He thumped his fist on the table, so that your glasses rattled in shock. 'Let's get another damned drink! I'm not a destroyer. I'm a Steppenwolf. Can't you understand that? You are meant to be intelligent, you damned jailbird, don't you understand the pain of being a Steppenwolf? Didn't you never read the German Hesse's novel? A part of society but always an Outsider … Christ, but this beer is piss. I swear they water it.'

'Yes, I did read *Steppenwolf*, you stuck-up prat! Hesse says a Steppenwolf has in him conflicting impulses of saint and profligate; that's what's tearing you apart.'

'So what? A Steppenwolf must once in a while take a good look at himself. When did you ever do that thing?'

'Oh yes, Caleb, you may not have done that but I certainly have. When were you ever in prison, tell me that!'

'I was in Franco's Spain. Does that count as a prison?'

You received a letter from Birdlip Hill, forwarded by your solicitors. It was from Abby. She made no mention of your daughter, she simply said that she was beginning her life anew. She wished you well, but hoped not to hear from you again.

A dismal letter, you thought, although her attitude was understandable enough.

Your father came to see you. Martin looked with contempt about your room before insisting you showed him the bath which served as bathroom, and the toilet. The toilet, having been tacked on to the rear of the house at a late date, was semi-outdoors; large black slugs slid about the concrete floor like animated turds.

'You've not made much of your life, old feller-me-lad,' he said. 'This is not the way we brought you up. Rotten luck! I'm sorry about it.'

He would not sit down. Instead he stood, hands on hips, gazing out of the window at the primary school across the street. 'The world's progressing, but you don't seem to be managing to do the same.'

'I'm studying with Open University, Dad, doing an advanced course in Earth Sciences.'

Martin ignored the remark. 'You've become one of The Poor, I'm sorry to say. Yet The Poor in the old sense are disappearing. What were once luxuries are now seen as necessities; take central heating for instance. Do you have it in this dump? No.'

'I can live without it.'

He turned to direct a look of sorrow at you. 'You say that now, yet a few years ago you were buying chateaux in France. We spoilt you and your sister, now all you've got is a second-rate job and one room in a slum like Blackall Square ... Time it was pulled down.'

You felt bad. 'Would you like a cup of tea, Dad? I'm afraid it's all I can offer. If you came here just to tick me off, don't bother. I feel bad enough as it is.'

He shook his head. 'I am not ticking you off, laddie. I'm just worried about you, as any good father would be. How old are you now? While you're rotting here, England is changing – rapidly, and for the better. We've got new drugs and new technologies, better ways of governing. The bad old days of booms and busts are over. Now we're capital-intensive and labour-saving. Your grandfather would hardly recognize the country if he came back –'

'Fine. Well, Dad, let's have a cup of tea together. Believe me, I did rethink my life while I was banged up.'

As you put the kettle on the gas ring he said, 'It's not just socialism, it's a world trend, at least in the Western world. Inexplicable really ...' He fell silent, musing. Then he said, 'You know, Britain led the world in the eighteenth century. We began the Industrial Revolution.'

'I know, Dad.'

'With the coming of mechanization, what did the Continentals do? They made little artificial singing birds in gilt cages, and little human-looking dummies who signed their names. All toys, really. Meanwhile, the British working man was digging canals and building bridges. It's something to be proud of. It's what has made us great.'

Listening to Martin, you felt ashamed you did not love your country more.

You poured hot water on the tea bags. 'You can buy circular teabags now,' he said. 'The old square ones are going off sale.'

'Evolution even in teabags ...'

'No sugar for me, thanks, Steve; I've given it up. Putting on weight ... Getting old. Got a touch of diabetes, as a matter of fact. The trouble with labour-saving devices is they are also labour-cancelling. Progress hits the old working class. There's not quite the solidarity there used to be. Sons are now going to universities! Can you believe it?'

'That's something to be pleased about, surely.'

He sipped his tea with undue caution. 'We were going down the drain, now it's the reverse. It's the West outshining the Soviets. Although I hate to say so, last year's Apollo 14, and the two moon walks, are an apotheosis of capitalism; adventure, initiative, innovation ...'

'I've never heard you speak well of capitalism before.'

'You claim you had a rethink when you were behind bars; I'm having a bit of a rethink too. As some chap was singing the other day, "The Times They are A-Changing ..."'

He shook your hand as he got up to go. After he had left, leaving you a fiver, you thought, 'Gosh, we actually had a conversation. Of a kind ...'

An Avon lady came to call on you. She was pretty, brightly painted, plump, in her mid-thirties. She wore a black two-piece over a white, well-filled blouse, a neat flared skirt and a saucy jacket with mock-gold buttons. Her shoes were red. Her lips were orange. Her eyes were green.

She was selling cosmetics; you said you had no need of cosmetics. She asked if you were married; you told her you were divorced. She was sympathetic, and remarked on how much you must miss female company. She crossed her legs as she spoke, revealing a shapely calf and thigh.

You admitted that you did miss female company.

'You poor dear,' she exclaimed. 'Come and let me give you a cuddle.'

You learnt later that her name was Judy. She wore black underwear. Her ministrations were extremely pleasurable. She liked you to be naked, but would never strip off entirely herself. 'I have to be businesslike, you know,' she said with a smile. She was cheerful, she was meticulously clean, she liked fornication, she liked sexual organs – her own and yours.

While studying yours on one occasion, she chuckled and said, 'They're funny, aren't they?' in a slightly puzzled way. 'Yet they produce such wonderful sensations.'

Judy never asked questions. In a sense, she was not interested in you. You discovered that she never voted; politics meant nothing to her; nor did the wider world. Yet it was not that Judy was unintelligent. The sensual world enveloped her. When you commented on her shining dark hair, which was kept short, Judy told you that she was a natural blonde.

You were surprised. 'I thought the ideal for women was to be blonde.'

'I dyed mine black because I thought with blonde hair, I looked like a tart.'

When aroused, Judy gave forth a delectable scent – a lure. You were permitted, indeed encouraged, to study her neat little lower purse. It amused you to think of it as plump and well-fed. You kissed its smiling lips and sank your tongue deep into it, lured by her strange, but irresistible, aroma. When your sessions in that bare blue room were over, she would dress herself, use your primitive toilet and go on her way.

She came to your bed every other Thursday.

The question of money never arose between you.

Some years later, as you passed through the cosmetics department of a big store, you saw Judy standing behind a counter, the same old Judy, possibly slightly plumper. The recognition was immediate and mutual. She gave you a slight smile and a wink, as if to say, without regret, 'We had a bit of fun, didn't we? Don't tell anyone!'

4

'We Don't Want No Trouble'

You were saying goodbye to Judy on the front doorstep one day. You noticed a taxi wending its way past the grim old brick tower of the Salvation Army fortress and entering the square. A taxi in the square was a rare sight.

It drew up in front of Number 12. From it emerged your Aunt Violet, who went round to the other side of the vehicle to help your grandmother, Elizabeth Fielding, put her daintily shod feet to the ground. Violet linked her arm with Elizabeth's to assist her into the house.

You showed the ladies into your room. Elizabeth you seated on your only chair, the blue-painted hardback. Violet sat on the edge of your rumpled bed. You stood, smiling and embarrassed. You noted Violet's covert response to the atmosphere of the room; she had identified the scent, which had not yet dispersed.

'Who was the woman who just left, Steve?' she asked.

'Oh, she was the Avon lady. I didn't buy any of her cosmetics.'

'What else was she selling?'

'Nothing,' you said, with perfect honesty.

Violet cocked an eyebrow above her spectacles but said nothing. She was looking much older than when you had last seen her.

Elizabeth spoke, possibly aware of a certain tension in your exchange. 'I saw on my television set ... Launched. The set. That the Americans have launched another rocket ... To the Moon, a rocket. It's so clever.'

You agreed that it was clever.

The ladies sat in their respective positions, regarding you. You offered to make them some instant coffee. They refused.

Speaking rather formally, Violet said, 'Joyce – perhaps you remember my daughter, Joyce – has a new job in a government planning office.'

She paused there until you said, 'Oh yes?'

'You know of the government scheme to demolish some of the country's slums, to build high-rises instead?'

Again she waited for a sign of your assent, frowning meanwhile.

'The scheme includes the demolition of Blackall Square. We thought you ought to know.'

You said nothing. You were shocked. 'When?' you managed to ask.

'Joyce says that March next year is the date set. It has yet to be announced; they're waiting till after the by-election.'

Elizabeth spoke, clutching the scraggy folds of her throat. 'Steve, you must come away. Must leave here. It's not fit. It's a good ... that is, it's better. My intention ... Let me say quickly. In my will, my intention ... it was to leave ... I mean, you, you some money. To leave. In my will. My daughter speaks ... hardly speaks ... Your aunt hardly speaks ... Bella hardly speaks to me now. She's earning in Brussels now ... Good money. Earning. Some money in the will, but much better to give now ... Give you the ... what did I say? Give the money now ... Just to help. To get you out of your bad time.'

'Elizabeth, dear, you –'

'Calle Galina. The house,' she said quickly, raising a hand to interrupt you. 'I have inherited. Dorothy ... my friend who owned ... it. The house ... She's Dorothy. I have inherited Calle ... You were there – Calle Galina. She, my dear Dorothy, has died of ... She nursed you once. On her, oh, her knee, yes, as a baby. There were complica ... Complications. I may go to live out my years ... final years. Let me do this. For you. Dear boy.'

'Then you can study,' said Violet. She looked at you as if you were a stranger. 'Lead a decent life. It's an absurd idea, living here like this. Particularly when your sister is doing so well in America.'

You were angry and troubled after the ladies had gone. You did not rejoice at this stroke of good fortune.
In fact, I cried ... I cried because ... it's hard to say. Because I did not deserve the good fortune. Because it seemed so arbitrary. Because – oh, I had a romantic view of failure.
And?
Later, I felt ... oh, I felt the closure was rotten luck on everyone who lived out their mortal lives in the rotten old square. Like woodlice under a stone.
Harming no one.
So you went and had a drink with Caleb ...

You were boozing in the Gardeners Arms, as usual. Caleb was the enthusiast. You had graduated from pints of beer to boilermakers – beers with whisky chasers. You were sitting in one corner of the room, elbows on the table. The pub was crowded and noisy, full mainly of men. The air was blue with smoke. There was a real fug, which was getting into your heads. This was 'The Life of Blokes' with a vengeance; many there found it fulfilling.

'I used to swim in the Med every evening in the summer,' Caleb said. 'As naked as I was born. I hated the tourists, bloody tourists. We lived in a village south of Barcelona, just a kilometre inland from the Med. It was okay, a bit primitive.

'Not many tourists came in our village. Not much accommodation. There was one thin guy, old man, with spectacles, too scholarly to be a proper yob of a tourist. Came several years with his daughter. She was pretty for an English woman. I fancied her – dark in a sort of Spanish way. Some nights the father he got rather smashed. Tipsy, you know? She'd take him home.'

Caleb scratched his blue jowls, thinking back to that time.

'This particular night, I looked in the bodega – our one and only bodega – with a pal. We'd been swimming. And this old man had gone and left a book behind, an English book. I took hold of it. I was trying to learn English.

'My first English novel! *Caleb Williams*. Godwin. That was the author's name, William Godwin. It's a masterpiece! I wanted to visit to that dark, villainous country Godwin described.' Caleb stopped suddenly. 'Why am I telling you this?'

'We were talking about the demolition of the square.'

'Oh yes.' Caleb sighed and took another swig of his beer. 'That summer, the village, my village, is demolished. Absolutely destroyed. We waked up one morning and already the bulldozers are at work. Rmmm rmmm rmmm. This was the Generalissimo's idea – for a coast road. So anything in the way of this road had to be destroyed, laid flat. Fucking high-handedness, you see? Fascism is like that. Fucking high-handedness.'

'So what are we going to do about Blackall Square before the bulldozers arrive?'

He threw his whisky down his throat, tipping his bald head back to do so.

'We get the fuck out of here,' he said. 'As we had to get the fuck out of our little village.'

You reminded him that your father was Undersecretary of State for Housing. You could appeal to him.

Caleb made a wide sweeping gesture, brushing your suggestion aside. 'Never appeal to authority. Once you show your face, you're in trouble. Take the word of a Steppenwolf. Never appeal to your father. What we shall do, yeah, what we shall do, is hold a protest meeting. Get the *Finsbury Chronicle* involved. Right? Are you ready for another drink?'

'I'm not a drunk, you know. I became a new man when I was banged up.'

'Good – have another drink to celebrate!'

You did not tell Caleb about your sudden good fortune. Your grandmother's kindness fermented inside you.

Blackall Square consisted of three-storey buildings, many with cellars, just like Number 12. They stood shoulder to shoulder, faced with grey cladding, capped with slate roofing. Iron railings stood a yard in front of the houses, guarding them. An indwelling melancholy had perhaps been there from the start, ever since the square came into being in the late nineteenth century. But in those days there would have been more vitality in evidence; carriages would have come and gone, street sellers might have cried their wares. All that activity had faded with the wars; nothing had replaced it. An active class of people had been succeeded by the unwanted – people sad, docile, but resentful of their fates. Big red buses roared along the main road only a street away, ignoring the backwater of the square.

The present inhabitants of Blackall Square had never previously experienced a protest meeting. Caleb stood on the top step by your door, beckoning people nearer, calling to them to get together, showing, you thought, great spirit. You went about the square, knocking on doors, trying to persuade people to come out, assuring them it was in their interest to listen because their homes were under threat.

'We don't want no trouble, mister,' some told us.

'It's not for us to say. Council knows best.'

'Clear off, mate, or I'll set the dog on you!'

'They may find us somewhere better to live, don't you think?'

All told, you managed to marshal twenty-two people between you, the majority being older women. The ex-sergeant who ran the bath place, Colin, had locked up and come along to listen.

Caleb began to speak, his voice rather controlled at first. 'This lousy government of ours has decided to pull down our square. It has planned to let it go to rack and ruin, so it thinks no one will care about it. So it guesses we will be glad to let it be destroyed. The bad news will shortly be announced, so we have to act now. This square is our home and we must fight to preserve it.'

'But you're only a lodger here,' a woman called out indignantly. 'What's it got to do with you?'

'I like this square. I live here. I pay the rent. Isn't that enough?'

He stood there on the step, half-pleading, half-challenging, his big ears glowing pink in the early sunshine. Admittedly, he was a strange-looking person. Your heart went out to him. Caleb saw all the shortcomings of the world.

'But you're a foreigner,' the same woman in the crowd protested – a scraggy woman whose life was not working out well. 'We don't know where you come from.'

'What's that got to do with it?' Caleb retorted. 'We must all present a united front. We must make it clear that not only are these houses our homes, but it will be our way of life that will be destroyed if the square goes down. Then we shall all be dispersed to different parts of London. Could be you will be forced to live in the suburbs. How will you like that? You wouldn't want to have to live in Walthamstow or Chingford, with the snobs, would you?'

'I wouldn't mind a little flat with a bath room,' said one frail old man, raising his hand to speak. The ex-sergeant answered him. 'What's wrong with my nice spotless bath place? It's just you're too bone idle to visit it.'

'Yeah! That's right. We must not be bone idle,' said Caleb. 'We must do whatever we can. I have prepared a letter to the Finsbury council. I ask every one of you to sign it. What do you say?'

'I'm not signing no letter to any bloody council,' a youngish woman with red-dyed hair said. 'They'd turn me out for a troublemaker.'

''Sides, they may put us up in a better place,' said her mother who was standing next to her. 'The housing here is a regular disgrace, that's what it is.'

There was a general murmur of agreement.

'You've got to fight, you stupid lot!' Caleb shouted. 'If you don't fight, you'll simply find yourselves shovelled into an old folks' home in no time – and it will serve you right! Do you want to die there, with a plate of porridge for breakfast and a matron standing over you with a whip?'

'That's no way to talk,' said the ex-sergeant. 'What are you, any road? A bloody Communist?'

That was when they all started calling Caleb names.

So the meeting broke up.

Caleb then began to drink seriously, punitively. His brow became darker, his mood more sullen. The more he drank, the more he ranted. You knew he was a vegetarian; now meat-eating became another of the objections he had to the rest of humanity.

'It's not just fucking meat-eating; that's a euphemism. You got to understand it, Steve.' He wagged a finger at you.

'You'll dislocate that bloody thing if you keep shaking it like that.'

'I'm telling you, chum, it's killing animals. Murdering without thought. Hateful! Those poor placid things in fields – cows, sheep, pigs, ducks, whatever – they are just there waiting for some farmer to come along and kill them. Ever seen the fear in a cow's eyes just before the chopper falls? No? Well I have.'

He took a deep drink of his whisky, followed by a sip of beer. You always bought the cheapest stuff the Gardeners Arms could sell.

He went on quietly. 'That wise old crank, Thoreau, said that as the human race improved, it would slowly give up the bad habit of slaughtering and eating animals. The big mistake he made was to imagine the human race was going to improve. How does it improve? It gets worse … And the more of us there are, the larger the population grows, the more our nastiness grows. Like an infection.'

'It is part of our nature to eat meat, Caleb.'

He squared up to you across the grimy old table. 'Does it occur to you all these animals could know that they are to be eaten? Suppose they know. Suppose the knowledge has been inherited. But they can't say anything, they can't escape, so they just have to live on and wait for the fucking chop, all the while bearing intense hatred of we humans. Just as we all feel intense hatred and fear, knowing we'll get the fucking chop one day soon ... Buy us another pint, will you? God, I'm thirsty. How I loathe this sodding pub.'

You admired Caleb's despair. You admired Caleb's independence of mind. But you took to avoiding the evenings' boozing with him. You pursued your studies, and welcomed the Avon lady when she called. You still worked in the warehouse – until your grandmother's money came through.

The pigeons, rising with a great clatter of wings, still enjoyed their daily flight above the square. Some Pakistanis moved into the house next door. You tried to make contact with them, but they were shy of it. Every morning, they would leave the narrow-shouldered house, leap on the saddles of their push-bikes and cycle away to the factory where they worked. They were as regular as the pigeons.

At three o'clock one winter morning, there came a hammering at your room door. It was Caleb, in a bad state.

'Let me in, Steve. Have mercy on me! I've got the bloody DT's!'

You sat up in your bed, rubbing your eyes. 'For Christ's sake, go back to bed, Caleb! Sleep it off.'

He banged again. 'I know you hate me. I know I am a social leper. I am dying. Let me in! Have some mercy on a poor Steppen fucking wolf, for Jesus Christ's sake!'

You put the light on and let him in. Caleb was shivering. He wore nothing but an old grey shirt and a dirty pair of underpants. You sat him down on your chair and threw the rug from the bed over him for warmth. 'Why weren't you a fucking Catholic, Steve? Like my mother, for God's sake.'

You tried to soothe him, to some effect. Lighting the gas ring, you boiled him up a cup of tea. He drank in noisy sips, groaning meanwhile.

'You're a true friend, Steve. I know I'm a bastard. I'm scared to go back to my room. Let me sleep here with you.'

'You can't do that. There isn't room for one thing. What the fuck's the matter with your sodding room?'

He looked ghastly. He stank. He buried his face in his hands, to pull the hands away at once as if they burnt his skin.

'Suppose I was fucking Jesus Christ, would you turn him out?'

'Jesus was not a fucking drunkard, as far as we know.'

He flung his scraggy arms up in supplication.

'Let me stay here. I'm safe here, you shit. I won't throw up, I promise. I never throw up.'

'Sorry, but you can't fucking well stay here. I keep telling you.'

'My light's gone out in my room. It's all dark. I'm scared. I thought General Franco was in there, the bastard.'

'You need to lay off the booze, Caleb, old pal.'

'Remember what Schopenhauer said? "Do your best for your fellow men, and if that's not good enough, then fuck 'em!"'

'If your bulb's gone, I've got another.'

So you took the bulb out of your overhead light. It left only the dim, 40-watt light burning by your bedside. You eased Caleb out of the chair and helped him upstairs through the broken-down night. He alternated groans with imaginary quotes from Schopenhauer, together with obscene ramblings. 'Just suppose I was bloody Jesus, just got in from Belgium or wherever, fat lot of good speaking to you in Amoniac, you so bloody inch – angular – East Angular, trying to sneak sanctuary ... insular I mean, how many more stairs are they in this goddammed billet?'

You propped him against the wall on his landing. By leaving the landing light on, you could see into his room. You untwisted the old bulb from his overhead light. Since he had wandered in after you, you handed it to him. He flung it impatiently on his bed as you inserted your functioning bulb.

Light flooded the room, revealing a scene of Dostoevskian squalor. There was no furniture other than the stark bed, beside which old hardcover books were piled. No curtain hung at the window to keep out the shabby night; no rug lay on the floor to cover the nakedness of the floorboards. Ranged round two of the walls were old milk bottles. Some of the bottles contained rotted milk, some a curious yellowish-orange mixture, which indicated what they had been used for.

Seeing your glance, Caleb gave a guilty grin. 'It's a long way down to the loo,' he said.

With that, he flung himself on the bed. Quickly following a crunching noise came his agonized screams.

You read everything that Dr Fraser had to say, and felt the better for it. You sensed within you what he called 'the operation of incomprehensible powers'. The change that had taken place in prison was still working within you.

You went to see Gerard and Helge. You happened to arrive at their office a week after their daughter Brenda gave birth to a baby girl in the nearby hospital.

'It's the Great Chain of Being, Steve, my friend,' Helge said. 'What a blessing it is to have a granddaughter! That we should live so long ...' She raised her right hand and gazed upwards. She had assimilated several gestures that you thought of as 'Jewish'.

Brenda clasped her baby, gazing down on her with love, as if nothing else mattered. The infant murmured contentedly to itself.

When I told Gerard and Helge about the proposal to demolish Blackall Square, Gerard spread his hands in resignation.

'No formal announcement has been made as yet, my dear friend; it could be only a rumour. But let us suppose they do demolish the square ... To be honest, it needs pulling down. The dilapidations! I should be compensated for the destruction of my property, since this is a country that believes in legality. Maybe I can find you a better place, but whatever happens, it will be for the best, I'm sure. We trust English law.'

'You're the only ones who do.'

'Steve, we shall see what happens.'

What happened was that a general election was called. The Conservative Party returned to power under Prime Minister Edward Heath. Harold Wilson and the Labour Party lost power. Martin Fielding lost his post in Housing.

It looked like a reprieve for Blackall Square, but Prime Minister Heath retained the housing plans drawn up by the previous government. Bulldozers moved in. The square was demolished; the inhabitants were put into old folks' homes, just as Caleb had warned.

By the time Harold Wilson returned to power in 1974, the year you became fifty, a brutish multi-storey car park had been built on the previous site of the square.

You bought Helge's granddaughter a blue teddy bear.

5

Some Family Conversation

A year may pass almost without notice; it is the weeks, those small slices of a year, which are felt to go by so quickly.

The passing weeks, with their accumulations, were full of work and study. You built a stable life for yourself. Your aims became more modest than they had been; the acquirement of knowledge became an increasing pleasure, as you tried to put away the old questions which had plagued you for so long. However, the question of Walcot sands remained; was it simply by a lucky accident that you had not died then? What would it be like to die aged four? What meaning would such a death have held for others – for your parents, for instance?

Dying in France during the war would have been quite a different matter, almost to have been expected. Almost to have been accepted.

Such reflections recurred with decreasing frequency. In your studies you delved deeper into a far more distant past, as if the answers to your ontological riddles might be buried there.

Your parents' old house in the Southampton suburb underwent changes; the modest porch was pulled down and a grander new one built, with Corinthian pillars to support it. Once you went inside, you encountered more change.

The chandelier which had hung lopsidedly in the hall had gone. Instead, new tracking lights had been installed. And the living room, which your mother had always called 'the lounge', had been extended into a large conservatory. A grey fitted carpet had replaced the old Axminster, and new pieces of furniture stood in new places. Gone was the old leather sofa you remembered. Gone was the old radiogram. Instead, a flashy cocktail cabinet stood at the entrance to the conservatory.

The conservatory itself was choked by rubber tree plants in pots. Your father's Russell Flint watercolour ('rather risqué' had been the judgement in the old days), had gone; in its place on the long wall of the living room were two large repro oils of African elephants, posed as if about to charge the visitors who thronged beneath them.

It was almost ten years since you had set foot in your parents' home. *Of course things change,* you told yourself. *How natural that the place should be modernized.*

Your parents had grown old. You had returned because Martin and Mary had decided to, as they put it, 'patch things up'; to celebrate your degree in Geological Sciences and your appointment as Geology Master in the private university of Ashford. What you did not tell your parents was that Elizabeth's kind donation had come through, and you had thought it advisable to make a contribution to the renovation of the Geological classroom there.

With the signs of encroaching middle class modernity went graver indications of the passage of time. Mary had shrunk and her face had withered. Her right arm and hand were never still, vibrating slightly in warning, so you feared, of worse to come. Martin had put on weight again and was being treated for diabetes. His cricketing days were long over; the bats that once lined the old hall had been given away to charity. He had grown a moustache.

He remained a member of the Labour Party; but had invested in farmland, the source of his mild prosperity. As is commonly acknowledged, the possession of acres of countryside induces conservatism and a tendency to be defensive when discussions of equality among men are raised.

As you shook hands with Martin, he congratulated you on your degree and your new position. 'The spell in prison must have stimulated the old brain cells,' he said.

You were peeved that he should bring up your term in prison. You replied to the effect that he had ruined several lives by executing the plan to destroy Blackall Square.

'You have to move on,' he declared. 'We all have to make sacrifices.' His old catch phrase: you smiled to hear it again. He said, as you might have expected, that the square was beyond salvation. He went on to remark that 'an old companion' of yours had been arrested in an illegal squat in Hammersmith.

'People like him should be kicked out of the country,' he said. 'He's just a parasite on society.'

'Who do you mean?'

'A troublemaker friend of yours. Arthur Blake, or Arturo Blake, as he likes to call himself.'

'Of course he likes to call himself Arturo; that's the name with which he was christened. He is also known as Caleb – his writing name, okay?'

'Steve, dear man, now you have a fresh chance in life, do stay away from such riff-raff.'

You felt a flush flood your face.

'Father, would it surprise you if I told you that Caleb is one of the best guys I ever met? I'm only sorry I lost touch with him.'

'You've also lost touch with your own wife and daughter. It seems rather to be a habit of yours.'

'Abby is not my wife. She's my ex-wife.'

Your father sighed heavily and turned away. He marched straight over to a serious-looking group of four men and a silent woman and began immediately to talk about the national water shortage. His parting shot had struck home. You had reason to feel bad about not seeing your young daughter. As ever, you had been swept along by events. There was also the knowledge that you would be highly unwelcome on Birdlip Hill, where Abby and Geraldine lived.

The family constitution as represented by those attending the party had changed as much as the furnishings. Claude Hillman, the erstwhile Justin, who had deserted your father's sister, Ada, had evidently been forgiven his sins. There he was, looking rather more subdued than previously, though he gave you a cheerful salute, standing with a younger woman called Phoebe – in your eyes not at all attractive, a thin woman with drab hair. Ada, however, was also present, though in a different corner of the room, drinking with a jolly young academic, often to be seen on TV – Beavis Bernard Gray. She was brightly painted and extremely cheerful. Her hair was short and streaked with scarlet.

According to your mother, 'Oh, serve old Claude right! Ada's better off without him.' A more tolerant remark than you would previously have expected. 'Beavis is an absolute dear. They're off to Jordan next week. He's doing a programme from there.'

You asked what the programme would be about.

'King Hussein, of course.'

'What about Joey and Terry?' you asked. She replied defensively that they were doing well.

'I'm sorry to hear that. And Abby and Geraldine?'

Mary shot you a quick look before turning her gaze to the party. 'I do keep in touch with Abby – for your sake, although I never liked her. I felt she was bad for you. She's become rather grand. Mind you, the Cholmondeleys were always rather grand, weren't they? I understand your little girl's doing well. Go and see them, why don't you?'

'I can't face it.'

With uncharacteristic spirit, your mother said, 'You can face anything if you've a mind to, however long it takes.'

Claude came over and shook your hand. 'Good to see you again, Steve. I'd like you to meet Phoebe, my new girlfriend.' You noticed he tinted his hair.

You shook hands with Phoebe. She smiled and said that Claude had told her all about you. Rather hastily, Claude asked you what you thought about all the Jamaicans coming over to Britain. You had given this matter little thought.

'They fought for us during the war, didn't they?'

Phoebe said she had been looking for digs and one landlady had said to her, 'You're all right but I don't want any racial people here.'

'There you are!' Claude exclaimed, as if his girlfriend's experience confirmed all he dreaded. 'I phoned our Tory MP, I said to him, "They may be black, but we have a duty to let them in."' He lowered his voice and held you by the sleeve. 'You know Joyce has got a black boyfriend. I don't know what you make of that.'

'They're here,' whispered Phoebe. 'He seems ever so nice, but still …'

'Yes, but he's not Jamaican,' Claude said. 'Been over here a while, I understand.'

To change the subject, you asked him about Joey and Terry. 'I hear they're doing well.'

He pulled a face. 'I don't know who told you that. They fell out over some financial deal. Had a bit of a scrap, so Joey told Phoebe.'

'That's right,' said Phoebe. 'Cos Joey had a black eye and I asked him about it.'

'Silly buggers,' said Claude. 'Anyhow, the long and the short of it is that Terry has up and offed to Canada. I can't think why Canada – Australia would have been so much warmer than Canada.'

You remarked, 'So Joey's still hanging around, is he?'

Claude said, lowering his voice, 'I gather he didn't do you any favours. He was bragging about it. I was sorry to hear it.'

'So what did you do about it, Uncle?'

'Told him to shut up, of course. Him I brought up properly …'

Several people whom you did not know were present to celebrate your degree and the new post at Ashbury. Uncle Bertie was talking to a few of them. Violet was not present; however, her daughter was. Joyce had arrived with her father and her boyfriend, who was more-or-less black, as Claude had said. Even at a casual glance, Joyce's resemblance to her mother was strong.

You accepted a glass of Sauvignon Blanc from the waitress, evidently a village girl, and talked for a while to your Aunt Belle, who had married a sportive Monty Pepler while you were in prison.

'Don't know why we're being so cheerful,' said Monty, grinning. 'Inflation at twelve per cent and rising, I mean to say.'

'Still, a space probe is on its way to Mars,' said Belle, winking at you, to establish the fact that she knew her husband's false gloom. 'That's progress, isn't it?'

'Probably going there to escape inflation.' Monty could not stop laughing at his own joke. You laughed politely too, for a second.

Belle sighed. Turning to you, turning her back on her husband, she deliberately changed the subject. 'Have you seen *Easy Rider*? Fantastic film! Dennis Hopper and Peter Fonda.'

'I was locked up, remember.'

'Drugs, bikers, rock 'n' roll, sex … I'd say it was your thing.' She gave you an old-fashioned look.

'You're very frivolous, Belle.'

'I've had a couple of glasses, sorry. I take life very seriously, let me tell you, don't I, Monty? I'm a civil servant now, with the prospect of being posted to Brussels.'

As you passed Mary and the group of women she had joined, including her sister-in-law, Flo, you overheard your mother saying, 'Yes, would you believe it, gave away half her fortune to Steve, on a whim, mind you, and now she's gone to live in *Venice*, of all places …'

Evidently that absurd phrase, 'of all places', rankled with Flo as much as it did with you, for she remarked, challengingly, 'Why not? Ruskin did! Byron did!'

But Flo was always inclined to be superior.

Smiling to yourself, clutching your glass, you wandered into the garden, where various guests were sitting talking under sunshades. It was gloriously hot and sunny. The grass looked dry. Among the ladies in summer dresses was a younger woman in a T-shirt, chatting to an Indian youth whose face seemed to radiate beauty. They had recently been sitting on a bench, and were now strolling about with glasses of kir in hand.

As you recognized her, she waved you over. 'Uncle Steve! Come and meet my friend, Paul Patel.'

You shook hands with Paul and gave Joyce a kiss, all the while trying to come to terms with the fact that this young woman was so clearly Violet's daughter. 'By this token,' you said to yourself, 'you must understand how you yourself have aged.' This was another time that it sank in upon you that you were no longer growing up but growing old. You would shortly turn fifty.

Dismissing the thought, you sat down with Joyce and Paul Patel. As you did so, Sonia strolled over with a distinguished grey-haired man who had in tow a younger chap dressed all in yellow. Sonia threw her arms round you, kissed you on both cheeks – that was a new continental fashion – and introduced Adrian Hyasent and another actor, Ralph Lyngstad, the yellow-clad fellow. On being introduced, Lyngstad pulled a yellow handkerchief from his breast pocket, flourished it, and dabbed at his narrow forehead. 'Enchanted,' he said.

'Here on a quick break,' Sonia said. 'England seems terribly small. On the other hand, the US seems terribly big.'

You were astounded to see that your sister's affair with Hyasent still continued, while you were prepared to dislike on sight anyone who dressed all in yellow; but they sat themselves down at a nearby table and all began talking at once.

A waitress came immediately and served them champagne.

'Oh yes, I have let my life drift,' Adrian declared, wrapping an arm round Sonia's waist. With his free hand, he made a drifting gesture in the air. He wore a bracelet tight on his wrist. 'Trouble is, I listen to too much popular music. Abba is a drug, wouldn't you say? It saps the will.' He gave a gesture of wry apology, exonerating himself. 'One is allowed to drift. It requires a particular talent.'

'I adore Chubby Checker!' exclaimed the yellow fellow. He started to sing *Let's Twist Again*, with appropriate shuffling move-ments. 'Surely they must have a record of it here, even in this endearingly old-fashioned place? I'd entirely *lurve* to dance.'

'Oh, Chubby Checker!' Sonia exclaimed. 'It's the happiest music since Schiller wrote his *Ode to Joy*!'

You noted how attentive were the men to your sister. She seemed somehow to have gained stature, not to mention a taller coiffeur.

'Who's Schiller? I haven't heard of him,' said the yellow man. 'Is he with Dire Straits?'

'Oh, *Fred* Schiller,' said Sonia, pretending to be cross.

'But you notice that even in that twist,' you said, attempting a more intellectual note, 'the element of nostalgia creeps in. "Do you remember when things were really humming?" – isn't that one of Checker's lines? The happier past! Nostalgia is like a virus creeping into modern life.'

'Don't you suffer from it, Steve?' Joyce asked. 'You must suffer from something.'

'I hate the past,' you replied. 'It's where all one's mistakes are stored.' You drank from your glass. It was the sort of afternoon for which Sauvignon Blanc had been invented. You secretly preferred it to champagne.

You sensed that the men were coldly uninterested in what you had to say. You swung directly to face Sonia, saying, 'So what about this film you were going to be in? Haven't heard another word about it. *Jocasta*?'

'Where have you been, dear?' she answered pertly. 'It's now in post-production. It's going to be big.'

'Yes,' said Adrian Hyasent, jostling you. 'You want to get out more, chum. Out of the slammer, for instance ...'

'You want to get out of my way, you tick!'

Paul Patel spoke up swiftly, moving between you and Hyasent. You had sensed that he and Joyce did not greatly care for Ralph Lyngstad. 'We can link nostalgia with immaturity. A longing for the past and the womb.'

'Oh, that's all garbage,' said Ralph, touching his cheek for some reason. 'Chubby would so laugh to hear that. I met him once, in New York. Brief encounter. A dear, a so fun man.'

Patel gave a ravishing smile. 'Fun or not, nostalgia is a contemporary problem, one of several that evolution has dealt us. Let me remind you that since humankind became bipedal, a narrow pelvis was a good structural adaptation. But we have endorphin-thirsty large brains –'

'Oh, look here –' began Adrian, but Patel was not to be interrupted.

'And those big brains really require a wide pelvis for the comfortable delivery of babies. So there is a conflict; wide pelvis or narrow pelvis? Intelligence or dimness?'

'Terribly boredom-provoking question!' exclaimed the yellow-clad one.

'Oh, so you opted for dimness, did you, you little prick?' said Patel, with sudden venom.

'Chill out, dear!' was Ralph's response.

'He's saying all this because I'm pregnant,' Joyce interposed, directing this remark at you.

'The narrow pelvis,' said Paul Patel, stroking Joyce's behind; he was pleased to have silenced the opposition, 'imposes an unfair burden on women.'

'Still, the evolutionary solution to the problem is rather neat. Our babies are born before they are really ready, before the cranium grows too large and hard to pass through the neck of the womb. A neat development. Of course, it does lead to later societal problems, such as a protracted immaturity.' He directed a dark gaze at Adrian. 'The evidence for which being such groups as the Sex Pistols and rock and roll. Reflect on how long it takes a human child even to toddle, whereas the progeny of wild animals, particularly grazers, is up and running five minutes after being born.'

'What's all this about, chum?' asked Adrian, looking offended.

'Hence the institution of marriage – at least for those not gay. A matrimonial pair staying together provide best protection for the baby's protracted immaturity.' He looked challengingly at Adrian and the yellow-clad Lyngstad. 'If you *chums* can understand all that –'

Before he had finished speaking, a young man wearing a floral shirt came up, clutching a glass, trying to conceal the fact that he was drunk. It was Douglas, Joyce's brother, full of cheer as well as wine.

He grasped Ralph Lyngstad's hand and shook it vigorously.

'I say! You're a picture! What are you advertising? Colman's Mustard?'

A little later, you were strolling with Joyce and Paul. Joyce was saying how amusing her brother was; Dougie was now a prominent DJ on Radio Caroline.

Paul was saying he regretted that he had been impolite to fellow guests. 'I can't stop swanking,' he said. 'The awful thing is, I always have a sense that there is a part of myself standing apart, aloof, watching the action. Not disapproving exactly, although in this case –'

'Disdainful?' you suggested, trying to remember where you had heard similar remarks before.

'Yes, more that.'

Joyce said, 'We all have that feeling at times. Detached from our actions.'

'I have it much of the time,' you said. 'If I stop and listen, as it were, it's there.' But you were feeling slightly tipsy. 'Read the *Upanishads* –'

'No, thanks,' said Paul.

'That sensation of something remote at your elbow may be what makes people believe there is a God watching over them,' Joyce suggested.

'Or vice versa,' you said, with a sudden inspiration for something to say. 'Maybe there is a God watching over us and we just mistake it for a part of ourselves.'

'Do you believe in *Doppelgängers*?' Joyce asked.

'In which case,' said Paul, ignoring her question, 'He – or possibly She – will have to look away for a while, because I intend to visit the toilet. Excuse me.'

As he departed, sauntering elegantly, you seized the chance to ask Joyce how her mother was.

'Violet and Dad quarrel hideously. And they don't much like the fact that I love my gorgeous Hindu. Do you like Paul, Steve?'

'Oh, massive approval. Loved the way he put Lyngstad down. And are you really preggers? It doesn't show.'

'Not yet. Give it a chance. Steve, you are a real bastard, you realize! I do know you were humping mum that time, when I was just a nipper. Maybe later, too. You shouldn't have taken advantage of her. She was in a bad emotional state.'

You were not displeased to have that happy occasion mentioned.

'Hang on, Joyce! I didn't take advantage of her. It was mutual. Maybe we were both in an emotional state, but what's that got to do with it? That's when you need a shag or two! For comfort, if nothing else.'

She gave a half-laugh and squeezed your hand. 'Well, I wanted to tell you I know what you were up to. It made a great impression on me as a kid.'

'So you've gone to the bad ever since!'

'What, me? Me with a career in job placement? That's where you see a whole country going to the bad. If we join the EU, it might save us. Here comes Paul. Glad you're not racist.'

'Count on me. Tell me, Joyce, did that little wretch Terry ever –'

But Paul was returning, strolling past Adrian *& Co.*

'What were you two talking about?' he asked you.

'Oh, I was saying I wondered if I could make a synthesis of my life. And I was wondering what a synthesis was.'

'Are you drunk?' he asked you, peering into your face. 'Let's get drunk, shall we? Do you think any of the folks here would notice if we three fell into a flowerbed?'

So you did, and they did.

6
Over Jurassic Sand

You stood at the casement of the room which was now your refuge, the place where you could pursue your new occupation, gazing out into the night. Beyond the walls of Ashbury University lay the Oxfordshire countryside, the landscape of which had been fashioned by countrymen over many centuries.

The great clump of trees which stood to one end of a broad meadow grew there by courtesy of mankind, of generations of farmers. Darkness turned it into a black mass which might have been mistaken, by anyone who had not seen it in daylight, for a gigantic and impregnable rock. The aspect of the land was transformed by the dark into something entirely more remote; the hand of man had vanished, leaving behind a footprint of wilderness.

Something here was real and true, but it proved elusive.

You were familiar with, comfortable with, your mood – mild melancholy being your prevailing mental weather. It did not vary with age. Indeed, it had lightened after your epiphany in prison: though the unresolved question of Walcot and its sands remained.

The night was now at full flood as you stood motionless. Countless points of light which lighted nothing were strewn like grains of sand above the old building in which you stood. A full moon had risen at this small hour and hung low over the horizon; it shone on a dew-soaked stretch of ground which, being level, gleamed as if it were the line of a calm sea, the tide of which had withdrawn far from any shoreline.

Your newly trained geologist's eye carried you to a greater isolation, as you reflected that this setting before you resembled a far more ancient scene. Your sleeplessness, your very consciousness, would have had no place four billion years previously, when that same moon was sailing much closer to its parent planet. Earth itself, as geologists understood, had then rotated more rapidly. Land areas would have been swept by powerful tides flooding miles inland, only to withdraw rapidly, and then as rapidly to return, to retreat again, in ceaseless repetition. Those tidal forces may have enabled early DNA to form in tidal pools, thus providing the very basis of life.

You stirred and sighed. The gentler tides at Walcot were but tepid imitations of those more ferocious floods played out in the early days of the planet, before anything lived.

And now here you were, on dry land, in the heart of rural Oxfordshire, at a small private university, discovering how little talent you had for teaching.

Even the Rector of the university, Dr Mathew Matthews, had seemed doubtful when he employed you. However, your donation towards a new classroom had had its influence. 'We live in troublesome times, Dr Fielding,' he had said, placing his hands together, with his fingers pointing upwards. He was a small, bustling man with a ruddy complexion, the sort of man, you felt, with whom you could never be really at ease. 'I speak as if there were times which were not troublesome, which I believe not to be the case.

However, industry is not expanding, inflation is rising. Tell me how you see our prime minister, Mrs Thatcher.'

An interview question. 'Well, she is certainly upsetting the trades unions … Not exactly a popular woman …'

'I'm asking for your personal opinion, Dr Fielding, not for a report on public opinion.'

'She certainly has her convictions. As a result, the working class is in trouble. Well, it's being broken up, because Mrs T is a tough lady when dealing with the unions …'

Matthews leant forward over the polished table. 'There you hit the nail on the head. We do not allow trade unions here at Ashbury. We are strictly private and do not permit outside interference. After the Winter of Discontent –'

'The oil price shock,' you pointed out, 'was hardly the fault of the trades unions.'

A black Labrador dog, lying by the table, rose and shook himself, as if the mention of trades unions worried him too.

The Rector tapped on the table with the sharp nail of his index finger. 'We try not to air our personal political preferences here, but I say this to you; England has gone through a ghastly period – the Sick Man of Europe. This university was almost forced to close. I believe that now, under Margaret Thatcher, the tide will turn. We shall see no more trade union bosses hanging about at 10 Downing Street – Vic Feather and all that bunch. Common sense, elected government and prosperity will return … Do I see you flinch, Dr Fielding? You are not afraid of prosperity, I trust?'

'No, Sir. Simply not used to it.'

'Well, let us hope that shortly practice will make perfect.'

'Excuse me, Sir, but we do have prosperity. The seven leading capitalist countries, which include us, have three-quarters of all the cars, passenger cars, in the world. That's prosperity, surely.'

'And three-quarters of the world's traffic problems.'

You reflected that you should not have argued with the Rector on that point, but he said mildly that if you were inclined to argument, you should meet Myrtle Eddington, the deputy head.

Myrtle Eddington was a woman of medium height, in her forties. Her hair was dyed a dull bronze; she wore an authoritative grey suit, and her manner was friendly, but brisk. You judged that she was unmarried. As she entered the room, the Rector's Labrador rose, shook himself, and went over to sniff her leg in a friendly way.

It was George Orwell's year of 1984, when you were almost sixty, though looking younger. You now tinted your hair, and kept yourself reasonably slender. You shook hands with Myrtle, summing her up as she summed you up.

'The Rector enjoys talking like a hard man,' she said. 'You will find he is a gentle person. We really don't fear the trades unions any more, he just likes to pretend he is fending them off.'

'I employ women but not unionists, Myrtle,' said Mathew, with a slight smile. 'Here we are labour-intensive. If we can be said to labour at all.'

You remarked that there was mass unemployment elsewhere in the land. The old working classes had fallen victim to new technologies, where mass-production lines were now run by computer and other machines. Privatization and increased prosperity had broken up working-class solidarity. 'As you can see by the gentrification of pubs,' you added. 'No more straw on the floor, no more spittoons.'

'More than that,' said Myrtle. 'Access to education. I was the first person in my family to go to university, but I come from the Birmingham working classes and I know what I'm talking about.'

'And you're always talking about it,' said Mathew, waggishly.

Ignoring him, beyond making a face at him, she said, 'I know how things have changed, how quickly, how dramatically. Remember segregation by clothing? Now everyone wears jeans. That's Americanization, in part – or globalization, I should say, since you are probably wearing pants made in Thailand or China – but when I was a kid, everyone had lower expectations. We lived in different places from the middle classes, even in different towns. We had different voices, different jokes. All stand-up comedians come from places like Liverpool, from terraced houses, from back-to-backs. You never see a duke treading the boards, do you?'

'When and if we do, we can celebrate true democracy,' said Mathew.

The word 'democracy' confirmed your view that this was a time of heavy conversation.

'I agree with you, Myrtle,' you said. 'Another way in which things have changed is that workers are more scattered and now live more privately than they did – in part because of television and videos. In the old days, I remember, the poor were forced to live in old railway carriages or pokey houses – rented houses – tied cottages in the country – so that their free time was conducted mainly in public; in pubs, on street corners, at football matches. Now old working class districts have been destroyed, including the one I lived in for a while. Destroyed, or gentrified – or ghettoized with workers from abroad.'

Mathew set his elbows on his desk and made a pyramid of his hands once more, fingers pointing upwards.

'Are you lamenting or rejoicing about all this?'

'Rejoicing, of course,' you and Myrtle said at once.

'Well, I preferred the days when everyone knew their place.'

Myrtle had the last word on this occasion. 'I knew my place and was eager to get out of it. Little did I know it would entail working for you at Ashbury ...'

Your first friend at Ashbury was a man who had been seconded in to run the Earth Sciences class until you arrived. He was a tall, shaggy fellow with a lumbering gait. He came forward, rather round-shouldered, with a big skull, a man of fifty but looking older, to greet you as you climbed from your taxi. He was wearing tight jeans and an old cricket blazer, to signify that if his heart was in the past, at least his legs were in the present.

'Welcome to Ashbury, my friend. Though it's not a great career move, I must admit. I'm Ted Loftus.' He laughed self-deprecatingly. 'Known as Lofty. Can't think why.'

You shook hands. You discovered soon that students called him, not Lofty, but Neanderthal Loftus.

As you lugged your suitcases into the mock-baronial main school, it occurred to you that the name Loftus was familiar. You remembered being twelve, when you had climbed a hill in France, with a master whose name was Loftus.

'Good lord!' you exclaimed, 'We met long ago, when I was a kid. Do you remember?'

He looked blank, then covered the expression with a polite smile. He shook his head and the shaggy locks trembled. 'Sorry. Where was that? I'm afraid I can't – well, my memory isn't all it should be …'

'In France.' A name came floating back. 'In France. The Roman villa – Beaussais, that was the name. Beaussais.'

'Oh dear … No. Beaussais? Beaussais? Don't actually recall … What year was that?'

You told him it was before the war.

Again the head-shaking, as if the skull were loose on the neck. 'I was a boy then. Well, I say a boy, just a lad. It must have been my father you met, Archibald Loftus. I could be wrong.'

You were embarrassed.

A further embarrassment came later, when you rounded a corner into the main corridor. Two people were talking by the notice board, the red-faced bursar, Jeremy Nash, and Myrtle, the deputy head. Myrtle had her back to you, and was saying, 'But he means well.' At a warning sign from Nash, she turned and saw you.

'Oh, Steve, we were discussing the forthcoming tennis match.' But she spoke in a forced way, which you knew meant she had been talking about you. So they thought you 'meant well', what a condemnation. No doubt your prison sentence had earned a mention.

Any faint intentions you had of forming a liaison with Myrtle died before they were properly formulated.

Breakfast was served in the staff dining room. Sunlight poured in through a stained glass window, modern and abstract in design. The bare walls were decorated only in one instance, by a stipple engraving of Thomas More, by Bartolozzi. Behind the buffet counter stood the cheerful Mrs Anstruther – Amy Anstruther, wife of the maths tutor. You collected a croissant, a plain yoghurt and a dubious banana, and sat at the common table. Amy brought you over a cup of tea, smiling amiably as she set it down.

You were sitting next to Ted Loftus on one side and Mrs Verity Nash, who taught English Literature and French, on the other. Mrs Nash was an attractive woman in her mid-forties, as far as you could determine. Her hair was dark and curly, drooping over her brow. Her face was pale and unsmiling. A dark mole rather coyly decorated her right cheek, high, near the eye. As she slowly ate a bowl of muesli, spoonful by spoonful, she peered through a pair of heavy-rimmed spectacles to read a French paperback.

You cautiously peeped over Mrs Nash's shoulder to read the title of the book. It was *La Tentation de Saint-Antoine*. At the same time, you caught a hint of her perfume. She was drably dressed in a fawn two-piece, with a wispy scarf tucked about her neck. She had barely given you a glance and a nod. 'Not friendly,' you said to yourself.

Dr Mathew Matthews entered, wearing black clerical garb, as was his custom. Accompanying him on a lead was his black Labrador, as also was his habit. The dog was almost as dignified as his master. Dr Matthews greeted everyone present, sat down at the head of the table, solemnly drank a cup of tea, ate an unbuttered round of toast, and then departed.

'Just to demonstrate to us he's an aesthete,' said Loftus, grinning to show a number of big, heavy teeth. 'Not that I mean to be unkind …'

You also departed to your classroom. One consolation was that you would see, among a largely unmotivated group, the cherubic young face of Heather Lambert. This morning, Heather was wearing a tattered pair of blue jeans and a tight blue sweater which showed off her breasts to perfection – or distraction, you told yourself. Although her odious boyfriend, Jasper Deakins (you were sure to remember his name) was sitting close to her, Heather Lambert paid attention to every word you uttered.

She sat, elbow on desk, pencil poised in the region of her miraculous ear and looked at you, her mouth slightly open. You wondered if that was a sign of admiration or of a tonsil problem.

In the afternoon, although rain threatened, you took the class out to the dig you had started in the rear of the college grounds. You had managed to persuade Dr Matthews to permit this excavation, saying that a practical exercise was needed for the teaching of geological knowledge to a group not alight with enthusiasm.

Jasper Deakins and two of his cronies climbed down into the hole. It was square, eight feet at a side, the banks supported by timbers. The spoil had been thrown on two tarpaulins spread nearby.

'We aren't going to find much here.' As he spoke, Deakins shaded his eyes with his hand to look up at you. 'Waste of time, if you ask me.'

'We weren't,' you said. 'Get out now, will you?'

Partly ignoring Deakins, you addressed the class. 'We have already learnt something about Britain. We understand that the dry land on which we stand was for a long time under the Tethys Ocean; for hundreds of thousands of years.'

You scooped up a handful of sand from the nearby pile and let it sift through your fingers. 'This is Jurassic sand. This part of Oxfordshire lies over vast beds of it. How deep is the sand? Sometimes fifty feet, maybe a hundred. A warm ocean, growing increasingly shallow as the land rose.'

'What made it rise, please?' That was Heather Lambert, standing with her legs slightly apart.

'The continents were shifting, as they still shift. Laurasia to the North was splitting from Gondwanaland to the South ...' But how could you convey to them the wonder of this ancient planet, the romance of the acquisition and accumulation of this knowledge of it? How force them to wish to know, to actually know, when there was so much you did not know yourself?

'The climate was changing, turning from warmer to cooler. Don't think of our world as stable. Geologically speaking, stability isn't on.'

'We're stable enough,' someone said. 'Ashbury House has been here long enough. Too long, if you ask me.' Several people laughed at this remark.

'You have to learn to think in far grander stretches of time.'

Deakins sank a small entrenching tool into the sand at his feet. 'We're not likely to find any fossils in this stuff.'

'"Stuff", you call it? This "stuff" is the past life of our Earth.'

But Deakins had a retort. 'It's nothing but sand, Sir. There's no life here, no skeleton, no bones. We're wasting our time.'

You felt compelled to return to the dig that evening. Ted Loftus accompanied you, hands in the pockets of his tight-fitting jeans. The sun shone through a light shower, which tailed off westward towards the White Horse Hills.

On the other side of the low stone wall marking the boundary of the university grounds was a field fringed by elm trees, which at one end crowded together to make a small copse. This field was owned by a Tony Abelhouse. Crows sat in the crowns of the elms, cawing in chorus.

Loftus gave a grunt. 'Dr Matthews is at odds with Abelhouse. He's suing him for cruelty to animals. I don't know whether suing is such a good idea, but there, opinions differ. Abelhouse isn't a very nice man, if I may express an opinion.'

Abelhouse professed to be a circus man, or at least to provide various animals for local circuses. A small brown bear had been kept cribbed in a narrow cage and had died there, of neglect. Dr Matthews had instigated a furious row which had got first into the local paper and thence into the nationals, and had featured on television. Confined in the field now were five horses of miscellaneous size and colour, but mainly white. The field itself was almost bare of grass, and presented a sorry sight. It had been trampled to death.

'Have a look,' said Loftus. 'Poor bloody animals. Well, mustn't swear, but just look at their condition.'

You went to look over the wall at the barren field. The horses came galloping up at a mad pace, eyes rolling, teeth gnashing. You stepped back, alarmed by their ferocity. Their great, sinewy necks stretched towards you. They whinnied savagely.

Seeing there was to be no help from you, the horses began to race round the field, a small white animal following the immense savage leaders. Their hooves appeared large, out of all proportion to their narrow legs. Their scanty manes flew, their great heads twisted one way and another, accompanied by furious neighing.

As you regarded the stampede, a memory of your friend Caleb's pamphlet, 'Guernica', returned to mind. You had regarded his account of Britain as a dark wilderness where persecution and injustice ruled an outdated portrait; but as a metaphor it still lived. These tormented beasts – presumably once placid enough – were the four-legged equivalents of many men you had encountered in prison; forever doomed to tread in the same wearisome circles of deprivation, deprivation of nourishment, mentality, even morality. Why had those unfortunates managed to accumulate the scrapings of the English tongue? Only, as Caliban growls in *The Tempest*, 'My profit on't, Is I know how to curse', for curse they did, forever in a storm of cursing their rotten luck. These victims of society, and many you met like them beyond the walls of that prison, had minds darkened like the untended regions described in that old book extolled by Caleb.

Wasn't England – and by no means England alone – a sham reasonable society where, below the successful and eloquent classes,

410

stormed a sea of the disappointed and lost? Why had you not formed this opinion firmly before now, as you stared over the confining wall? What mattered the great events of the globe when all the while – in the past, now, and inevitably in the future – men, women and children were in the grip of a huge hunger never to be allayed?

From this horrifying picture of what you saw as a profound, indecent truth you turned away, sickened and saddened by your vision. By the place where the trees stood thickest, the horses paused and, with their huge yellow teeth, savagely gnawed off pieces of bark. Then off again they charged, hooves thudding, wild, savage, starving. You watched them with pity and horror. Round they galloped again and again; unable to cease, in a torment of hunger.

There seemed nothing you could do. Alarmed, 'Shuggery-bees!' was all you could say.

You directed your attention away from the scene. You climbed down into the excavated hole. Ted Loftus stood staring, hands in ragged pockets, at the horses on their crazed circuit. Shadow lay on the sand that the shower had patterned. You thought that if you were a painter like, say, Tiepolo, you could not paint the light separately; you would have to paint the light on sand.

The sand had changed since the afternoon. The confused pattern the raindrops had drawn made it look more like the sand you would find on a beach; more alive – sand that still knew the sea and the tides. Yes, it was beautiful. You could not understand why you felt sad, or why you felt so alone. You gave a grunted attempt at amusement to think how lonely it would be to be the one man impossibly stranded in the Jurassic Era.

A voice coming from behind you said, 'Hello, Mr Mystery Man.'

Even before you turned, you knew Heather Lambert was there.

You looked up at her looking down at you. Her jeans were streaked with a yellow dust, pollen from a flower she had brushed against on her way. From this angle, her neat little chin was in evidence, as were the tilt of her eyelashes and the lids of her eyes over her hazel pupils. And the tilt of her breasts under the sweater.

'No sign of life here,' you said lightly. 'Or not until you came along.'

You watched her behind descend as she climbed into the excavation with you. 'Are you thinking great thoughts?' She wore sandals and had painted her toe nails scarlet.

'I'm wondering why you think I'm a mystery. There's no mystery about me.'

'That's not what I think,' she said with a hint of mischief in her voice. She looked up at you, and now the innocence you thought you saw in her face was replaced by something sterner. 'You do have mystery. It's not just because you're older, it intrigues me, I guess. I have a problem. I suffer from anhedonia, so they tell me. You know what that is?'

You shook your head. 'Never heard of it. Is it catching?'

'Could be, if you try hard enough. Anhedonia is the inability to feel pleasure in situations which are normally regarded as pleasant.'

You regarded her sympathetically, although not without a stirring of lust. 'How do you contract this condition?'

She gestured dismissively, as if it was not worth talking about. Her breasts shifted under her sweater. 'Search me. My ma was German and I hated going out with her, walking with her. Her family was well-connected but she was lame. It always embarrassed me, that lameness of hers; hobble, hobble.'

'Is that enough to bring on – what is it – anhedonia?'

Bored with the subject, she asked, 'Have you got religion, Steve?'

It was the first time she had used your first name. You made a note to use hers at an early opportunity.

'If you can be religious without believing in God.'

'You didn't come down here to think about that.'

'As a matter of fact, I was thinking about my daughter.'

'Ah, that's more like it. So there is a mystery, I guess.'

'What do you want, Heather?'

An impatient gesture. 'I don't know what I want. You tell me what I want.' And she looked smilingly up at you mouth open, waiting, inviting.

And so you were lying together on the damp sand, kissing each other, her mouth soft and moist.

'Ooh, you're not that old,' she said.

'You're not that young.' Lucky some girls have a father fixation, you thought.

She began kissing you again with her tender mouth, as you stroked her hair. In that eternal moment, the hooves of the starving horses could still be heard, drumming on the earth of the bare field, like a detached heart. You had forgotten about Ted Loftus. Tactfully, seeing the arrival of Heather, he had lumbered off, hands still in pockets.

Finally, your lips disengaged and you were laughing. 'You weren't enjoying that?'

She was laughing. 'Anhedonia comes and it goes. Just now, it went. Cool.'

You were feeling under her sweater and she was lying back, letting you, when the rain came on again. You had a hand on her left breast and her nipple between your finger and thumb.

'Fuck!' she said.

'Come into my room,' you said. And you both made a dash for cover.

'We can have a serious talk,' she said, panting.

So you did, among other things. The perfume when she was aroused enveloped you, becoming the very atmosphere of your desire. Heather, gasping, finally said she thought she enjoyed every-thing you did, but there was always something in her mind that stood apart, not happy when she was happy, not miserable when she was sad.

She propped herself up on an elbow and stared at you with large, dark eyes. She thought all this meant she was intended to be religious. She had been thinking of leaving Ashford at the end of the present term, but now ... 'Things are a bit different, I guess.'

413

You were not too sure about that. You could foresee trouble ahead if Dr Matthews discovered you were having a love affair with a student. It would mean dismissal and another blot on your CV.

You turned up at the tennis courts on the following day to watch Heather play in the finals of the so-called Ashford Cup. Although she was not a brilliant player, her athleticism on the court was attractive. She won the first set with ease, but was in difficulties in the second set, up against an opponent who was beginning to warm to the game. You found yourself sitting on one of the uncomfortable metal seats next to the self-contained Verity Nash, ensconced as usual behind her ebony-rimmed glasses. Her husband, the bursar, was nowhere to be seen. The only other member of staff watching the match was Myrtle.

You felt you had to say something to Verity Nash. Heather was flashing her neatly filled panties at deuce when you said, without taking your eyes from that glimpse, or the possibility of another, 'Tennis provides a good opportunity for the celebration of human consciousness.' Something intellectual, if asinine, seemed to be demanded. 'It combines rapid movement and balance, with coordinated judgement of spatial dimension. I don't imagine australopithecus played tennis, do you?'

You had not exactly expected a response from this remote-seeming lady, but she said, flicking a half-smile at you, 'That's the physical aspect. The psychological aspect is that you need to make rapid guesswork about the enemy's responses.'

'That's so,' you said, rather surprised.

'That's where I went wrong,' Mrs Nash said in lowered tones. 'In tennis as in life.' She then stared rigidly ahead at the play on court, her body language saying, 'No more talk, I have already overstepped the mark.'

You too concentrated on the game, and the panties, while thinking that there was more to Verity Nash than one would have at first imagined.

Kissing the succulent Heather had been the impulse of a moment, prompted by both hunger and curiosity. Had the wish come initially from her? Were you simply lonely? It was a long while since you had lain with a woman. Supposing it had been one of the other girls in the class ...

Had it been her breasts or her mind that attracted you? Once you were alone, you thought hard about these matters. 'Anhedonia.' It sounded like an arid country in North Africa.

You came to no precise conclusion. There seemed to be no word for what you felt.

> *Here, you need no language. Everything you have done or even thought is recorded and is transparent.*
>
> *I am supposed to be comforted by that?*
>
> *You will become comforted in a while.*
>
> *But why not comforted then – that vital then, when I was alive? It seemed to me there was no one course of conduct, no single response to be offered, or indeed, no set of definite rules to be followed.*
>
> *Better that than an inescapable 'Way' you might have been set to follow automatically.*
>
> *Why better? Why are we planted on this mysterious kind of assault course of life? For whose benefit?*
>
> *This is what you were given, what you call 'life'. 'Timelife'. It was what we were able to provide. You could perhaps have enjoyed it more.*
>
> *Oh? How could I have 'enjoyed it more'?*
>
> *By not regarding yourself as a failure. By less melancholy. By less self-regard. Now you tell me!*

You were made to feel even more provincial, more than ever 'out of the swim', by the release of director Brandy Bethlen's movie, *Jocasta*, starring your sister. It was proving a great draw at the box office despite its highbrow aspirations. 'The greatest, grandest recreation of Ancient Greece ever to hit the screen' – *Time and Tide*. 'Dig the Trojan position!' – *The Sun*. 'Deeply, darkly erotic in its stately

415

way' – *The Independent*. 'Young Antigone is lip-lickingly attractive' – *Sight and Sound*. 'An Oscar, surely, for authentic seeming costumes, authentically worn!' – *Empire*. 'Sonia's Jocasta's wonderful portrayal of combined guilt and innocence makes her a woman for all time' – *Observer*. 'Like Oedipus, you can but love her' – *The Times*.

You noticed among the rolling credits *Adrian Hyasent: Costumes*. The bastard!

Over the Easter break, you went with your parents to see Sonia's movie at the Southampton Odeon. There was no doubt that the Hungarian director had been inspired. As Jocasta's dilemma gradually became more serious, the Technicolor began slowly to fade, until the climax was played out in sepia. Your sister was first imperious, later overwhelmed, and in both phases unassailable.

'Well, we must take some credit for her success,' said your mother afterwards, moist of eye. 'I need a gin after all that.'

'That's nonsense, Mary,' said your father. He had suffered a stroke and was afflicted by a tic on the left side of his face. 'Sonia has managed despite …' He began to mumble.

A little later, while Mary was refreshing herself indoors, you walked out in the garden with Martin. He required a walking stick. There was something he wished to show you.

A little fire was burning on what had been his vegetable bed. A thin stream of smoke rose into the still air. You both stood contemplating it. He was breathing laboriously.

'I've kept it burning continuously for fifteen days now,' Martin said, with pride. 'It's never died out.'

'How do you keep it going when it rains, Dad?'

'I cover it with that old zinc washtub.' Chuckling at his own ingenuity, he tapped the washtub with his stick.

'I simply keep it going as long as I can. Rose clippings, mainly. As long as I can …'

You stood there in the gathering dusk, listening to the fire crackle, watching the smoke rise up. Your father stood beside you, linking his arm in yours for support, watching the smoke rise up.

7

Another Invitation

You caught an infrequent bus from Ashbury and went in to Oxford. You wanted to buy some books at Blackwell's. In those days, there was an old-fashioned bookshop in the Broad called Thornton's. Before visiting Blackwell's, you went through Thornton's hallowed doorway.

You climbed a rickety, uncarpeted stair. You were looking for a better copy of Lyell's *Principles of Geology*. But a section to which was attached a yellowing label reading 'Eng.Lit.' caught your attention. On these shelves stood many old novels, now no longer read or, if read at all, read not for pleasure but because they were set texts. Richard Blackmore, Richard Cobbold, George Gissing and Charles Reade mouldered there, among others.

Among the illustrious dead, you saw a copy of *Caleb Williams* in the Rinehart Press edition of 1960. Your thoughts flew to Arturo Blake, alias Caleb, your friend of Blackall Square days. You pulled the book from its resting place.

As you did so, a voice, in tones of surprise, said, 'Hello, Dr Fielding!'

You had been aware there was another customer in the pokey room, rendered almost in outline by light dimly entering through unwashed window panes, as if sketched by Daumier; a vague figure, probably female, hunched over a book, a beret on its head.

This figure, moving a step nearer, revealed itself as Mrs Verity Nash, wearing her heavy spectacles.

'How charming to see you here, Dr Fielding.'

You returned the compliment and fell into conversation with her. She commented on *Caleb Williams*, which she characterized as crude and awful, but nevertheless still highly readable. You confessed you had never read it. You knew of it, of course.

'Do buy it and tell me what you think. It's so nice to have someone at Ashford who reads for pleasure.' She said this as one attempting more brightness than she felt.

Thornton's had no copy of Lyell. You paid for the Godwin and you and Verity left the shop together, the book under your arm – no bags for books in those days.

You found yourselves in a nearby coffee shop. You realized she was not so much unfriendly, as shy. She seemed greatly cheered by your company, and put away her spectacles.

'Oh, this is a treat! It's very kind of you, Dr Fielding.'

'Steve, please.'

'I'm afraid I suffer from low self-esteem.' She gave you a brave smile. 'It does tend to make me stand-offish. Perhaps I'm really stand-offish, and it's stand-offishness which accounts for the low self-esteem, rather than vice versa.'

Your heart went out to her. You thought of Caleb again, complaining that the British always ran themselves down.

When you mentioned her husband Jeremy, the bursar, she was evasive, seemingly more interested in the starving horses in the field behind the university grounds.

'Can't something be done about them?' you asked.

'That'll soon be settled,' said Verity. 'Abelhouse has to burn down all those lovely elms on his land – within a week, what's more.'

You were surprised to hear it.

'It's Dutch elm disease, you know. All the elms in the country are going to have to be destroyed. It's terrible, isn't it? The face of the countryside will be absolutely changed.'

'Bad luck on the birds too. Dutch elm disease? It's a fungus, I imagine?'

'I believe it is. Some say it comes from Holland, some say Canada.' She had brightened considerably. When smiling and animated, as now, she looked attractive, with a round face and dimples in her cheeks which came and went when she talked, as counterpoint to the mole by her right eye.

'Rather like syphilis; to us, the French disease, to the French, the Italian disease.'

Verity laughed and began polishing her spectacles vigorously. 'Whereas we take French leave, the French "*s'en filer a l'anglaise*".'

'You speak French fluently? You teach it?'

She looked up with a moody expression. 'My first husband was French. A bastard, what's more.'

Later, you learned that her second husband, Jeremy Nash, was also a bastard. It seemed at that stage that she was a woman who collected unfortunate marriages.

'And you have made a discovery in that dig of yours?' she asked.

You told her guardedly that you had dug just a metre farther along to the right of the original hole and had come across something.

'A skull, someone told me?'

'Well, could be. It's a bit early to tell. Probably not important.' You could not say that you hoped it was important. You could not know that it was to be very important.

Sensing your reluctance to say more, Verity changed the subject. She asked you if you were comfortable with your present rooms in the university building. When you said you were, she said that perhaps you might be more comfortable if you took rooms in her and Jeremy's house in Sandy Bassett, only three miles from the university. She said that her husband called it 'Nash Villa' – 'You know, after Nashville, where Americans make a lot of music, I believe. You'd have a view of the downs?'

She saw you were doubtful. She said that she and her husband would not interfere. 'You might like the village?' She would not overcharge. You could have breakfast in your room if you liked? There was a bus? Her manner was distinctly questioning.

You did not want to move digs, at least for the moment (thinking of Heather Lambert).

What was more, she continued, it was quiet in Sandy Bassett. A pretty little stream. Oh, and a wood. And they had lots of books? English books as well as French? Though Jeremy did not read much; he preferred the pub.

You thanked her. You would certainly think it over.

And they had a nice little woodland garden? No gnomes. She tittered at the very thought. You were amiable as you left the table, picking up the bill and *Caleb Wiliams*.

You asked Ted Loftus about Verity. He shook his head. Lowering his voice, he said, 'Look, this is not to be repeated, but rumour has it that Jeremy is a bit of a brute to her. I shouldn't be telling tales, but … She is a touch irritating, but it seems he, Jeremy, knocks her about. Of course, that may not be the case, but she did come in once with rather a black eye. Oh, that was all of two years ago, three, possibly. No, two, more like. Could have been an accident …'

'I found Verity was rather a nice woman. Not happy, possibly.'

'Yes, she's all right. I mean, I get along with her. Just a bit, well, withdrawn.' Ted wobbled his head from side to side in order to indicate that something, to which he could not commit himself, was not as it should be.

There was a letter for you stuck on the staff noticeboard, from Colbert & Kolberg, the solicitors Geldstein had recommended. You took it to your room and opened it anxiously. Abby, as you knew, was now, at last, actively seeking a divorce; so far, the fact that she had deserted you had stood in her way. Denis Kolberg stated that she now demanded divorce on the grounds of your adultery with a woman named as Heather Lambert.

You were horrified. How had Abby's lawyers acquired Heather's name? And so promptly? An old-fashioned phone stood on a side table in the corner of your room. You phoned Denis Kolberg. He did not know who had acquired the name of Lambert, or how; he had received an anonymous note, posted in Oxford.

Your daughter, Geraldine, was well, he had learned. He asked you if you wished to fight the case, in which case he could recommend a good lawyer, not too expensive.

You rang the solicitors back half-an-hour later: Kolberg was out. You spoke to his secretary and said you would not fight the case, provided the name of Heather Lambert was left out of the charge.

Opening up your computer, you sent an email to Abby, saying that since she had deserted the marriage while you were in prison, honours were pretty even. A court case would be costly; only the lawyers would gain from it. Why could you not both simply agree on a divorce?

You then sent another email to Geraldine, telling her about the wild horses in the next field. You had taken to emailing her every other week; she responded when she felt like it. Why did you love this girl you had scarcely seen? True, you had fathered her with a woman you had loved; yet it was as if the sperm involved had carried a secret code, demanding response, within its DNA. DNA was thicker than water.

When you thought about it, you realized you no longer hated Abby as you had done. Something of your earlier love had surfaced again. It was a signal that your temperament had become more equable. The thought was reassuring.

An unusual noise impinged upon your consciousness. After a while, you rose and went to look out of your window. You were in time to see a tall elm crashing down in Abelhouse's field. You had heard the spiteful snarl of chainsaws biting into living wood. Several men were in the field, some working with machines, dragging trees already felled into a great pile in the centre of the field. The starving horses had already been taken away.

The sight of this destruction was upsetting. You closed the computer and went downstairs to get a drink at the little bar in the tutors' common room. It was a convivial hour. The bursar, Jeremy Nash, was there, having a pint with Dr Matthews. Verity, Jeremy's wife, was sitting apart by the window, looking lost, a book open, unread, before her.

Jeremy was a hefty man, his cropped hair seeming to emphasize the squareness of his head. Despite the warmth of the day, he wore a polo neck sweater under his blazer.

'How does it feel to have a famous film star for a sister?' he called, in a hearty way that indicated he was not so much seeking an answer as airing his knowledge of the world of cinema.

Dr Matthews summoned you to sit with him and Jeremy. You took your whisky over and told the men about the destruction of Abelhouse's copse.

'Yeah, we heard,' said Jeremy.

You remarked you were sorry to see the elms go down.

'Well, it's got rid of those poor confounded horses,' said Matthews. 'We hope the RSPCA are now tending them.'

'What's the betting they'll be back, once the elms are burnt?' said Jeremy.

'I'll see they don't jolly well come back,' said Matthews. He gripped the handle of his glass so tightly his knuckles showed white. 'I got Madge to phone the RSPCA again this morning. They'll have to act this time.'

'Poor starving things,' this from you. The old black dog got up from Dr Matthews' side and scratched itself.

The Rector of Ashford gave you a look of contempt. 'They're in such a deplorable state. Diseased. Mercy demands they should be put down.'

You thought that perhaps the horses would see the matter differently, but said nothing.

Jeremy seemed rather more friendly. After a glance across at his wife, he invited you to supper with them on the evening of the next day. 'You don't have a car, do you, Fielding? I can give you a lift in the Jag to our little pad in Sandy, "Nash Villa", as long as you don't mind walking back. It's a nice country walk – under three miles. You'll like Sandy, I know. And Verity's not a bad cook when she sets her mind to it.'

You thought it a good idea to accept, and summoned some enthusiasm to do so.

Before that event, Heather came to your room. She was familiar, as if you had known each other for months. It was a part of her charm. Going over to the bed, she snatched up the letter from Colbert & Kolberg. Dusk had gathered. You had had a second whisky with the men; you did not want to be bothered with the girl.

'That's bloody private,' you said.

But Heather had seen her name in the body of the letter. She gave a shriek. 'What's this? You're married? You're dragging me into divorce proceedings?'

Attempting an explanation was useless; she would not listen to your explanations. 'How did I know you were fucking married?' she kept asking.

You did not switch on the light in your room. That might have encouraged her to stay longer. She was upset. You understood why she was upset, yet you were impatient. It was not your fault, yet it was your fault. And the bizarre yellowish flickering of sunset grew more intense.

She was standing by the window, still waving the offending letter. You rushed over and grabbed it.

'I don't want to know you any more, you arsehole!' she cried. 'You've been bloody using me!'

Outside was a great fire, flames waving tall into the sky, sparks flying still higher, whirling away to die in the blue. The elms were burning in Abelhouse's field. At this time, finely balanced between day and evening, but ever inclining towards the blue of night, smoke was hardly visible, only flame, gigantic sheets of it, ever steady, ever wavering. And figures of human beings were black against it, dancing. Women and children and a man; those you could make out capering round about the blaze, as if at a witches' Sabbath.

'Look at it, Heather! The primitivism of it! Is there music? Do you need music?'

She wrenched open the window. A great roaring was to be heard, like an immense chimney fire. Some shouts, some shrieks. No music. The stream of golden sparks pouring into the sky seemed music enough for those who danced about the blaze.

Staring at the majesty of the conflagration, you and Heather forgot for a moment your own concerns. Then she said, in a subdued way, 'You're a real shit, Steve, sorry to say, and I don't want nothing more to do with you.' And she left, closing your door quietly behind her.

It was a week and a few days since you had uncovered the skull in the university dig.

8

Supper at Sandy Bassett

Jeremy Nash drove like a madman to Sandy Bassett. Sometimes he forced his black slug of a Jaguar to bump over the grass verge, sometimes he commanded the middle of the road. His wife rattled about on the back seat, despite her safety belt. Jeremy tooted fiercely on the rare occasions that another car approached. Little quiet country cars ran into ditches rather than face Jeremy head on.

You disliked the man even before the brakes squealed outside the front gate of the so-called 'Nash Villa'. Verity climbed from the Jaguar, slamming the car door behind her, and went without comment into the house. She did not glance back.

Jeremy looked at his watch. 'Record time!' he said, with evident satisfaction. A gust of wind blew the gate shut behind him.

It was a pretty cottage, with a scarred wooden door, and windows placed symmetrically on either side of the porch. Window boxes stood on both windowsills, flaunting bright red geraniums.

The walls were painted white and the roof was thatch, wired to keep out birds.

You followed Jeremy's broad back into the house.

'Welcome to our humble abode,' he said, standing and almost filling the hallway. He grinned and rubbed his hands together. 'Let's get ourselves a drink and discuss what we imagine Thatcher and Reagan think they're up to. Nuking Moscow, let's hope!'

He called to Verity, who had disappeared into the back regions of the house. 'Bring us a couple of glasses, dear.'

He led the way into their front room, the window of which looked to the quiet village road. 'This used to be a worker's cottage, but it suits us pretty well.' He gave a hoot of mirth. 'We're humble folk, worse luck.'

'It's very cosy. You've got some good beams.'

'Bloody things! I'm always banging my nut on them.'

Indeed, there were sturdy beams crossing the ceiling, which was so low that Jeremy ducked his head as he crossed to a drinks cabinet with cut glass panes in its doors. The cabinet stood beside a wide stone hearth, where ashes of a dead fire lay.

Jeremy indicated the fireplace as he was about to take up a bottle of Johnny Walker. 'It's cosy enough in the winter. We burn logs; I pinched some of old thing's elm logs from the field next door. Of course, we don't need a fire just now. Why hasn't Verity cleaned the bloody hearth out? Women! I don't know …'

So extensive seemed his lack of knowledge on this subject that he sighed heavily.

Removing his blazer as if stripping for action, he flung it across a chair. The polo neck sweater was revealed in all its grubby glory. He poured two generous slugs of whisky into the glasses Verity produced. 'Do you want a nip?' he asked her.

She shook her head. 'I'm just getting the supper ready, Jeremy.'

'See there's some wine with the chops, will you, dear? There should be a bottle or two of Merlot in the kitchen cupboard,' he added, with a grin at you. 'Nothing's too good for our guest.'

She disappeared without answering. He gave you a wink, as if you were two men indulgently sharing a knowledge of the oddity of the female sex.

'She calls herself a "chilly mortal"; likes electric fires. I can't bear the horrible things.'

'So you don't have electric fires,' you said, mildly. The deduction was so obvious, Jeremy did not bother to reply.

'But you have electric lights,' you said, pursuing the subject. 'How are you on smoke alarms, for instance?'

'Oh, them!' Jeremy gave a chuckle. 'Fashion accessories! No, no, you see, Fielding, this is an *old house*.' He wagged a finger to make sure the phrase got through. 'Not likely to catch fire, is it? Stood here for centuries. All stone. Good solid stone.'

'Except for the beams.'

'Of course the bloody beams aren't stone. What do you expect?'

You sat yourself down in what you recognized as an Erko chair, and sipped your whisky. Jeremy remained standing.

'Tastes awful, does whisky. Think how much of the stuff you could drink if you liked the flavour.' He made the remark thoughtlessly, as if it was a witticism he had uttered many times before.

'You get used to it,' you replied.

'Here,' he said in a moment. 'You're a geologist of some sort or other. What do you make of this?'

He reached up and took from where it lodged on the top of the drinks cabinet, a skull which you had already noticed. He balanced it in the palm of his hand. The lower jaw was missing, as was a tooth in the upper jaw. Otherwise it was intact, with a sweep of bone curving above the vacant eye sockets.

'Dug it up in the garden a few years ago. Chap in the pub told me it was a couple of million years old.'

'A couple of thousand, more like,' you said, when he handed it to you for inspection.

'Some poor bugger probably died in the Black Death,' Jeremy said. He poured himself another tot of Johnny Walker.

'Not if it was two million years ago.'

You decided to give Jeremy something to consider. 'Did you ever wonder why skulls survive in the earth so long? It represents an odd case of evolutionary overkill. Just making the skull so strong, nature neglected greatly to enlarge the brains inside. We're supposed to have large brains; they would have been quite a lot larger if some of the growth energy absorbed in bone growth had gone into the grey matter inside.'

You had appreciated Geldstein's lectures on Aristotle. Jeremy evidently disliked lectures. He looked at you blankly. 'If someone whacks you on the head, though ...' He did not follow the supposition through.

'How often does that happen?' you asked. 'Surely preferred methods of attack are to break your leg with a stave, or slice your head off with a sword.'

'I see. Well, anyhow, I've got a thick skull to protect me from these beams. That's what evolution means to me, old chum.' He paused. The subject had been dismissed. You visualized a 'thinking' cloud above his head saying, 'What a nutter!' 'Why isn't that bloody supper ready? Now what's she up to?'

He marched out of the room. You heard him shouting in the kitchen. 'Get that bloody cat out of here!' There were noises of what sounded like a shriek. You put the whisky glass down and stood up, undecided. More shouting, footsteps, the clatter of plates smashing on a stone floor. A curse. Going to the hall door, you listened.

Muttered voices: Jeremy's, angry; Verity's, defiant.

You were finally summoned. Supper was served in a small back room, its one window looking out on the back garden. Verity had put two lighted candles in china candlesticks on the table. She had a dish of pork chops before her, which she endeavoured to serve. Her hands were trembling so much she dropped her fork. It fell on the floor.

'Clumsy today, aren't you?' said Jeremy reprovingly.

'Feeling terribly ill, what's more,' she said. 'Ill and unloved, if you must know.' Dropping the fork on the tablecloth, she covered her spectacles and her eyes with her hands, and burst into tears. 'Sorry. Oh, sorry. So sorry. So, so sorry ...'

Jeremy stood up. 'Oh, get out, woman! What's wrong with you? More bloody hysterics!'

'But she's really upset –' you began, in protest.

Verity showed some spirit. She jumped up, shrieking, 'How I hate you, you fucking bully! I won't live with you!' and rushed from the room.

Jeremy clenched a fist, muttering to himself, 'I'll give her fucking bully.'

He stood with his head to one side, looking upwards as Verity's tread sounded on the steps of the open stair. On his face dawned a look of comic resignation, as of one who has weathered this kind of thing often before.

'Bloody hell,' said Jeremy. 'Women! Unmanageable!' He shook his head. 'Sorry about that. You have to be patient with them. Well, she'll be back soon, may as well get on with the meal before the chops get cold, eh, Fielding?' He gave you a would-be jovial laugh.

Although the chops were succulent enough, you had no appetite for them. Jeremy was telling you of his previous employment, in what he called 'an amusing Northern town'. You were bothered by a flickering light entering the room from outside. Bored with what your host was saying, you rose when he was punctuating his account with a good pull at his glass of Merlot, and stared out of the window. Beyond what Verity had described as their little woodland garden, a fire was blazing, seeming to gather strength as the world darkened into night.

You exclaimed about it.

'Remain calm, Fielding! It's that bloody fool Heath, my neighbour, rot his socks. Fancy setting fire to his dead elms when a wind's getting up!'

'Sparks are flying everywhere.' Indeed, the sparks from the fire were whirling upwards in a fury, starring the sky with their glow.

The hot winds carried up with them numerous little fragments of the materials that fed them.

'Have another chop, old fellow. A few sparks won't worry us. Let me pour you some more of this Merlot. Pass your glass. As I was telling you, the mayor of this dump – it was rather funny, actually – he turned up unexpectedly and there we were, neither of us with a stitch on …'

He continued with his story. You ceased eating and concentrated on the wine, wondering when you could excuse yourself and begin the walk back to the university. Certainly the wind must be getting up. The loud roaring and crackling was only partly attributable to the nearby bonfire.

When unease got the better of you, you jumped up again to peer out of the window. Jeremy also jumped up and tried to pull the chintz curtain over the window, shouting, 'Night-time! May as well close down.'

But you tore the curtain away.

'Christ, Jeremy, your fucking roof is on fire!'

'It can't be!' He thrust his great head against the window-pane. The thatch was ablaze in two places, flame shot upwards, smoke billowed down. 'Jesus Christ! Ring the bloody fire brigade! Quick! I'll sue that stupid sod Heath for this. I'll get every penny he ever owned off him!'

'But Verity–'

'What about my fucking Jag! I forgot to register it …'

With that, he flung down his table napkin and ran for the front door. For a moment you stood there undecided. You could smell the burning. Then you rushed for the stairs and ran up to the first floor. Choking smoke confronted you, billowing down from the ceiling, where plasterwork had fallen in.

'Verity! Where are you?' No response.

A loud crash came from one of the rooms, followed by the crackle of flame consuming something dry. You threw open the nearest door.

It was the main bedroom, stretching, as far as you could gather, from front to back of the cottage. Of the two twin beds, one was already on fire. On the other Verity was sprawled. An oak beam had fallen in and lay in part across the empty bed. The bedclothes were burning fiercely. The heat was intense. A windowpane cracked like a twig snapping.

'Verity!'

You thought she stirred. It was difficult to see across the room. You waved a hand in front of your face, fruitlessly, in an attempt to clear away the smoke. A mass of flaming thatch fell at your feet. You jumped back, but the fire had to be crossed if you were to get to Verity. Flames were spreading with horrifying rapidity as you hesitated.

So you gave a great yell. You plunged forward through the flame, scattering fragments of burning straw everywhere. A rug by the dressing table, hitherto merely smouldering, burst suddenly into flame.

You reached the bed. You endeavoured to lift Verity. As you did so, you saw, on her bedside table, a bottle of white tablets. The top was off the bottle and some tablets had been spilled by an empty glass. With a mighty effort, you lifted up Verity's inert body, hefting it over one shoulder. Staggering, you plunged back through the smoke and flame. One of your trouser legs began to burn.

You managed to carry Verity downstairs. You phoned the new hospital in Oxford, you phoned the fire brigade, then you carried her out into the flickering dark of the front garden. Jeremy and his precious Jag were nowhere to be seen. You knelt by Verity on a patch of grass, nursing her head, until an ambulance arrived. Her body was limp. She gave an intermittent shuddering breath.

'Stay alive, Verity,' you whispered to her. 'You mustn't die, poor darling. You mustn't die ...'

Behind you, the blaze took firmer hold of 'Nash Villa'. The racket and roar of it all drowned out your pleas to her.

9

Tolstoy Unread

The years seem to pass more quickly as you grow older. Spring, summer, autumn, winter – all blur into one another. You fail to notice the changes about you.

Not until the late eighties, when President Gorbachev was emerging from the Soviet Union to visit Western capitals and in the streets of New York and London, crowds were acclaiming him, calling 'Gorby! Gorby!', did you realize you had entered the consumer society. You were then planning to purchase a house.

You received an invitation to address the Institut fur Geologische Wissenschaften in West Berlin. You accepted almost by rote, for a new house was foremost in your mind. That and your mother's continuing illness.

You had a particular house in mind. It stood not exactly in town, nor in a suburb, rather it was in a conurbation, with open space on either side of it. It stood in a quiet road as regards passing traffic, though not exactly quiet with regard to passing planes overhead, readying themselves to land at London Heathrow. Quite close was what had been a park in Edwardian times, when it had been surrounded by open country. A supermarket now stood within easy walking distance.

A branch of Barclay's Bank was also close, just a street away. Unlike the shops and a delicatessen surrounding it, the bank remained closed on Sundays, but there was no longer any difficulty in getting your hands on cash to spend; the bank had installed a cash slot in its wall and money was now available twenty-four hours a day, every day of the week. The installation of cash-slots outside banks made the spending of money far easier for everyone, everywhere.

You had been spending money. You had money to spend. You and your wife had accumulated antique and reproduction furniture. She had developed a liking for expensive glassware; the eighteenth century goblets from which you drank your wine were much admired by your many friends. These friends were new friends in the main. They also had possessions they valued. On your dining tables you enjoyed the work of Dublin silversmiths, Italian plates and Swedish candelabra, while on your walls hung, if not costly oils, then original watercolours by the likes of Copley Fielding, Birkett Foster and John Sell Cotman, artists who strove to represent something resembling the real world. In your study you had framed first proofs of G. B. Tiepolo's *Scherzi*.

Not that there was anything particularly ostentatious about this mode of life. In no way did it compare with the accounts you received now and then from your sister Sonia, in California. It seemed that when not filming, Sonia was aboard a luxurious yacht in Antibes – no matter if it never left harbour – or skiing off-piste on some hitherto unknown Alp. All this among the famed, or would-be-famed, of the film world. It was, as she reported, a hideously expensive business simply being a star.

Whether ostentatious or not, your possessions had a habit of multiplying. For this reason, you and an estate agent were now looking round this large, empty mansion. The garden, though at present rather neglected, had been landscaped. You admired a waterfall pouring from a rise in the ground, supplying a stretch of water on which, in due season, water lilies blossomed. Under the flat round leaves of those lilies, carp nosed about with an indolence suggesting that they too profited from the consumer society. This stretch of water encouraged many different kinds of bird to live among adjacent trees. A small apple orchard was, as you remarked, not displeasing. You approached it along a path sequestered from the main lawn by hedges of kolkwitzia, towering above your head.

You were inclined to purchase. Firstly, your wife must come to view and approve.

You were calm, although well aware that in Beijing, on the other side of the world, students were being massacred in Tiananmen Square. Sorry though you might be about that, it would not deter you from buying a house. You had little interest in the fact that behind the slaughter, a new and economically powerful China was being born.

The estate agent was a polite, deferential man, half your age. Together you emerged from the main gates, where you had a discussion regarding when it would be most convenient to return. You were standing near the 'For Sale' notice when you were surprised to hear your name called by a man some way down the road, just emerging from a BMW. The estate agent departed. You remained where you were, jiggling your car keys, while the newcomer approached.

He was of modest height and wore a double-breasted suit. His shoes shone brightly. You recognized him – it was Pief Geldstein. So then you went towards him, shook his hand, clutched his arm.

Pief was pleased to see you. When you suggested you went somewhere for a coffee and a chat, he explained regretfully that he was too busy. He had gold rings on his fingers and leopard-skin on his shoes. As you remarked, he looked prosperous.

'I am prosperous, my dear Steve. Because I am a hard worker. While I was working for my father in his restaurants, I was studying engineering and its principles. I don't care for the restaurant business; it belongs to my father's generation. I'm a modern man. I have a degree in engineering and now I'm boss of my own firm. It is a tad small as yet, but it expands.'

'Well done!'

'Yes, I really think so, but not done yet.'

As you stood there, outside the empty house, in the mild sunshine, Pief explained the nature and function of his business. First of all, he said, showing his teeth in a wide smile, he married a clever woman, not a great beauty, not even a Jew, but a good woman to help him plan the future. And by the way, he had changed his name to Goldstone. Better for business – there were still some shits about, he said, clamping down on the smile.

'You, Steve,' he said, 'I know your success comes from sand.'

You wondered what Walcot might have to do with it, before realizing he was referring to the exhumation of the famous plesiosaur at Ashbury.

Without waiting for your response, Pief went on, 'But my success comes from the present. I make and deliver complete bathrooms. I buy in some components, I issue plans and I give firm estimates, I plug in whole toilets and lavatories, women's and gents', to new factories being built. I hardly bother with private houses, small projects like that. Me, I do all the plumbing, the urinals, the jakes, the hand-driers, the wash basins, the mirrors, everything necessary; lighting, towel machines, French letter machines – sorry, condom machines – I do it all. My staff I'm talking of. My company is Sale-Safe. That's what it's called, with good reason. Sale-Safe pic. I do everything, right down to tons of toilet paper and gallons of liquid soap, all at preliminary costing. When the builders are there, I am in there like knives. Construction is everywhere today, the economy expands, my men, they come in quick, they work quick, do a faultless job, get well-paid – depends if they are illegal immigrants – so I make my plenty dosh.'

He nodded in agreement with himself, smiling again, full of pleasure with his own success. Tapping his head, he said that Sale-Safe sprang from his own brain.

'You see, Steve, it's a time of opportunity. You suss a niche, you go for it.' He asked you why it was that Britain had abolished the old, antiquated monetary system of pounds, shillings and pence, answering his own question by declaring that computerization was changing everything, including the way everybody thought.

'In the age of the computer, you have to have a decimal currency, together with standardized paper sizes. Standardized globally.' He saw this unification as a great, unacknowledged advance. 'Steve, my car has a central locking system. That's computers. You should treat yourself to one. The day will come when cars won't need human drivers any more ...' He shook his head at the wonder of his imagination. 'Another child of the computer is credit cards. I don't need money in my pocket any more. I won't deal in cash with nobody.'

'That reminds me,' you said. 'I must get to the bank.'

'Credit cards simplify everything. Speed up life. It's just a beginning.' He produced from an inner pocket a wallet in which he displayed a dozen plastic cards. 'Very soon, cards such as these will unlock our front doors, switch our TV sets on and off, draw the blinds, set our meals cooking. All sorts of things.'

You shook your head. 'You make me feel old-fashioned, Pief.'

He bestowed one of his smiles on you. 'You must dine with me some time. Then we can talk. You are old-fashioned, Steve, let's face it. But you have values I don't. Maybe when I am old, which God forbid I will, I will read Proust and Tolstoy.'

You liked Tolstoy, which conjoined storytellers from both East and West.

Glancing at his gold Rolex watch, Pief said he must hurry. He shook hands with you. He turned one way, you another. Then he stopped and called back to you.

'Hey, I almost forgot, Steve, so much on my mind. I was looking over this plot of land. It's a prospect for Sale-Safe. Planners got planning permission to build a new shopping trolley factory here. If you like this house up for sale, forget it! Don't buy. Take my word, don't buy – not unless you got a big thing about shopping trolleys.'

You were grateful for his warning, but you said to yourself as you drove away that Pief was so full of himself, he never even thought to enquire how your darling Verity was.

10

Violet in Her Bath

You and Verity were flying back from a brief holiday in Corfu. You had stayed in a pleasant, small hotel on the north-east coast, where you swam regularly and virtually lived on a diet of retsina that washed down fresh fish, taken from the sea just before dawn. The skies remained every day a gentle blue, unbroken by cloud. You were sixty-five, a little grey at the temples, but very much content with life, and with Verity, who had by now recovered from her burns and was in exuberant spirits.

It was September of that remarkable year, 1989, when the pilot of your plane, instead of advising passengers to keep their safety belts fastened, announced that Hungary had opened up its frontiers in order to let refugees and others through to the West. It was a sensational decision. In Warsaw there was unrest. Gorbachev was about to visit the German Democratic Republic, a visit that would signal the downfall of the Honecker regime. The Communist world was in stress, breaking open like a rotten melon. After the uncertainties of previous years, there was reason to be cheerful, and to hope that the armed division of East and West might at last be drawing to a close.

Nevertheless, as the plane crossed the tidy English coast, with its bars of damp shingle and its parade of rainswept promenades, so unlike the informal bays of Corfu, with their welcoming tavernas, melancholy filled your mind. You could not understand it, nor escape it.

'Are you sickening for something?' Verity asked.

'No idea. Perhaps something's sickening for me …'

Once you were grounded and rang home, you understood. You were told your Aunt Violet had committed suicide.

You pushed past the faded mauve door of 19, Park Road into the hall, where Joyce greeted you.

'It's good of you to come, Uncle, I knew you would.' She kissed the air by your cheek, clutching you tightly, looking pale and drawn. The years had thickened Joyce's figure. Paul stood rather helplessly in the background.

'When did this ghastly thing happen?'

'In the night. About two o'clock this morning, according to the coroner. Dougie and I were asleep; we never heard a thing.' Joyce managed to keep her voice level. 'Oh, I feel so awful. I knew mum wasn't feeling too good – depressed, you know – but I didn't do anything about it. She and dad had had a terrible row. He was so unkind. And you know we were going to the cinema again this evening … He called her a spendthrift and a witch and I-don't-know-what-all.' Joyce's hands fluttered about her like lost pigeons, she choked over her words. Her blonde hair straggled, despite a ribbon tied to keep it in subjection. 'Of course she liked to spend money, but that's not a crime, is it?'

You were still lingering in the hall, against their heavy hallstand. From a rear room, Dougie called. 'Who is it? Is it the hospital again? Visitors? People who live in prisons roaming the streets?'

440

'Dougie's in a terrible mood,' Joyce said, speaking quietly. 'Thank God Paul is here.'

'And Bertie?' you asked. 'He's here? Where is he?'

She shook her head and more strands of hair escaped from the confining ribbon. 'I say he should be here, looking after us at the least, the scumbag ...'

Still she made no move to leave the hall. You said, 'Hadn't we better ...?'

'Okay. Listen, I'm glad to see you, Steve. Thanks for coming.' She took your arm and led you into the sitting room. Paul Patel followed.

French doors looked onto a small back garden, part of which had been terraced. A bed of bewildered French marigolds lived out their existence. The doors were open. Paul went to stand on the terrace, his back to the house, smoking a cigarette, away from the fray. He gave you a sad smile. 'We'd taken Violet to the cinema yesterday,' he said. 'We went to see a movie produced by Roger Corman, *The Drifter*. Wasn't very good ...'

'Yeah, we sat in the cheap seats,' Joyce added.

Dougie was a solid man in his late forties. He wore a plastic jacket over a T-shirt which said 'Famous DJ's Can't Spell D J' – a gentle hint that he was by now a famous D J. He rose from an armchair and came to shake your hand. His expression was gloomy.

'Good of you to come, Steve, unlike the rest of the lousy family. This day of all days. I took the day off. I'm a refrigeration engineer, in case you didn't know – hence the frosty reception – thinking of giving it up since D J-ing takes up more and more of my time; but what's time for, if not to be taken up? And a fine state we're in.'

'Oh, do shut up, Dougie,' said Joyce, and was ignored.

'It's the worst day of my life. Poor old Dad – he's cleared off. Dead wives don't come any deader. Can't blame him.'

'You can blame him,' said Joyce quietly. 'It's his cruelty to Mum drove her to commit this terrible thing to herself.'

Dougie scowled at her, then turned to you. 'She keeps saying that. What was Pop supposed to do? She'd used up all Dad's money;

441

we all knew what a spendthrift Mum was. She spread money like honey. Poor old Dad – deep in debt. I knew he was upset but I didn't do anything about it. What'll happen now? It's beyond me.'

You saw that Joyce was working herself up. 'You keep on saying that. Dad was so weak, he encouraged her. It's our fault too, we encouraged her. I encouraged her, I admit it. But then I loved her so much.'

'Don't get into that,' he said. Dougie's face was growing redder. 'The fact is that architecture never paid. Nothing he ever did ever paid. Mum would not face facts –'

'He was too old-fashioned,' said Joyce, throwing you an appealing glance. 'Wouldn't adapt.'

Paul Patel flung the stub of his cigarette away and re-entered the house. 'Shall I make us all a cup of tea? This is really not a fitting time to quarrel, not when poor Violet is newly demised. Life is horrible enough –'

'I'm not quarrelling,' said Joyce sharply. 'I'm merely defending my mother's good name. You agree with me, don't you, Steve?'

'I loved her too,' you said, with sorrow. 'I'm sure you both loved her. Perhaps your father loved her too much, couldn't be firm with her, or face telling her the truth.'

'That's tosh,' Joyce was saying, when there came a rap at the front door. Someone had found it open and walked right in. The someone proved to be your Uncle Claude, bringing with him a young woman in a tight pink blouse and a miniskirt, with a dragon tattooed on her right upper arm.

As Paul disappeared into the kitchen with Joyce, Claude came round, shaking your hand and Dougie's. 'Heard the bad news. Came right over.'

'Where've you been, Uncle?' you asked him.

Although he was looking older, his usual blustering manner was still in evidence. 'Joey's emigrated to America, the blighter. I told you Terry was in Canada, didn't I? Britain wasn't big enough for them.'

'We're better off without them.' You could not resist saying it.

'Never mind all that. They're still my kids. Dreadfully sorry to hear about Vi. Anything I can do? Do you want some flowers? I know the very place where I can get them cheap.'

You asked him what he was doing.

'I run a garden centre down in Brighton. Ideal for my old age. Come and look it over some time.' Claude was wearing a hairy green suit, evidently a sartorial reference to his new trade. You had heard that his previous job had collapsed under him.

He turned to Dougie.

'Don't mind me barging in, do you? Terribly cut up to hear about your dear old mum – one of the nicest people in our ruddy family, was Vi. Never did anyone a mischief. You want someone to sing her praises, it's me.'

His remark about mischief made you wonder over again if Violet had been mischief-making when telling you that your parents had hoped you would drown on Walcot beach. Even if it had been as she said, discretion might have preserved her silence on the matter. You would have been saved years of perplexity.

'So who found the poor old dear?' Claude asked. As Dougie was explaining, Claude's girlfriend nudged him in the ribs. 'Oh, by the way, this is Dusty Straw, a new friend of mine. Laughable peasant name, admittedly, but a sweet and charming lass, aren't you, love?' He leered at the young woman who, on closer inspection, was less young than she had at first appeared.

Dusty Straw giggled. 'If you say so, Claude.' She curled her left foot about her right.

'Oh, but I do say so,' Claude declared, feigning seriousness.

Joyce re-entered the room with a plate full of biscuits.

'So you found her, Joyce, old gal?' Claude kissed her cheek. 'In the bath, right? Bit of a shock for you, I'd imagine. Wrists cut, bath full of blood … Nasty! What did she do it with, if you don't mind me asking?' He grabbed a biscuit.

Dougie took charge of the answer. 'She used the bread knife. Do you want to see it? Do you want to see the blood-soaked towels? The empty gin bottles? Why all these nauseating questions, Claude?'

'They must be asked. Suicide is a serious business. You have to face facts, whether incriminating or not,' Claude stated, possibly with an echo of his old profession. 'Why isn't Bertie here – the erstwhile Hero of Kabul? I hope he's crying his little eyes out.'

Paul emerged from the kitchen carrying a tray loaded with six mugs of various colours and vintages. Claude immediately grabbed one.

'Nothing stronger, eh? Any sherry, to name but a few?'

'We can't afford anything stronger,' said Dougie, impatiently. 'We're bust, you understand! Bust, got it? Why do you think mum killed herself? We're deep in the red.'

Claude gave a snort of laughter and winked at Dusty Straw. 'She certainly died in the red in the bath, didn't she?'

'You lout!' Dougie exclaimed. 'This is a fine time for your coarse jokes!'

'Bit of a joke to lighten the atmosphere. You're a touch touchy, Dougie – absolutely understand how you feel.'

Joyce, ignoring this exchange, walked about the room, tugging at a lock of her hair. She stopped suddenly and attacked her brother again. 'How dare you say Mum died because we are in debt? You know darn well it was because of your father's hostility to her. She just felt that life wasn't worth living after years of that. Guilt and misery, that's what Mum died of, poor darling.'

'It's not the first suicide in the family,' you reminded them. You thought, or the attempt, as in Verity's case.

Which of the siblings was right, you wondered. Why could not both be right? After all, as you now realized, your dear aunt had been of a fragile nature. Could her two suffering offspring not come to a conclusion, and comfort each other instead of quarrelling? But, you had to admit, this painful time was scarcely a period for reason to flourish; you too suffered, although not as they did.

444

As if tired of the discussion, Dougie turned with his mug of tea and went to stare down the garden. 'There's that bloody tabby from next door again. If I still had my air rifle, I'd shoot him right up his jaxi. Anyhow, Mum's dead, and no argument will bring her back. It's Dad I worry about now.' Glancing at his watch, he added that the police should arrive soon.

Joyce breathed a deep sigh. Claude said, 'Dusty will give you a hand cleaning up the bathroom, if you like.'

'It's been done,' Joyce said, shortly. After a silence, she added, 'I feel so desperate. I feel one of us should shoulder the blame.'

'No,' you said. 'That won't help, Joyce, dear. Blame always follows a suicide; the guilt thing. You remember when Aunt Flo's son, Sad Sid, killed himself? It's enough that we grieve for a life lost. You'll never forget your dear mother. Nor will I.'

'She spoilt me rotten.'

'Then you were lucky.'

'There are worse conditions than rotten in this context,' said Paul.

Paul set his mug down and said, 'Remember Violet's life. Don't just remember her being dead in the bath. Remember her love for you, remember what a nice person she was, remember her living, and breathing. Maybe she had her faults, as we all do, but just remember what a nice person Violet was, and how she cared for you. Remember we all loved her.'

'Hear, hear,' said Claude. 'And remarkably pretty when young, eh, Steve? When's the funeral?'

The funeral was later in the week. Later in the year, Nicolae Ceausescu, the dictator of Romania, was shot, together with his wife, after twenty-four years in power. You viewed his downfall on television. In November, the Berlin Wall, brutal symbol of oppression, was also to fall – and you would happen to be there to witness it. It was an example of the way in which the face of a nation could change in a few days; whereas an individual takes longer about it.

These great events meant little to the family when weighed against your beloved aunt Violet Wilberforce's death.

Uncle Bertie went into a home for the poor, and was subsidized there by contributions from the family. You visited him once, to help him settle in. His little room was painted cream; even the sparse furniture was painted a thick, indigestible cream. Bertie wanted to talk about Violet. The more he talked, the more strongly you felt he had no idea of her inner life; but then the question arose, *Did you understand her inner life?* Your aunt had left no suicide note. Such a note might have held, if inadvertently, a clue to her inner life, and what really drove her to kill herself.

And knowing, you reflected, would have made you a little happier, perhaps even in an Aristotelian sense. You had loved Violet; you hoped she had been at least content with her life, her character. She had loved and cared for her children. That was a virtue and a blessing.

You tired of hearing your mother trying to justify her long hostility towards your aunt. 'I know people. I never trusted her. I trusted my instinct. I always thought she was unbalanced, and this proves it. Of course I'm sorry, sorry for Joyce of course, but –'

You cut off one of these monologues, saying, 'If you'd been kinder, Mother, and had offered her some support in her difficulties, instead of ostracizing her, Violet might still be alive.'

She flinched backwards as if from a blow. 'How dare you? How dare you? Whose side are you on?'

And she left the room.

You talked the matter over with Verity. She inclined to the idea that much of what one tends to think of as 'character' is actually just an accumulation of accidents and contingencies which occur to you by dint of your being around, much as, she added unflatteringly, the flu virus passes round from one person to another on a winter's day, just because they happen to be present. Looking back on your own life, you could not but admit there was some truth in this point of view. If the bullying Jeremy Nash had not

446

invited you to supper on that certain evening, if there had not been an outbreak of Dutch elm disease, if there had not been a high wind just then, if he had not shouted at Verity … why then, you two would never have married.'

'Still,' you told her, 'there's more to it than that.'

'Oh yes, the inward thing, I agree,' she said. 'Like the accident that there happens to be two sexes.' She put an arm round your neck and kissed you. 'Had a thousand people rescued me that evening, I would still have loved you.'

You heard later that Uncle Bertie was ill. You had been so busy that you had gone only once to see him in sheltered housing, where he had a small room.

You paid him a visit clutching a small bunch of flowers and a bunch of seedless grapes. A nurse in a white overall showed you to Bertie's room. The one-time hero of Kabul was sitting up in bed, wearing a dressing gown and smoking a cigarette. He looked much older than when you had last seen him.

'I'm all right, old boy, thanks. Got over it with the help of my nurse. Like a cigarette? She's Nurse Marya Bird. Was Marya Deschutski, or something, but she got married to an English chap. She's a Pole.'

'She treats you well, does she?'

He blew out smoke and stubbed his cigarette end in a conveniently placed ashtray. 'There's not many people you can talk to here. Half of them are daft – you know, past it. Marya likes to talk. Look, she brought me this pear.' He indicated the fruit, its nose cocked at an angle, sitting on a saucer on his bedside table. 'I haven't eaten it yet. Don't seem to have much of an appetite these days.'

'What's the food like, Uncle?'

'Not too bad.' He laid his head back on one of the pillows that were propping him up. He looked weary. His moustache drooped. But for the moustache, his might have been a woman's face; he was still masculine, but age and defeat had taken away his maleness.

The nurse he had been talking about came in smiling, carrying a little tray.

'Here's your Bovril, Bertie dear,' she said, setting the tray down on the table beside the pear. With a surprisingly quick movement, he seized her hand in his weak grasp.

'You're a darling, Marya,' he said. 'How about eloping *avec moi*?'

'And you're a naughty old man!' Her bright little thin face broke into a radiant smile.

When she had gone, he said, 'I'll drink that stuff when it's a bit cooler. They always make it too weak. My throat's so dry.' He lit another cigarette. 'Do you want one? Player's Navy Cut. You see, we went to war over the Poles, and much good it did them. We bit off more than we could chew, I'd say. When you think about it, who won the war? It was the bloody Russians, wasn't it? Or perhaps it was Adolf Hitler. He bit off more than he could chew there – he conjured up the monster in the Kremlin who went on to swallow up half of Europe, in –' – a bout of coughing made him pause. He took a sip of the Bovril before continuing – 'including Poland. That's why she's here, Marya. She'll never go back to Potsdam, where she came from. Sorry, Poznan. She'll never go back there now. She reckons the British were too nice to fight properly. That's what she said, too nice. Whereas the Germans and the Russians, well, terrible lot of hooligans … She knows all about it, does Marya.'

You recalled the group of old men in Wehrmacht uniforms whose lives you had spared in the Ardennes struggle. This little nurse in her white overalls probably knew more about the real horrors of war than you did.

Bertie went on talking about her. He was still talking when the nurse looked in again. 'You haven't drunk your Bovril up yet, you old scamp! It's good for you!' Turning to you with a smile, she said, 'Oh, what a terrible trouble is this one. Never does he what he's told.'

When she had gone, to prevent any more monologue about the war, you asked Bertie, 'Do you think much about Auntie Violet these days, Uncle?'

He peered at you in a vague way. 'I bit off more than I could chew there, old boy.'

You felt an affection for him then you had never felt before; he had summed up his life's situation in a well-worn phrase. Bertie was defeated – after all, defeat was not an unusual fate for the old – yet seemed reasonably cheerful. And he enjoyed the good fortune to have happened on a nurse who was evidently fond of him, and of whom he could be fond.

11

Flight to Austin, Texas

You were flying from Washington to Austin, Texas, to attend a meeting on museum technology, to be chaired by Professor Tony Pekhovich. You were pleased to find yourself seated next to Pekhovich in business class. The year was 1983.

You took two bottles of vodka from the air hostess and began to talk, idly at first and then more intently when you discovered you had both been involved in the war in Europe, almost forty years ago, in 1944.

Tony Pekhovich was a small, neat man with a goatee beard now threaded with white. He had dark eyebrows and grey, penetrating eyes. He was pleasant in appearance and spoke with a deceptively languid delivery.

'I served in Intelligence under General Patton,' he said. 'We were more scared of Patton than we were of the Germans, madman that he was. I never hated the Germans like I hated the Japanese. My brother, Devlin, he was prisoner of the Japs, taken prisoner on Bataan. He's four years my junior, but you'd take him for a much older man, thanks to the way those little yellow cocksuckers treated him.'

You told him that although you were fifty-nine, you felt younger now than you had done during the final months of the war.

'Now there's more trouble on our hands,' said Pekhovich. 'President Reagan has been taunting the Soviets again, calling them the "Evil Empire". It surely only stirs up more trouble. I don't like it, but maybe that's on account of my family being of Russian descent.'

You rattled the ice cubes in your plastic glass and took a sip. 'You may have heard we have a new prime minister, Margaret Thatcher. She's apparently as warlike as Reagan. The nation's in bad shape. To my mind, she needs to look to the country and forget about international affairs.'

'You think so?' He regarded you musingly. 'I'm no isolationist, unlike many of my colleagues, and I see all the world as uncomfortably united – the way two boxers are united in the ring.' He lowered his voice to say, 'You may have heard the US Embassy in the Lebanon was blown up in April. We were taken off guard; the embassy was all but destroyed and over fifty people were killed.'

'By the Russians? Surely not.'

'By Muslims; Shi'ites. Well named, you might think. There's more trouble brewing up everywhere.'

A trolley was approaching along the gangway. 'Here comes lunch. Eat, drink, and be merry. Tomorrow we die.'

'Isaiah, I believe,' he said. It was tortillas for us, and Tony ordered champagne. You tried to pay but he insisted that you were his guest, from what he called, 'an almost foreign country'.

So you were convivial and, as befitted those who frequented museums, went on to consider the past; in particular, the past with all its follies and wickedness, such as the war you had both soldiered in. The question arose of how human wickedness could be conquered. Tony Pekhovich asked you if you had read H. G. Wells's *Time Machine*. You admitted you had not done so.

'Good health!' he said, and you both raised your plastic glasses. 'It's a fine book, published less than ten years after Robert Louis Stevenson's *Dr Jekyll and Mr Hyde*. And what do these two short books have in common? They are both about the duality of man – the good and the bad. Wells raises the stakes by showing us the whole of Victorian society bifurcated. Eloi good, Morlock bad. This has always been taken for social criticism, but I believe it goes deeper. We all have the good and bad in us. Do you want a crackpot theory, Steve?'

It was the first time he had used your Christian name. You looked out of the window at the plains of Oklahoma below, unsure whether or not you wanted a crackpot theory. But Tony had bought you both champagne.

'Go ahead.'

He leaned slightly towards you, to speak confidentially. 'Not only do I prize the past, where forgotten human life is preserved in museums, I look to the future, as well. In the museum in Austin there is a precious little relic, it has a showcase of its own. Floodlit, it rests on green baize, so's you can view it best. It is the first lens that Galileo Galilei ever ground, in order to construct his *occhiale*, his telescope. You know what the Medicean stars are?'

His habit of asking such questions was a minor irritation. This time you knew the answer. 'Galileo ground his own lenses for his telescope. When he turned the telescope towards Jupiter, he saw four small bodies in orbit about the giant planet. For his own protection, he named them after the powerful Medici family.'

Tony nodded vigorously. 'That's it exactly. Four moons of Jupiter! Which was proof that the Copernican theory of Earth's rotation round the Sun was a fact. That perception is one of the tender shoots that formed our modern world.'

You smiled, unable to discourage him. 'And those Medicean stars we now know as Io, Europa, Callisto and, what's the other one, the largest moon?'

'Ganymede. Now for my theory: I foresee the day when men – and women, we hope – will make a landing on Ganymede, establish a colony there. That's not too far-fetched. Think how unlikely the walk on the Moon would have seemed in Galileo's time. And Ganymede is the size of a small planet.'

'We've yet to walk on Mars, don't forget.'

'Hear me out, I am talking of the future. The Ganymede settlers would be lit by Jupiter, as well as generating their own power. Think how beautiful the night skies would be. And, the settlers would be distant from our turbulent Sun. What a difference that would make! They could live calm lives. My belief is that it's our Sun that affects us with aggression; no one has ever thought about that before. I am making notes towards a book on the subject.'

At which point, a man in the seat ahead of you rose up, turned, and glared down at you, red-faced. 'Gentlemen, I'm hearing what you are saying, and it is all hogwash. To leave this planet on which we were born is against God's teaching. You are defying all that the scriptures say. Does the Bible mention this Ganymede? No, no way. So cease to blaspheme, okay?'

Tony Pekhovich was calm, saying mildly, 'What are you doing on this plane, friend? Have you not left this planet? Progress is unstoppable; sit yourself down and think about it.'

An alert air hostess came and asked the challenger to sit down and fasten his safety belt, since you were about to enter a region of turbulence.

'A region of turbulence, yes, that's one of the reactionaries we have to cope with.' Tony looked undisturbed, but he changed the subject, abandoning the future to talk again of the past.

So you amused yourselves until reaching Austin, without offending the man in the seat ahead. And in Austin, Mrs Annie Pekhovich was waiting to greet her husband at the airport. They had met in London, during what he described, laughingly, as 'that much maligned World War'. She greeted you warmly. She had been born in Ilford, Patricia Ann Evans. The days of that conference were more enjoyable for their company.

What did you make of tho man Pekhovich's remarks?

I'd quite forgotten old Tony. And his wife. Very pleasant couple, I met up with them on another occasion, with Verity.

Never mind that. What did you make of his remarks?

I haven't thought of them from that day to this. My apologies, this is not at all a day –

Pekhovich made a prediction about mankind settling on Jupiter's moon, Ganymede. I step beyond the bounds of my instructions to tell you that Professor Pekhovich was not the superficial man you may have thought him. The time came when human beings indeed settled on Ganymede. His prediction was correct.

Oh? He never published the book he planned. What happened to Tony? He died of Alzheimer's disease.

Oh shit. It may visit us all in the end. And did that distance from the Sun bring those benefits of peace he anticipated?

His Sun theory was nonsense. The settlers fought one another for every kilometre of that barren moon.

You feel ashamed of the human race?

I am ashamed of our bad programming.

12

*The Future of
the World*

The time came when you had to go to West Berlin to deliver your lecture to the Geological Institute. It was winter and you and Verity were busy moving into your new house in Maidenhead, where the Thames flowed by at the bottom of your garden.

You were met in Berlin by a small delegation that escorted you to your hotel. In your room, you found a note addressed to you; it came from a Frau Heather Pieck.

You read it hastily. 'I am interested to learn that you will be in West Berlin. I am curator at the Geological Museum here. My name was Heather Lambert. I married a German guy six years ago – my mother was German, as if that explains our love for one another. (I write that to warn you!) We used to know each other at Ashbury, many years ago. I will attend your lecture and will be curious to meet you again and introduce Helmut, if that is possible.'

Heather had signed the note with a flourish.

She was curious. So were you. Smiling to yourself, you recalled making love to the young woman in a hole in the ground. The affair had been consummated either there or later in your room; memory was a little vague on that detail. It would be instructive to learn what she had been doing with her life; one advantage of growing old was that you found out what had happened to people you once knew, and how character and circumstance had worked together to weather the other.

You showed Verity the letter; she read it over and handed it back. 'Yes, you knew Heather quite well in those days. It'll be interesting to meet her again, I hope you won't be too disappointed.'

'You knew about our brief affair?'

She gave one of her abridged laughs. 'The whole school knew about your brief affair!'

'And you're not jealous?'

'What! It's a bit late to be jealous, isn't it?' This time her laughter was unabridged. 'Besides, your Heather may turn out to be a Flora Finching.'

You recognized the reference to the character in Dickens's *Little Dorrit*, which you had read together with Verity the previous summer.

A limousine collected you and drove you to the Institute. You were warmly received and escorted to a smart anteroom where drinks were served. You toyed with a glass of tonic water while chatting to your confrères. It was the 9th of November, 1989, and the geologists wanted to talk about nothing but the *Aufregung* in the DDR, where there were mass demonstrations against the Communist government of Erich Honecker; Honecker had just resigned.

'And now they demonstrate just across the Wall in East Berlin,' said the chairman. 'It is really most unprecedented –' He was an old man, and portly, with a florid friendly face across which a white moustache was draped.

'All because of Gorbachev,' said his secretary, butting in – a fair-haired young man by name Edschmid, who was keen on promotion.

'Not the mighty Gorbachev alone,' said the chairman, to keep the youngster in his place. 'The DDR is bankrupt, financially and morally.'

'But the immediate cause for this disturbance,' said Edschmid, excitedly, 'is because the Hungarians have opened up their borders with Austria. Did you not see it on the television? This has enabled many thousands of East Germans – our dear friends and enemies – to make the escape to the West, where they can enjoy the benefits of democracy, and pornography, and decent food – not necessarily in that order.'

'We had best to move into the council chamber now,' said the chairman, stiffly. 'There I will introduce you.'

The council chamber was thinly attended. 'I fear that politics have intervened, as so often in the course of our German lives,' said the chairman, with a sad wit.

You rose to speak when the introduction was over. You had already identified Heather Pieck; she was seated in the front row of chairs. Her husband, Helmut Pieck, sat next to her, a reedy little man in a neat suit, his sandy hair receding, his hands clasped together on his knee. Heather had spread. She wore hornrimmed glasses and was refulgent in a long, bright dress, possibly chosen carefully for the occasion. She gave you a tiny wave as you stood to speak, hand against an ample bosom so that others would not notice.

'The disciplines of the geologist and archaeologist represent a remarkable combination of the workings of scientific method, together with the imagination, in which the public have largely collaborated. Most educated people now accept the vast, geological time-scale, and its division into eras and periods, which has been created only over the last century and this century. Many eras, such as the Mesozoic and, before that, the Permian and Carboniferous, have become vivid to our understandings. And of course, movies about the Jurassic period and its large reptiles are popular. Children take pink felt tyrannosauruses to bed with them.

'Yet we must understand that it is the painstaking study of rocks, together with a mere truck-full of bones – not more – which has delivered this awesome panorama of past Earth over many eons. The patient delver in an arid-seeming rock stratum has his training and his imagination as guide, but not only that. The work of many men and women now deceased provides the foundation on which he builds. This represents the essence of our culture: *continuity*, that continuity which insures the allied labours of science and imagination.

'So much for context. Now I shall be more specific, more technical, and speak regarding our work in the Chicxulub crater, which may prove to be –'

You were interrupted by a messenger, who entered the chamber and thrust a note into the chairman's hand. The chairman read the note and looked flustered. Then he caught you by the sleeve – just a tweak on the cuff. 'Oh, do please excuse me, Dr Fielding.' His countenance, already rubicund, had flushed bright red. 'It's most incorrect to interrupt our speaker, but it's most unprecedented, most – most – *beispiellos*, yes, unexampled.' Turning from you, he addressed the sprinkling of audience. 'Fellow colleagues, the Berlin Wall is being attacked from the east side!'

Cries and shouts came from the audience. All immediately stood up, looked round for reassurance, and then began to rush from the chamber.

'I'm so sorry about this,' said the chairman. 'So sorry, but history, well, you know all about history ...'

'Yes,' you said. 'And sometimes it happens when you are standing talking.'

Although you sought to hide it, you were considerably annoyed by the interruption. You felt your speech was important; how could an attack on the Wall be of equal or more importance? After all, the Wall must have been attacked many times. So you were annoyed with the chairman, and annoyed with Mr Gorbachev, who had stirred up trouble in the Communist states.

Later on, when you discovered the momentousness of the situation, you were annoyed with yourself. But for the time being, you cold-shouldered the chairman.

Out on the steps of the Institute, Heather was waiting for you, her reluctant husband beside her. She was wearing a light coat over the bright dress. She put an arm round your neck and kissed the air by both cheeks before introducing Helmut. He was polite, verging on frostiness. A little man in a brown suit, with long artistic hands and fingers, his handshake was a weak, limp grasp.

'You have become very celebrated, Steve,' she said, her eyes gleaming behind her spectacles. Her manner was slightly flirtatious; you wondered if you remembered it.

'You haven't changed,' you said gallantly. But her face was puffy and pale; powder had been injudiciously added.

She gave a brief laugh, dismissing this compliment. 'I've had two children, you know.'

A great commotion was taking place in the street, with crowds moving mainly in one direction, towards the Wall. Many women carried clothes, some carried bedding, while men carried crates of lager, or pushed baby carriages containing medical supplies, or groceries. Two small boys ran in and out of the crowds with comics under their arms. An ambulance made its way slowly forward, its siren sounding. There were cars and motorcycles moving at two kilometres an hour among the pedestrians, who filled the streets from wall to wall.

Heather locked her substantial arm in your arm. 'Like old times, *nicht war*?' she said, with a short laugh, much like a snort.

'Ah, *die alte Zeit!*' you echoed, although you could not remember that she had ever taken your arm before. You were uncertain about her intentions.

'I must buy some cigarettes. Helmut, get us some Philip Morris, will you? A carton.' She explained to you, 'If those poor devils get over the wall, they'll be in need of a smoke.'

The Wall could be seen ahead now. Searchlights were playing, police were shouting through megaphones, trying to order the

461

crowds, three fire engines were manoeuvring for position. Troops were standing by, clustered beside a tank and looking bewildered. Cheers went up from the crowd as more East Berliners appeared on top of the Wall. They waved back delightedly.

'What a scrimmage!' Heather exclaimed.

'We should not get so near,' said Helmut. She ignored him, pressing on. In the hubbub, swamped by the good-natured crowds, you lost Helmut. Or perhaps he preferred to lag behind in safety.

There was some slight danger as you pushed your way forward. Men on top of the Wall were attacking it with spades and picks; fragments of concrete and stone were flying. A youngster up there with a banjo was playing and singing *All You Need is Love*. Westerners were picking up the song, waving and shouting. A woman on your side of the Wall, poorly dressed in an old raincoat, was battering the Wall with a round stone, yelling expletives as she did so. Music was coming up from both sides now – non-military music, Western music, love songs, pop ... Mouth organs from the East, and the odd ghetto blaster.

Now a metal ladder went up against the Wall. A man climbed up it, to help down a woman and a small boy, but the gates had been thrown open and Easterners were pouring through, many waving arms above their heads, yelling in delight.

'*Freiheit! Freiheit!*' – that precious word on German lips – 'Freedom! Freedom!'

A middle-aged man in ridiculous clothes, with a Union Jack wrapped across his chest, stood on the Wall and began broadcasting in English.

'Hi, folks, *Gutes Nacht*, bon soir, not to mention Good Evening! Here's your favourite DJ, Dougie the Demon, Demon Dougie, speaking to you from Radio Charlotte, the Station with Good Vibrations. I'm on the Wall – no, not the Pink Floyd Wall, but the Wall that divides Democracy from Communism! A world is ending, folks, and a world's beginning – not with a bang but a vodka –'

'Good god,' you exclaimed. 'It's Dougie Wilberforce!'

'That's ever so trendy of you, Steve!' exclaimed Heather, impressed.

It seemed as if the whole world had decided to embrace. Women and men from the DDR flung their arms about whoever happened to be near. Women and men from the West flung their arms about anyone who approached. Many women caught up little East Berlin boys and girls and kissed them over and over, until the children wriggled to escape.

Heather had let go of you to join in the general rejoicing, clapping and waving. Two men pushing forward grabbed her and kissed her, one on one cheek, one on the other, all three laughing with happiness. You were seized by a tall, gaunt old lady, scantily clad in the cool night.

'*Liebchen!*' she said, and began pouring out her history of oppression, while Heather disappeared into the throng.

'Sorry, I don't understand,' you said.

'You are where from?' she asked.

'England.'

'Englandt, mine God! Hey, this man is from Englandt, everyone!' she cried to the passers-by.

A man grabbed your hand and shook it. 'Good luck!' he said and was gone.

Flags were being waved. Trabants were moving slowly into the streets of the West, the stink of their exhausts adding another element to the absolute frenzy of the crowd. And now the Wall was being seriously demolished, from both sides! A young woman, possibly a schoolgirl, danced naked on top of a Mercedes. Two men with old-fashioned bellows cameras were photographing her, encouraging lewd postures.

You happened on Heather an hour later. She had lost her glasses and had given her coat to an East Berliner. Her gaudy dress was torn under one arm.

'It's never happened before, never,' she said. She was crying for joy and flung herself into your arms. 'Oh, this moment, this very moment. It's history!'

'Let's get a drink, Heather, it's impossible here. Come back to my hotel and get a drink there. You look whacked.'

'You're not up to your old tricks?' she asked, with a smile.

You kissed her. 'Don't be so hopeful.'

She gazed up at you flirtatiously, saying, 'But on such a night, eh?'

'You're pretty safe. I'm sixty-five and happily married.'

'Who's happy that much?'

You were pushing your way through the masses of people. The crowds were thinning as you advanced. You met a group who had lit a bonfire in the middle of the street; men and women were dancing beside it, dancing and kissing. A radio was playing.

'Where's Helmut?' You had to shout to make yourself heard.

Heather shrugged. 'Not dancing, that's for sure.' She stopped. 'Come on, let's dance too. I feel like a dance, don't you?'

One of the women dancers took your arm, insisting that you join them. So you did, really not caring. Heather began singing in German, joining in with the song some of the other dancers were singing. The bonfire crackled as if it, too, rejoiced.

You whirled round and round, suddenly jubilant. The motions of the dance, the sense that this could never happen again, liberated something in you. The end of the DDR? The end of Communism? It was something impossible, something to celebrate. And a suspicion crept over you that after all it would be pleasurable to have Heather in bed with you, just this once. It was not being unfaithful to Verity. Why, you said to yourself, it was almost a duty to Germany. 'England expects this day that every man will do his duty.' That sort of thing.

You laughed aloud.

'I'm sweating like a pig,' Heather said.

But the pair of you went along towards the hotel nevertheless.

'I told you a little white lie, Steve,' she said, clinging on to your arm. 'I'm not the curator of the museum. In fact, I'm just a minion there, the curator is Dr Carl Hartrich, a nice kind man. Sometimes even says good morning to me.'

She gave her short laugh.

464

'But you've evidently found your niche here,' you remarked, consolingly.

'What niche? True, I like Berlin. Y'know, I go back to England occasionally to see my sister. I don't care for it any more, everyone's so rude.'

You evaded a laughing gang who were trying to stop passersby. Beyond them, a Trabant by the roadside was quietly burning, emitting clouds of heavy black smoke. A policeman in a yellow coverall stood nearby, immobile, deep in thought.

'So you're reasonably happy, Heather?'

She asked instead of replying, 'How's your life turned out?'

'Better than I dared wish for. I've been lucky in love –'

'I don't know whether I'm happy or miserable. That's the truth, Steve.' You thought you remembered her saying something of the kind back in Ashbury days.

'But Helmut –'

'Oh, Helmut. Yes, he's sort of kind. I can boss him about. But sex –' She made a face as she turned down her thumb.

You pressed on up the crowded street. Elsewhere, car horns were sounding.

The normally staid foyer and lounge of the hotel were in a hubbub. Crowds of people, mainly male, were celebrating, those in evening dress jostling with those in cheap grey clothes or T-shirts. On every side, glasses were being raised and toasts drunk. The dining-tables further in were crowded with laughing people, while to those tables waiters struggled to make their way, trays of drinks balanced overhead like open umbrellas.

A band was playing swing at full blast. Couples were dancing or standing hugging each other, or falling over, to the music. Glenn Miller was back in force.

'Sit down and I'll get you a drink,' you told Heather. 'What do you want?'

'A lager and a Fernet-Branca. Thanks. Phew, it's hot in here.' She fanned herself with one hand.

You made your way to the bar, where many men fought for the attentions of the besieged barmen. You began calling for attention with the rest.

A man in evening dress with a long, leathery, outdoor kind of face put an arm round your shoulders, saying, 'It's a case of the survival of the loudest. Darwin would be interested.'

'I'd buy Darwin a drink if he were here.'

'He'd see the human race at its best. Let me buy you a drink, buddy. I'm a pal of all Limeys.'

The leathery man turned out to be one of a party consisting of three Americans, of which he, Henry Dice, was one. There was also an Englishman and a French woman, smartly attired and smoking black Balkan Sobranie cigarettes. Her name was Violane. One of the Americans had a young woman on his knee, they were kissing when you joined them at their table. The Englishman drank without setting down his shot glass, elbows on the table.

You and Dice were carrying eight bottles of lager between you, together with a small bottle of Fernet-Branca. You held two of the bottles in your hand and had another bottle gripped precariously under each arm, high up in the armpit. The Fernet-Branca bottle protruded from your jacket pocket.

'Can't stay. Got a girlfriend over there. Just a quick drink.'

It transpired that all but the girl on the knee, who had come from Leipzig, were members of an EU trade delegation. The two Americans were arguing about what was happening at the Wall. One claimed that trade would benefit, that once the Easterners had seen the prosperity of the West, they would no longer tolerate their wretched lot and Communism would die the death. There would then be a whole new nation to trade with. He was rather drunk and his pronunciation was indistinct.

The second American, the one with the girl on his knee, denied this. He claimed that the Easterners were not going to return to the DDR once they had escaped. Their nation would soon be emptied of its population unless they were stopped. Western

466

Germany would sink under the weight of, well, he had to say it, Communists, fascists and savages.

'No, we are not savages,' said the girl, suddenly speaking up. 'This indiscipline which you see here in this hotel would never happen in our land.'

'What about the Stasi?'

The Englishman in the party said nothing. He drank steadily, a sip at a time, regarding you with unrelenting hostility.

Henry Dice was not exactly sober, not exactly drunk. He said to you, seriously, 'Is this one night's aberration or are we witnessing a profound shaft in geopolitics? I mean shift, a shift in geopolitics? Just last week I was in Moscow. The dump was in a ferment. I don't doubt that Communism is about to disappear up its own arsehole, they're fucked up economically and agriculturally.'

'Not true of Hungary.'

'Admitted, Hungary is an exception. Believe me, buddy, the world is about to turn on its axis. The people in the slave nations will be free at last. It's America saving Europe again, thanks to President Reagan, with a tad of help from Mr Gorbachev.'

'And Mrs Gorbachev, Raisa,' said the French woman from behind a veil of smoke. 'Isn't she a revelation? So smart, so appealing. Gives a whole new slant on Russian womanhood, isn't it? I believe that from now onward women have a new chance. Look at this little slut here' – she pointed with her cigarette to the young woman now smooching with the man on whose knee she was sitting – 'product of an evil system. Never had any chances. Give her a good shower and have her hair attended to and put her in decent clothes and you would transform her.'

Then, as if suddenly changing the tactics of her argument, she said, bitterly, 'And after all that, she would still be a *putain!*'

'But that's because of poverty,' you told her, swigging lager from the bottle. 'You know very well that prostitution is a product of disadvantage.'

'No, of disposition,' she shot back.

'Nuts,' said Dice. 'It is because women have pussies and pussies mean money. Age old, the trade in pussies. Come on, Violane, we're a trade delegation, you should know that.'

'That is not what cons mean!' she said. 'And I despise this euphemism, "pussy".'

He belched relaxedly.

'You think? Why else do you figure we men would put up with you women if you hadn't got cunts?' He was bellowing now, only half jovial.

The silent Englishman at the table switched his malevolent gaze from you to Dice.

The various arguments went on. At other tables, people were convulsed with laughter or waving their hands above their head for greater self-expression, or trying to stand up, or making speeches, or telling jokes, or kissing, or arguing, while the band played on. They had just reached *Speedy Gonzales*.

A waiter came round with a pillowcase. He said he was collecting for the refugees from the DDR. Violane fished in a little beaded black bag and produced a fifty deutschmark note. It fluttered into the already swollen pillowcase. You too found some notes.

Dice told the man to clear off. 'It's a scam! The cash will go straight into your own goddamned pocket!' When the waiter had moved on to the next table, Dice said by way of explanation, that he had met that type of fraud elsewhere, 'including in San Francisco, I might add'.

The Englishman, who had not stirred, said nothing, continuing to stare with a look of hatred, first at Dice, then back at you again.

Belatedly, you remembered Heather. You rose from the table, lager bottle in hand, Fernet-Branca bottle in pocket, and left the trade delegation. You never said goodbye. No one remarked on your going. You made your way with difficulty through the throng. It was impossible to tell how sober you were or were not, because drunkenness was in the very air you breathed.

Heather, when you found her, was red in the face. She was dancing with an elderly man, and drooping over his shoulder. He was bearing much of her weight, even her eyelids were heavy.

You tapped him on the shoulder. 'Sorry, this is my girl.' Even as you spoke you wondered at the possessive article. He was indignant and spoke no English. He made it clear, however, that the woman was unwell and he was about to take her up to his room.

'Oh no, you don't, I'm taking her with me. I've known her for years.'

A struggle then ensued. The man kept a hold on Heather and fended you off with his right arm. *'Bitte! Bitte!'* he kept saying.

'I used to shag her!' you shouted in the man's furry ear, to sharpen the argument. 'When she was young, and pretty.'

He swore at you, rather despairingly. His trophy was about to be snatched from him.

'Heather! Heather, you're coming with me, aren't you?' You called to her from her distance.

She roused and said she was coming. She said further that she had never met the other man and did not know who he was, only that he had bought her drinks. She added, touchingly, that she felt sick and wanted to be taken to your room.

Although you were unsure how much you wanted her, you needed to establish ownership. The old man backed away, swearing. You got Heather to the lift and ascended to the third floor, where you trotted her along the corridor to your room. She was emitting something between a giggle and a shriek. As soon as she was in the room, she rushed for the toilet. You went and lay on the bed, flinging the Fernet-Branca bottle to the floor.

'A most unattractive proposition,' you said, at the sound of Heather vomiting.

You plunged into a deep sleep, leaving the future of the world undecided.

13

An Arrival from Venice

The year was 1999. England's extraordinary display of grief over the death of Princess Diana two years earlier had died away. You and Verity had discussed that extravagant display of emotion. 'People wept for the sorrow of their own lives through the passing of hers,' Verity concluded. 'It must have been a placebo effect.'

The family lived on. You and Verity Fielding were preparing to celebrate your tenth year of marriage with a party. You resided in a sprawling, late eighteenth-century house outside Cambridge, in Waterbeach. As you said when you moved in, no relation to Walcot beach.

With you lived your and Verity's daughter, May, the prized daughter of your later years. Verity's son, Ted Nash, by Jeremy, was a year or two older. Ted was in Australia for a gap year. Those painful years when you were being divorced from Abby, and Verity was getting her divorce from Jeremy, lay far behind you.

Now was a time to be grateful and throw a little party.

You were working out the phrasing of your party invitations on your iMac. Verity was away at present, lecturing at Cambridge on 'The Trail of Responsibility in the English Novel, 1719–1939'.

You were now moderately prosperous, even distinguished. A tide had turned for you some years ago with the skull found in the Ashbury dig. The past had come to your rescue. Your students were moderately excited as you went down on your knees with a brush, to reveal more of the bone. You were careful to disturb nothing.

The brush uncovered a hard whitish line of bone. It converged with another. Finally, one side of a small neat skull was revealed, together with some neck bones. Your class yelped with excitement.

'Gordon Bennett, we've dug up an ichthyosaurus!' Deakins exclaimed.

You corrected him. 'No, it's certainly not an ichthyosaur. Ichthyosaurs had elongated jaws, this is a more sophisticated critter. My guess is it's a Jurassic plesiosaur. It has a long and flexible neck and, if we're lucky, we may be able to uncover bits of the skeleton. A little more careful digging is required.'

Young Heather Lambert clapped her hands. She had reverted to Deakins for a lover after her fury at discovering you were married. Age would make her less choosy in that respect.

But you were right, your students became enthusiasts. As they lengthened, under your supervision, the vital trench, the skeleton of a plesiosaur was slowly revealed. Even Deakins regarded it with awe. Both media and academic worlds were in rapture – you had discovered a skeleton, all but complete, with every vertebra of its beautiful long neck intact and in place. You marvelled, as did everyone, at the delicate architecture of the great fish's remains, that fish from long ago, beached in Oxfordshire.

In those exciting days, you bought a VW Golf and drove every day to the John Radcliffe Hospital in Oxford to see Verity Nash, still recovering from her burns. She had undergone a series of skin grafts. When she came out of intensive care, she lay in a small ward with three other women. Soon she was looking up at you with eyes of love. You held her hand. You hoped and expected that she would recover fully.

Meanwhile, you supervised the extended dig in the Ashbury field so that, with tantalizingly slow care, the mighty neck, the slender body, the large paddles which had once propelled the plesiosaur through the warm, shallow seas – as Bill Heyne on Radio Oxford phrased it, 'of what in the course of eons was to become Oxfordshire' – finally, yes, there it was, with only a few fragments missing. The bones of the tail were revealed.

Dr Mathew Matthews was supportive and generous. He funded a tent to protect the excavation and encouraged the Earth Sciences class to stay on without charge at end of term. He provided them with free meals and refreshments.

'The least I can do,' he remarked, 'in view of your generous bequest to the university. You have done us a great service, Steve.'

There were benefits for Matthews – suddenly, Ashbury was news. The Rector saw to it that you appeared on the television news and on a special BBC 2 programme, always speaking of you as 'our distinguished geologist, Dr Stephen Fielding'.

The skeleton held a special attraction which made it news-worthy. Only a few inches beneath the skull and leading vertebrae, a second skeleton was uncovered. It was the skeleton of a small plesiosaur, measuring just over a yard long. Although its delicate bones had snapped, it remained recognizable. MOTHER AND CHILD DOING WELL, declared a tabloid headline, above a photograph of you kneeling by the bones, for all the world as if presiding over a delivery. The image went straight to the sentimental hearts of British tabloid-readers.

Archaeologists and other experts came to visit the site. A ticket office was hastily installed by the entrance gate and ordinary visitors were charged for entry. Many more students enrolled at Ashbury University. You were the hero of the day.

When the Smithsonian Institute in the United States mounted a reconstruction of 'Mother and Baby', you were invited to lecture at the opening exhibition. Before you flew, you proposed marriage to Verity.

She had an unexpected fit of modesty. 'Why should you want to marry me, Steve?'

'I just thought it would look good on my CV.'

Despite your flippancy, Verity gladly accepted your proposal. As soon as you returned from the States, you and Verity were married at Wolvercote Church.

You were so busy. You came at last to an agreement with Abby, and were allowed to see Geraldine at weekends. Geraldine was of a placid disposition. She was delighted when Verity gave birth to May, preferring May to any doll. You accepted a good post at Cambridge University, which you held ever since.

The Iran–Iraq war filled the nineteen-eighties. You and Verity scarcely noticed, although half a million people died in the war and twice that number were wounded. Even the coming to power in the USSR of Mr Gorbachev, and his subsequently being supplanted by Yeltsin, and the fading away of the Cold War, meant no more to you than did the pressure of everyday things, and the passage of weeks and months. On Christmas Day of 1991, you saw on television the resignation of President Gorbachev and, before the year was over, the Soviet Union was dissolving into its component parts.

'I would never have believed it!' Verity cried. 'Thank God, oh thank God! It's the death of that hideous ideology.'

'Some would claim that it really marks the final end of World War Two.'

'Some would claim anything, dearest.'

As you embraced her, you said, 'But someone has to pick up the pieces.'

'That's up to the Russians,' she replied. It proved a realistic remark. The following summer, you made a tour of Lithuania, Latvia and Estonia, all now free of the Russian yoke. By that time, not only you two, but England at large was becoming more prosperous.

Sometimes professional demands took you abroad, most notably to the Yucatán peninsula, where you worked with American colleagues near the site of the Chicxulub crater. Your equable disposition made you popular. While you were in the field in Mexico, your Aunt Belle phoned to tell you that your grandmother, Elizabeth Fielding, had died in Venice. This was in 1995. You felt truly miserable; for a while you sank into gloom.

Verity kissed you. 'Many causes for grief,' she murmured. 'A good woman can rarely be replaced.'

'Yes, and not only grief for her and the past she represented, her dignity, her generosity, but for us too, and for the triviality of my life, which has been so self-indulgent. She perceived that Abby and I were "not spiritual", as she put it.'

Verity shook her head and smiled.

'At least we have some time to reform, my love, if we only knew how.'

Elizabeth's body was flown from Venice back to England. You also flew back to England, from Yucatán, to attend the funeral. Most of the family, young and old, gathered in the cemetery.

Giving a short oration, you spoke in affectionate terms of your grandmother. 'Elizabeth was approaching her one hundredth birthday, and was certainly very frail. We understand that human beings are living longer; in that respect, my dear grandmother was a trailblazer. Towards the last years of her life, she became unable to speak. On occasions, she would scribble a few words on a piece of the paper she kept by her side. I have here the last such scrap on which she wrote, when I visited her at her home in the Calle Galina in Venice, the year before last.'

You produced and unfolded the paper to show it to the mourners standing by the graveside. On it, in a shaky hand, Elizabeth had written in pencil, 'No longer in human race'.

You continued, 'Grandma had for many years struggled with language. Towards the end, she could no longer speak, and so she considered herself ruled out of the human race. Perhaps she merely meant "human society". Even though it was untrue, we all understand how she felt. We believe that it is the gift of language which makes us human, and which forges our societies.

'Yet recent exhumations of a cousin of early *homo sapiens*, whom we call *homo heidelbergensis*, reveal that even those primitive beings probably had a form of speech. In the ear are curiously named bones: the hammer, the anvil, the stirrup. We have them; *heidelbergensis* also had them. The inference is that these bones of the ear equipped them to hear at frequencies of from two to four kilohertz. It's the range that covers normal human speech.

'We cannot but wonder at the life of this long-extinct tribe, which existed perhaps four hundred thousand years ago. What did they say to one another? What dreams and affections could they convey? Elizabeth Fielding had a speech impediment of long standing. Nevertheless, she conveyed her meaning perfectly well; a meaning always full of love and good intentions. She was my benefactor.

'Now, alas, her voice has died forever from the stirrups of our ears. We can only wonder at her life, and at her determination – her determination for instance to live in Venice, a city she adored. But at this solemn time, when we commit her remains to the earth, we must wonder at all intelligent life.

'Those long extinct people, the *heidelbergensians*, we cannot know what they said to each other, what their fears and hopes were. But we can suppose that they lived then as we do now, half-aware, hoping and fearing, captives of the enchainment of day following day following day, until our night falls, as Elizabeth's has done.'

Your Aunt Ada and her second husband – nowadays he had a little white beard – threw a posy onto her mother's coffin as it was lowered into the ground. She clutched Beavis Gray's arm, perhaps afraid he might fall into the forbidding hole. Tears blurred her vision, as yours too was blurred.

Both your parents were dead. You had never brought yourself to ask them if there had been a period of their lives – for this was the way you tactfully phrased it to yourself, in silent rehearsal – in which they would have liked to be entirely rid of you. The question had never been asked, certainly never answered; so that the problem of your days alone on the sands of Walcot could never be resolved.

Your mother in her coffin looked so small and frail as you stood there, bidding her a sorrowful last farewell. The lines of discontent about her mouth had faded away. In death she appeared young again. You wished then ... but wishing was useless.

A year later, standing at your father's graveside, head bowed, you thought with some affection of old Martin Fielding. 'At least he tried to do something for his country. That counts,' you told yourself. 'He knocked up a century at the game he loved, he wrote a book, he served in the Labour government, and perhaps it was a good thing, after all, that he had the old Blackall Square slum pulled down.'

Moreover, you were consoled to know that the multi-storey car park which had succeeded the square had recently been pulled down in its turn.

You were gloomy at that time.

Sonia did not attend father's funeral. I felt she should have been there. Even if your family's not all it might have been, there is something precious about it.

You speak in retrospect.

I saw Sonia once during this period. She did attend the reception after Elizabeth's funeral. It was all a matter of timing, she said. She flew over by Concorde, on her way to make a movie in ... I think it was Hungary. It was hard to hold a conversation with her, she was with what Dad used to call 'a fast set'.

She had no time for you?

Let's not get into Time.

Anyhow, towards the end of your father's life, when he became more dependent than ever on the NHS, Martin had acquired some religious belief. He defended what he saw at first as a weakness, by claiming that no individual intellect was capable of grasping the truth of Christ; that truth came to a body of people as a whole, just as football fans forfeit their identities to merge within a greater mass of support; that the truth of Christ's Resurrection could be known, not through logic, but through revelation; and that this revelation had been preserved through the faith and medium of the Church; and that the Church was one of the most stable factors in Britain, more stable than government or politics.

He saw no hypocrisy in this line of unreason. As his hold on religion, or religion's hold on him, strengthened, his interest in politics weakened. He had never supported Tony Blair and New Labour.

You thought solemnly of how you and he had stood side by side watching his tiny fire in the garden, the fire he strove to keep alive day after day, and of the intent way Martin had watched the trail of smoke rise into the clear sky and disperse. That had been a moment of companionship and reconciliation between you.

Towards the end, Martin had become a milder man, but it was too late for Mary to assert a more dominant role. She remained until the last the nonentity she had always been.

These thoughts, compassionate and puzzled – for what was meant by human character? – ran through your mind as you watched the clods of earth land with a decided thump on your grandmother's coffin.

A light rain began to fall. The mourners hurried into their cars for shelter. The drivers drove them to 'Bacton', yours and Verity's house, for some refreshments.

'A touching and academic oration you gave, darling,' said Verity, in the car. 'If a touch pedantic. You'll miss your dear Gran, I know. Elizabeth was a remarkable woman.'

You simply nodded. You held her hand, the hand of a woman you loved more deeply than you had any other. As the car was pulling into the drive, Verity, her thoughts still occupied with your family, asked you what you most regretted about your marriage to Abby.

'We virtually threw away our dream chateau at Tremblay.'

'Oh, but that's only property. Nothing else?'

'Not knowing Geraldine, but fortunately I haven't entirely lost her. And I've got you.'

She laughed. 'Don't make it sound like a deal!'

'You mean a good deal to me, sweetheart.'

'Bacton' began to fill with cheerful mourners. A younger generation now predominated. Ted, Verity's older son, was acting as host and seeing to it that everyone was looked after. You had more or less patched up the divide between Abby and yourself; once free, Abby had gone social climbing and was now Lady Abigail Wade-Warren, her husband currently being British Ambassador to Ecuador. Rumour had it she had learnt to speak fluent Spanish. However, your daughter, the placid young Geraldine, was present, and making eyes at Ted Nash. Ted was ostensibly keeping his eyes on your daughter May. Various Frosts and Hillmans, together with Joyce and Dougie Wilberforce, were there with their friends.

Joyce had decided three months previously to live with Paul Patel, and was already expecting his baby, as she proudly announced. She had had an earlier pregnancy, but had miscarried. Despite the solemnity of the occasion, Joyce put on a CD of The Cure. She and Patel were dancing together in a corner of the room. Patel was now a wealthy man. He had bought a declining brewery in the Midlands, where his own light beer, 'Shabash', was brewed and canned. 'Shabash' had spread from Indian restaurants to bars throughout the land.

Paul Patel spoke teasingly about his success. 'To think I studied erotic Eastern art as a youth! Now in middle age I'm a bloody old plutocrat and philistine.'

You teased him. 'That's so English. Really, Paul, you're so English! Do you feel English inside?'

'No, no, it's all a pose.' He wagged his head, smiling. 'You mean under my brown skin? Equally, when I ask myself if I feel Hindu inside, I find that is equally a pose. What's a poor chap to do?'

Looking cheerful, he accepted another glass of Australian Shiraz.

'Why, he brews a wonderful beer that all races can drink,' said Joyce, clinging to his free arm and looking admiringly into his face.

Your sister Sonia was now a grand dame of the international stage and screen. She had changed her name by deed poll to Sonia Gleesorro. She had finally disposed of Adrian Hyasent and was now escorted by a gay young man called Wayne Ellison. She sat at a side table on a hard-backed chair with a drink at her elbow, receiving homage from many in the room. She had played a cameo role in a Hollywood sci-fi comedy called *The Dark Light Years*, as a result of which she was dependably rich.

And an old friend of yours was also present on that occasion, Gerard Geldstein. Gerard had come with his son, Pief, a handsome and exotic man escorting his wife, Veronica Vera Goldstone, CEO of a mobile phone company. Pief had still not read any Tolstoy.

As you and Gerard embraced each other, Gerard said, 'You'll think I'm an old fool, but I am standing as candidate for Mayor of London. England is quite kind to its Jews and, if I am elected, I shall try to repay that kindness.'

'What's your main concern? Inner-city poverty, traffic, the state of the Underground? All that stuff?'

Gerard chuckled. 'Well, all of those, of course. I would like to bring a little order to the general untidiness. I once ran a museum, in another lifetime, if you can remember. But in particular, cars are my passion, my aversion. You remember what Aristotle said, that the virtue of a thing is related to its proper function? The proper function of a car is to be moving. That's why it has wheels, eh? But stationary, not moving, it's a curse.'

You agreed, smiling. You reminded him of the way in which Blackall Square had been demolished to make way for an ugly multi-storey car park.

'Exactly and precisely,' Gerard said. 'It was that act of vandalism which set me on my political career. Though to speak truth – as if one should ever speak otherwise – I would rather be back lingering and lazing on that beach at Assos Island. You remember how we swam in the waters where Aristotle had swam? Swum? Oh, these highly irregular verbs! When we were young and able? Surely we gained a little sagacity there, didn't we?'

You shook your head, not quite knowing whether to smile or grieve.

'Gerard, my dear friend, I was never there on the beach at Assos – not with you, not without you.'

He looked confused. 'What tricks the mind plays on one when one grows old. Of course. It was never a beach but a forest where we first met and encountered one another.'

'Yes, and you pulled a gun on me. That I remember clearly!'

And you both laughed, rather ruefully.

After your grandmother's funeral reception, you and the helper stacked all the glasses in the dishwasher. You went and sat down with Verity, who had kicked off her shoes and put her stockinged feet up on a pouffe.

'How about a Metaxa to wind down with?' you enquired.

Verity gave a thumbs up. You settled on the sofa with her, cuddling against her. When she asked about Gerard, you told her how supportive he and Helge had been after you were discharged from prison.

'He seems a cheerful and good man,' she said.

'I believe he is, when he might well have been broken and wicked.'

One of Verity's many virtues in your eyes was the way in which she so rarely quizzed you about your past life; you lived now in the present, for preference. But at this relaxed moment, perhaps under the influence of that final Metaxa and the sense of a cosy ending to a mainly sad day, she asked you about your trial.

You had no wish to go into detail, or indeed to open the question. 'The scene was electrifying,' you said, flatly.

She caught the implication as well as the intonation.

'I wonder how people described scenes before electricity was invented,' she murmured. 'Gaseous?'

You admired her for her ability to combine tact with wit. You turned and kissed her. She inserted a Greek-flavoured tongue in your mouth.

14

The Known Unknowns

That October, you gave a talk in the Castle Museum in Norwich. Your subject concerned the site known as Grimes Graves, in the heart of Norfolk, where the subterranean chalk beds had been tunnelled into by miners seeking a stratum of flint.

You concluded by saying, 'The flints mined in the forests of Thetford were the subject of international trade. They were traded all over Europe. So Neolithic people would have had no problems with joining the European Union, or the European Monetary Union.'

Subdued booing emerged from the crowd of listeners. You had expected as much, and added crisply, 'As you know – or as you should know – Spain has just adopted the euro as its official currency. We should do the same, at least if we wish to trade freely, as did the miners of Grimes Graves.'

You sat down to scattered applause. Norfolk had always been an insular part of the nation. Your podiatrist came to mind. She was an intelligent, middle-aged woman, a single mother with two kids to look after. As a confirmed Tory, she was also against the European Union. 'We don't want to be like the French and the Germans, Dr Fielding, do we now?'

'But we are like them, Ursula. Our traditions are much the same, we all share the same rather soft culture nowadays. It makes sense to unify.'

'I for one don't wish to be ruled by Brussels.'

You smiled down at the woman. 'You dare tell me that while you're kneeling at my feet!'

Verity was with you in Norwich, as was May, now a sixteen-year-old, by turns flighty and morose. She had been allowed to roam the city while you and Verity attended a dinner given in your honour.

After the dinner, you both sat in the lounge of your hotel to await the return of your daughter. Verity started to chat to a local couple who were drinking Patel's Shabash beer nearby. When Verity admitted that she did not know this part of the country, the man, who introduced himself as a Mr Jim Whiteside, proved himself keen to describe the beauties of Norfolk. He had a strong, musical local accent.

'As for the coast,' he said, 'as got a perticler booty. You want to goo up and see for yooeself. There's some pretty lettle ould places up there th' he'n't changed since I were a booy.'

You asked if he knew Walcot.

'Walcot? Corse I knoows Walcot. I bin fish'n' orf of that beach many a time, ketch'n' mack'rel.'

You turned to your wife. 'Let's go and have a look at the coast in the morning,' you said.

You rose from your seats and were starting to leave the lounge when Mr Jim Whiteside called out, 'None of them furriners up there eether.'

Turning, Verity said, 'Enjoy your beer, Mr Whiteside.'

*

Contrary to Mr Jim Whiteside's claims, even Walcot had changed since your boyhood. You had revisited that stretch of coast once, after you'd been forced to quit Blackall Square. That was many years ago. You had travelled in low spirits, hoping for a release from melancholy.

Come unto these yellow sands
And there take hands

Such music crept by you on the waters; but the well-remembered spot was disappointing, its inhabitants sunk in poverty.

Gone were the beautiful wheatfields of your extreme youth, where cornflowers and poppies once punctuated with their blue and crimson blossoms the thickets of wheat. Instead, caravans clustered as far as the eye could see: caravans that intended never to move again, caravans up on bricks, caravans with little privies like sentry boxes by their doors, caravans with clematis climbing on trellis nailed against them, caravans with water butts, green or black. And by those caravans were old people, mooching in and out of their doorways; old men in shirt sleeves, their trousers suspended by braces; old women in flimsy dresses with curlers in their hair; younger men sitting on what served as their door-steps, reading racing papers; younger women gripping plastic pegs between their teeth, pegging out clothes to dry; kids playing with plastic soldiers in the dirt. Old dogs and ageless cats, a canary in a cage, singing its heart out.

You exclaimed with displeasure.

'Omega' still stood at that time. Archibald Lane had become a real road, paved and straight, but the bungalow looked as it had looked all those years ago, except for the veranda, which had been demolished. A cheap corrugated square of plastic now hung over the door.

You parked the car on a patch of grass and locked the doors. As you walked along the road to the sea, you remembered the North family who lived in the railway carriages on top of the dunes. A longing possessed you to see them again, but not as they might

485

be now, rather as they were then – the boys in their grey shorts, with their freckles and honest brown faces, their mother in the old frock pale from many washes, watching for you from the dunes to see if you were safe. A fruitless longing.

And with that longing came a longing for the innocent happiness of childhood, and bathing costumes and wooden spades, and the smell of salty towels, the sun forever at zenith, burning you benevolently, before you knew anything of evil, when a day seemed to last for ever and there were shrimps for tea, and strawberries and cream too, if you were lucky.

Nothing seemed to be as it used to be, except for the lulling sound of waves on the shore, tirelessly, ceaselessly, casting themselves up on the shingle and withdrawing, to come again and then again withdraw, the sea breathing like a living thing.

It was high tide at Walcot at the time of your earlier visit. The beach was covered by grey and languid waves, laced with white foam. Directly at your feet was a red metal wall stretching away in both directions, a hideous fortification against further coastal erosion – an inevitable and unwelcome reminder of wartime fortifications, rather than weather.

A little old man in a shabby grey suit was standing on the dunes, looking out to sea.

You asked him if he lived nearby. When he said that he did, you asked him how he liked Walcot.

He shook his head. 'Mustn't complain,' he said.

You thought of Caleb with all his grumbles against the English.

You stared out to sea, shielding your eyes with your hand, in the manner of mariners, trying to recover something you could not name.

That visit had been all but twenty years ago. But how past and present became entangled as you grew older. Now Verity, your beloved wife, was with you, and your daughter, May. You were ageing but more happy and established than you had ever been. And once more Walcot had changed.

Archibald Lane seemed very short. On either side were modest new bungalows, tidy and prim. Sand still blew everywhere. Where the caravans had been, a small village had appeared, neat and organized. Its bungalows were surrounded by tidy gardens. A lawnmower's roar could be heard. The picture was one of modest prosperity.

May raced you to the edge of the dunes.

Verity clutched your arm. 'So this is where you played as a little boy. Has it changed much?'

You gave a laugh that held joy in it. 'Not as much as I.'

Something else came back to your remembrance, floating up from the past. You told them of the iconic thing that had appeared to you one day, a golden figure like a small man. Putting the incident into words made it sound preposterous.

'But the uselessness of trying to put anything of the past into words –'

'But if words are all that remain ...'

The golden visitant had asked you various religious questions. You could not remember precisely what the questions had been: something about your soul? Perhaps that was a modern interpretation.

'I bet it was the vicar,' said May. 'Or a bishop – bishops sometimes dress in gold. On special occasions.'

'No, it was much more heavenly than that. I think I believed it was God. Oh, it's so long ago, I hadn't thought about it for years ...' You lapsed into silence. 'It must have been a vision.'

Verity asked gently, 'And do you believe your parents realized how dangerous it was to leave you alone to play all day on the beach?'

You hesitated before saying that your mother was rather lazy.

May was silent, looking up at her parents' faces, trying to interpret your expressions.

As she found nothing there relevant to her, the girl began to search about at her feet for pretty stones. Stones were fairly scarce here among the tough marram grass. May came up to you with a pure white stone in the palm of her hand. 'Look at this! Just like a gull's egg.'

On your previous visit, all those years ago, ugly red metal sea defences had been erected, very much cheap and post-war. Now there were imposing concrete ramps, studded with pebble, to resist the erosion of the sea, and not unattractive in their massive stability. Certainly there had been great change over the years. Now the country had reached a period of stability, too. Much as you had. Only global warming threatened a greater change to come.

The tide was retreating, revealing a skirt of golden sand.

'I want a swim,' said May. 'Can we have a skinny dip?'

'I think the wow factor might be too heavily involved,' you said, using one of your daughter's phrases.

'But it would be cool,' May said, with the hint of a whine.

'And the sea would be cold.'

'Oh, why not let her if she wants to?' Verity said. 'Go on, May. We'll keep an eye on you.'

You all climbed down the steps onto the beach. Gulls rose up screeching. May slipped out of her clothes and waded into the water, with many a shriek at how freezing it was.

After some consideration, Verity said that inevitably there were things we knew, and things we did not know, but it was a gain if we recognized that we did not know them. They were labelled 'the known unknowns'. She said she considered that most people held in their minds unknowns; the more educated had 'known unknowns'. Unknowns were like a knot they couldn't untie.

It was not comfortable to have such locked areas in the mind, or rather, it was more uncomfortable to know they were there, she presumed, than not to know. One of the penalties of intellect was that one understood one had known unknowns locked in the mind, impossible of resolution. Knowing they were there, one naturally wanted access to them. It was in general impossible to open these unknowns, she said.

'You will always have this particular unknown to worry about,' she said, giving your arm an affectionate tug. 'There's this peculiar quality in the human brain.' She gave a chuckle. 'Perhaps it's a, well, a sort of design fault.'

It is remarkable how ordinary humans frequently touch on a para-universal truth.
As Verity said, we have committed design faults. Yet some of you manage to remain sane, or to attain sanity of a kind.
Of a kind? I suppose you have every right to be condescending.
Every right, certainly.

All the while a mild wind blew off the sea, and the sea continued to sound. May was swimming strongly, breasting the waves. 'It's lovely and warm,' she called.

Your answer to Verity was that your particular unknown covered a vital area. If it was opened, then you would know whether your parents had loved you or not.

Verity shook her head. 'Surely you know the answer to that one. For whatever reason, their ability to love, even to love one another, was not particularly strong. So give up on it. You and I love one another intensely, let that suffice.'

'You're right, sweetheart. It doesn't matter any more.'

Verity agreed before, looking hard at your face, she demanded, 'But why did you never ask your mother why they left you alone all day on the beach, without looking after you?'

Your words had to be forced from you. 'Because I dreaded to know the truth, I suppose.'

May came shining from the sea and stood shivering, hands clasped together over her chest. Verity towelled her vigorously with her own skirt. 'Get yourself dressed, you awful child.' She combed her daughter's hair, bending a benevolent smile on her. 'Come on, let's go somewhere for lunch. Shall we try Mundesley?'

She and May turned to go. You stood for a moment longer, staring down at the tide now uncovering the beach. 'The known unknown' indeed! You thought it was not merely the beach that held an unknown; here, poised on the edge of the North Sea, you reflected on how much of your own character was unknown.

And you had gone and married a stranger. What luck that that, at least, had turned out well, just as Verity said.

Then Verity tugged you away. The three of you returned to the car. You learned that Geraldine had flown out to Ecuador to rejoin her mother and her adopted father. You were moved to write to her.

My dear Geraldine,

Once when I was a boy, I had a vision of a golden creature who visited me on a beach. You were the real golden creature who visited me, and I have always regretted I was unable to share all the golden days of your childhood. Can you believe that I loved you intensely although we were apart?

In those days, I was weak and misled. Only in recent years have I become strong enough to admit to that weakness. I fear it may have injured you. There was a hole where your father should rightfully have been. I can only advise you – and perhaps I have not earned the right to do that – NOT To BE INJURED! Surely we can choose our injuries as we choose our activities. And so I presume to tell you not to brood over any injuries I have caused you, as I once brooded over injuries caused me in extreme youth.

We all get such knocks. To employ an old phrase, 'If it isn't one thing, it's another'. Becoming adult should mean to grow out of those knocks. It is better to look to the future, where the hope of avoiding, or at least of dealing with, further knocks is greatly enhanced.

You will find much to engage your attention in a new country. Forgive your father, if you can, not for his sake, but for your sake, to make you free to grow up and be a happy and contributing citizen of this world. (I don't speak of other worlds, since I have even less jurisdiction there than I have here.)

Be happy, my dear girl!

Your loving

Father

15

The Sacrifice

A mild and damp day. A Saturday, a special Saturday. This was
New Year's Eve, AD 1999. You were a spry seventy-five, marriage
to Verity agreed with you.

Spry, yet not entirely one hundred per cent. You had recently
suffered spells of fatigue and dizziness. According to your doctor,
you had suffered an ischaemic event. He had prescribed atenolol,
without telling you what usually followed from such events.

You rose in the unfamiliar hotel room and padded over in your
pyjamas to the electric kettle to make Verity and yourself a cup of
Jackson's tea. As you waited for the kettle to boil, you swallowed
down an aspirin and two atenolol capsules with a glass of water.

'Wonderful,' said Verity from the bed. 'I refuse to wake up until
you press the mug into my hand.'

'I was thinking. All that keeps me alive are these bloody pills.
Three at night, three in the morning; our human biology is

much more ramshackle than was that of the plesiosaur.'

'You don't know that.'

'They lived for millions of years. You can't claim that of us.'

As you took the mugs of tea over to the bed, Verity sat up, lodging a pillow behind her shoulders. She was wearing her scarlet silk nightie.

'Do you wish we had met years earlier than we did?' she asked. The mischievous expression on her face told you that she was setting a small trap and planning to tease you by contradicting what she expected you to say. You took evasive action.

'I'm simply glad that good fortune rolled up when it did.'

'If by good fortune *rolling up* you are referring to my weight … I may have put on a few pounds, but look at the way we live.'

You snuggled beside her, spilling the merest drop of tea on the sheet.

'I don't know how I endure your quibbling.'

You kissed over the cups.

'What happiness you have brought me, Steve, my darling.'

You told her, 'To celebrate the end of this century and the beginning of Number Twenty-One, I have written, well, I have extruded, let's say, a verse. As follows:

I shall think of the woes of the past
Ere I go to my ultimate rest,
How the best love of all is the last,
And the last years of all are the best.

'This, lady, is my sonnet to your eyes …'

All the church bells in the kingdom were ringing in the new century. The magical quality of three noughts in the year had excited everyone, so much so that you and Verity had booked yourselves a suite in the Savoy Hotel. And not you two alone; this was a time for the gathering of the clans. Your children, Ted and May, had adjoining, but separate rooms; other rooms were occupied by Ronnie and Barbara Nash and Barbara's sister, Lulu; by Paul and Joyce and their little boy, Sanchi; by Freddie Frost and his partner, Hy Donaldson; by Geraldine Fielding and her girlfriend, Kyle Clifford; by Betsy, Belle Hillman's daughter; and by old Claude Hillman. Nine rooms or suites in all had been booked for the clan, many of them looking out towards the River Thames.

'I doubt I'll see this new century out,' said Claude, with a gruff, patent laugh. A year earlier, he had undergone a triple heart bypass. 'Better drink up while we can, eh, Steve?'

Despite his brave words, Claude was but a shadow of his former self. 'I hope the sight of Sonia won't upset you too much,' you said. You steadied yourself against the back of a chair. You were feeling slightly dizzy again.

Verity regarded you. 'You're looking pale, Steve. Is everything all right?'

'Could be worse.'

'No, truthfully?'

'I'm fine. I'm just worrying about Sonia's appearance. We've grown away from each other. It's been so long. She said she'd be here.'

Your wife took your arm. 'Let's go upstairs and take a little rest. There's plenty of time.' She had weathered well. She still dyed her hair, approved by you, while her lined face preserved a grave, senior beauty.

'Plenty of time?' you found yourself saying, in a puzzled way. The dizziness persisted. You ascribed it to the tension of the approaching evening.

Up in your suite, you studied yourself in the bathroom mirror; it was not an inspiring sight. For want of anything else on hand, you swallowed three Viagras with a glass of water. Although it was more than you had ever taken at one time, you hoped they would restore you.

You and Verity were in bed together at teatime, while most of your guests were out enjoying the sights of London. You began fondling her in a way she knew well.

'That's enough of that, sweetie,' she said. 'You know I'm work-shy. Have a rest, you need it.'

You rolled on to your back. 'Thank God for bed, for you – and for Viagra!'

'Not necessarily in that order, either.'

You felt as pale as the pillow. Suddenly, you sat up, 'You see, Walcot –'

You were unable to complete the sentence. Your head fell back on the pillow.

'Oh, Steve, dearest –'

Later, both you and Verity were dressed smartly for the occasion. Gazing at yourself in the mirror, you said, 'All dressed up and nowhere to go.' The words came distantly.

'Don't be so self-critical. You look splendid,' Verity said. 'Besides we must look our best to welcome in the new century.'

'And to welcome in Sonia.'

Verity regarded you quizzically. 'You're worrying. You're not well, have a swig of whisky. It's Sonia, is it?' She added with a smile, 'Don't want to call it all off, do you? We could creep out the back door and sneak off to Waterbeach …'

'I'm fine, really. I just hope the next century is going to be less violent than this one has been. No, I'm fine, my love, though in Hamlet's words, what does he say? "How ill it is about my heart."'

'You're getting old, my darling. You need a drink, and you're not the only one.'

Soon there was a glass in your hand. But you stuck to the blessed San Pellegrino.

I felt for you, Stephen. It was as if you were moving nearer, and seemed to know it.

Ha, I didn't know it. All my life I've been so damned ignorant.

That's better than the pretence of being all-knowing.

There were more, and stronger, drinks to come, and dinner, and the arrival of Sonia. That Sonia had agreed to be present was in itself a triumph. Your sister's change of name by deed poll to Sonia Gleesorro had brought her increased acclaim. Despite her age, she was now perched at the height of her career. She was a dominant Hollywood legend, a kind of trophy of time, a great exception, playing the role of Jocasta in the film *Time of the Tyrant*, based on Sophocles' drama *Oedipus Rex*, and set in the Old West, to universal applause, even from those critics who despised the film's happy ending.

'Garbo and Brando in One!' *Variety* had exclaimed.

Among most of the Fielding clan, some nervousness prevailed. They were unsure how they should receive this luminary, whether as formidable Auntie Sonia, or as the lauded Movie Queen, the so-called Grandmother of the Movies. Rumours circulated about her malevolence. The clan was proud to have a living legend in the family, and was prepared to go through the rituals of obeisance before her; yet there was an undercurrent of suspicion that she might be, in the words of Ted Nash, 'the poxiest party-pooper west of Warner Brothers'. To which his half-sister May had said that he meant east, not west. And Ted had said he was going the long way round the globe to try and find another such appalling pooper.

So they all trooped down to the lounge of the Savoy, dressed in their best, to toast, with the Savoy's most expensive champagne, the New Year and each other. You experienced the lights continually fading and flickering; no doubt the demand for electricity all over London was at its height. The world seemed to have gravitated to the capital to welcome in the Twenty-first Century.

You could just hear the music. An orchestra played tunes from the era of Cole Porter, Gershwin and Irving Berlin. Many couples danced, often with strangers from other parties. You danced sedately with Verity; her hands were cold. Joyce and Paul danced, while their son trailed them rather forlornly round the dance floor. Euphoria was the name of the mood. Heaven, they were in Heaven, and the worries that beset them through the week had now become amazingly antique.

After the party had enjoyed an eight-course dinner, the orchestra struck up again. A firework display started on the terrace overlooking the Thames. Coloured series of transient lights arched and banged over the waters, to be reflected below.

Amid the hubbub, you were struck dumb. Like the flowing Thames outside, the onrush of the years suddenly overwhelmed you. What good fortune you had enjoyed, how wonderful life was, and here you were surrounded by everyone you loved and who, with luck, loved you, Verity above all. So wasn't it enough? Were you not sated? Did a part of you not long for everything to cease? Suddenly, satisfyingly, to cease? To go while the going was good … You suppressed these unlucky lucubrations and turned to speak to Ronnie.

The music stopped suddenly. The conductor held his baton low, and the orchestra then struck up again with a blast of *In the Mood*. Dazzling light burned from the night outside. Through the swing doors of the hotel entrance, where doormen bowed deep, appeared la Gleesorro's contingent: two heavies leading, then an escort of three polished young men, indistinguishable from each other, then a lean, bearded man in a biscuit-coloured overall with a badge declaring him to be a paramedic, then Sonia herself, ablaze, absonant, abrupt, the ablative absolute among adults, then her lady's maid, followed by two more heavies. All of the escorts in this contingent, except the paramedic, were in evening dress.

You were amazed that Sonia had actually appeared, this amazing sister! Had she sold out, you wondered, or had she bought into an expensive – almost exclusive – legend? And did you feel up to meeting her – you with your sense of being somewhere else?

Sonia was dressed in a white ivory, ankle-length gown, which trailed behind her. 'Classical reference there', said Claude, determined to exhibit no awe. He was drinking mineral water these days – mineral water diluted by Scotch. Her gown of eider down was chased with pearls and besieged by sequins. Sonia's throat, stringy and thin, was enveloped and enhanced by a diamond choker. More pearls and silver glittered amid her ample, dark, dyed tresses. The very atmosphere opened to her progress.

'*Parbleu*, it's Mae West redivivus!' said Verity in your ear. You patted her bottom reprovingly.

Sonia moved forward like a great painted wooden effigy, like the Juggernaut worshipped by Hindus at Puri, or carried through the streets of Seville at Easter, conjuring up the fears and cheers of the crowd, and those obeisances which peasants pay to beauty or beatification. Aided by Botox, liposuction, and a few facial tucks, carefully painted, bekohled about the eyes – eyes freighted with artificial eyelashes, eyes strengthened by contact lenses – Gleesorro was a lay idol, was a picture, if not of youth, then of age's pastiche of youth or, if not a pastiche, then at least a grand act of reclamation, of restoration, a fortification against the years that had been, that were to come. Look on my works, ye mighty! declared every inch of her. Looking close you saw her complexion resembled that of stale sponge cake, where every pore was caked with powder. You could not help but admire the determination involved in this brilliant art of deception. Her smile was more dazzling, when she permitted it to emerge, like a credit card from its slot, than it had ever been in those days when she bore an imaginary hunchback, in a youth long forsaken, as she held out her hand to you. That hand, admittedly, was veined and stained by age, yet it had been powdered over and its nails dressed in scarlet shields.

Evading the claw, you seized careful hold of your sister and blew a kiss very close to her encarmined lips. 'Well done, darling,' you said, speaking low in case she was also wired for sound. 'I hardly recognized you.'

'No surprise there, honey. I'm not the old me any more, don't aim to be.' The words were delivered in a croak. 'Neurochemical change has taken place. The old me don't wanna be recognized. Or frigging well remembered.'

'Great to have you with us, anyway.'

'You've sure changed – one with the illustrious dead, eh, Stephen?'

497

'I wouldn't say that, but thanks for coming. I'll introduce you to the mob later.'

'Don't bother. I thought I'd like to maybe put in an appearance. I was passing through Europe any case.' As she spoke, her dark, reinforced eyes were staring searchingly at your face, looking for something she could never find.

'Anything I can get you immediately? Would you like to sit down?'

'Woofie's in the car, I didn't wanna bring the creature in here. Mustn't scare the punters. Woofie's kinda like my costume jewellery. Part of me.' She gave a dismissive gesture, slow but sure.

'*Woofie!* What is it, cat or dog? Let me guess …'

'Cheetah, fer God's sake. Don't you read the scandal sheets? It's okay, Woofie's tame. We keep her drugged, like she's a fucking cheetah.'

'Won't she tear the car to bits?'

'So what?' This was spoken, as was the rest of the conversation, with Sonia erect and without facial expression, as if mummification had preceded mortality. You were trying to suppress the belief that there was something malevolent about this transformed sister, dry as a stick, rustling like distant leaves whenever she moved. Everything was pale, Gleesorro herself, her tongue, the stage through which she moved. Weird, you thought. You could not believe this was happening.

You led her and her entourage to the rear lounge. Sonia walked slowly, at one stage muttering to herself. The entourage kept their distance, pace for pace. The lady's maid muttered into a mobile phone. Relations and onlookers fell back as from a leper before the pair of you.

You had come to an arrangement with the management; there was to be no charge for yours and Verity's suite, as long as you consented to allow Sonia Gleesorro to remain within public gaze in the lounge for half an hour. The half-hour began with cameras clicking and flashes blinking. The Savoy had informed the press of her presence, to the advantage of their publicity machine. Sonia simply maintained a fixed smile, ignoring this intrusion.

'Steve, come back to me,' Verity was saying faintly. Her voice somehow vexed you. Nor could you tell where she was ...

Sonia had taken your arm, fobbing off her young men. You steadied her down three shallow steps. Maybe she was *on something*, you thought. You were confused, thinking for a moment you were marrying an unknown woman, in an unknown place.

'Whole lotta fuss. All these creeps ...'

'Do you mind all this crap?' you asked, between laughing and weeping, feeling bad.

'Honey, it's like I live and breathe this crap. While I'm wow factor material I need all of this crap same as a babe needs breast milk.'

You admitted to yourself she had acquired a Californian accent. Or was it Brooklyn?

'So my Gard, this is all the goddammed family? Kinda grown, hasn't it? Which one's your Aunt Violet you were so hot on?'

'Oh, she's dead, Sonia. Years ago. The old family's dead. We are the old family now, you and I.'

'So you're meaning to say we're – what's that word again?'

'Dead.'

'Great vocabulary you have. You never utter that word in Hollywood.'

'Would you like to sit up, Steve?' You imagined it was Sonia's maid who spoke, as cameras flashed your images back to waiting computers.

Sonia gestured with one hand. 'We all gotta go some time, just don't be in any hurry, make the best of it while you're still warm. Whatever "the best of it" means. Fuck knows, I don't.'

Hardly thinking, you said, 'You could give all this up. Come back and live a normal life with us.'

She flashed a look of contempt. 'You call it life? This is about the best thing that could happen. Give this up? Dream on, baby! Get a life!'

'But a normal ... normal –'

499

'Life, you mean?' Someone said it.

'Who're you talking to?' Sonia's thin lips hardly moved. 'Normal sucks in my book, hon. I'm worth a million, every breath I take. Why would I want to come back here, of all places?' She was using her mother's old phrase.

Sorrow filled you, for her, for yourself. This was the point life had brought you to.

You might be old; you could be dead; your sister had become embalmed in a kind of eminence. You could almost hear the scornful voice of your old Blackall friend Caleb saying, 'Get real, Steve, don't sell your soul!' Caleb was there in the crowd, with a camera. You thought you saw him. Then he was gone.

Sonia had seated herself on a kind of throne that had been prepared for her. She lowered herself stiffly into it while her three brilliant young men held their breath. When she was gone, they would lose their jobs. Where else could they find such well-paid humiliation?

Verity hovered nearby, half-amused; you could not read her expression. Although the family gathered round, and various paparazzi, you noted that many other hotel guests turned away indifferently, or maybe in envy. The smartly-dressed heavies ranged themselves about the throne, unsmiling, occasionally waving away any camera fiend who got too close. The three identical young men hustled about, fetching unheeded water and cocktails and olives and canapés. The maid, to whom Verity said, sarcastically, 'Run short of gold and frankincense and myrrh, have they?', lingered behind her mistress, erect and poker-faced, ready to repair any defences that might need it.

All this attention, more ostentatious than Royalty would have received. It made you dizzy.

'Sonia, I can't believe it! How can you bear all this fuss?'

She gave you a quick glance before resuming her stony smile ahead. 'It's okay, honey, it won't last. I can sure tell you one thing, fame's better than being fucking unknown.'

'But this excess of fame.'

500

'Ferget it. I go for excess every time. Famous, you can get your revenge on everyone.'

You thought she had no real wish to communicate, that she was divorced from common feeling, but you were mistaken. After a silence, she said, 'Remember the unreal atmosphere they brought us up in? Remember all the pretence? Remember that phantom kid of Mother's? – Valerie? yeah, Valerie! – well, that was good training for all this. I'm their stupid fucking pretensions writ large.'

She had no need to explain who the 'they' were of which she spoke. She turned away.

'Come back,' you begged. 'I hear what you're saying, but you are a success in your own right. Don't knock it. I envy you in a way.'

'Don't bother to pretend. Envy works both ways. Think I don't read your contempt of me? You, a jailbird, Steve! Come on!'

'Stop it! I'm just astonished at how you've changed. And aren't you imprisoned too?'

'"Bird in a gilded cage" kinda thing.' She spoke without interest, turning her head slightly to accept something – a pill? – from her maid. 'How much you've changed! You're ashen, Christ, the walking dead, us both. We got that in common.' Lights were dimming again.

You frowned, angry with yourself. 'It's difficult to talk. We're so public here ...' You kept thinking to yourself that, unbelievably, you were brother and sister.

While Sonia was engaged with her maid, you turned to the paramedic in the biscuit overall. 'How is Sonia's health?'

'Classified.' The word emerged as if chewed.

'Look pal, I'm her brother. Haven't seen her in years. I don't want to make anything of it. I just want to know how she is.'

He put his long, neat head down and regarded you from under an eyebrow. 'Think Grade One Alzheimer's plus Obraxis symptoms, okay?'

'What are Albraxers symptoms?'

Expressionlessly, the paramedic said, 'Obraxis. Obraxis. Occasional outbursts of mental cruelty. You a candidate? You're about right age.'

'I'm okay, I think. Just faint.' You could not make out his face clearly.

A card was produced all of a sudden, like a conjuring trick. 'Any problems, call me. Runs in families. Private treatment. Total confidentiality.'

'Thanks.' But the man had already turned away.

'Look more pleasant, will you?' Sonia was saying to her maid. She turned to you with a gradual move of her body through forty-five degrees. She was chewing.

'I wanna meet your current spouse, Stan. Vanity? Valerie? Verity! Yeah, introduce me to your Verity!'

'It's Steve, remember? Like we used to be brother and sister.'

Verity was her usual witty and pleasant self. 'I loved your latest movie, Sonia. The sea certainly looked good.'

'Fulsome praise indeed,' croaked Sonia. 'They warmed up the whole goddamned ocean for that one shot.' She emitted a controlled laugh. Verity laughed. You laughed. The young men, standing apart, who had not heard the joke, also laughed.

The film to which Verity was referring was Sonia Gleesorro's greatest triumph – an adaptation of Euripides' play *Iphigenia in Aulis*, entitled in this case, *Beauty on the Beach*, the summer mega block buster which had also been granted grudging critical success.

The scene opens on a grey dawn, grey as in a dream, pale as in a coffin. The sea is calm tonight, the tide is full, the moon lies fair. At anchor rides the Grecian fleet, becalmed. The viewpoint drifts to shore, where Agamemnon's army is encamped. A camp fire gives the one quick tongue of brightness to a sombre screen. Men emerge in armour next, to stand about their swords, awaiting dawn. This is the brotherhood who plan to fight the Trojan War.

A primitive belief holds them to the Aulis shore. They believe that the ashen goddess Artemis, the many-breasted Artemis, will not permit them to sail until Agamemnon has sacrificed his daughter, Iphigenia, played by Sonia Gleesorro, to the goddess.

Grey-haired Agamemnon is plotting with others in his tent.

A cruel scheme is hatched, whereby Iphigenia is lured to Aulis. We see her in the grand wilderness of her mountain home, far away in Argos. She has become a Wise Woman, living alone in a tower a few metres from her noisy family. In several beautiful shots we watch her leave her table where she has been studying, put on sandals and walk out on the slopes dominated by distant blue mountains. The tower stands behind her, already old. Iphigenia wears a light grey robe with scarlet hem. She walks among scattered weeds and scattering chickens to see her family, where her old uncle lies dying.

Other women stand about, inside and outside the cottage. Two small boys linger by their mothers' aprons. No one speaks. A hound sprawls, panting, by the threshold.

Iphigenia's uncle lies propped on his rough bed. A messenger has just brought word to the dying man that Achilles wishes to marry Iphigenia. Achilles is with the army on Aulis. Iphigenia protests, but her dying uncle insists that she must go and must consummate the union, for the honour of the family is at stake. Her young brother hugs her and congratulates her. A group of women, assuming statuesque poses, laments her fate. One younger woman runs off down the hill to spread the news in her village of Iphigenia's turn of fortune.

Iphigenia makes the sea voyage. After many adventures, and the defeat of sea monsters, her ship arrives at Aulis. She is almost dragged from the deck. A man in a black gown with cowl, standing thigh deep in the flood, tells her she must die. War must be waged. We see her face as suddenly, involuntarily, she turns to look back across the sea. Soldiers lead her, no longer visitor but captive, through the surf to Agamemnon. In Agamemnon's tent stands Achilles. He knows nothing of the ruse that has brought Iphigenia to Aulis. Agamemnon, weeping, tells his child she must be sacrificed to appease the gods. Achilles fights to save her, but is overpowered.

She is resigned. They lead her to a sacrificial stone. The director of *Beauty on the Beach*, Fritz Shetzenhammer, who is of German-Jewish-Ukrainian origin, does not make the mistake of the Jocasta/Oedipus movie – here there is to be no happy ending, only a dreadful logic, leading like all life eventually to death.

While a great storm rages, with snow blowing in gusts from the bare hillsides, Iphigenia submits for the greater good, giving herself gladly to the ancient rituals of sacrifice, lying unaided on the sacrificial stone. It is her father, Agamemnon himself, who raises the sword, hesitates, then brings it down on his daughter's womb.

Blood flows; and on that blood the fleet can sail for Troy.

You and Verity, and most of the family, had seen this drama in the cinema, and were moved by its primitive vitality.

'Yes, primitive vitality, but also some modern sophistication,' Verity said, over a coffee, when you sat in a café near the cinema after the showing. 'Shetzenhammer and his scriptwriters have married a slice of Euripides with a slice of Aeschylus's *Oresteia*, that ghastly family drama.'

'What's "Obestia", Verity?' little Sanchi asked. Paul and Joyce had left Sanchi with the nursemaid while they were with you in the cinema.

'*Oresteia*'s about wives slaying husbands, sons slaying mothers, written about five hundred years before Christ, I believe. The opening of the film shows Agamemnon receiving word that his wife, Clytemnestra, will slay him when he returns from the invasion of Troy. So that's the frame within which we see Agamemnon having to destroy his daughter to appease the goddess Artemis.'

'I liked Artemis,' said Ted Nash. 'She was really scary.'

'So we see that Agamemnon is also doomed.'

'But who are all these Greek people?' asked Sanchi, in an aggrieved voice.

Verity and you had to laugh. 'Their actions and motives have held audiences for two-and-a-half thousand years, Sanchi. Basically, I suppose, it's all about actions of love and hatred, over which the law has little power.'

And you said in agreement, 'That must be more or less the case today or MGM would not have spent forty million dollars on the movie.'

Verity had greatly opened up her character since the days of her divorce from Jeremy Nash, being no longer circumscribed by fear. She had a warmth about her to which many people readily responded, including, it seemed, even the great actress, Sonia Gleesorro.

'I can see you have made Steve so much happier,' Sonia said to her. 'What's the secret? Plenty blow jobs?' She emitted an instant's cackle. She was clutching a concoction the golden young men had brought her, as if for tribute. From it she took an occasional sip. Otherwise, she sat motionless as a statue, staring straight ahead. 'The humbler the person, the happier.'

Suspecting insincerity, Verity said, 'I'd say the opposite is at least partially true; the happier the person, the humbler. Are you not happy with your renown?'

'Renown is in itself a form of happiness. Or so they claim.' She spoke with indifference, above dispute.

'That too works both ways,' Verity said, dismissing the subject. 'Tell me, when you were on that slab, did you know you were going to freeze the blood of the audience? Did you want to freeze the blood of the audience?'

'It was uncomfortable. I was meant to have some foam rubber support under me, but it didn't show in time for the shot. I hoped we would scare the daylights out of all those little arseholes who had bullied me at school.' She thought a while, took a sip from her small glass, and said, 'No, I didn't. That was later. I was in the part. Just terrified of that cocksucking sword ...'

Fireworks were going off outside the large windows of the Savoy. It lacked only fifty-five minutes to midnight, the birth of the new millennium, and the death of the old, and we talked of the ancient Greeks.

'I hope you're going to stay here with us overnight, Sonia,' you said.

'No way, baby! Stay in this place? You're joking.'

'Oh, we think the Savoy is terribly posh,' said Verity, good-humouredly.

'We got a suite at Claridge's. I'm staying there with Fritz Shetzenhammer.'

Her dark eyes were alert in the dead face, looking from one to the other of you as if peering through a mask. She said, 'I got a little surprise for you. Call it a New Year gift. Have you got some place private we can go?' It seemed to be a remark indicating friendliness.

The publicity half-hour was over. The manageress of the hotel came and thanked you. You escorted Sonia in the elevator up to your suite. Her entourage followed in a neighbouring elevator. Sonia looked with practised distaste about her.

She went to the bedroom, where the bed was still unmade after your recent rest period. There you lay still. You were hallucinating. You were on the rock.

Sonia demanded of her maid that the bed be made up. Turning away from this work, she stood staring out of the window, showing neither pleasure nor displeasure as she watched for a minute the illuminated boats floating on the Thames, and the hundreds of people who lined the banks.

'So, another century.' She spoke flatly, addressing nobody in particular.

'They're two a penny these days,' you replied. 'Cheaper by the dozen.'

Without further comment, she went and lay on the bed.

She waved you away, saying, 'Gimme five minutes, okay?'

You and Verity joined the rest of the family, who were arriving in the outer room. Verity raised an eyebrow at you; you shrugged in return.

'Can't you get her out of here?' Ted asked you in a low voice. 'We want to enjoy ourselves.'

Barbara squeezed his hand. 'She's *Sonia Gleesorro*, for God's sake! We can put up with her for an hour, can't we? I'm just thrilled to be in the same room as her.'

'That's right,' Sanchi piped up. 'She's the Movie Queen! I'm really scared of her.'

'She's got a surprise for us,' Verity said. 'Can't guess what it will be.'

'Maybe she turns into a dragon?' Joyce suggested. 'It couldn't be a very big step for her.'

The bodyguards were carting in new equipment. The new equipment included a screen, which snapped into position, also a number of light folding chairs. The family were ushered into these chairs and sat facing the screen. A metal box was set up beside the screen and plugged in.

You heard an ambulance siren, wailing down the street. 'Here comes the ambulance,' said Verity. 'I'm coming in it with you.'

'Don't leave me ...' You clung to her arm, again confused.

The maid went and assisted Sonia off the bed. Ten minutes later, Gleesorro appeared, this time in a flowing gown with a scarlet hem, her hair piled high upon her head.

Her manner was abstract. Her gaze was fixed somewhere above her audience. One of the polished young men drew a curtain over the window to avoid external distraction.

The room was darkened. The screen lit. Once again, ancient Greeks plunged splashing through seawater up to their thighs. You believed you recognized the beach.

'Why do the classics still hold meaning for us?' Sonia intoned to her audience. 'Because they gave us the means to express our inner torments. We sacrifice and are still sacrificed. We still have to wade through the deep waters of life.'

Saying this, she had lost her American accent and was again speaking in unaccented English. Still the soldiers plunged through the waters. Now Iphigenia was among them, skirts flying and adhering wetly to her delectable thighs.

'You are watching a clip from my movie. It is also a clip from my life, from your lives. Reality is transformed into fiction. Fiction must hold the secret truth of real life. Fiction is greater than life because it has meaning.

'I'll let you into a secret. These scenes were shot not in Greece, but on the islands of Guadeloupe. My director, Fritz Shetzen-hammer, has an estate on Guadeloupe. We filmed there, like Bergman on his island, right? And another secret, these scenes were shot only five years ago, not in two hundred BC.'

Someone in the select little audience clapped.

Now the soldiers and the scantily clad woman were running across bare sand. The sand as it had been, bare, warm, scrupulous. Timeless. Mrs North stood again looking down from the dunes. Motion was slowed. There was no music. Sonia ceased speaking. The naked legs seemed to work mechanically.

'Oh, another secret – those ain't my thighs.' Sardonic chuckle. 'Another secret truth of real life.'

The bracing of feet against sand, the bend of the ankle, the action of the knee, all could be studied as the actors raced over the beaches towards the sacrificial stone.

The audience almost stopped breathing, their backs to the sound of rockets exploding beyond the curtained window of the hotel room, where the drama of the calendar was taking place.

The box by the side of the screen opened like lips parting. A perfect baby girl was revealed. She was naked, and her little fists were clenched in sleep over her chest. Gasps came from the audience. The infant was a perfect dream child, unrecognized by the hand of time.

And now the false Iphigenia came forward with a sword. She raised the sword above the sleeping babe.

One of the women in the audience – it was Joyce – shrieked. Sanchi cried out, 'No, no don't, Sonia! Don't kill that baby!'

The actress paid no attention. She lifted the sword until its hilt was above the level of her eyes. She held it there for a moment.

The infant slept on.

Then down plunged the point of the sword, down into the baby's stomach. Blood instantly welled out, tiny arms were thrown up in shock, then dropped. The audience broke up, everyone jumping from their seats in horror.

Lights came on. Sonia stood there, mouth slightly open in a laugh of some kind. The baby had vanished.

'The kid was a hologram, punters!' she said. 'Just kidding. You like blood, don't you? That little act is my millennium gift to you all. Exclusive!'

'You're disgusting, disgusting,' you said weakly.

'Aw, come on, Steve. That was young Valerie slain, okay? Ma's dream child, okay? Belated catharsis, okay? Have a laugh.'

Choking with anger, you shouted – but you were whispering – 'Let's hope the twenty-first century will not be one half as bloody as your imagination!' But the words seemed not to register. The banging and popping outside were closer now.

She gave a scornful laugh as she turned away. 'Human nature don't ever change.'

Paul and Joyce were trying to comfort their little boy, who sobbed uncontrollably.

'They're all archetypes,' said Paul, consolingly. His face was close to yours.

The equipment was being rapidly packed away by the body guard. You and Verity escorted Sonia down in the elevator.

'Which were you?' Verity asked. 'Iphigenia or Clytemnestra?'

It was your prison cell again. You were confused. It drifted in leisurely fashion, and yet seemed to be plunging uncheckably to the ground floor.

Sonia appeared pleased with herself.

'You like a bit of drama, don't you?' she said, stepping out of the elevator. She took the maid's arm to steady herself. 'Horror – the stuff of life!'

You crossed the hotel foyer to the street. Mystifyingly, the foyer was now totally deserted, cold, and in semi-darkness. It seemed to be empty of furniture. One of the three Gleesorro youths had called Sonia's chauffeur on his cell phone, so that the stretch limo was awaiting her out in the street.

You approached the long, black, hearse-like vehicle reluctantly.

'It's been great to meet you again, Steve, Verity.' Sonia spoke in her customary flat tone. She raised her face to be kissed. 'There's been a ...' You could not think of the word 'mistake'.

She turned to the vehicle with some rapidity. No one was yet there to open the rear door for her. She pulled it open impatiently. As she did so, the chimes of Big Ben began to ring out the midnight hour, and the birth of a new century. The chimes were amplified in the lounge of the hotel, from whence now came cheering and clapping.

The banging and popping were louder now.

Sonia paused.

Woofie, the cheetah, saw its chance. It bounded from the limo and ran, ran in a lissom swerve round her mistress – ran for freedom.

Sonia screamed. 'Oh, my love! Steve, quick, catch her!'

Without thinking, you rushed into the roadway. It was at that midnight moment free of traffic. The cheetah had paused on the far pavement, rump high, head and forebody close to the ground, ears back, staring back at you. She wore a collar. She was crouching in fear as rockets exploded overhead, filling the London sky with stars of many colours.

You went cautiously towards her. The cheetah did not move. She looked at you with an expression you read as a mixture, an almost human mixture, of hope and despair. You held out an open hand to her. You hesitated.

Such was your concentration, such was the noise of the fireworks exploding overhead, you did not heed the cries of Sonia and Verity.

A car with its roof open came speeding along the Strand on an erratic course. It had no lights on. Drunken passengers stood with heads and shoulders through the open roof, waving paper flags, blowing plastic bugles or singing. The vehicle bore down on you in all its blackness. In trying to back out of its way, you slipped. It struck you full on the body as you fell.

You were thrown against a stone wall, already dead.

The singing in the car changed immediately to screaming and yelling. The car swerved across the road and hurtled through a plate glass window. The cheetah disappeared down a side alley.

Verity ran to you, falling on her knees to lift your head, as once you had lifted hers. But she was too late. For you, everything had stopped.

In the hotel, guests had linked hands and were still joyously singing 'Auld Lang Syne'.

All along the Thames, a wall of light was spreading into the new century.

16
A Fuller Understanding

Stephen Fielding conceived that he was making his way through deep water, almost as if the tide had caught up with him at last. There was light of a kind – of a kind hitherto unknown to him. Inasmuch as he had any sensations, he felt that his consciousness had waned, and yet that he consisted only of a fragment of consciousness.

Although everything presented itself to him as paradox, paradoxically he accepted it as normal. He was reduced to an electron, yet he experienced a great opulence.

That great opulence expressed itself in many ways, in warmth, in distant singing, in drifting colour, all of which constituted a womb-like wealth.

Now he was emerging into an immeasurable space, wide as infinity itself.

'Oh, of course', it seemed he said to himself, though the 'of course' was the last thing that could have been anticipated. Nothing could have prepared him for where and what he was.

The shades of many people drifted about, deflected through a haze that was not exactly a haze, but rather a version of eyesight. Indefinably, he stood at last – but he was not 'standing' at all, and there was no 'at last' defining divisions of time – before a concentration of light and energy, a solid block of something that he could only interpret as light. Congealed light: the gaseous element light in its solid state.

He gloried in the miraculous – as everything had always been secretly miraculous. Secretly miraculous. *Of course.*

The block formed a perfect square, yet its dimensions were elusive. The block was addressing him. He understood it to be at once almost impossibly remote, and yet it was, he recognized, his personal block; his saviour.

'Now you have entered what you may consider the great Afterwards, Stephen. This is really a true beginning, when you become an integral part of a, shall we say, multitude?'

'Oh, an Afterlife? I'm in an – the Afterlife? Is that it?'

'No. You still need a little orientation. This *is* life, the *real* existence. What you have been undergoing was an experiment. What you regarded as the Earth or, perhaps, the Universe, was our experiment on rather a modest scale. We wish to apologize to you for the discomfort and confusion you experienced.'

'Wait! Let me try and take this in.' So it seemed to him he said, although the nature of the transmission was obscure. It could be that he had sometimes had doubts about whether there were large elements of deception in his 'life' ... 'Are my parents here?' An affirmative answer came. He wondered how drab had been his mother's inner life.

'Rich, rich. Enclosed, but extremely fertile. Some who cannot speak, or fulfil their natures, like your mother, enjoy whole meadows of monologues.'

He had no forehead to clutch. 'This is real life! I thought I'd died. I simply can't take it in.'

An eon passed like a solitary chord on a harp.

'To help you truly "take it in", I will tell, show, *reprise* for you, your entire projected existence. We will begin, if you are ready, when you are no more than three years old, when you first venture onto the beaches of Walcot.'

'No, wait, please ... I'm not yet prepared.'

So then there was another gulf of some kind. And then he was somehow prepared, and the block was projecting, 'We will review your entire life, from when you play on Walcot beaches. And from there we will proceed throughout the "twentieth century" as you think of it, until your emergence here, freed from unreality. Do you understand?'

'You put an emphasis on the twentieth century. Why do you do that?'

'We set up the experiment on a time-limited basis for ease of study. There was only the time-stage you knew as "the twentieth century". Nothing else.'

'But my plesiosaur ...'

'All that you thought of as having gone before was a, well, let me call it a computer simulation, for ease of understanding. Your so-called past, the past centuries, have never happened.'

'Steve' was unable to feel faint. He merely stammered that he did not understand. 'Explain about the fossilized Jurassic fish I discovered. Was that a simulation?'

'It was another prop, simply, to make you, and everyone else, believe there had been a long past. All your hard-earned knowledge, I fear, as false as your "sister's" film. In fact, your entire world – that "special effect", you could call it – opened quite arbitrarily at a date we decided to code-name "The Twentieth Century". Such matters may become clearer to you as we rerun your story.'

It was too much to comprehend. He was dazzled and deafened, fighting to adjust.

'I can't see you!'

Comprehending, the block projected, 'You are contained in me. Your senses have yet to accommodate to your new specifications and forms. Be quiescent and we will reprise your whole story for you.'

'...'

'Are you ready?'

'Yes.'

'At high tide, the sea lapped close to the dunes, leaving little sand to be seen. The remaining sand above the high tide mark was as fine as sifted salt. Spikes of marram grass grew from it like quills from a porcupine. No stones were visible. The small waves, white and grey, seethed against their limits. How lonely it was, this wild coastline.'

The sand above the tidemark was as fine as sifted salt. The dwindling sea re-enacted its harmonies. It was once more August, that August. The August sky was once more blue overhead, without a cloud, the air was fresh. A small sun-tanned boy set out across the shore of Walcot to follow the retreating tide.

He was once more that little boy; once more without a care in the world. Once more totally happy on that beautiful beach. A happiness like homesickness.

He was to have his time again.

The whole story of this existence unfolded.

The Steve-being did indeed take it in, with all its length rolled into a tolerable format. He relived everything. He did – it seemed unavoidably – grasp the overall, ungraspable situation, which prompted a vast horizon to roll out before him, carpet-like, into a creditable imitation of eternity.

'It was all an experiment. All my life. All everyone's life. My parents', Violet's, Stalin's, the cheetah's. To what end?'

The block replied. 'It is a thought experiment, perhaps flawed from the start. Your lifetime, or "timelife", to employ a better word, was a kind of examination. Now is your, well, transcendence; your entry into the eternal life of what you may call "the spirit", the "essence".'

He could scarcely formulate the question. 'Have I passed the examination?'

'You mistake my meaning. We were under examination, not you. Now you have come through, the whole gravamen of timelife is that it is reviewed and rethought.'

Did Steve think before he responded? 'So you really were the known unknown of which … my dear Verity spoke … But, now you can give *me* the answer, did my parents leave me to die, to drown, on the sands of Walcot when I was a small boy?'

'You did not suspect that threat for some years. Then the possibility was brought to your attention and you commenced worrying about it. It was that suspicion which was your burden; it coloured your life.'

'You don't answer my question.'

'But I have answered it. You were unable to deal with a problem you had yourself, in part, conjured up and sustained. I spoke of our flawed experiment – one flaw was in the construction of the human brain. These admittedly low-power perception-machines we installed sensed things, but could not always resolve them.

'To give an example, in your churches you sang of God, "Help us to see, 'Tis only the splendour of light hideth thee". A good guess at the truth. We were most entertained. So close, and yet so far! What you reckoned to be the all-pervasive light speeding through your universe, that light registered by your instruments, was in fact our thoughts of you; they were the background noise of our survey. Not light but thought.'

If there had been a function for sadness, Steve would have been sorrowful. He said, 'It is dreadful to believe that all that glory, that amazing mixture of misery and joy, was just your … box of tricks. What of all the dreadful wars of the century? The bloodshed, the despotism, the famines? They were just for your entertainment?'

'Not so. Once the experiment was under way, we were unable to interfere.'

'But those things happened. There must have been a major flaw in your original project.'

As usual, the block was answering without hesitation. 'To put it briefly, a major flaw in our project was the way in which everything was designed to prey on everything else, up and down the food chain, in order to achieve adequate energy-input. The method encouraged callousness. When we close down this particular timelife experiment, we shall install a better system.'

'What else will you change?'

'We are rethinking the clumsy use of planets. Your planet, your Earth, if you could see it, that ball forever trailing its one eternal night behind it like a dark tail, round and round ... So unaesthetic ...'

The dumbfounding entity fell silent, as if in contemplation. Steve dared not speak.

'Also, we are considering in our next experiment that it must be staged in a more stable element than time. We have something in mind.'

'Steve' grappled with the statement, finally asking what this other element, superior to time, could be.

The block replied without hesitation – it seemed even before the other's sentence was completed – that even if it explained, Steve would be incapable of understanding, since he had been a creature of Time. 'Suffice it to say, it is a nexus we are designing.'

As silence fell between the two, the light began to change.

'Can I have my beloved Verity back?' But even as he asked, he knew that so great was the transformation that he had no need of her in this eternal Now, was indeed unable to need her.

The block was silent, at peace. It knew that 'Steve' now understood. Completion had been reached.

'Steve' then said, or possibly did not say, 'The circumstances in which I lived, the images of them and of myself, were something I engaged, fondled with my senses, those precious senses. My salvation then was a kind of intoxication with life, with its pleasures and sorrows. The cleverly designed icon of my being – my soul, my psyche! – was always present in my mind, though distorted in representation by dreams. Am I right there?'

The response was immediate, superimposed on the question. 'Although mainly pleasurable, those dreams were your flaw in our composition of your cerebral organization. Arbitrary though that entire scheme of timelife might be, it seemed logical at the time, as it was, I assume, intended to be.

'All men and women were forced to confront something unresolved in their lives, some knot forever knotted, some element of puzzlement, unreality and dream, their glass forever darkened. They could not be permitted to realize the truth, or our experiment would have been spoiled.

'As the light dies, they see clearly. And in that perception, in that moment when they gasp, "Oh, I see!" in a sigh of relief, the enigma of life is fulfilled.'

'It is possible, I admit, to accept it in that aspect.'

And slowly, the light gathers up its mighty skirts, the light of understanding, of an intense cerebration. All timelife humanity would weep to see it happen.

The darkness divides into bars. At first there is only a silver bar, low, encircling the gigantic space like a ring; with it comes a kind of solemn music, like, but also unlike, a breath, unheard by human ear.

The brilliance sinks from silver to gold, and suddenly the dome overhead is suffused with a glorious scarlet that has about it a stirring finality, so that those elements reach up their imagined hands to it. Almost immediately, the scene changes. All has been digested and understood and forgiven. There exists now only a slender bar of light, of the most tender non-colour, along the supposed horizon.

And then the great eyelid of creation closes, leaving only darkness.

Virtuous thoughts of the day laye up good tresors for the night, whereby the impressions of imaginary formes arise into sober similitudes, acceptable unto our slumbering selves, and preparatory unto divine impressions: hereby Solomons sleep was happy. Thus prepared, Jacob might well dream of Angells upon a pillowe of stone, and the first sleep of Adam might bee the best of any after ...

– Sir Thomas Browne of Norwich
On Dreams

Notes

Some of the books and texts mentioned in this novel have an existence in the real world. They include:

The Museum of Unconditional Surrender, by Dubravka Ugrešic. Phoenix House 1998

The Duchess of Malfi, a play by John Webster. First published 1623

My Five Lives, by G. F. Stridsberg. William Heinemann 1963

The Old Red Sandstone, by Hugh Miller. 1841

Of Time, Passion, and Knowledge: Reflections on the Strategy of Existence, by J. T. Fraser. Brazilier, New York 1975

Caleb Williams, by William Godwin. 1794

Steppenwolf, by Hermann Hesse. S. Fischer Verlag, Berlin 1927

Miscellaneous Writings, by Sir Thomas Browne, edited by Geoffrey Keynes. Faber & Faber 1921

The Nicomachean Ethics, by Aristotle. Penguin Classics, 1976

The Man without Qualities, by Robert Musil, translated by Sophie
   Wilkins and Burton Pike. Picador 1995
Dover Beach, by Matthew Arnold. 1867
Jocasta, by Brian Aldiss. The Friday Project 2014
The Oresteia, by Aeschylus. Oxford World's Classics 2002

My thanks to Emily Gale for her good advice and encouragement.